I0687696

Also by Susan Shepherd:

A Vampire Story
Killing Esther
Killing Andy
The Grain God
Soul Of Rah
City Of Rah

Returning Rah

Book Four

Of the

Saga Of The Rah

SUSAN SHEPHERD

ISBN: 0692974768
ISBN-13:9781549890741

"Mystery enough at noon.
The blinding, unfrequented paths
Above the too frequented sea
Hold labyrinth and mask enough.
No need to twist beneath the moon.
Here on the rising secret cliff
In this white fury of the light
Is mystery enough at noon."
John Fowles, "The Magus"

* * *

I met a traveler from an antique land
Who said: "Two vast and trunkless legs of stone
Stand in the desert. Near them, on the sand,
Half sunk, a shattered visage lies, whose frown,
And wrinkled lip, and sneer of cold command,
Tell that its sculptor well those passions read
Which yet survive, stamped on these lifeless things,
The hand that mocked them and the heart that fed:
And on the pedestal these words appear:
'My name is Ozymandias, king of kings:
Look on my works, ye Mighty, and despair!'
Nothing beside remains. Round the decay
Of that colossal wreck, boundless and bare
The lone and level sands stretch far away
Percy Bysshe Shelley, "Ozymandias"

* * *

"You have received The Law by the visitation of Angels and have not kept it."
Acts of the Apostles, 7:53

CHAPTER ONE

Rah emerges from the canal half a mile south east of the People's Temple. It is dark, and the rain has passed. Stars are peeking out from behind wisps of ragged clouds, and in their light he can make out the white stone bulkhead, rising several feet above the water on either side of the channel. A lanterned walkway borders either side, and stretching out to the south military barracks are stacked like loaves of bread. Rah can hear an infant cry in the distance, a dog bark, a nightjar call.

"For soldier family," he murmurs to himself in Greek, shaking his soaked curls. Treading water, he waits, using his acute hearing to pick up sounds behind him, in the slave district. A whip, a cry, a murmur of many voices, perhaps a communal prayer amongst the Hebrew slaves behind closed doors, but the streets are silent. There is a curfew in the slave district of the Zababa, were even the slave keepers and traders shut themselves in and bolt their doors at nightfall.

"No can go there," thinks Rah aloud. "Maybe keep go, leave this Babylon to Wolf, swim through."

But another turn in the canal brings him in view of the Zababa Gate, where a heavily guarded fortress squats like a sphinx, its head lighted from within by many torches. Along the bridge stretching over the top of the Zababa Gate, men at arms pace, their swords glinting, warning approaching merchant ships that they will be stopped and boarded. Below, a great double wooden door blocks all entry and exits, a system of pulleys and weights making it possible for the guard

to open and close the device with the help of slave manpower.
"Maybe go under," says Rah, drawing in a good breath before slipping beneath the surface of the water and swimming, eel-like, toward the submerged bottoms of the doors. There is room enough for him to slide between the silt bottom of the canal and the bottom edge of the great wood door, upon which has been fixed a long row of fiercely sharp iron spikes. Rah's golden belt is hooked on one momentarily, but he does not panic. He flips himself face up within the golden circlet and then, pushing himself downward and backward with a wave of his opened hands, he unhooks himself from what could have easily been a bloody and ignoble grave.
On the other side of the gate he follows the bulkhead out another hundred feet, then shoots to the surface. Except for the torch light along the walkway above the gate and the lanterns within the fortress, there are only the stars blinking in an indigo sky, to illuminate the night. The rain clouds have departed north, and for a moment Rah's attention is captivated by the brilliance of the Pleiades directly above.
"This like night when Rah become god," spits Rah, treading the black water, "Ileah come, take Rah to mountain, Rah is fly, play with doves. Now go back, go to Knossos, finish what priest he start. No more volcano, no more wave, no more war. God is angry. Wolf is stop priest, but God want Rah. On mountain. Sacrifice. Or volcano, wave, war, is never stop." Rah pulls his gaze from the night skies, and looks toward the southern shore of the canal. "But need horse first."
He breast strokes through the water, silent as a fish, then pulls himself up on the southern bulkhead. Then, his head still bleeding and pounding, his arms and legs a purple-brown blur, and his silken Rainbow Rah costume trailing in the dirt, he sets off along the base of the southern wall of the city to retrieve Ono.

On the far side of the city the palace sleeps. Amegan guards walk the ramparts above the river, and Amagan sailors the small vessel portal below. Teams of Amegan watchmen patrol the seven entrances, two on the west, two on the north, the Lion's gait and the two servant's entries on the east. But inside, only a handful of staff remain. Noblemen, patricians, the amelu and their wives have not yet returned from the theater. The servants are to bed, the stable is silent but for the munching and blowing of the half dozen Turkoman still remaining in it. All of the other horses have been sent downriver by ship, loaded the very day that Amega took Babylon, by none other than the Palace Stable Master, Hatu-Hadu. They were shipped downriver to the fork of the Tigris and sent to Hattusha on the assassin's orders. And Ono, unbeknownst to Rah, is among them.

But the King's Turkoman, tall as an eland and gold as any coin in the King's vault, still occupies the stall farthest from the stable entrance, closest to Hatu-Hadu's chamber. Sharing his wall, in an adjoining stall, Pala, Petuk's gelding, sleeps on his feet, his golden rump to the aisle, and across from him Hatu-Hadu snores through a broken nose in the Stable Master's chamber. He has not had a decent night's sleep since he fell from Pelek, whom, against his brother's advice, he insisted on 'schooling' himself in Peleshet's absence.

"He is in the Terror's favor, that man, and I will not have you babying his mount and ruining him for battle, for I will then have to face the man myself to explain where his courage has gone." The gelding, normally obedient and brave, had not been ridden in a fortnight, and he was instantly spooked by the stable master's crippled arm. It took two men to hold him while Hatu-Hadu mounted. Even so, Hatu-Hadu made it half way around the training arena at a mincing trot before the animal made an unscheduled war-kick, jumping a clean three feet off the ground and twisting with such force as to send the man sailing a good two strides out before he struck the ground. Hatu-Hadu landed hard on his face and left side, cracking his nose, two ribs and his left patella. This would have been insult enough, except that the horse then struck him in the back with a hoof as he galloped past him.

Hatu-Hadu had been walking at an angle ever since. His knee, no longer swollen twice its original size, was making progress, nevertheless, and the doctors believed he would bend it again one day. The ribs were healing, though it was still advisable not to take too deep a breath, and his nose, once so narrow and handsome, was crooked. He dare not complain, for if he did, his brother Buhuru-Hadu reminded him he might instead be happy to be alive at all.

The Stable Master's chamber is the width of two stalls. The chamber is decorated with many ribbons and tokens of honor from his days of greatness, though his brother now does most of the training and Hatu-Hadu's importance rests more on the sickle of removed flesh upon his cheek than on his history as a horseman. It is the fact that he survived the assassin's blade, withered arm though he may have as a reminder of that meeting, which earns him honor now. And no amount of skill in the training of colts can elevate his brother to that status. Because of this, Hatu-Hadu continues to occupy the Stable Master's chamber while his bastard brother, Buhuru-Hatu, while technically the new Stable Master, remains in the feed room guarding the grain, though no one east of the Nile has the mettle to steal from the Wolf of the Hatti, nor enter without being summoned what is now referred to as the Eastern Palace of Hatti by that very Wolf.

It is upon this cozy arrangement that Rah stumbles in the early hours of the last day of June. Trailing his silken tendrils across the packed earth aisle, his head pounding, his stage paint smudged and running brown, he pads softly toward the stall in which he last saw the dun Amorite mare. He finds himself staring instead into the cream tail of a Turkoman mare, beside which totters a newborn colt, as gold as the dawn.

"So beauty, you and baby," whispers Rah, noticing instantly that the mare has pinned her ears and moved her rump closer to the door upon which he leans. He takes a step back, purring under his breath and turning his gaze away instinctively.

"Yes, you protect this baby. Good mama. Not know Rah. Best be careful. Maybe I steal him." He moves toward the far end of the aisle, wincing at the recollection of the Stable Master striking him with his crop and slicing open his ear in this very spot. He picks up Hatu-Hadu's light snore behind the door opposite Samsu-Titana's stall. He stops in his tracks, dripping a mud puddle onto the floor. Still as a stalking cat, he waits.

Hatu-Hadu makes a little cry in his sleep. And then, "The Wolf!" he cries in Amorite, and "Not my arm!" and then he is weeping, a low, heartbreaking sob. A snort. Stillness.

Rah waits another minute, then feels the fluttering of breast-soft lips against the back of his head. The King's Turkoman has stretched his long, elegant neck over the stall door to greet him. He makes a pleasant whinny. You are golden too! The elastic lips gather a curl at Rah's nape, mistaking it for hay.

Rah giggles, a lovely, dusk sound, half-boy, half-man. "You are beauty, too, King Turkoman. I call you King Turk for short, yes?"

The animal raises its head sharply, then jerks it again, up down. Up down. A stallion's nod. He is flirting and preening, alert that the mares in estrus down the aisle have put their heads out of their stalls to see what is going on. It is too early for grain! Is he getting his grain now? The head mare strikes her door with one hoof.

Rah understands this, but takes Samsu's reaction as an omen, nevertheless, an affirmation. This is the one he will ride. The very best for the very best. Rah has forgotten his pounding head. He steps back, assuring the mares that no one is being grained before them. He is only here to choose a mount.

There is a shuffling in the chamber across from him. Then a loud bang. Amorite cursing.

"Sound like Bad-Hatu, he wake up with Wolf on him, too. I think he is not stop Rah take King Turk. He be scare to touch Rah now." He scratches the stallion's forelock.

"Prob'ly even help Rah, hey? What you think, King Turk? You let Rah ride?"

"Devils be damned! Will my nightmare never end?" cries Hatu-Hadu from his open chamber door. He is leaning on it, not half dressed, a misery of bent and crippled appendages.

Rah regards the Stable Master.

"What happen to Bad-Hatu? Wolf come try even you up other side?" Rah smiles, his eyes sparkling blue beryl in his melting-colors face.

"You! Why do you return to my stable, demon? Have you not done enough damage? Look at me, are you not satisfied?" Hatu-Hadu stumbles back, ready to slam his door, retreat into the gloom of his chamber.

"Bah," pouts Rah, "What Rah do to you? You do this to self, Bad-Hatu." He lifts one hand, a graceful wave to cover Hatu-Hadu's woes, head to toe.

"Here," he points to the gimpy arm, "This for hit Rah. Here," he gestures to the rest, "This for scare horse. Same thing, over, over. Never learn. You hit, you scare. You not big like you think. Always someone bigger than you, can hit, scare you too. All this you do," he sweeps an arm toward the mares at the far end of the aisle, toward the arena archway, "All this hit and scare, it come back to you, no?" He punches Hatu-Hadu in his weak arm, "Bah! Here come Wolf! Could maybe cut off all together and hit you with this arm, hey?" Rah turns his back to the Stable Master, gently pulling another blonde curl out of Samsu's fingering lips. He gives the stallion a scratch under his chin and the animal leans into it. Do me here! On the neck, yes! Just there!

"You better be talk to horse with love. You give horse heart. He give back to you. Bigger heart. Bigger love." Rah turns from the stallion to look about for his tack. "Where King Turk saddle is?"

"This is the King's Turkoman, you little fool," snarls Hatu-Hadu, backing into his chamber as he nods at the beast. "Even your Wolf will not save you if you try riding him. He will kill you before you have gathered your reins. I will have no part of it! The man will break my neck for aiding you!" and he slams his door and throws the bolt.

Rah frowns at the door. Behind his back, Samsu stretches his golden neck, straining to capture another ringlet of his hair.

"Is okay, King Turk," says Rah, turning to breathe deliberately into the animal's nostril. An exchange of trust is made in that instant. Samsu blows.

"Rah is ride you no saddle. Rah is light, Rah is strong. Balance." He snatches Samsu's bridle from a hook beside the stall door, slips the iron bit expertly into the stallion's mouth and buckles the throat latch. Before he opens the stall he tears a long strip of silk from a tendril of his costume. He dips the silk into Samsu's water bucket, which is a brew of hay, the stallion having a habit of making his own version of Mead every night by soaking his dinner portion in his trough. Rah twists the rinsed silk around the stallion's brow-band, covering the golden palace emblem. There is little he can do to disguise Samsu's breed, but at least his is no longer immediately identifiable as the King's own and finest Turkoman.

Rah leads the beast down the aisle, a crop in hand to discourage the mares from their strident flirtations with the stallion, for should such a flirtation be allowed to begin, even 'the best horseman in Gaul' could not prevent its culmination. Under the arch of the stable entrance Rah takes a handful of the stallion's cream mane with his left hand, giving the animal a scratch at the wither as he does so. All the while he is talking, deep and soothing sounds, in his native tongue. He sets his right palm flat onto the beast's back just above the hip joint, and like air, lifts himself up and into position. His ankles tuck naturally into the hollow behind Samsu's elbows, his heels and toes fitting to the space like a boot. Gingerly he picks up the reins, playing with them in his fingers and using his own inner animal to determine points of aid, method and strength of communication with this particular horse. Samsu is well-trained, but nervous of his rider. Rah notices with a few paces forward that his mouth is hard against the bit. He is protecting himself from a heavy hand. Rah gives him room to stretch, scratches his wither, holds him lightly with the tuck of his own rump, an open knee, a firm thigh.

"Stupid Bad-Hatu, he get what he deserve," Rah spits, "King Turk he have soft mouth, like butter, but Bad-Hatu he lean on it, ride with hands. No good. Now how he is going to ruin soft mouth? With just one arm, heh? Rah give you back mouth, King Turk. You see. Rah is no ride on your tongue. Rah is ride with balance, with seat. You going to like Rah, King Turk. We like each other."

It is still dark when the pair explode past the Amegan guards posted at the bridge, spraying pebbles in the faces of the sailors sleeping on deck of the barge below, and galloping out of the city through the Royal Gait, which has been opened for early traffic, and before a single man has become aware that the god-slave of Knossos has slipped through the Wolf of Amega's teeth once more.

CHAPTER TWO

Not far west of Babylon, along the great Euphrates, a lone rider gallops east through fields of barley in a broiling noonday sun. It is July, and the storms that chased the ash cloud have been followed by a hot dry breeze which has quickly absorbed the moisture left behind by the tempest. Peleshet rides with Media comfortably seated in his lap, his red cloak wrapped about her to protect her from the baking sun. The Queen of Cyrus has been stoic, indeed cooperative, since their night together in the Aleppo inn, and she cuddles now, quite contentedly in the curve of the man's breast.

"We will stop here to water the horse, Madam," says Peleshet, pressing his lips to the cloth at Media's ear, for they are so near the river now that his voice would otherwise not be heard above it. "Are you hungry?"

Media lifts her head, pushing back the fabric of the cloak to regard him. She smiles sweetly. "You have a noble face, Peleshet, and piercing eyes. Has anyone told you? You have the look of eagles."

Peleshet stifles a chuckle. Is this the wildcat I caught in Arwad? he thinks. Washed and returned to sanity, she has been a pleasant companion, as demure and grateful as she had been shameless and wild. He shakes his head at her.

"You have not answered me." And pulling up his reins, he halts his mount, jumps down and swings her down easily beside him.

"In Caphtor I had a vast wardrobe of footwear, my handsome Sir, and one pair in particular comes to mind now, which could have put my crown aligned with those broad shoulders," she smiles up at him, a mouse on tip-toe before a lion.

"Little queen, you have no need of such footwear." He lifts her from her waist, which he can circle in his hands, so that her eyes are level to his, "When I only need pick you up, like a vase of lilies, to admire you."

The Queen giggles, and Peleshet sets her down gently, then bows to one knee, crossing a single fist over his heart. The bow of a courtier to a noblewoman.

"You have learned fine manners somewhere, Sir, and not on the battlefield! Have you been to Caphtor? You bow as they do in the Pearl City, in Knossos."

"I have been to the Pearl City. My Master sent me there on two occasions, though well before he found the Grain God."

"The Grain God? Is that what my kitten is called in Amega?" responds Media, tilting her head at the words. Has she heard them before? Did she know that the boy from Knossos was a god? Yes! Yes, that is what her husband called him, when he dreamed that the boy would destroy the world.

And suddenly Media is no longer staring into the hawk-bright eyes of her Amegan kidnapper, but into the waters of a scrying bowl. And she is in the tomb of Heritas, in the Hall of the Kings, and in the bowl a vision: a wild sea rising up and sweeping over the cities in the north, destroying all but Knossos. And earthquakes consuming the walls of Cyrus, and fires and terrified crowds fleeing the city, and darkness, and ash, covering all of Caphtor, for the little Grain God of Knossos, son of the Moon, had been taken by the assassin.

"Yes," she closes her eyes, her knees weak, "Yes, the little Grain God. I too was under his spell, Peleshet. I could not see that he was the very thing that would destroy us. My little kitten, had we only protected him from the one you call Master, Caphtor might still be. And my kingdom, and my people…"

"But it is this same man, little queen, who has summoned you. He intends to build a new kingdom for his Grain God on the very ash that you accuse him of dumping on your island."

"But we are heading toward Babylon, Peleshet. Who is the assassin there, in the city of the Amorites, if not a prisoner?"

At this, Peleshet must stifle another chuckle. "A prisoner? The Babylonian king is dead. My master has taken his throne, and so you must address him as King while he sits on it. Nevertheless, I have no doubt that he is still "called the monster from Amega" behind closed doors there.

Since the disappearance of his prized possession Rush has taken up residence in the Palace, spending his days wine-drunk and collapsed on the King's throne in the theater, where Eliabus struggles to keep him amused with his best dancers.

"They have all the grace of a gobble of headless jakes," belches the new King, throwing a half empty amphora of wine onto the stage over Eliabus' head. The choreographer, now quite used to ducking, incorporates a deep bow into the movement.

"Quite so, Greatness, who in your divine wisdom must compare them to the lost god, the Rah. But what mortal dancer can withstand such comparisons?"

Satisfied for the moment by this mention of Rah, Rush reaches for a fresh amphora, which a nearby slave inserts gingerly into his enormous fist. "You make my point, Choreographer. No one can compare to him."

"No, Divine King, no one can. Yet do remember that the very god you find these falling short of deigned to dance with them. Surely he would not dance with such vulgar creatures as you describe. Surely he himself, being pure dance, found some commonality with those he chose to share the stage?"

"My King," announces Peleshet, who has been forced to march across the stage and shove Eliabus down into the choir pit in order to gain the assassin's attention. He bows low, then nods to the little queen of Cyrus at his side to do the same. Media, however, merely lowers her eyes.

"Ah, it is my Peleshet!" burps the wine-besotted assassin. "Come home with the Cyrian Queen, as ordered." He stands, wobbling on his tree trunk thighs, and puts one enormous paw on the shoulder of the nearest slave to steady himself. The man flinches, but manages not to fall over from the blow.

"And is she mad as a spring rooster? Our little god is flown the coop and cannot cure her," and he gestures loudly toward the stage, effectively bringing the slave who has been holding him up to his knees. "Alas, fair Queen, be mad then, for you will find no sanity here in Babylon either," he collapses back onto his throne, clutching his amphora to his chest. "We are all mad here," he mumbles into the head of the vessel, then tips it back to take another loud slurp.

"Master, she is quite sane," answers Peleshet. "The other queen I could not bring back with me, for she is the mother of an infant girl who resembles you so completely that I dare not hazard their journey."

"Hah, a daughter, you say?" and for the first time the assassin smiles, putting down the amphora beside his chair and leaning forward to nod his approval. "That is best, for a male child from those two parents would be one too many monsters on the Aegean. A girl. A little she-wolf. How sweet. I shall give her a wide berth, else we kill one another for sport one day. But this one? This one comes willingly? Does she know of my plan?"

"She knows only that you mean to reinvent the island kingdom," answers Peleshet. At this Rush booms a laugh that causes even Media to flinch, while sending the servants in flight down the four sets of stairs leading to the theater floor.

Rush stands, puts the amphora to his lips, chokes on a final guffaw while attempting to swallow, then tosses the vessel into the arms of a servant standing nervously at the bottom of the stairs The man manages to hang on to the jug though the force of it nearly topples him. Rush trots down the stairs, leaps onto the stage using only one palm for balance, and takes Peleshet in a bear's hug.

"Good man, Pele, good man. Yes, I mean to reinvent it. The Minoan gods have turned it to ash, such was their anger at the people who inhabited it. And why? Hmm? Has anyone given me an answer in the two years that I have waited, with utmost patience I might add, with amazing tolerance, to claim it for my own?" He is pacing now, back and forth behind Peleshet and the queen, his stride so powerful that his pass lifts the hair of Peleshet's beard. "Was it because they failed to worship the proper deities? At the proper seasons? Offering proper sacrifice? What sort of conceited gods are these, hm? Capricious and vain. Dangerously shallow-minded. Not like my little cat," and now he brings a hand up to squeeze thumb and index finger against the arch of his brow. The theater is silent, all eyes riveted on this unrehearsed scene, a scene more enthralling than any they have ever prepared or executed. Does the Wolf weep?

Peleshet has taken Media's arm by one elbow and drawn her back, giving the Wolf all the room he needs to command the theater.

"Not like my little Grain God, who hates…. not because he is given too little, for I have buried him in gold. Because of me the world is his. No, he hates me because I killed. Because I killed that which I have every right under heaven to kill! A beast. And an enemy king!"

"WAS IT THAT?" booms Rush, stopping center stage with arms outstretched. His voice carries up into the open sky above, as if beseeching the Babylonian gods. Behind a curtain to his left Eliabus watches with eyes big as duck eggs.

"My gods," he hisses at Horus at his side, "He is magnificent! What an actor he might have been!"

CHAPTER THREE

It is daybreak on the coast of Anatolia. Rah has been riding for three days, never overtaxing his new mount, but resting as the horse needs rest, four hours at a time. His animal brain has adapted quickly to his independent freedom, and reverted to the habits of his childhood. When the moon is high, he leaves the horse tied at a fence or stand of trees with sufficient vegetation to keep it occupied foraging. Then he slips silently into a farmer's field or through a gate and down a deserted cart path to find a hen house, a grain bin, a cold cellar stocked with apples or pears, carrots or onions. He steals without guilt, for in his world, everything is everyone's. Need is the only license required for pilfering food for himself, grain and hay for his ride. A lamp lit in the main house does not discourage him, but in fact invites his thieving, for if the farmer is inside and the lamp still lit, he is sitting down to table after a hard day's labor, complaining to his wife or scolding his children, hardly likely to hear an acrobat's soft tread, or the start of an owl, or the lowing of a cow.

In this way, Rah and the King's Turkoman have made a long journey easy, and when they arrive at the cliffs of Amega they are refreshed and rested.

"Is good time, we find Josepha," says Rah, patting the Turkoman's golden shoulder. "She is be feeding dove maybe. Lady always feed her dove before sun is come up. Feed dove before even she eat. Eh, up there!" And he points with confidence at a tiny figure moving across a wide balcony on the roof of the assassin's quarters.

"This be her, this be Josepha." And with another pat on Samsu-

Titana's withers he gathers his reins and urges the gleaming animal forward, down a steep rise, toward the gates of Amega.

Three days later the Wolf of Amega receives word, via the now famed runner, Akintunde, that his little cat has returned to his very fortress on the coast of Anatolia, and is making demands that only a god would dare make of the lady of that house.

He must have a ship, his twenty horses, gifted to him by the Wolf himself, and a promise from Josepha that his troupe will shortly follow him back to the island kingdom of Minoa.

"There is no reasoning with him," continues Akintunde, still panting from the day's labor. It is nearly summer and the air is hot and heavy, his face grayed, his lips white from the dust he has swallowed on his journey. He has rehearsed this message repeatedly, with each footfall, for two hundred miles. These are the very words Josepha gave him on the day he left, and he has lost not a single one.

The assassin paces back and forth across the pearl and jade tile floor of his enemy's war room. Along the walls Babylonian weapons gleam in the morning light that filters through the clerestory windows facing east. Several Babylonian runners stand at attention at the entry, waiting their turn to be swift or be dead. But Rush has no use for them. He will send no answer back to his wife, for in the end he is a wolf and a wolf works in secret. No one in Amega must know his plans before their time of execution.

Except for those who can read his mind, and there is always an advantage in that, when you are a wolf.

"You will remain here, Akintunde. My wife will do nothing without my answer, and that is sufficient. Let him see how far he can get without my hand holding open the door. Little fool, he runs into the trap like a baited animal." He turns, his blood red cloak lifting like a red tide, then settling about his gold-embroidered tunic. Today he wears his Hatti general's helmet, a bronze headpiece with a red-dyed horsetail plume rising from the poll. The costume gives him the aspect of a dragon whose fire spouts not from his maw but from his crown.

"Have the Black ready for me," he tosses the order behind him, toward a footman. "And you, Petuk, give Captain Nikolaos my orders that he will remain in command of the city until my return."

At the House of Seven Cisterns, Mochlos the priest is overseeing the rearrangement of the Temple Of The Rah. The High Priest has been in unusually high spirits since the disappearance of his creation, and Awiti has lately overheard him humming Minoan lullabies across the hall upon awakening.

"Henceforth, there will be a continual prayer here in the Temple of the Rah, Nipu, and these two torches will never be permitted to extinguish. They must remain ablaze, here in the south and east windows, so that the entire city of Babylon is reminded that the spirit of the Rah remains present, though his body has ascended into the heavens to live among the gods. Therefore there will be perpetual worship of the Rah, and the Temples of Marduk and Ishtar must be cleansed of all of the vile and distorted practices that their gods demanded. I shall appoint my own priests to oversee these temples and the proper worship of our little savior within, so that the fields of Babylon may continue to recover and indeed to thrive."

"Some say it is the ash cloud from the Minoan disaster that replenishes our fields, Holiness, and not the Rah. Some say that the Rah has fled, and that there is no 'Soul Of Rah' in the temple, that it is a hoax, a foreigner's idolatry, and that the sons and daughters of Baal should be slain for allowing this blasphemy against their deity."

"Some say a goose is a flightless bird, Nipu, but I say they have never traveled beyond their own barnyards. There are gods in this earth with powers beyond Babylon's imagination," Mochlos raises a fist for emphasis, "I have brought the greatest of these to Babylon, and I intend to be recognized for my skills throughout the land!"

When he is not in the stable, working and grooming the horses he intends to take with him, Rah is pacing the lyceum, drawing a constant if fluctuating audience of men and servants around him as he pantomimes his story, extolling his deeds as a god and pleading his case for his return to the lost island world where he was made. At first, Tyrus, priest of the Bull God, and Enenoch, priest of the Sky, ignore his presence, going about their duties before their own altars with little notice. But as the crowds continue to gather about Rah, drawing their own assemblies from them, the two High Priests abandon their oblations and join the spectators.

It is Tyrus who makes the first attempt to challenge him.

"The Island is lost, Rah, perhaps blown clear off the face of the earth by the fires of Thera. There is no home to return to. If there were, do you not think that we would have heard something? Wouldn't the Egyptians, second greatest sailing nation but to Minoa, have by now sent word that they have taken it and are rebuilding the great cities? Repaving the roads? Sewing new crops in the ashy earth?"

"Greek is be first," nods Rah, as if in agreement. "No Egypt. Is Greek be first. This why Rah have to go now. If Greek come first before Wolf, wolf is angry, make more war. Wolf is no let Greek take Knossos. He think this Knossos his city, like he think Rah his god. You think Wolf is sit by," and now he is sitting on the stone base beneath the Bull God, arms crossed over his chest, which is noticeably broader than when last he held the attention of an audience in the lyceum of Amega, though as sleek and hairless as ever. "Like this?" And now he leans back, as if on a couch, crossing his legs at the ankles and lifting an invisible amphora of wine to his lips. He casually gulps a mouthful, spilling a bit on his skirt, which he pats with an unseen napkin. He puts the jug down at his feet. "You think Wolf leave Knossos to Greek?" he chides, looking about at his entire audience. A man in front snorts and shrugs in answer, looking back at his companions.

"Hah," says Rah. He slips off the platform upon which Tyrus' bronze bull, God of War, commands the lyceum from the south wall. The figure hurls his immortal bulk forever forward in an attitude of attack: head down, golden horns gleaming, nostrils flared, ruby eyes glittering, one front leg lifted as if it readies itself to leap over the heads of the congregation.

"Wolf need to follow Rah now to Crete, before Greek there. Then maybe no war. Just maybe some Greek try march up Bridge Road into city-" and he is marching, arms and legs stiff and chin set, his naked feet slapping against the floor stones as hard as boots. "Then!" and Rah whirls, and he is slashing and spinning his way through his audience, unseen crescent blades held high over his head. Taken in by the pantomime, some of them crouch and fall, playing their part, so that the assassin might singlehandedly lay waste the imaginary Greek battalions that are attempting to disembark from their warships.

"The Wolf, as you insist on calling our Master," responds Enenoch coolly from his position under the Sky Dome, a towering mural of blues and golds that dwarfs even the bronze Bull God and reaches up from behind the Sky altar into a curved point. The mural has only recently been completed, and the artist tips forward on a ladder high above his head, stroking the final touches of the golden framework. "The Wolf of whom you so easily speak is still in Babylon, as we all know, having taken that city as quickly as an osprey takes a fish, and, though unlike you I would hardly dare to guess his plans, he is surely in no frame of mind to leave Babylon, The Star of Syria, to strike out for a dead hump of ash and rock that must float now like a bloated turtle in the middle of the Great Sea."

"What you know, Enenoch, hey? You know Sky? You tell King sky is fall, eh? No! Enenoch tell nothing! Because Enenoch *know* nothing. Priest of Sky he cannot predict Sky. How he predict Wolf?"

The Sky Priest frowns at that, for he has no answer to it. He makes a little huff of exasperation and flattens his features into a mask of unconcern, though he shoots Tyrus a "do something!' look as the crowd turns back to watch Rah strut across the hall toward the altar of the House of the Moon.

Cara is arranging lilies on either side of the immense altar, which spans twenty feet across the north wall. Behind her the gleaming golden emblem of the House of the Moon, two crescent moons flanking the full, challenges the Bull God across the lyceum like a giant's war shield. She has been listening to Rah's tirade with calm humor. He is the same, she thinks now as he marches up to the altar platform, takes the five stairs in two steps, and launches himself atop to stand amongst the flower pots.

"This Rah temple!" he cries, taking her upraised wrist and pulling her easily up beside him. "This Rah priestess!" he spins her into his embrace, pressing a hand into her back and bending her over so that her silken cape and hood fall away from her.

His crowd hushes. Tyrus takes a step forward, his hands outstretched as if to catch the priestess from his own altar. Enenoch presses his eyes with the fingers of one hand, shaking his head.

Rah has lifted the priestess' chin with his free hand and gazes into her eyes, his mouth so close to hers that she can feel the bristle on his upper lip. His breath is puppy sweet.

So strong! thinks Cara. He lifts me like a child. And taller too, though he will never reach the Assassin's chin. You are grown into a man, sweet Rah, and you are not man, but divine.

Rah's kaleidoscopic eyes stroke her face, settle on her mouth. He dips her, loosening his grip on her waist imperceptibly so that she suddenly feels herself let go of and must snatch his shoulders to prevent herself falling. She sees the corners of his mouth turn in a sly grin just as he opens his lips and brings them down on hers, his cleft tongue hidden in the depths of that mysterious place, though his audience imagines it has plunged into her mouth.

There is a wave of giggles in the audience, mostly those of maids and ladies, before he releases her carefully, sets her back on her feet, and leaps off the altar to the lyceum floor.

"All this for Rah. Wolf give to Rah. Make Rah god here Amega. Wolf now he want return Rah to Knossos. He want Rah take ship, take all horse. Take new moon priestess, this Cara." He gestures to the flustered Cara, whose cheeks are now pink from her ordeal. She wobbles, then climbs off the altar to stand beside him. "And Sun too," he adds in an afterthought.

"You disobey Rah, you disobey Wolf! You see what he do! What you think? You think Rah is come to Amega with Wolf no want? Rah come because Wolf want Rah come. Take what his. Go back Crete, where Rah is born. Make good for Wolf, all kind things come from Rah. Good crop, good fish, good horse. Be island where Rah can raise, train all horse for Amega, Babylon, what else Wolf he take." He struts toward the far archway and disappears.

Later, in the priest's wing, Tyrus and Enenoch are settled on chaises around a low table in their joined sitting room enjoying their evening meal when Crispo and Cara enter unannounced.

"I would offer you something, Sun, only I know you feed yourself better than you do us. And you, Moon, you live on such white and meatless fare that you would find nothing on our table to tempt you," Tyrus says with a tired smile.

"Still, recline and enjoy the Master's last stores of Minoan wine," offers Enenoch, rising to his feet at the sight of the Moon Priestess to offer her his couch.

"Stay where you are, dear Sky," returns Cara, waving off his offer. "I can make a comfortable enough place for myself on this sheepskin."

"And I," joins in Crispo, "Will need help rising if I recline as you two do, like the Egyptians, on the floor to eat."

"Stand then, you pastry," laughs Tyrus, "And I will pass you up a cup

of this delicious fruity red."
When everyone's cup has been filled and raised, Crispo offers a toast. "To the Grain God of Knossos, and to our continued good fortune in his service."
"Hah!" Tyrus chokes on his sip. "That from the man he has demanded must sail with him back to the charred remains of Caphtor?"
"He will demand you soon enough, Bull. He only insists on his own priestess and on me because he believes he cannot survive without the one and he cannot eat without the other."
"That is certain," responds Enenoch ruefully, "he will demand us all returned to the land of the dead. Unless he realizes upon sight of the coast that the place is a Tartarus, uninhabitable and fit for neither man nor god. Perhaps he will not land at all the, but return to Amega with his tail between his legs."
"Really?" Tyrus raises his brows at his associate, setting down his cup and nodding to a concubine to refill it and those of his companions. "And when did you ever see that blond bobcat with a tail between his legs? It is a wonder he can carry his head on his shoulders at all, agile as they may be, with the weight of it, since he has become the property of the Aegean Demon. No, we shall all be hauled off to the fried island of the damned," he gives Crispo a nod, raising his cup. "I have no doubt of it. What we must consider is how we might take advantage of it. We shall be the first, shall we not? It will be in our best interests to look upon this new turn of events as a means to an end." Tyrus puts down his cup, jarring the cedar table, causing Cara and Enenoch to flinch in unison.
"This is no bull fight, Tyrus," snaps Enenoch, frowning. "You cannot convince me that there is any advantage to a handful of priests on a scorched island. For all we know Knossos has tumbled into the sea, along with Mount Ida and every city along the coast as well. A priest requires a city, a gathering of believers. That land, if it can be salvaged at all, will require an army of warriors to hold and another of craftsmen and laborers to rebuild it. Where does a foursome of dandies such as ourselves fit in to that nightmare?"
"You have said it yourself, Sky!" counters Tyrus. "The warrior and the workman needs his gods, too! And priests to placate them. The former requires his deity to protect him in battle, also to give him something to fight for. The latter requires his deity to give his work

purpose. To sustain him in his drudgery. To give him hope that he will one day be rewarded."

"And what of Mochlos, brethren?" asks Cara suddenly. "Am I to become High Priestess of the Moon in place of the one who made him?"

"Wasn't that always the plan?" Tyrus raises his brows at the priestess. "And why that smug weasel was forced to make you also? Certainly the Rah himself will not chose him over you, and the assassin would leave him in Babylon to tend the flock of Marduk, where his self-important sadism can do the most good!"

"He is not so bad as you think," murmurs Cara, looking down. "He loves the Rah, in his own way," she trails off.

"Hah! And would loves him to death if he had the chance!" Crispo counters, setting his own cup down on the low table with a bang. "I for one, gentlemen," and here he gives Cara a smile and a half-bow, "and lady, will go where the Rah demands I go. If it were not for him I would still be on the island kingdom, a puff of ash amongst the bones of the ancients now twice roasted in the City of the Dead. I owe him my life, as do all of you. As does all of Amega and Hattusha if you would be honest about it. For without the Rah, the plague might have taken the one and the Amorite, Iamhad, the other. I believe in the Rah's magic. I believe he saved us all from the destruction of Crete, and that if we fail to honor and obey his wishes now, we bring upon ourselves, and our houses, the wrath of his god."

The room is silent, but for a small gasp of alarm from Cara. The priests of the Four Houses look from one to another, the jovial flavor of the meeting having dissipated with Crispo's words like smoke dissipates in a puff of wind. Finally, Tyrus speaks.

"Well, we had none of us thought of that, had we," he frowns. "But this too can be seen in two lights. Yes, we will have to go where he demands we go, for within him is the will of our god. But with a little luck, and some fortitude, this can be our salvation. Let's face it, brothers and sister, we are of no use to the assassin sitting comfortably here in Amega preaching to a congregation of killers. If we are in fact the first to return to the island, and under the umbrella of the protective claws of the assassin, our futures are guaranteed. We need to start considering how we can make this happen in a way that is most beneficial to us, and not sit here glumly like a gaggle of old hens, assuming the worst. Center your attentions on the worst that can happen and the worst will center its attention on you, let me tell you. I have lived a whole and healthy life by this maxim and I know it to be true."

"Bull is right," sighs Enenoch, slapping his knees and rising. "Even if the island is not more than an ash heap, we are better off doing as the Rah demands. How can we not and maintain our credibility? And if we have no credibility, what are we? And if we wait, and let the Rah return to Crete without us, and the Amegan Devil returns to find us sitting here with our thumbs in our asses, doing nothing to protect him as is our duty as his priests, what then? He will skewer us like mutton on a spit and find himself our replacements in Babylon, where priests are bought for a song, and have been re-trained by our good friend, Mochlos."

CHAPTER FOUR

Rush is three days out of Babylon when he has a sudden change of heart.

It is not the sort of thing that happens to him often, and at first he dismisses it from his mind and gallops on, hoping to make Amega before sunset. But the thing that claws at his heart like a mother leopard guarding her young, as he rides through the Table of the Gods, is a sense of defeat, an inability to settle a score, a thing that Rush, being Rush, cannot tolerate. It closes his lungs, narrows his vision, until he must stop, transfixed and all but blind, as he approaches the spire under which he found the Rah wailing the night he rescued him from the headless ghosts of Babylon. And he is beset by walls of hate and vengeance, walls that even he cannot scale or break through to continue south toward his fortress.

He is remembering Rah, remembering how he found him, crouched and yowling, there, a broken thing, a lost child.

A deposed god.

He pulls the Black up short, circles the spire, pictures the boy again, on his knees, shivering, twisted in on himself like a wounded bird, unable to utter a human word. And he remembers how he would have gone into battle with the dead at that moment, raised his blades to the very author of the underworld, to stop that howling, to soothe that boy.

His mouth is clamped with rage. But it is not the dead he wants, it is not those unfortunate and headless multitudes that lurk here, awaiting vengeance. It is the one who took Rah from his mother. Seventeen? Eighteen years ago? Far north, in the land of the Sun

People.

Barbarians. Some tribe of thieves pushed north by the heat, scavengers from Gaul moving on foot in small clans, filth who called themselves 'warrior' because they had the brute strength to wield a mace or an axe, entirely ignorant of any real meaning of the word.

They would have meandered, boldly, through the land of the evening sun, perhaps in late spring or early summer, after the thaw, in search of furs and amber. They would have killed whole villages of the peaceful people making their permanent homes along the riverbanks and lowlands, people who traded their furs and amber for bronze.

They would have come upon some small tribe living in long houses in a dense wood, or along a waterway. They would have slaughtered any males over thirteen summers, raped any woman not a grandmother, and taken the children to trade as slaves. They would have killed Rah's father if he were home to defend his family. His twins.

They would have raped and killed his mother. Did they kill the sister, did they take the boy's tongue as well? Or did these things happen later, during the terrible course of the boy's child-slavery.

Rush feels the saliva collecting in his mouth like a wolf who smells blood. He whips the Black around, certain now of what he will do before he returns to the Minoan island to reinstall the Rah, along with his two queens, Media and Ephtheta, and his four priestly houses. As surely as he knows his many names: Rush The Assassin, Ameg the Merchant, Minoan Priest of the Dead, Amorite mercenary Samal-Etatani, and Greek warrior Antaris, he knows that neither he nor any of his guises will rest without the sweet delight of revenge, the evening of scores, the symmetry of his capture and enslavement of the beast who killed Rah's mother.

That he might also thank the man for giving him his nemesis, a boy so beautiful that he could not take his head, a creature so strange and otherworldly that he would forfeit his own sanity to have him, does not escape him.

"I have two reasons to find you, little man. You and your nest of vermin. One, for killing his mother, and two, to thank you for my own enslavement. Death is too good for you, too quick, to final. You I will take for a slave and put on your knees that you might worship and praise from morning 'til night the very boy you made an orphan and sold into bondage."

"But where will you live, Rah? What will you eat?" Josepha sits at her weaving stool in her inner chamber. Her loom stands before an open double doorway overlooking the sea. This morning the sky is like crystal, as if the ash cloud somehow sharpened the lens of the sun, rendering the heavens in finer detail. It is blue as a robin's egg, while the sea roils, white lions raking the sand with emerald claws. How strange, thinks Josepha, that the Rah desires Crete, though Crete and the sea twice conspired to kill him.

"Not everyone die, Josepha," says Rah. In bad weather servants close the doors, which open onto a wide terrace, but today the sun beats down on Rah's curls, his scalp long healed from the injury of his tearing off his diadem. It has been four weeks since Rah's return, and Josepha has become accustomed to his daily visits to her chamber to plead his case. He must return to Knossos, where he was born. He must be sacrificed as the priest, Mochlos, planned from the beginning. This is his purpose among men. This is his destiny.

"What do you mean, Rah? You were there when the quakes and the floods foretold the end of the Minoan world. You were aboard my husband's ship when that world exploded in fire and ash. How can you say these things?"

Josepha looks up from her work, a rendering of the clouded waves of the sea below. She is struck, suddenly, by the changed profile of the Grain God of Knossos, who is no longer a beautiful boy, but a beauty of another sort altogether. Not yet a man, though the platinum bristle along his jaw might suggest that he is. No longer a child. Your legs are longer, Rah. Your chest deeper. Your shoulders broader. And your face, though never having lost its innocence, could not be taken for a girl's. The brow, the forehead, the cheekbones, more male now. Though never have I seen one so beautiful.

Rah nods, his eyes never leaving the horizon. He looks always to Caphtor, thinks Josepha, to the land of the Philistines, to the isle of Crete.

"Some still live, I see in here," and he taps his chest, "Ting Ya, she show Rah. Knossos no. But east, yes, and south, no Cyrus. But more south. Many people survive. Now Greek, they come, come before Wolf is come. Wolf is go north. No come to Amega. He go north first, go where Rah is baby. Look for man take Rah. Too much love for Rah. Wolf is need come back to Knossos, Josepha. Forget man who take Rah. Is all gone. Too late. But Greek they come to Crete. Come from east. Soon they plant. Good soil now. But no rain. Not without Rah. Need Rah."

Josepha sighs, returning to her loom. The boy has become a man since Knossos fell to the sea. Now he determines his own fate, slave or no. Antaris or no. He will find a way to return to the island, while her husband chases phantoms in the land of the Sun People, looking for vengeance and symmetry. But when he returns, will he find his Rah? Or will his Rah no longer be his Rah, but something else entirely.

Rah turns from the window, picks up the sheepskin he has been carrying with him for days, and moves to go. As he passes her bench, Josepha reaches for him, and though he is quicker than she, he allows her to hold his wrist a moment, as if assuring herself of his pulse.

Smoke, a dark hall. Stairs. A doorway leading out onto a veranda. It is evening, and the night air is moist, and rain is coming. She hops onto the balustrade, which is no wider than the heel of her foot. And suddenly she is looking down onto the upturned face of her beloved, who stands on the balcony twenty feet below. And the look in her husband's eyes…at first she forgets she is not herself. And the look bites her heart, she nearly reels from the desperate love in it.

"I will climb that wall with my teeth and eat you whole!" he screams, his fingers crawling over the slick Iberian marble, desperate for purchase. And then she remembers. She is Rah now.

And she hears herself barking from the depth of her lungs in the lashing rain, "Wolf is kill King!" as she tears the emerald diadem from her head, flinging it down at him, though a warm breeze gentles its fall so that it only wafts like a golden dove into the palm of the assassin's upturned hand.

"Rah, it is done in every city," says the Wolf, lifting the circlet to his muzzle to inhale the scent of it. "The king must die. Or the city will never accept its conqueror. I am your king, Rah. And the new King of Babylon. And you have danced for me. Come down, boy, I cannot lose you thus," he mouths the words.

"Kill, kill, kill!" she shouts down at him, and she is walking back and forth along the ledge as easily as if she had the floor of a stage upon which to balance. "CAN YOU MAKE WHAT YOU KILL? No, even chicken you no can make. Only what is make *you*, can make chicken to *feed* you, feed your army. Kill cat, kill king. Always kill. No more for Rah. Now Rah take what you love, Wolf, and kill. You see. You see."

And she makes a half turn, lifts her arms above her head and she is spinning back and away on her hands along the ledge and she is slipping like a seal down a rain pipe into the canal.

"Josepha see," says Rah, who has been watching the Wolf's mate with eerie patience. Josepha frees his wrist, looks up into the blue-green sea in his eyes, and falters. She draws her hand into herself, as if burned. She gives Rah a repentant look.

"Maybe see too much, eh?" says Rah, a small sinister curve twisting the very edges of his lips as he sits down beside her. "Josepha see," his voice is a low, buttery growl, his eyes no longer the lost, innocent eyes of the boy-slave, but so dizzyingly clear, certain, unconquerable, that she is for a moment frightened of him.

"Rah, I-"

"Josepha always like Rah, yes?" he whispers against her lips. The back of her throat shivers closed. "Maybe like Wolf is like Rah, eh?"

Her eyes can no longer hold his. They drop, only to slip over the tawny shoulder, down the well-muscled pectorals, lingering against her will on the pierced, peach nipples, to the golden arrow of fleece peeking over the lip of his skirt.

When she looks up into his face again his smile has tucked a dimple into one cheek. His brows twist up, amused, indulgent. "Josepha like Rah," it is a statement of fact now, and she feels the heat of his mockery reddening her cheeks. "Want to touch Rah. Want to feel what inside Rah." And it is true. She did want to touch him, to know what was inside him, so hidden, so inaccessible.

She took what was not hers to take. He let her.

"Want to take." It is as though he reads *her* mind now. He is teasing her. "You take maybe Rah is no want to give. Now maybe Rah take, eh? But Josepha she *want* to give."

"Josepha like Rah when Rah is slave. Is okay. Rah is be slave for Josepha. No touch. Only Josepha touch." He draws his arms behind his back, a trussed slave.

Her head is swooning. This is not her love. This is not the one who loves her. The one who saved her. This is the boy, the child, the sweet child.

What has happened to that sweet child?
"Sweet Rah," is all she can answer. Before she has formed another thought his mouth, soft as the nose of a kitten, has brushed her own. Posed, slave-like, with his arms pinned behind his back, he nuzzles along her jaw, that wounded tongue finding her ear and flicking at it, creating oceans.
"Oh, no, Rah!" It was meant to be a demand, at least a plea. But it softens into a sigh in her throat. She had meant to pull his arms forward, had she not? Yet somehow she has lost her way looking for his hands, and found instead the long, lean muscle along his sides. He snatches her hands.
"Take Rah, Josepha," says Rah. He leans back to rest on the bench, pulling her hands behind him so that she must come with him.
The movement puts her on top of him, and she is at first chagrined. She is too plump. She will crush the breath from him! But then she feels the stiffness of his member through the linen of his skirt pressing, unrestrained, into her belly.
"Let me go, Rah," she manages, awakened by that hardness. He is a man now. I must remember, this is a man. And he is every bit as dangerous as a man.
And as suddenly as she was drawn down on top of him he has lifted her, righted her on the bench, and he is standing, his back to her, his head hung as if in shame.
He is pantomiming. The voice in her head is loud. He is always pantomiming, her mind answers it. Then follow his lead, says the voice.
"I'm sorry, Rah, I understand. I had no right-"
"Nobody have right, Josepha," answers Rah. "But everybody take. Now is maybe time for Rah to take." He turns to face her.
And in the immediate beauty of his face there is also a warning, a keen light in those prismatic eyes that heralds a new age.
"Everybody think Rah stupid. Rah can dance like," he tosses his open hands over his head, "like falcon can fly, but Rah be stupid. Empty head," he taps his temple. "Rah can make three-horse chariot for war. Change fight forever. This all Rah. But still, Rah be stupid. Just baby head," he taps his temple a second time.
"Baby because always slave. Somebody always tell what to do. Can no think for self." His brows are low, the foxy feathers have become a single line. His eyes are blue ice. "Rah want to dance for king,

baby want to dance for king. Put king in box. Think Rah is no see Wolf because Wolf is dress like king maybe dress. Still have kill-kill hood, still have all weapon all over!"

He crisscrosses his body with a wave, adjusts his invisible belt, hooks his thumbs through it, and he is the Wolf, decked with weaponry, leering over the railing of the King's Theater Pavilion.

"But Rah see, Josepha. No need to touch to see," and Josepha flinches at the accusation, though she cannot pull her eyes from his face. "Rah see, see before thing come sometime. Maybe Wolf is go north because Rah is send Wolf north. Maybe Rah know Wolf like Rah know dog, eh? Put scent down, dog go. Rah put scent down, Josepha. And Wolf is go north. Go find what is already dead. Wolf he want to find man who take Rah, take Iliah, kill tribe. This seventeen summer ago, Josepha. You think this Wolf is find this man now? How he do that? You think man who kill kill all the time kill is be living seventeen summer? Somebody kill him long time ago. Maybe Wolf he is chase shadow now."

"You are telling me that you deliberately sent him north, Rah? On a false trail? For what purpose? Why have you done this?" Josepha has risen from the loom bench to meet Rah's eyes, only to find that she must look up now, for he has grown in the year that he has been gone.

"Why you think, Josepha? Maybe Rah no so stupid everybody think. Maybe," and somehow he has stepped forward and slipped one arm around her middle before she has had time to react.

And those satin lips are on her throat. And there is no fight in her, not even if her husband where to slam through the double doors of her sitting room, blades drawn. She is a quail in a snare. Her head drops back, willingly, allowing him access to her heart.

"Rah is go back to Crete." He mumbles into her décolletage, pressing her back down onto the weaving bench. "Maybe Josepha no want Rah to leave," his voice is deeper than she remembers, only shades lighter than her husband's. The timbre sends a warmth down into her belly that threatens to release the most intimate of moistures. "Want Rah stay here, with Josepha, maybe, while Wolf is north," He lifts his head. His ultramarine irises are eclipsed by his enlarged pupils. "You want Rah stay, Josepha?" He blinks, dropping his eyes down to scan the neckline of her dress. The tip of his bitten tongue peaks from his mouth to moisten his incisors.

She opens her mouth to speak, but only offers a silly squeak.

"Ta-hah," Rah graces her with both dimples. "Josepha she can no talk now. Rah talk okay now. Josepha like have bad tongue. No easy to speak with this tongue, Josepha," he slips the tip of his tongue between his lips to show her, and the sight of that damaged sweetness completes the release of intimate wetness that his new, man-voice, had begun.

Yet there is no moisture in her throat to lubricate her voice. She sits dumb, watching him rise from the bench with a sly erotica in his movement. He is dancing, comes the voice in her head. A performance. For me.

Suddenly his seductive demeanor is gone. He stands over her, a stubborn scowl flattening his brow. His pupils are gone, his irises frosted cerulean.

"Rah need ship, Josepha. Need men to sail, take Rah to Crete. Rah give everything. Give rain, bring good crop, stop plague, give Wolf three-horse for war. Save Amega, save Hattusha, save Babylon," he lifts his hands and gestures to the north, to the south, to the east, the west. "But nobody give Rah what he need when he ask. So maybe Rah take what he can take, until somebody give Rah what he need."

And he picks up his sheepskin, and pads, barefoot, to the double doors, taking care to close them soundlessly behind him.

CHAPTER FIVE

The caravan from Babylon arrives on the following evening. Light is spilling into the lyceum clearstory windows, blinding Crispo, who is completing his evening adulations before the great bronze sun disk that is the central feature behind his alter. Above the disk, which is as wide as a man is tall, the eastern sky is a lavender cape, waving from the shoulders of the sinking sun. Crispo finishes his invocations, struggles to his right knee as best he can, and bows to his sovereign. Who am I to love the sun? he thinks, climbing to his feet. A god who can rise on a breathless morning, without so much as a puff of air to lift him, does not need a priest who cannot lumber to his feet from a genuflection without straining and panting. I belong in the kitchen, creating delights for the tongues of men, while one as golden and lithe as the Rah serves you and your church. He has only managed to turn, lifting his aprons to descend the steps of his alter, when a commotion out in the hall brings his head up.

Enenoch has already left his own podium and reached the archway into the entrance hall when a tall man with a red cloak and a bronze helmet shoves past him. His horsetail plume is black, signifying his rank as a special-forces officer for the Wolf of Amega.

Behind him the rise and fall of excited, if exhausted, travelers filters past him to fill the lyceum.

"The troupe!" cries Enenoch, turning to call the Sun priest from his frozen position at the top of his altar stairs. "It is the troupe of the Rah!" But he has no sooner said it than the lyceum begins to fill, the dusty travelers pushing past Peleshet to mill about the much changed auditorium.

It is Tyrus, just now entering the hall from an interior archway, who spies the second group of travelers, in finer garb yet reticent, behind the others.

One petite and fully-veiled creature has stepped into view to the left of the red cloak, and beside her, a second female, this one dressed from crown to toe in yellow silks, clings to her arm.

Presently a third female, wearing the elaborate headpiece and the saffron robes of a Minoan royal, steps forward from behind the red cloak to take a position on his right, and with brazen self-assurance, takes the man's free arm.

Tyrus is instantly striding forward to make his introduction to this third female. Enenoch, seeing his fellow cleric's quick assessment of the situation, follows at his elbow. But poor Crispo, whose has yet to descend from his altar to cross the length of the lyceum, must fight his way through a sea of dancers, costume designers, prop builders and gaffs before he is close enough to hear the little Minoan's reaction.

"Oh, how extraordinary! To find that not only has the boy-god, Rah, survived, but that all four priestly houses of Knossos are among those whom the Terror rescued from the cataclysm! Well I have not introduced myself. I am Media, and I was Queen of Cyrus. Your enemy, I suppose, in another age, but now, here, finding ourselves among fellow Minoans, I hope your friend. Why, we were utterly convinced that the entire north coast must surely have fallen into the sea on that terrible day! And surely you, who were among the few that the Terror was willing and able to take with him, thought the same held true for the south coast!"

Media has been chattering fluently and without interruption at the two high priests, and she pauses only briefly to nod to Crispo, including him in her conversation. But a hush at the far end of the hall brings the room full of magpies to silence and she lifts her eyes to peer over the three priests' heads to see whose entrance has silenced the prattle. She sees a softly plump, plainly dressed woman with one unadorned, dove-brown braid draped over her right shoulder. The woman is obviously a central figure here, for several soldiers, milling about the lyceum after paying tribute to their personal gods, have fallen to their knees and struck their chests at her entrance. But Media barely notices the lady of the house. She has been eclipsed.

Beside her, taller, broader, paler than she recalls but unmistakable, stands the Grain God of Knossos. Media releases a groan of utter delight. Her hands clench involuntarily and her sharp nails nip her escort's arm. Her free hand moves to her throat.

"It is he!" she sighs, releasing Peleshet and pushing past the priests surrounding her to get to him. But the crowd of performers is too thick. They, too, have spied their doyen. As the mob packs toward the eastern wall of the lyceum under the altar of the Sun, a dozen ram's horns blare from the open balcony above the Bull God, and a squad of Amegan archers are suddenly lining the railing, bows pointed down at the line of newcomers closest to Josepha and the Rah.

Media, hopping on her toes to see over the heads of the mob of dancers in front of her, fixes her gaze on Rah's face. The kitten is a tiger now. The planes of his cheeks are glittering with the start of a pale beard. His whiskers frame his heart shaped lips, creating the illusion of an imperceptible grin. The fleecy brows are determined. Rah looks over his admirers, barely turning his head. His thick-lashed eyes are at half-mast, needing no Egyptian liner to accentuate their cat-like tilt.

"Oh, he is even more beautiful!" she hears Awiti murmur. And as if he has heard her, Rah lifts his muzzle, spies her.

His eyes flash.

Now he is pushing his way through the subdued crowd. He shoves Dimius aside, strides past Aros and Pyrus without a word, gives Crispo a stroke of a glance, causing the corpulent priest to gulp and step away, giving the Grain God access to his first concubine.

Rah takes Awiti's hand, lifts it, plants a kiss against the pink of her palm.

The crowd begins to murmur appreciatively, moving back and away from the couple, giving them room. Rah tilts his head at his concubine seductively. She looks about, mortified.

"I cannot dance, Rah!" she hisses as he draws her into an embrace and then spins her away from him, to the end of his arm. His eyes are full of mischief as he circles her, stalking, his shoulders back, his feet stealthy. He spirals closer and closer. She turns round and round on her heels to follow his movement. He lifts his arm, drops his chin, his eyes hot and fierce under the ruff of blonde brows. Now his fingers extend like claws reaching for her, while his torso pulls back as if fighting his own longing for her. Awiti giggles. Instantly he launches her into a delicate spin. She twirls into his open arms. He bends her backward and slips one knee beneath her arched back. He leans over her, his face a portrait of the immortal longing of love.

After a moment of stillness, Rah's passionate face decomposes. He smiles, dimples popping, and winks at his heroine as he holds her like a bouquet of lilies over his thigh, one arm supporting her, the other drawn back and away from his body.

"Don't need to know how to dance, Awiti," he says in his dusky, thick-tongued voice to the girl in his arms. His troupe is laughing and clapping. Even Dimius must smile in spite of himself.

"He could make a cow dance," he mutters, as the dance troupe engulfs Rah.

"You are to come with me, ladies," says Ham to Media, Ephtheta and Awiti, when Rah's little performance is completed. He waves off the three priests, who move to join the group, and leads the women out into the main hall and up a shallow flight of stairs to the colonnade overlooking the lyceum where, moments earlier, a line of ferocious archers had aimed their weaponry at their hearts.

"Not a very welcoming introduction," murmurs Ephtheta to Media, sotto voce.

"The Lady has had these wings prepared for the Rah and his temple," says Ham, who has reached the end of the colonnade, where a north/south hall bisects the one they stand in. "The High Priests, Enenoch and Tyrus are already installed, along with their households. The House of the Bull, down this way," he gestures down the southern corridor, "The House of the Sky," he waves a hand toward the northern extension. "The sun priest resides directly below, where he can be nearest the kitchens, in order that he might prepare the meals of the Rah."

He raises an arm toward Mochlos' sanctuary, which extends down the far end of the passageway.

"The High Priestess of the Moon," and Ham offers a polite nod at Cara as he continues down the hall, "Has controlled the House of the Moon alone since the Rah's ….flight from Amega. When he reappeared, he naturally returned to the rooms he was accustomed to, and to her. The priestly staff of the Moon remains in residence here.

I believe there are twenty." Ham gestures to the rooms lining the passage.

"Wouldn't it make more sense for Mochlos and his house to occupy the eastern rooms?" asks Media, stepping away from the group when they have passed under an archway into the entrance hall of the House of the Moon.

"I am not one to question my master's will, Madam," answers Ham, with a tight smile. "But I would imagine he gave the most important house, that in which the Rah dwells, the most attractive rooms. As you can see, these are larger, more accommodating, and have an exquisite view of the sea. Now that his two Queens are arrived, it is most favorable that they, too, reside in the House of the Rah."

Media tosses Ephtheta a curious look, but the eyes of the deposed princess are unreadable.

"You speak of 'the two queens' as if our arrival had been foretold to you, Ham. But how can that be? Before the disaster, the Rah knew two queens, that being myself, Queen of Cyrus, and Nanaea, Queen of Knossos. The former princess of Babylon is no longer a princess, and so can not be a queen."

The women have been milling about the room, which is the size of a small training arena, two stories high, ringed with clearstory open air windows and lined with colonnades along each side. Ham guides the women to four arched doorways behind a short colonnade along the southern end of the room. Ignoring the inquiry, he points to the first of these.

"Queen of Knossos," he bows to Ephtheta, whose draws herself up, her amber eyes opened so wide that they have lost their tip-tilted appearance. The archway is covered by a red and gold screen of strung beads. The design on the undisturbed curtain is a seated lion, symbol of Babylon.

"Queen of Cyrus," he makes a light bow and a sweeping motion toward the next archway, which is strung with a similar beaded curtain. This one is jade green, with a design of gold beads depicting a rising sun in the center. A crease at his lip is the only indication of mischief on the house servant's face as he lifts the shade to allow Media to pass through.

When she has done so, he lifts the blue and gold bead curtain of the third archway, nods at Awiti.

"First Concubine of the Rah." Awiti takes only a moment to curtsey and patter past him into her new lodging. This curtain depicts a dove sailing on extended wings over a mountain.

Ham gives the ladies a few moments to explore their chambers. Each one faces the sea, and each opens onto a joined balcony overlooking the cliffs of Amega. When the ladies have returned to him, Media points to the fourth chamber.

"This one is for the priestess, Cara, then," she states with certainty.

"The high priestess occupies the nearest of the two chambers you see along the western wall. The furthest is reserved for his Holiness, Mochlos, and remains empty at present," answers Ham.

"Then whose is this?" pipes Awiti, "this room joins my own with an inner door…" she trails off, not a little alarmed, for she is suddenly transported back to Babylon, where, rushing down the unlit stairwell to give Mochlos the good news of Rah's arousal she stumbles into a black breathing wall of fury and is hoisted by the neck against the cold stone wall.

"This is the chamber of the Rah," smiles Ham, lifting the white and yellow curtain, depicting the same bouquet of five heads of wheat that is embroidered on the back of the priestly robes of the House of the Moon. The ladies peek in, surprised to see two unadorned pallets against one wall, and a third, as low and simple but this one loaded with down-stuffed linens and several goose-white lambskins. There is a Minoan trunk beside it, and a small vanity against the wall between the two unadorned pallets, above which hangs a bronze mirror. A small round stool is tucked beneath the vanity.

"Why three beds?" asks the Minoan Queen.

"His dresser and face painter," answers Ham, moving toward the double doors leading out to the balcony. As he unlatches them and swings them outward, the ladies gasp. This view of the sea is more extraordinary than the view from their own rooms, although all four chambers share the same parapet. The view encompasses the sheer sides of the Amegan cliffs, and just now the salmon-colored evening sky is melting away above them like a soft fire. All along the clifftops at varying intervals men stand guard, though it is clear that even these cannot see the steep and crooked trail that has been cut into the side of the cliff, dodging in and out of brush and outcroppings of rock. The path will not support two men abreast, but if one, physically exemplar specimen chose to use it, and be willing to risk a fall that would surely break his back upon the rocks below, he might indeed

make his way to the base of the fortress.
"Is there access into the house below?" asks Media, who has stepped out onto the terrace to lean over the crenelated parapet.
"The Minoan Queen asks many questions," responds Ham, taking her arm gently and guiding her away from the low wall. The sea air is sweet, and Media resists him momentarily. She looks up into his face. "For she is used to governing beside her figurehead king. Here in Amega, the Minoan Queen will learn that this can be a dangerous habit. This king is in no need of the assistance of his womenfolk in securing his battlements."
"But why does the Rah choose to share his chamber with his servants? These men are part of the theater troupe, no? Or is he painted and dressed daily here in Amega?"
Ham gives the little queen a pleased nod, and was that a wink? "This is his way, Madam. Some days he demands to be painted, most days, he pads about on bare feet wearing nothing but a Minoan skirt to shield us from his nakedness, but I have also seen him in full costume, striding about the citadel as if deeply ensconced in some imaginary role. Of course, he has had to create his own faces and costumes up to now. For he will not tolerate any but his own Minoan staff, the Knossans, Aros and Pyrus to touch him."
Ham allows himself a sigh of exasperation as he leads Media and the other two ladies out of Rah's chamber.
"It has been a strange month," he adds, perhaps to himself.

CHAPTER SIX

The Sun People have camped for the night at the head of the river. The Sun Priests, seven in all, are dressed in their white-hooded robes and standing in order of their importance in a broad circle around the Sacrificing Bowl, and as his two assistants hold the trussed day-old lamb over the lip of the vessel, Aghi, head priest of the Sun People, readies his blade in the cauterizing fire. All around the circle of priests, the Sun People chant and dance in the dying light. Their only instruments, the lurs and drums, are silent. No music will be played again until the tribe moves on from this place, and the tribe will not move again until the river is fished out. Aghi raises his blade, a short, curved edge used only for sacrifice. He pulls the lambs head back and makes one short swift cut across its throat, efficiently silencing its terrified bleats and losing none of its blood to the thirsty ground. He launches into his Prayer for Good Waters, and the mass of bodies collapses around him, giving homage to the Sun God, their faces in the dust, as Aghi quickly wraps the body of the lamb in a skin sack and motions for Gudrun, his son, to take the meat away to his tent. The blood he will ladle out of the bowl and sprinkle on the heads of his supine flock. Later he will offer the best parts of the lamb, the heart, the liver, the brain, to Hakon, the chief of the clan. But old Hakon will decline these parts, asking instead for only the hind legs for his family. In fact, Hakon has no teeth and can no longer masticate the richer portions of the lamb meat, nor does he possess the gall to digest the sweet entrails. The once hale and hearty leader of the Sun People is now sustained by the fish gruel and berry mush that his daughters-in-law make for him, his five wives having all predeceased him either bearing his children or his rages.

The evening prayers and sacrifice complete, Aghi makes his own oblations to the setting sun, then leaves his assistants to wash the Sacrificing Bowl in the waters of the river. Tomorrow the camp will settle more firmly into their new habitat, and a long thatch hut will be built for the priesthood. He will have a decent pole tent for his personal use, and the fine albino elk skins that have not yet been unpacked will be hung at the door, displaying the importance of his position in the clan. Only old Hakon has a finer tent, the entrance decorated with two enormous elk heads in full horn, the exterior overlaid with albino fawn skins. Soon enough his oldest son, Ari, will inherit the chieftain tent. But until then, Aghi can look forward to a good lamb dinner every seventh evening, when the sacrifice is performed.

It is at the first hour of the moon that Aghi is awakened from his lamb-drunk slumber by an unexpected coolness over his bare legs. His tent door has been hitched open, allowing the damp river air to breathe a chill over his nakedness. But how is it that he is naked? When he lay down on his skins that evening he had drawn his deer hide rug over his body. Aghi always retired in the same fashion, stripping naked, washing his private places in a basin of warmed river water when water was available, and settling himself down on his skins like a corpse laid out in a burial mound, flat on his back, ankles together, wrists crossed over his chest, under a blanket of fawn skins.

Grudgingly opening his eyes to see what had caused the tent flap to hitch open, he perceives something, a thick darkness, in the entry hole of the tent, and he blinks, thinking that the thickness must be in his eyes.

And then the thickness moves.

And he is choking. Something has clamped shut his windpipe. A bear? is sitting on his chest growling.

"Tell me," says the bear, in a voice so low he can barely make out the words. The bear has a thick accent, quite beautiful actually, if one were not on one's way to unconsciousness.

To his shock, a second voice, this one a voice he recognizes, pipes up in a nasal whisper, "You will tell the Bear Man the name of the child thief."

The grasp on his throat has lifted. He takes a panicked breath and sputters, "What? What thief?"

"The Bear Man wants the name of the slave trader. He knows the Sun People hunt and steal children from the peaceful Forest People. He will return to cut out your eyes if you give him a false name."

Now Aghi places the second voice, the Bear Man's interpreter. It is Tryggvi, the amber trader. Twice a year Tryggvi brings copper and bronze north by ship to trade with the Sun People for amber and furs. Tryggvi speaks the language of the Sea People. But he refuses to carry slaves away from their homes in the north to labor and die in the parched land below the World.

"I do not know the name of the man. But I can tell you how to find him!" answers Aghi, feeling the stone fingers of the Bear Man begin to close again around his throat as if he understood what he was saying.

"Tell me," says the bear again, his voice a guttural purr.

"Quickly, Sun Priest," says Tryggvi, stepping forward in the dark, for the Sun Priest is a reliable paying customer for his Hatti bronze work and Egyptian beads. "He kills swiftly, Aghi, I have seen it."

"The man you seek lives in the mountain!" squeaks Aghi, who has again been given a reprieve from his strangulation and has taken advantage of it, drawing in a powerful breath. He might have bellowed the words, unwittingly waking the entire camp, but for the Bear claw regulating the outgo of his lungs.

Something is said in a purring whisper, and the Bear Man's muzzle is now so close to his face that the distinct heat of cinnamon, rare as rubies, burns his nostrils.

"Waste no time, Aghi, for this is not a patient beast. What mountain? He wants the trail, or he will take you with him and gut you swiftly if you fail him."

"Take the western trail along the river, five hundred paces, no more. It is invisible but for the boulder at its base, hidden in the briar, marked with the rune of the Axe. Follow the trail to the fork, where the root of the triple oak plows the earth. You will cross a small stone bridge across a stream running fast down the mountain. Just past the stream, in a Troll hole big as a man standing, lives the Slave Trader. The one you call 'child thief'. He sells the children of the Forest People to Hakon for a fair price, and Hakon sells them to the Sea People twice a year."

Why Aghi has added this bit of useless information he cannot even imagine, except that talking keeps him breathing. Now he has run out of words, and sure enough, the Bear Man's fingers close around his throat like the roots of the triple oak. Oh Thou, God of Day, prays Aghi as he loses consciousness, let me live to see you rise again.
In the morning, Aghi awakens with a brutal headache, a bruised neck, and a cracked rib. The choicest parts of the sacrificial lamb, which he had hung carefully from the ridge pole of his tent for this evening's dinner, is gone, and in his right hand is the ornate carved handle of his now bladeless sacrificial knife.

Mochlos has journeyed five days on ass-back. His own ass is bruised and tender from the jarring ride on a wooden-treed Amorite saddle. He rides behind the old gentleman, Mafali, whom he has come to regard with some affection, and the man's two young retainers. Neither is older than the Rah was on the day he purchased him, that day that seems now a lifetime ago, when the blue sea beyond the north facing second floor veranda of his beloved villa competed with the azure Aegean sky for brilliance, and the peach and blood red roses climbed through the railings from the trellises beneath with such speed during the summer months that the gardeners could not keep them off the seaside murals. Now and then Mochlos takes a moment to pull his sodden handkerchief from the sleeve of his traveling robe and wipe his dust-streaked brow. He has shaved his Amorite-friendly beard, for he has been instructed that renowned High Priest of the Rah or nay, he will be cut down like a bald cornstalk in this country sporting the thing. Indeed, even Mefali, who has not been without his facial hair since his youth, has removed his waist-length whiskers. In deference to the safety of the small caravan, he has also refused the comfort and stamina of a palace Turkoman, and is riding a sister of the animal Mochlos straddles, while the two lads are mounted on the barb ponies pulling the priest's belongings.
Mochlos taps the sides of the she-ass he rides to come astride her sister. He offers Mefali a weak smile, then digs in an upper pocket of his robe to find the last of his stash of sugared dates to offer the older man.
"Take them, Sir, they are my last. I see the crests of the cliffs ahead, and we will be descended upon by the Wolves of Amega before this

noon day heat has broiled my scalp right off my skull. By supper time we will have had a good bath and a nap in the fortress of the Beast. You could use the color in your cheeks before you meet the Lady of the house."

"Is she really as kind and mild as I have heard, Your Holiness?" Mephali has pulled his mount up short beside the priest's, and accepting the offering, speaks through a mouthful of honeyed dates.

"She is, Sir," responds the priest, pursing his lips into a thin line. "Though I have never reconciled the image in my head, I will admit, of him and her…" he shakes his head, then chuckles softly. "Strange world we live in, Master Mefali, when a wolf can bed a lamb without the lamb becoming the wolf's dinner."

"No stranger than a priest being sent away from the very city he has restored with his magic, Holiness," answers Mefali, chewing the last of the dates. "I understand my own exile, for I am the lady Ephtheta's friend and property, and I understand the Wolf, against his own liking, has taken quite a liking to her, and would keep her as happy as she can be under the circumstances. But you, Mochlos, what is your crime? Did you not do what you were asked to do? The ash cloud has followed you from Caphtor to fertilize our barren fields, and Babylon thrives. What need does Amega have of you, when there is a priestess there to serve the Rah, should he in fact have fled there. Why uproot you now and send you south again, when you have only just established the Temple of the Rah in Babylon?"

"I was told it is a temporary move, Master Mefali, a hedge against the return of the Rah's illness. I am sure that once it is established that the diadem can hold the god within his living vessel, I will be returned to my sanctuary in Babylon to serve the people there." Mochlos involuntarily slips his hand into his robe to feel for the hundredth time today the comforting shape of the mail circlet, which has been securely stitched into the lining of his garment.

Mefali sighs, waves to his retainers to begin down the crest of this last rise and launch their descent into the heath that surrounds the cliffs upon which the stronghold of Amega crouches.

"How beautiful it is here, under his awful brow," he mutters, as to himself. "The sky above is a ripe persimmon, and the meadow below so brilliant with wildflowers that a princess would be proud to lay her head upon such a pillow. Look here," he reaches down to cup the white and lilac bowl of a wild iris, which is as tall as his jenny's shoulder, "Not even the ripe fields of Babylon can boast such a display of natural beauty, nor have I ever inhaled such a floral banquet there, and yet," he sits back into his saddle to gaze with distress upon the toothy shoulders of the Wolf's lair, hunched on the highest cliff, as if waiting to spring down on the little band and devour them whole.

"And yet the gods have loaned it to a monster," finishes Mochlos beside him. "Downright creepy." He purses his lips into a frown.

"Well I have been dealing with that particular injustice since I created the Rah, my dear Mefali. It is the same. For how does the world allow it? Are we to believe in a benign godhead when such a ghoul is given to possess a creature of heaven? Where is the symmetry in that?"

"Funny you should bring symmetry into it," Mefali smiles ruefully. "It is said that the Wolf has an oddly balanced mind, and that his dreadful artistry is built upon it. Tit for tat. An eye for an eye. Perhaps there is the symmetry you look for. There the justice."

"Pah, he is no more just than a common cuckoo," grumbles Mochlos, pulling his kerchief from his sleeve for the hundredth time to wipe his nose, "who sacks the sparrow hawk's nest and then has the gall to lay her own egg in it." He stuffs his sodden wipe in his sleeve. "Let us waste no time attempting to make this sow's ear into a silk purse. There is no justice in it. One must be satisfied in one's own integrity," he gives a self-important sniff. "And pray one's own wits will see one through."

Rah awakens on the evening of Mochlos' arrival, folded in the arms of his concubine, his priestess, and his Minoan queen, at the sound of his High Priest's mutterings.

His own small pallet was far too cramped for his caprices, and it is Mochlos' enormous platform bed upon which his tribe of ladies now languish, exhausted and sated from their lovemaking. Rah has become a man, and these three ladies are the first to realize it.

Sweaty and caked with dust from his long ride on ass-back, Mochlos is in no mood to share his private suite with the three ladies, let alone his bed with a naked and sexually spent Rah. He has made his way to the Chambers of the Moon without Ham's assistance, having been informed at the fortress door that except for the installment of the

Cyrian queen, the Babylonian princess, and his "hermaphrodite", all is much as he left it so many months ago. Now he crosses his great room, his belongings to be brought up after supper by Amegan house slaves. But hearing the tinkling of laugher in his own bedroom he stops short, only then noticing the blue and gold pile carpet that now spans the hall, depicting the repetitive pattern of a loin-clothed blonde acrobat standing astride a trio of white horses.

"They are not the *only* alterations made in my absence," mutters the priest as he studies the exquisite carpet. He is shaken from his contemplation when the giggling trio of nude females dart across the hall to disappear behind the beaded drapes of their own chamber doors.

"What the-?" Mochlos nearly turns to follow them, intent on demanding an explanation of this outrage, when his eyes meet the vision of a mildly drunken Rah, his hair tousled, his face a familiar shade of chartreuse, his eyes flattered by a line of indigo which runs along his lower lids and across his temples into his hairline.

"Is priest," says Rah in his guttural purr, scratching the golden fur on his belly. "What priest for here? Wolf send? Rah is no need priest. Have priestess." Dimples popping, he glances toward Cara's chamber. "Better. Much better for Rah."

"Better my sore ass," answers Mochlos, trudging toward Rah, who continues to lean one uplifted arm against his chamber door and scratch at his belly with his free hand.

"What were you doing, tearing the emerald from your head?" spits Mochlos, shoving past the boy, whom he notices no longer looks up at him but across now, nearly eye to eye. "Grown a bit, haven't we?" snipes Mochlos, looking Rah over. "In more ways than one, I see."

"Priest maybe move," says Rah, his gaze piercing despite his half-mast lids. His dark voice is thick, muddied by the mix of wine and a wounded tongue, but the base purr somehow finds the nether reaches of Mochlos' nerves and tickles them. "Rah is maybe take Priest bed. Nice, big, fit more women. What Mochlos need big bed for, heh? Can no even one woman."

Mochlos narrows his eyes at the boy, for one exhausted moment thinking he might have heard Rah say he was taking him to bed. Then he realizes the omission was in the last, and not the first sentence.

"You are leaving out words, you cloth-headed rabbit. However, I have caught your drift. You would put me in a closet and have my chamber, yes? Well, do it, and I shall get right back on that jenny I rode in on and take your soul with me to feed to the spirits of all those dead babies in Babylon. Did you think of that?" he pauses before adding, "Whilest you were riding my high priestess?"

As he enters his once pristine and sexless chamber, the high priest moans. The fragrance of women is heavy in the bedclothes, and overpowers the light and pretty elegance of Rah's hyssop and cherry scent. Mochlos frowns at the ravaged bed.

"Well I won't be sleeping in *that* tonight. You may have it!" He sniffs. "I shall take your pallet for the night. Only give me a bath and a meal and I shall find it heaven after that thankless ride back to hell!" He turns back for the door, and refusing to meet Rah's blue-green gaze this time, shoves past him.

Rah watches the priest's retreat as he makes his way toward the white and yellow beads that drape the doorway of his own little chamber, which he has been sharing with Pyrus and Aros as in the early days of his godhood. The priest's traveling cloak is caked with dust, and the embroidered heads of wheat are barely visible.

"Priest be mad now," he mutters, turning to face the rumpled bed. Ladies garments are strewn across it, and a yellow veil rests in a soft pile on the lambs wool rug. Rah sets the ball of one foot on the platform as if to fall back into the bedclothes, then thinks better of it and turns to kicks about through the undergarments scattered on the floor for his loincloth and skirt. He dresses sloppily, mumbling to himself, then catches his own reflection in the mirror over the long vanity opposite the bed. He points at it with clumsy authority.

"Rah is no be feed dead babies of Babylon!" he growls, stumbling over to the mirror, and tipping forward on his toes he stares at his lime green likeness. "This priest he try to hurt Rah now, maybe, heh?" he narrows his eyes at his visage, "No!" he slams the palm of one hand down on the top of the vanity. "No more can hurt Rah. Look! You see?" he flexes his muscles at his image. "You no need Wolf now, Rah. You is man now. Can take care of this priest! Akh!" he spits at the floor. "No let this priest feed Rah to dead. Maybe Wolf he no come this time, heh? Run far, north, crazy wolf, can no save Rah from dead like on Table. Wolf is maybe never come back, find nice girl look like Rah up north, ya." He pulls his mop of golden curls up into a ponies tail at the back of his head, makes a coquettish face in the mirror, fluttering his painted lids. He puckers his kiss-bruised mouth, a Nordic lass, flirting with the Terror of the Great Sea.

Tiring of his own mime, he picks up an ornate, pearl-handled brush from Mochlos' vanity.

"What he use this for? No hair on head. Stupid priest." He sniffs the bristles. Akk!" an image of Mochlos petting his privates with the thing causes him to hurl it spontaneously at his reflection. "Stupid priest!" he pouts, shaking his hand out as if it had been burned.

He studies his lime-green face, considering. A thought brightens his eyes

"Rah be smarter than this priest," he nods at himself in the dented bronze mirror, ignoring the results of his temper. He winks at his reflection, a slow, deliberate wink. He straightens up, chews his lip watching himself. He leans toward the mirror again, tilting his face so that he is looking up at himself under his brows. He works them, settles them into a mixture of innocence and fear, and his face is suddenly transformed into the boy he was the day the priest first examined him. One unruly dimple pops.

"Ya, this like what he always want from Rah. Crazy priest. I think maybe Rah can change this priest mind."

CHAPTER SEVEN

The Sun People have made camp at the head of the river. The longhouses are nearly raised, and the skinning huts and cooking sheds are built and functioning. The Sun Priests have their own house, made of white birch and sycamore, thatched with straw and willow. Their dwelling has four doors, the eastern and western doors having awnings of fine albino elk hide and the north and south made only of fawn skins, for the Sun God walks through the house of the Sun Priests by day, west to east, and must be welcomed and honored, while the spots on the fawn skin doors north and south are meant to confound the river trolls who come in the night from these directions to bring chaos.

But Rush is finished for now with the Sun People camped at the head of the river. He has taken Triggvi and followed the western trail five hundred paces into the wood. He has found the boulder marked with the rune of the Axe and he has followed the trail it marks up the mountain to the triple oak and over a bridge made of boulders across a swift stream. And he has found a troll hole big as a man standing, though not as big as he, and he had to crouch and maneuver his shoulders to get into it. He lies in wait there now, knowing that the slave trader, the child thief, the Barn Smyga, as Triggvi called him, would return to do business with Hakon, Chief of the Sun People, very soon, now that the Sun People have reappeared in the north to hunt and trap.

But the slave trader will not be selling the children of the Forest People to Hakon this spring, nor will Hakon sell Forest children to the edge of the World come summer. All this will end now, for the bear that has made its nest in the Barn Smyga's hole is determined to make it so.

Rush waits five days in the Barn Smyga's den. He snares a hare on the first day, traps a hen on the second. There are berries and roots to eat in the wood, and the stream is teaming with salmon. He is a well-fed and contented bear on the morning of the fifth day, when the mourning doves nesting outside the cave startle, filling the air with the whistle of their wings, and the crunch and snap of feet in the leaves only a moment later confirms that the troll who lives in this hole has come home with his haul.

Rush sits up on the Barn Smyga's thatch sleeping mat. He wears only his assassin's leggings, his upper body naked but for his weaponry. He has trimmed his beard himself, having had little else to occupy his time while he waited for his prey to return. He hears the Barn Smyga shout an order in a reedy voice, then a sharp slap, flesh on flesh. A soft cry. Weeping. A yelp.

Still he manages to control his thirst for this throat long enough for the troll to crouch through the cave hole with a rush light.

He waits for his face to be made out by the rheumy eyes of the Barn Smyga. When the old man sees his pale countenance in the dark he starts so hard he trips backward on the tails of his own boot laces and smacks his head against the cave wall. He drops like a dead bird, this thing that torments children, now a mere heap of smelly leather skins.

"Bugger," growls Rush, rising to tower over the unconscious man. "Do not die on me, smear of shit," he winces at the thought of touching the smelly heap, and pushes at the man's head with the toe of his boot instead.

"Triggvi!" he booms, and a moment later the trader's silhouette has filled the cave hole. "He stinks of urine and runs with lice. He is a pestilence. Wait here for him to wake, and then assure him that what he saw was not a ghost, nor a bear but far worse. My knives are sharper. And I will gut him like a pig and hang him in a tree while he lives unless he can tell me what I need to know."

Rush pulls the trader into the cave and throws him on the packed dirt floor beside the child thief. He crouches to squeeze himself through the cave hole to inhale a lung full of fresh, cold mountain air, but he chokes on it when he finds what the troll has left outside. Five children, all tied together at the waist, shoeless and dressed in rags, are lined up along the path. The smallest, a boy of no more than three summers, is lying still at the end of the line, bleeding from the nose and eye.

"Triggvi!"

The four standing children have shrunk back in terror at the sight of the assassin, pale as gypsum, tall as a brown bear, his naked chest and waist strapped with black leather holsters and glittering blades. They have never seen a black braid or beard, nor such bottomless, pitch eyes. If the troll was Fendinn, the trickster, this is Fenrir, the wolf-god, who tore off the hand of the god of war.

Triggvi has come out of the cave to blink in the morning light beside the Wolf. He wipes his hand over his mouth, sweating despite a soft mountain breeze.

"Does he live? Or has his own cowardice killed him."

"He lives, Sir," answers Triggvi, and hopeful, he looks up into the assassin's face, but finds a scorching anger burns in the wolf's fathomless eyes. "But whether he shall wake…"

"Tie his hands and feet with this," Rush tosses a length of leather which he has removed from one of the children at the trader. "Tend to this little one," he nods at the struck boy. "And untie and feed the rest. I will wait for my answers."

Rush watches in silence as Triggvi finds a doeskin in his own pack and gentles it under the unconscious child's head. He unties the oldest, a girl of ten summers, and hands her a scrap of woven cloth.

"Take this to the spring there," he says gently in her language, "and get it good and wet for me, yes?'

When she has returned with the wet cloth he takes it and applies it to the boy's forehead.

"This is your brother?" He nods at the little boy.

"Yes, sir," she answers, taking a furtive look back at the Wolf-god, who stands at the mouth of the cave as still and dangerous as a Forest Shadow Archer.

"He will not harm you, child. Nay he is here to save you. He is a friend of children, and wishes to find the clan of another Forest boy he saved many moons ago."

"What boy is this, sir? That I may help him find the clan," answers the child.

"A twin, and the sister a girl. They were fair as the silver moon. Taken as infants from a beautiful mother with yellow hair that hung in a single braid to her feet."

"You speak of the White Elves!" she cries, delighted and for a moment too distracted by this game to notice that her brother has come to with the cold cloth against his temple. "The Fire Trolls came from the south to take their women, who were more beautiful than sunlight. The White Elves wore their hair in one braid, not two, like us. It is said that they were born from the flowers of a great white elm that stood in the center of the Lakes. And they worshipped the tree, and were a peaceful people. The Tree God forbid them to cut a single limb, nor harm a single beast that walked beneath her. They rode white horses, and raised white sheep. And so they made their huts of thatch and lived on fish and birds, roots and nuts and berries. In homage to the tree the White Elves did not cut their hair, and some maidens wore it to their feet! And the children were like squirrels, and could jump from tree to tree and not be seen!"

"Yes," says Triggvi patiently, nodding as he gently presses the cloth against the back of the boy's neck. "I know the story, child. But you must not tell the Bear Man fables, or set him on a false trail, for if you do, he will discover what you have done and return to eat you."

"Oh, no sir!" whispers the girl then, glancing fearfully at the pale face of the assassin. "He must not look for the White Elves, for he will never find them. The White Elves are gone now, wiped out by the Fire Trolls. They came up from the Four Straits and raided the Lakes Region for furs every spring, for as long as anyone remembers, but when one spring they discovered the beauty of the White Elves, they slaughtered their men, and took the women. Back to Snorri…" she trails off.

"You tell me fairytales, child. But the Fire People I know. They are nomadic horsemen, barbarians. They roam as far south as the Great Sea and as far north as the Lands of the Sun People, stealing and killing and burning, and if he goes looking for his revenge among them, they will kill him for his trouble, for they are a bloodthirsty race." Triggvi sighs, considering the danger of being the first to give this information to the Bear Man. Still, he cannot leave it to the child to tell him. He gentles the boy into his sister's arms and rises from his knees.

"See to your brother, child." He slouches toward Rush, a dog expecting to be beaten.

"I have some information, Master," he says, not meeting the assassin's gaze. "It is not information that will please you."

"All information pleases me, Tryggvi," responds the assassin. "It is the lack of it that I disapprove of."

"The child tells me fairytales. That the clan you seek were known as the White Elves, fair as the sun. She claims that they lived in the lakes region, farther north, and worshiped a great tree. And their children could jump like monkeys through the canopy of their forest. She says they were peaceful, horsemen and sheep farmers, and that they were wiped out by the Fire People, who came over the Four Straits to steal their women."

Rush is silent.

"I have heard stories of a clan of the Lake People who were known for the beauty of their maidens," Triggvi clears his throat and continues. "They wore their pale hair in one braid, and did indeed worship a great tree." He studies the ground, unable to hold the assassin's hot black gaze.

"Pale?" Rush presses. "Blonder than these?" He motions to the tawny-haired children.

"To you it is all yellow hair here. But these people's hair was like the moon, almost white. You see these girls, they braid their hair in twins. But the Lake People wore only one braid down their backs," Triggvi swallows, "Like you, Sir."

"Go on," says Rush, his black eyes somehow grown blacker still with his attentiveness. He is not a bear, thinks Triggvi then. He is a wolf, as the girl calls him, a wolf with a wolf's keen eyes. May I never be at the business end of that gaze.

"Sir, she speaks of the Fire Trolls, the Black Elves. It is a myth. But perhaps the stories overlap. Perhaps the Fire Trolls could be the Fire People, a barbaric tribe, marauders, called Fire People because they burn down the villages they have raided. They come up from the Four Straits each spring to plunder and steal from the Forest People of the north. They carry their spoils back to the Great Sea to sell, furs, amber and slaves. Perhaps when they heard the tales of these beautiful women they came for them. But they are gone now, returned to Gaul."

"I have feet, Triggvi. I have a horse with four." Rush lifts his head, hearing something stir behind him in the cave. "Ah, my own troll awakes." And he is gone, ducked back into the hole. No sooner has he disappeared than the Barn Smygga has tumbled out of the aperture, having apparently been tossed by the scruff of his neck and the seat of his pants. He lands on his face in the path at Triggvi's feet.

"My gods what is it?" he sputters, his mouth full of grit.

"Say rather, what can I do to please it, child thief, for it is a mother bear who seeks the one who stole her pup and it is spoiling to open you with crescent claws," answers Tryggvi dully. He is unimpressed when the assassin slips back out into the light, drops onto the back of the Barn Smygga and presses those very blades against either side of the man's matted neck.

"Agh, he is crushing my back, trader! His knee!" yelps the troll. "He is the weight of a bull moose! I will do whatever he wishes, only what good am I to him crippled?"

"He asks that you remove your knee from his spine there, Sir, that he may serve you in any way you wish," says Triggvi, his hands now drawing in the three children who have come to stand at his sides. "I beg you, sir, do not remove his head in front of these," he says more softly, "Let me take them down the hill a little."

Rush has taken some of his weight of the Barn Smyggas backbone. He considers the three youngsters, looks down at his crescent blades, glittering in the morning sun.

"I am not a monster," he mutters, a bit abashed at his own lack of discretion. "Did I not tell you to feed them?" he barks at Triggvi. "Take them down to the spring and give them the rest of the bread and dried mutton from my pack."

Triggvi rummages in the assassin's food pack, finds the loaves and smoked mutton, and waves it at the children. "Come, little ones. Let us have a picnic by the spring now. And we will soak those bruised feet of yours." But the children are so transfixed on the assassin's strange blades that they are not seduced by the food, though they are little more than bones themselves.

Rush glares at them, lifts his lip, snarls a deep, vulpine snarl, and the children jump and run behind the trader, who has turned to start down the path. Only the injured boy and his sister remain.

"Would you leave the weakest behind?" Rush booms, holstering his blades, "What is wrong with these people?" he mutters as he lifts himself off the troll, "Move and I will eat your liver," he adds. He approaches the children, sighs again, and lifts the dazed boy into his arms as the girl stares up at him, dumbstruck. The boy rouses as he settles him on his right hip, his ice blue eyes fighting to focus on the assassin's face.

"Fenrir!" he gasps, and begins to yowl.

Rush grimaces. He looks about for some solution, sees that the girl has not moved from his side, lifts her into his free arm and bounces her on his opposite hip to steady her. The movement causes her to throw her arms about his neck. But her proximity has calmed the boy. He whimpers, reaches for her hand.

"Ilse," he whispers across the assassin's chest. "Fenrir."

The girl is smiling, wide-eyed. "Fenrir!" she exclaims to her brother, and the boy smiles back.

She looks up into the assassin's face with shining eyes. She and her brother have the same coarse, tawny hair and colorless irises.

Rush meets her gaze, gives her a stern, parental nod. She returns it with a coquettish flutter of eyelashes and a smile, then reaches up to finger the black curls of his beard.

"You are not so afraid of me, are you girl?" Rush tilts his head, pulling his rough from her fingers. "Females," he sighs, "You are a dangerous lot."

The boy has settled against him as well, and Rush starts down the path with the two children in his arms. When he comes upon the trader and the other youngsters they are already settled on the mossy bank munching provisions and drinking from a shared gourd water they have taken from the spring.

"He is come to," says Rush, setting the siblings down on the moss. The boy sits down immediately beside the trapper and snatches the crust he is offered. The girl is more difficult to release, for she has taken a hold of his braid. He winces as he untangles it from her fingers.

"This one is named Ilse," he says as he sets her on her feet beside her brother. He pauses, regards the brood. "Perhaps they are all of one family, eh? All dun-haired, and ice-eyed."

"It is a common look here in the north," answers Triggvi, who is busy steadying the water gourd against the boy's lips. "But I will ask them. What is your name, lad?" he asks the child in his own tongue.

"Ole," answers the boy hoarsely.

"And are you all of one mother?" the trader looks at the girl, Ilse.

"We are," she answers, "Our father was an archer. He was killed defending our village from the Sun People. Our mother died the year before. We are orphans now," she adds, her tears welling up.

"And who sold you to this man? For he did not take you himself."

"The Sun People sold us," answers Ilse.

Triggvi squints at her. "Which Sun People, Ilse? There are many tribes."

"The ones who always come, each spring, in caravans from the south. They carry a great bronze sun on one of their wagons, and they bring their cattle too, and graze them in our meadows. They take children every year to sell to the People of the Sea who live in the parched lands below the earth. Snorri!"

Tryggvi looks up at Rush, exhausted by the effort of deciphering the girl's tongue, which is barely comprehensible to him. It is as if she has not spoken for so long that the liberty to do so has made her speak in rapid bursts, for she cannot know when she will be allowed to do so again.

"That is the noise a flock of seagulls makes, fighting over a single fish," Rush shakes his head in amusement. But the lilting language is reminiscent of Rah's articulation of every language he ever twisted in that wounded mouth.

"The child is a bard. The children are orphans, all of one mother, both parents dead. They were taken by a tribe of Sun People," he nods down the mountain path. "Not these."

"There are more than one?"

"There are. This clan," Triggvi makes another nod toward the river, "Worship the sun you see above you. The other worship a bronze disk they carry with them on a cart. I have seen them myself, though only at a distance. Their cattle decimate the lands they drive them through. They are like locusts, coming north not to trade fairly but to steal. They take the furs and amber these people work all year collecting, raiding their homes for slaves to sell to the Sea."

"And these are not the Fire People she spoke of earlier?"

"The Fire People are worse," answers Triggvi wearily. "They leave nothing but death and ash behind them."

Rush is silent.

"Will you yet hunt them?" asks the trader cautiously. "Will you go to war with a tribe of devils?"

Rush turns his head south, sniffs. He wears the open-mouthed grin of a wolf who has run long in the heat and now stands on a ridge, intoxicated by the heavy aroma of his prey drifting up from the hollow.

He makes no answer, turns and lopes back up the mountain path toward the cave and the trussed troll he left in front of it.

CHAPTER EIGHT

"No want to stay here, priest," murmurs Rah into Mochos left ear an hour later.

"Whah?" Mochlos lurches away from the tickling stubble of Rah's immature beard. It is too reminiscent of something far too horrible be awakened by.

"Do you hate me so, boy?" he grumbles, realizing that it is only his creation, leaning on one elbow alongside him on the little lambskin bed. "You do not think beyond that fluff of gold you call a head. The monster would make a mosaic of my pieces for his bedroom wall."

"What you talking, priest. Rah be nice to you," Rah flops back down on the down-plumped linens beside his maker. He is so close that his naked thigh burns the high priest's hip through his sleeping gown. Mochlos attempts to put some distance between them, but it is impossible. He would have to roll over Rah to do it. And so he presses himself to the wall beside the pallet.

Rah takes no notice of the priest's discomfort. He is picking at a stray thread in the hem of his skirt, leaning against a stack of pillows so that his chin rests against his chest.

"Priest be so stupid," he chuckles. His wine-laden breath is tinged with a hint of blueberry. "Always he want Rah, no? Now have Rah where he want him and too scare to have happy," he plucks out the thread, his gaze drifting to Mochlos' ashen face. The priest grits his teeth and swallows. Rah giggles and dangles the thread over Mochlo's nose.

"You ridiculous nuisance," snipes Mochlos, but he cringes from the end of the thread as if it were the point of a blade.

"Rah is no ridicule," Rah murmurs, lowering the string to tickle the priest between his eyes. "Priest be ridicule. Priest want to feed Rah to dead baby spirit in Babylon." He turns onto his hip, effectively corralling the priest against the wall. His prismatic eyes are at half-mast, dulled by blueberry wine.

"Why you want hurt Rah, heh?" he purrs, leaning closer. His lips part sulkily.

Mochlos, at his nerve's ends, pulls himself up into a sit and hurls himself off the end of the pallet. He falls on his knees, trapped by his own robe. Rah chuckles as the priest crawls to his feet.

"You take my words too seriously, boy," he announces, straightening his gown. "Can you not put yourself in someone else's sandals for once? I have had a very long ride on donkey-back and I am not in my most pleasant mood. I wish only for the comfort of my bed, and find you in it with a triplet of naked women. Am I welcomed? Am I offered the smallest apology? On the contrary I am told that I shall be living in a closet and sleeping on the floor henceforth, or perhaps in your next divine breath, in the henhouse with the layers!" Mochlos takes a breath, draws himself up, smooths a hand over his pate.

"I have come here for one purpose only," he plows on, adjusting his belt. "To keep you intact! And I have risked life and limb on a very dangerous journey, I might add, to do it!" He begins to pace, but the room is too small to give him adequate room and his agitation only serves to put Rah into a paroxysm of silent giggles. Mochlos stops in his tracks. His outburst has exhausted him. His face is drawn. Perhaps he has taken a wrong turn here. After all, he is speaking to a nitwit.

Rah's giggles fade as the priest composes himself.

"I only mean to say that you are more than just a good looking performer," Mochlos sighs, "Though getting that idea into your thistledown cranium is beyond me. You are the vessel of the Rah, and if it were not for me, you would still be lying 'in state' in Babylon, your soul wandering for all eternity in the land of dreams. You think your high priestess could have brought you back? She is a fledgling. More adept at fornication than fortification. Only I can protect you from the many pitfalls and dangers of the spirit world."

Mochlos pauses to gauge Rah's reaction. But the boy is looking up at him with cool disinterest. His eyes are smoky with intoxication, which only serves to make them heavy-lidded and alluring. The high priest collects himself, then struts over to his traveling garment and slips his hand in to feel about for the shape of the emerald diadem. When he finds it he rips the stitches that enclose it, triumphantly pulling it out into the light for Rah to see.

"It was my magic that saved you from your sickness. When you were separated from the emerald, you were vulnerable to it. We must have your hairdresser weave this band back onto your head. And you must never be parted from it again!"

Rah pouts. "Why priest say he be give Rah to baby ghost to eat in Babylon?"

You believe I can do it, and that is enough, thinks Mochlos. He pastes an awkward smile on his face, takes a step toward Rah, and whispers, "Let us forget I ever said it, shall we? You and I need each other, and that is enough."

"Yah, priest he need Rah," says Rah, hopping to his feet. He hangs one well-muscled arm over the priest's narrow shoulders. His blueberry breaths pat the priest's cheek. "Rah, he need priest, too. Need priest to get boat, take Rah back to Knossos." He tosses his head toward the breakers beyond the open balcony door. "I think maybe this priest be so smart, can do this for Rah. Maybe better do soon, too, or Rah is be maybe wrong time in bed with priest, heh? Maybe Wolf is come home Amega and find Rah sleep in bed with priest, what you think?" He gives Mochlos' shoulders an alarmingly robust squeeze, plants a rose petal kiss on his brow, and leaves him standing stunned in the center of the little chamber.

The sea is calm, the moon lies fair upon the still shore. It is five days since the incident in her weaving chamber, and Josepha has had little sleep since. Tonight she has taken her husband's secret passage through the sea-facing walls of the fortress, down to the beach. Guards, seeing her pass, stiffen and raise their eyes over her head. They see nothing. For which one of them is brave enough to tell the Wolf that his wife walks this way, knows what he would not have her know, dares what he would not have her dare? Which one has the heart to tell him that he has seen the lady after dark at all? Or in her sleeping gown? Or outside the fortress walls under a moon?

Josepha follows the shoreline north and east, at first, picking her way along the stony rubble, causing more than one guard above to flinch watching her stumble or fall on her hands. Still she continues, oblivious to their eyes, or to their distress. By the time she reaches the sand her hands and knees are bleeding. The salt stings, bringing tears to her eyes. A breeze lifts her loose hair, swirls it about her neck like a noose. The soft waves break yards from her bare feet, but the only sound she hears is the sound of her own moan.

She walks a mile up the beach, until the chill in the damp air brings her to her senses. She is unmindful of the handful of wolves following her at a respectful distance, nor does she consider her near nakedness before the eyes of her husbands' men, men who are well aware that they will be relieved of those eyes if ever the assassin discovers they have seen what only he may see. For them it is the lesser of two evils, better blind than dead, and they will surely die if the Lady of the House of Amega comes to harm on their watch.

Josepha has fallen on her hands with the vigor of one great sob.

An arms-length to her right a pair of oystercatchers materialize from the sand and dash toward the surf at the force of her fall. Her breath catches in her lungs. She has disturbed a nesting pair, their sand-colored trio of eggs lay bare in the bed of shell-lined beach that is their nursery. Chagrined by her self-absorption she crab-walks backward, away from the nest. The pair dart back to their brood, peeping with displeasure.

"Oh, my darlings," whispers Josepha, putting her hands over her sand-streaked tears. "Oh my darlings. What have I done? What have I done."

"I am chief now," smiles Rush narrowly as he settles himself back on his haunches, pinning old Hakon's belly to his bed of skins.

"For pities sake, let him be! He is an old man, half blind and hard of hearing. He has no issue with your boy or his people. He-"

"Silence that bag of bones, Triggvi, or I will do it myself," pouts Rush, folding his arms over his chest. "I cannot stand another day of this gibberish. Why do they speak to me, when it is evident that I cannot understand them?"

"They are a talkative lot, Sir," answers Triggvi, taking Hakon's eldest daughter-in-law by the shoulder and pushing her toward the exit of the chief's tent. When she slips his grasp and attempts to shove past him back into the tent he grabs her arm, makes a slicing gesture across his own throat, and tilts his head toward the assassin. She peers past him at Rush, who squints at her and lifts his lip in a growl.

"The Bear Man will silence you, this way," he slashes his throat again, "If you cannot silence yourself."

"Filthy beast," she hisses, making a protective sign over her heart and then spitting on the dirt floor. "Evil thing!"

Triggvi gives her a good shove out of the doorway and lowers the flap.

"Tell this toothless mole what I have told you," grunts Rush, resting his hands on his crescent holsters.

"Hakon, Chief of the Sun People of the Upper River," begins Triggvi formally. "The Bear Man has disarmed your warriors. He has marked them as his own. They wear the Tear of the Bear on their cheek, as you will now do, for whoever sees him and lives is his property."

"I can see nothing," wheezes Hakon weakly. "He is a blur of black, heavy as a bear, scentless as a clear stream. Whatever this man needs, he need not mark an old man waiting to die to take it."

"He says he is an old man waiting to die, Sir, and that you may take what you wish, only leave him be."

"Old but not senseless," answers Rush. "A shrewd old fox. Tell him I will mark him twice for that. I will have a thumb." He flips his dagger from his ankle holster and grabbing the old man's chin, begins his work.

The old man makes no move to fight him.

"Tell him," says Rush, taking the man's left hand. He has splayed the fingers and pinned the thumb before Triggvi can open his mouth to repeat his words.

Hakon's eyes widen in disbelief as the assassin holsters the dagger, pulls a single crescent blade from his side and slices the first joint of his thumb clean off. He howls in shock and pain.

Rush leans down to growl in his face, "You heartless bastard. How many children have you sold into slavery? And yet you cry for a thumb?"

"He cannot understand you, Master," swallows Triggvi. The daughter-in-law has rushed back into the tent. Two other women, younger but no less homely, step timidly in behind her.

"He understands me well enough," says Rush. Rising to his full height he towers to the ridgepole. As he turns in the torchlight toward the women, one swoons and collapses at the feet of her sisters. "And I, him." He holsters his blade and moves to the tent flap. The two vertical women shrink out of his way as he moves past them and out into the morning.

Outside the aroma of grilled fish takes his attention. He has not made it twenty meters from the chief's tent before he is trailing the clutch of Forest children. Rush does his best to ignore them. They have taken to him like a litter of orphaned puppies since he freed them from the Barn Smygga, put Triggvi in charge of their care, and brought them into the Sun People's camp under the protective umbrella of his claws. They have seen their Wolf God turn their people's great and terrifying enemy into a pack of boot-licking hounds overnight while they slept in the wood with Triggvi and the trussed and gagged Barn Smygga. They themselves have risen to the status of chieftain first-borns, and now walk and play and even mock and tease those they feared above all else. How he managed it they have no doubt. Fenrir has no master, no commander, not even Odin. He can break every chain, and not even the entire heavenly council of gods could accomplish his capture. He took the War God's hand for trying.

The children, well fed now after several days in the Wolf God's care, prance and play about his feet. Now and then little Ole pulls at his leggings, looks up at him with eyes wide as a deer's, and begs to be lifted into his arms. Rush takes the lad's upraised hands together in one great fist and lifts him high up over his head and the boy screams and giggles, convulsing with glee when Rush flips him onto his shoulders for a ride. Ole knows he is the favorite, though at home he was the least of his siblings, a sickly lad who would never make it to adulthood. A waste of meat. He does not question Fenrir's choice, for he himself saved a starving wolf pup once, bringing the limp ball of fur, no bigger than a hare, home for his mother to feed and pick clean of ticks. When the pup was on his feet she let him keep it, and it followed him about as if he were chief of the clan, until the Sun People came and killed it when they raided the village. Surely Fenrir knew of his kindness to the wolf pup, and had come to save him in return for it.

Rush strides past the cooking sheds, the skinning huts, the priests' white birch longhouse. On the night he returned to the camp, leaving the children, Triggvi and the trader in the wood, he had entered this house first, tearing the fawn skin off the south door deliberately and kicking the nearest priest in the kidneys for good measure. The priest yelped dutifully and the house was roused, as desired, in time to witness Rush exercise his crescent blades on the stream of axe-wielding men who came at him from all four directions through the longhouse doors. There were fifteen bodies on the packed-mud floor of the priestly domain before Hakon wobbled through the eastern doorway, supported by two of his daughters-in-law, to call off his last two surviving sons. The boys were happy to oblige, both being in their teens and hardly matched for such a battle. Rush set his left blade in his teeth and took the younger by the front of his tunic, knocking the axe from his hand with a back-fist from his free right hand. Then he removed the crescent blade from his teeth with the same hand and put the two edges neatly against the boy's throat.

"What do you say, Sun King? Truce? Or do you die without a son?"

Hakon needed no interpretation. He fell to his knees, his hands clasped before him in supplication. The seven priests quickly crawled to their knees to do the same. With only his two teenaged sons alive to lead his men, Hakon he had nothing left with which to defend his village, save what remained of his wits. Fortunately, being a clever old Norseman, there were quite enough of those to save the day.

Rush ducks into the priests' house, the boy, Ole still perched on his shoulders, clutching the assassin's muscle-roped neck for balance. The four earthbound children gather around his legs, still unsettled by the sight of the Sun Priests in their white robes. In their own village mothers threatened their children with stories of the Sun Priests of the Upper River catching children who disobeyed their parents and boiling them in a lamb's blood soup to feed their god. Ilse makes a play to take the assassin's left hand, but her fingers can only manage to gather his fourth and pinky.

The Priests are on their faces, hands stretched out on the mud floor before them, before he can pass the first one to see what is in their communal cooking pot for breakfast.

"Not fish I hope," he leans over the steaming kettle, picks up the ladle leaning on a brace and dips it into the gruel. He starts raising the bowl to his lips, thinks better of it, and lifts it up to Ole. The boy sniffs it, then grabs the handle and empties it greedily.

"What's the verdict?" asks Rush after he has given the lad time to wipe his mouth on his sleeve.

Ole, understanding none of Rush's Hittite but desiring another ladle full reaches out for the handle of the dipper.

"Not fish, then," nods Rush. He takes another ladle full of the gruel and offers it to the nearest child at his feet, who is Stig, Ole's older brother by three years. Stig empties it, smiles up at Rush and rubs his ribs in a circle.

"Mmm," he offers.

Rush tousles his hair, looks about at the others, shrugs. The children giggle.

"Fenrir eat," Ilse beams up at him. She is the proud owner of a dozen Hittite words and wastes no opportunity to utilize her upper hand with the Wolf God. "Good!"

"Fenrir eat," agrees Rush, taking a ladle for himself. He finishes half, passes the ladle down to Ilse. "Mmm, good," he says, leaving the dipper in her charge. Turning from the children, who are now crowded around Ilse waiting their turn for breakfast, he looks about at the still prostrate priests.

"It is no wonder you stink," he frowns. "Fish gruel and berry porridge. You needn't have raised an axe, this diet will be the death of me. I shall check my snares."

Outside he finds that one young priest, the one named Gudrun, is following him at a distance. He allows the young man the illusion that he has not been noticed and continues into the wood where he discovers a pigeon has been caught in one of his traps.

The animal is exhausted from its struggle to free itself and has broken the leg upon which the snare is wound.

The dove is white. Blue-eyed. A gold ring circles its neck.

Something catches in Rush's throat and he lets out a gasp. Gudrun starts at the sound, a hollow moan. He is turning to flee when the assassin raises a hand, beaconing him.

Rush has sunk to his knees and taken the dove in both hands. He holds it now against his chest like a prayer. His head is bent over it, and he is groaning like a bear whose lung has been pierced by an arrow.

Gudrun extends his hands cautiously, sinking to his knees beside the assassin with utmost circumspection. The Bear Man looks up into his eyes. He is a broken monster, his remorse unmistakable, though why this madman should grieve for a bird he himself has snared he cannot comprehend. Gudrun nods at the dove, points to the broken leg, then points to himself and says in his own language, "I can set it." He lays one extended finger on the palm of his other hand and closes his hand over it. "So."

A light flickers in the assassin's pitch eyes. He squints at the priest, then carefully extends the dove, which has quieted in the maw of his fingers, feet up. The priest gingerly loosens the snare. He finds a twig, tears a thin length of cloth from the hem of his sleeve, and binds the leg.

Rush is watching the priest with the quiet patience of a shark. He has regained his composure during Gudrun's ministrations and now regards him with predatory curiosity.

"A useful priest," he says. His soft Hittite vowels suggest a complement to the priest's untutored ears.

Gudrun makes a game attempt to smile.

"I will not eat it," grunts the Bear Man. He shoves the dove into the priest's hands. "You," he pokes a finger into the man's sternum, "Take it back," he tosses his head in the direction of the settlement, "Keep it alive or I," he makes a slash across his own throat with his index finger, then pokes the priest a second time, "You."

Gudrun takes a moment to digest this. Then he cradles the bird like a tiny baby against his heart. He searches the assassin's face.

Rush nods his assent. Then, thinking better of it, he points to the bird again, to his own mouth, and makes another slash across his throat.

Gudrun repeats the pantomime. No, sir, it will not be eaten.

"Good man," Rush brings himself to his feet, helps the priest to his. He takes one more fleeting look at the dove, who seems remarkably content in the priest's embrace. Then he marches on up the path to his next snare.

CHAPTER NINE

Cara is singing.

It is daybreak in Amega. The surf against the cliff is rough today and there is an absence of shore birds, indicating that a storm is coming. Cara stands at her balcony, her long brown hair whipping about her face and shoulders in the wet breeze. Her song began in her bed, in a lullaby, for she had been awakened early by the sounds of a whimpering, growling, thrashing Grain God against their shared wall. She had listened to him for a time, wondering if Pyrus or Aros dare awaken him and end his torment. Eventually he seemed to quiet without the interruption of his friends. Then she lay awake herself, unable to return to the land of spirit, prophesy, and dream.

Pulling a sheer, gold-spun shawl over her shoulders she steps out onto the western terrace, which joins her suite to that of the High Priest, but Mochlos rarely ventures out upon it. Content with the luxury of his own rooms, which have been thoroughly aired and the bed linens washed after Rah capriciously returned to his own chamber several days ago, Mochlos had in fact bolted his veranda doors, and installed an Egyptian lock on his own chamber entrance. His justification for this was that his various religious oils and concoctions could be harmful, indeed deadly, in the wrong hands. It was understood that one pair of hands he was concerned for was that of the Grain God, who had been behaving more and more moodily in the past few weeks, having had no success in convincing anyone to help him get back to the Minoan island. But Cara believes that there was a second motive, one related to the Assassin himself. This is curiously ironic to her, for Mochlos more than anyone else should know that the Wolf would not be deterred from entering a room, least of all one in his own house, by a lock. Perhaps he simply wanted a bit of forewarning, again, hardly guaranteed by a lock, a bolt, or even a brace of guards.

Cara sings the lullaby she sang the day she understood that the world loved Rah because the boy was like love itself, light as air, bright as morning, free like a wild animal is free, to the point of madness. An otherworldly grace, fleeting as the deathbed heartbeat of a loved one, beautiful unto sadness. But most of all fleeting. Fleeting. Like childhood. Like his own childhood, which was leaving him forever.

There is no owl to sing to this morning, like that morning in Cyrus that now seems a thousand summers away. There is no death and destruction surrounding her, as on that terrible morning in the City of the Dead, and no pale halo of ethereal light coming toward her out of chaos, the boy's radiant head.

"Lady sing," she hears Rah's too-deep voice coming from his own veranda and she starts. But she cannot see him. His own balcony is unattached to hers. Unless either of them stands along the balustrade, they are invisible to one another.

His voice is tired, and substantiates that his sleep was interrupted by a nightmare. He is exhausted, she thinks, though he sleeps more now than he ever did.

Cara continues her lullaby, moving to the edge of her balcony and lifting her lovely voice to the Grain God to soothe him. And her voice carries in the soft summer breeze, and strokes his ear.

"Lady be sing for Rah," comes Rah's disembodied voice when she has finished. "Day Rah be sacrifice on mountain. You promise, Cara. You promise Rah, you sing for Rah that day. Sing Rah to sleep."

But Cara will have none of it. This talk has taken on a life of its own, and doesn't it always with Rah? He rides ideas like he rides a horse, giving them their heads, allowing them to take him where they would go, too far, too fast.

She lifts her left arm so that Rah can see it from his perch. His silence tells her that she has his attention. Her index finger is not bleeding today, the nail is intact. She raises it, just so: center note.

The chaos she seeks to control is not in the world around her today, but in Rah's mind.

Still she is startled by the Grain God's dusky chuckle. Can the

simple-minded beauty that is Rah really comprehend what she has said?
"Cara be like lullaby," the deep tones of his purred response are disconcerting. More than anywhere else, she has noticed the man replace the boy in his throat.
"Always be try to put Rah sleep, like baby." He tips his upper body over the balustrade of his parapet and the shock of his naked goldenness sends a yet another jolt of surprise through her body.
"Rah is no sleep, now, Cara. Rah be awake. Stay awake now. No more lullaby for Rah. No more pretend, like dance. Like play. For real now. Rah grow up." There is something akin to pity in his eyes. "Bad for you, no let Rah be Rah." He moves out of view, leaving her puzzling over his words.

For seven days Rush remains with the Sun People of the Upper River, allowing the children to eat as much and whenever they wish and play and sleep as children should. During the day he is with them, but when night falls, he disappears into the Forest, searching the Lakes Region for answers, clues that might lead him to even a single survivor of the White Elves that he now believes must be Rah's tribe. But the Fire People's extermination of that ethereal clan seems complete. The information he gains from his nightly excursions only confirms what he has learned from Ilse and Triggvi, that the legendary Fire Trolls are in fact a group of marauding barbarians who roam the whole of Gaul, pillaging and decimating whole villages, their claim to fame the torches they carry to set aflame every living man, woman and child they have not taken as a slave.
Rush fights to put the image of the burning City of the Dead out of his mind. Did Rah remember? On that day, that day that he heard Cara singing on her knees in the midst of that smoke and death, did the boy recall his own beginnings then? Did some part of his infant brain keep fast the memory of his own village in flames? His own mother's rape?
On the seventh day Rush saddles the Black. He plants Ilse in front of him, Ole on his shoulder, and Stig behind. Triggvi rides a dun fjord pony, a gift from the Sun People, and the two remaining children ride with him.
The children have gained most of their flesh back since their rescue, at least as much as the Barn Smygga has lost. The troll has been

carved with the Tear of the Bear, as have all of the grown men of the Sun People, including the seven priests. But the Barn Smygga will spend the rest of his days in slavery. He is now the property of Hakon, for that is the bargain that the assassin and the chieftain have agreed to, that the child thief will serve as a fair trade for the children Rush is taking with him, pound for pound an even bargain. This arrangement saves the old chief some face with his people, while allowing Rush to leaving this place knowing that the Sun People of the Upper River will never again trade in children. If they do the Bear Man will return to even the score, pound for pound, according to the weight of their sin.

Rush reaches the first of the Four Straits on the morning of the second day of travel. Here farmers living along the broken coastline make a second living navigating their wide, flat-bottomed canal boats across the three mile gap between the Land of the Sun People and the Greater Island when travelers require passage. Rush finds a farmhouse and sends Triggvi in to discuss a price. He has already secured the children and horses in the man's boat by the time the ferryman and three of his sons arrive to take them across the channel. When they reach the opposite shore the ferryman is all but blinded by the gold Rush throws at his feet for his service.

"He says you have overpaid him, sir," remarks Triggvi, when Rush ignores the man's fawning gratitude and makes to disembark. "He will gladly send his younger son with you to the next jetty, where his cousin has a good boat."

"I know the jetty," answers Rush. "Leave the boy here and give me direction to the man's home. I would cross the island by nightfall."

In this way, leapfrogging across the three islands by ferryboat, Rush makes his way to the mainland and to Gaul, with a vision of vengeance pressing him south and east into the Dark Forest.

The fires light the night sky, leaping from thatched roof to thatched roof across the narrow dirt paths between the maze of long houses along the rivulet. The little forest village, quiet enough yesterday that one could hear the babbling water over the stone bed of the brook from the Father's house, is a crackling blaze of screams. From the hilltop, Rush can hear them, the screams of the women and the children who have been taken to be raped to death or sold south along the Great Sea for bronze and gold. His acute hearing can make out the tiny voice of a newborn, too young to travel, roasted alive in the fire. He has left Triggvi and the children deep under the canopy, away from the sight and the sound of the horror below. The Black will not tolerate the descent into smoke and ash that gallops up the hill to greet them. Rush leaves the animal behind, pulls on his assassin's hood and lopes down the hillside toward the inferno.

The wailing of the captured women draws him south, upwind, around the back of the blaze. His pace is swift. He plunges into the gully, instinctively disguising his own sound and scent in the running water. His assassin's rags and Iamhad's boots are soaked through by the time he reaches the band of Fire Trolls who hold the village women and marketable children while their comrades torch and butcher the remaining village men.

The black beast that springs from the gully behind them is upon them like the first burst from a volcano. It is a nightmare made of glinting, whirling weaponry and rage. It slashes and whips, cutting throats and slicing limbs with sickening accuracy, as the women and children, trussed and lying over the backs of pack animals or on the ground, their rapes interrupted, watch, dumbstruck.

The whirling black volcano that is Rush is quickly left standing alone in the middle of his own destruction. He takes a moment to slice through the bonds of a girl on the ground, relieves a corpse of its dagger, and puts it in her hand, nodding at the woman lying beside her. The girl is a good choice. She has blood and flesh under her fingernails. A blackened eye. A fighter. She nods back at the single-eyed monster, grabs the blade handle, plunges it into the back of the man who had been raping her, already dead.

Rush smiles under the hood. "Free your sisters," he says, and leaps to his feet. He is gone, disappeared into the smoke and ash that was the village.

Starts Fire is having a fine day. It began when the tribe discovered a new path in the Dark Wood, a path clearly human, marked with notched trees, winding around marshes and skirting caves suitable for bear to bed in. These human attributes suggested that a settlement lay at the end of the trail, and Great Axe halted the caravan to choose three men to lead a band of looters on a raid. Meantime the rest of the tribe would continue south toward the steppes, which was their homeland. A good haul of fur, sheep, women, and child-slaves would be a great honor for the leader of this attack, not to mention pick of the women and a generous portion of the spoils. Starts Fire had been earning his name over the past several raids, and he had hopes of being picked to lead this assault. But when Brown Wolf was chosen, he was not surprised. Brown Wolf was Great Axe's nephew by his favorite brother, his twin. Starts Fire considered himself blessed to be chosen at all. He was young yet for a raider, barely eighteen summers. Starts Fire took up his brand and released his axe from its strap on his back and followed behind Brown Wolf into the heavily canopied wood. He drove his pony hard, making sure he remained on Brown Wolf's flank. He was a good rider and a fierce raider, and he wanted his exploits to be recorded in Brown Wolf's mind so that he might gain favor and status in the tribe.

The path led west down a ridge and crossed a small brook. Brown Wolf plunged his pony across, and several of the raiders followed after, shoving past Starts Fire in their excitement to reach the virgin colony of simple forest folk they knew must be at the end of the trail. But Starts Fire kept his wits, and several of the men, having been on past raids with him, understood that he had an uncanny gift for tracking. Four waited alongside his pony until their voices could be heard over the stampede of the departing team. When their pounding hooves faded, Little Elk, Seven Foxes, Red Beaver and Storm Shadow followed Starts Fire, who had already found a hidden secondary path leading north again, well hidden by the growth of spring vegetation, but evident beneath the new leaves and vines. Little Elk, who was Starts Fire's youngest brother, winked at the others and pointed to the marked stone several meters down the path.

"My brother sees what is hidden!" he boasted. "Now we will be the first to take the village and earn great respect among our people!" This of course meant that they would be chosen more often as scouts for the raids, thus being given even more opportunity to be the first men to come upon the spoils of their attacks on the simple folk they lived on much as hunters lived on their game. For the Fire People there was no drudgery, no toil, in their livelihood. There was no toil, for effort and amusement were one.

Now Little Elk has propelled his terrified pony past Starts Fire to plunge down a ravine towards his brother's find. But Starts Fire halts his mount, holding up a fist to keep the others back. His brother has made a critical error. His impulsive nature has sealed the fate of both he and his pony. Out of view, they crash through a stand of diminutive pine, clutching to the side of the chasm with shallow roots. Starts Fire can hear the silence of their descent. His brother will not scream, not even now, when he sees his final resting place hurling toward him. A mob of guinea fowl explode from the trees below, their cries deafening for a moment. Then stillness. Starts Fire feels the thrill of fury burst forth from his loins. His brother is dead, or broken. A pony lost. Starts Fire does not blame his brother's nature. It is the fault of the people they come to plunder. He will take his revenge upon the men and women and babes of this village, which is now his to obliterate because he has lost a blood relative in this attack. Red Beaver, Seven Foxes and Storm Shadow move past Starts Fire, careful not to follow Little Elk's impulsive plunge over the break of stubby pine into the ravine. They will lead the way, so that Fire Start may view his brother's fate without fear that the humiliation of his grief might be noted by the other warriors. For the Fire People, there is no grief in battle, only cause for rage.

Brown Wolf leads the group at a trot down a narrow path that skirts the hidden chasm. He hears Starts Fire's pony stop briefly behind them, then catch up at a canter, the three beat gait as easy for his ears to distinguish as the stillness of the forest nearing a village, or the mewl of a hidden infant in a basket. He urges his pony into a canter, but Starts Fire has charged ahead of him, the path widening now. Brown Wolf hears the babble of a brook, then the soft murmur of voices, the pleasant chatter of a little village enjoying their communal evening meal. Starts Fire has heard it too. He snatches his pony's reins, slamming the iron bit against its bars so that the animal spins to a stop, nearly launching him over its shoulder as he fumbles with his flint and lights his torch. The others follow his lead and light their own.

Another two hundred yards and he is upon them, his war cry lifting into the darkening sky like the tongues of flame from his torch, which catch the dry thatched roofs of the little huts like tinder.

CHAPTER TEN

Rah is asleep when the tremor rocks the little pallet upon which he sleeps, shattering a sweet dream of his first dance as a god in Knossos.

As suddenly as he is catapulted to his feet by the vibration, he has bolted through the curtained archway of his chamber and down the Hall of the Priestly Houses, across the catwalk overlooking the lyceum, and down an interior staircase past the kitchens. Crockery shattering in the bakery chases him further down the stair, further than he has ever been, down past the root and wine cellars, down and down into the bowels of the fortress. A cat looking for safe ground, looking for the earth upon which to cringe, he does not stop his downward descent until the stairs level off onto a stone floor and the passage continues ahead of him in full dark. He has found his way to the Assassin's underground lair beneath the family wing. No torch lights his way. It is dark as death here. Still he feels along the cold, wet walls of the narrow passages, one turn leading left, another right, his feline instincts urging him into the smallest spaces, the tightest openings, until he is funneled into a room that opens onto rough-hewn rock walls, a room filled with the heavy air of secrets, mounds of gold, silver and gems, a kings fortune, an assassin's hoard.

As Rah shudders and pants, exhausted by his fright, in a nest of pearls and precious things, the Wolves of Amega clear the fortress above. The aftershock of the quake finds not a living soul within the stronghold, only the bronze Bull God trembling in the empty lyceum, and the Grain God trembling in the wolfs lair several levels below.

Josepha, the twins, the four houses, cooks and clerks, surgeons and slaves, musicians and dancers, stand out in the chariot grounds in a confused group, jabbering like mocking jays, waiting for permission to return to their beds. In the excitement and haste, no one has noticed the missing Rah, who is in any case notorious for rising early to work his horses and not expected to be among them.

At the stable, Hagga had begun the daily task of choosing chariot horses for practice when the quake shook the timbers, driving the animals into a panic. As the dust rose from the packed dirt floor and descended from the mud-brick roof above, covering his head and filling his eyes with its orangey gloom, he made the only rational decision he could. He stumbled to the doors leading to the practice ring and flung them wide, then began opening stalls, nearest first so that the animals would not trample one another in their frenzy to exit. The practice ring was bordered on all four sides with high brick walls, walls that even Rah's Halix would not leap. The twenty Minoan Arabs had never been pastured with the Amegan chariot horses, but Hagga knew that their terror would keep them from harming one another until the tremors subsided. They would race in a circle around the enormous field, their equine minds believing always that speed was safety. By the time the quake had passed, they would be hot and exhausted and need to be cooled down individually. Then the worst part of this day would begin.

Two of Rah's mares were in estrus. There were five stallions among the war animals and all of Rah's colts were whole. Without Ghedi, he would need the boy to collect his own animals, and there again was the strong possibility that his head would be separated from his shoulders as a result. Rah would no doubt mount his lead mare to accomplish the task, which, in Hagga's opinion, would without question be the most dangerous place to be in Amega in half an hour.

Now the aftershock has passed and Hagga has collected several of his best horsemen to begin the job of catching his animals, one by one, with a bucket of grain and a lead rope. Thankfully none of the horses had had time to finish their morning portion before the quake struck, and grain would be a strong motivator. The men are instructed to begin with the quietest animals, and as a result are able to catch two and even three at a time using the grain bucket as bait. Lysius and Keret are leading theirs into the barn when Pelet runs toward him from the front entrance, his face red with exertion.

"The Rah!" he pants, collapsing as he reaches Hagga. "The Rah is missing! Is he here at the stable? Have you sent him out in the field? The Lady is demanding he be found and brought to her immediately!"

"The Lady?" Hagga blinks, confused. "What are you saying, boy? The Lady Josepha has never demanded so much as a cup of water from a house slave. What Lady do you speak of?"

"Lady Josepha, Sir," answers Pelet, looking past Hagga out into the chariot practice field. Four more horses are being led in by Keret and Lysias, and behind these, the others can be seen raising clouds of dust as they stampede round the track.

"I will need a dozen more men if I am to save these animals today. I have not seen the Rah this morning, but he must be on his way here. There is nothing he cares for more than these beasts, and he will know I have had to release them together." He waves at the clouded field as Keret and Lysias settle their animals into stalls.

"She is mad with fear," says Pelet, turning to carry his message back to the fortress. "She paces and wails and tears at her hair! There is more to fear in Amega today than a few injured horses!"

"Well, mother of the gods, if his animals are harmed on my watch we will all be beheaded! I need help here! Send me Kleitos and Thymus at least!"

"I have been sent to find the Rah, Sir," Pelet shouts back over his shoulder on his way out of the barn. "If I do not succeed, we will none of us be in need of a horse from this day forward!"

"And to die thus," mumbles Hagga, turning to catch a lead rope off a hook and go out into the field himself. "After all of my years of service to you, Master. What have I done to deserve it?"

Inside the fortress Mochlos, the High Priest of the Rah, is summoned by Ham to the Lady's inner chamber. When he arrives, he is shoved forward into the center of the room by two burly guards, and he nearly topples over a sight that turns his blood cold. Josepha is on her knees on the red and gold carpet. About her are strewn a half dozen broken dresser drawers, baskets of jewelry making materials, the rug slippery with pearls freed from their necklaces. Her fingers comb the rug, searching blindly through the disarray. Her hair is a mat of tangles hanging in knots from her shoulders. She is moaning, like a woman who has found her infant dead in its crib. Mochlos looks back at the two stone faced guards, then at Ham, who has remained at the door. But the old house servant only shakes his head. He has no answers. Clearly it is up to Rah's priest to conjure a solution to this calamity.

"Can I bring sanity to the senseless?" sighs Mochlos, raising his hands at them. He turns halfheartedly back to face the challenge that is the Wolf's wounded mate.

Her face is grey, twisted with grief, wet with tears. She is moaning softly, rocking on her haunches like a lost child. Then, spotting a stray pearl, she makes a little gasp of relief, throws herself upon it, takes it up in both hands like a baby bird. She studies it, crying, giggling, "There you are, my darling!" she whispers to the pearl. But no, no, this is not the one. Her face clouds, she lets out a terrible moan, she drops the pearl and clutches her bosom, rocks and sobs.

Mochlos swallows the saliva that has gathered in his mouth. He scuffs across the carpet, careful not to jostle the pearls. When he is an arms-length from Josepha he sinks to his knees.

"Mistress," he says softly, holding a hand out to her, palm up, "It is not the pearl you seek."

Josepha looks up into the High Priest's eyes, startled. "Not the pearl?" she whispers. "Oh but it was of great price, of great price, Mochlos. He loved the boy so, he gave his most precious for me to make … make into the earring…" she drifts off, her eyes raking the priest's face for comfort.

"It is not the pearl, Mistress," answers Mochlos gently. "That pearl is on his ear, as it should be. That pearl is with him." He extends his hand a bit further, and Josepha, to Ham and the guards' surprise, drops the lesser gem into the priest's open palm.

"Oh, Mochlos, what have I done?" she whimpers, pleading. "Oh, what have I done?" Her voice is whining, insipid. Mochlos grits his teeth against it. Is this what you were, he thinks, before he found you? Was it the Wolf who gave you strength all along? But to her he offers a soothing refrain.

"Nothing the world over has not done, my dear, again and again. We are all of us sinners, led astray by temptations we cannot resist in our humanness. You have desired a god, and a god has desired you," and here he pauses, for he has heard the swords of the two guards behind him slicing free of their scabbards. Still he plows on. Let them behead me before her, right here on their Master's finest carpeting, if they must. I will not be silenced.

"If it were not divinely conceived, should it have happened at all? Calm yourself now, it is done. The boy has followed his own path, also divinely conceived. It has nothing to do with you, nor with your perceived improbity, it is who and what he is that has sent him into a panic, just as it did in Cyrus when the earthquake came. Did he not flee then? Did your husband, and the good Captain Nikolaos, not discover him in the labyrinth beneath the palace?"

All of this Mochlos has heard second hand, but speaks as if he had been there, putting Josepha's fears into a context she can manage. The boy is not lost. He did not disappear forever, like a startled ghost, because she held him, longed for him to be inside her, betrayed her husband with her heart, if not yet her body.

Mochlos hears the two guards holster their swords behind him. The danger is past. He may have just as easily lost the hand that he'd extended to the Wolf's mate as found it still holding the lesser pearl. Now he looks about at the disarray around him. Broken drawers, gemstones and jewelry work covering the knotted Babylonian carpet. Mochlos begins gathering the items spread about him and depositing them in one of the less damaged drawers. He glances over his shoulder at Ham, gives him a firm nod, join me now! and turns back to Josepha, who has taken his lead and begun to gather the pearls nearest her into a small leather sack. Ham takes his cue and moves to assist the two, nodding first at the two guards that their services are no longer required. The two husky men drop to their knees, bow to Josepha, who pays them no mind, and leave.

"Where is he, Mochlos? He cannot live. He would have fled immediately to the stable to save his horses, and they say he has not been seen there today."

Mochlos shoots a relieved look at Ham. Ham nods in return. At first the old house servant had thought that an overabundance of black bile had been responsible for his Mistresses affliction of the mind, but her reaction to the Rah's disappearance has confirmed a more sinister suspicion. Now the resourceful priest seems to have managed some magic with a stray pearl to call her back to her senses, albeit with the use of some dangerous insinuations. Ham cannot speak for the guards, but as for himself, he will say nothing of this exchange to the master. It was, after all, he himself who summoned the priest in the first place, believing that Mochlos was the only person who could give Josepha an educated guess as to where the Rah might be. Therefore if fingers were to be pointed at some later date, they would ultimately point back to him.

Ham touches his fingertips to his heart, bows his head, 'thank you'.

But Mochlos brushes the deference off. He takes a deep breath then answers Josepha with as little concern in his voice as possible knowing that his already tenuous value to the assassin will plummet to zero if the Rah is not found.

"Let us put our heads together and consider the boy, My Lady. He will have been sleeping when he was startled out of a dream by the tremors. Would he have been able to consider anything at that moment, when the ground was shaking under his bed, when the walls were threatening to crumble about him, than his own safety? He is no hero, Madam, I have known him long enough to vouch for that."

"Little cat," squeaks Josepha, then chokes on an inhaled sob and covers her face with her hands.

Mochlos peers at her.

"Antaris called him that, 'Little cat,'" she pipes through her hands, gasping through her tears. "Oh he called him 'my little cat' don't you remember? My little cat." Her voice is lost in her weeping.

"Josepha!" the priest's voice is a tiger's bark. It is enough to send the two guards back into the room, weapons drawn. Even Ham, who has remained on his knees collecting trinkets, starts. But Mochlos pays them no mind. Here is power. Would they prefer their Master return to a mad wife? Her sanity is in my hands.

And as if by magick, Josepha's uncontrolled lament is cut off. She looks up through her fingers at the High Priest, a little girl admonished.

"Enough now," Mochlos continues, his voice soft again, hypnotic, compassionate and prevailing at once. "Hysteria is rarely helpful. Whatever has happened between you and the boy must be put aside now. It is your husband you must consider, for if he returns to find the boy lost…. or worse…" his words trail off. Josepha is studying his face with a child's trusting gaze. "Consider your husband, Josepha, to whom you owe much," finishes the priest.

"Yes, Mochlos, yes. My own feelings are of no consequence now, and I will not be a party to his broken heart!"

Heart indeed, thinks Mochlos, keeping his face neutral. As if that inferno could feel anything but its own fury. But to the wolf's mate he says, "We must work together now. For you and I know the Rah better than anyone else alive. What you say is true. He is a cat, and a cat thinks of its own safety first. He will not have gone to the stables. He will have found a tree to climb, a fence to jump, or a dark place to hide in until the danger is past."

"But Mochlos, in Cyrus he could not find his way home. He had been driven into such a feral state that-"

"Another valuable observation, Madam. And one I had not thought of. No he will not return to us on his own if he has lost his human senses. This happened again at the Table of the Gods, where your husband rescued him from the headless and undead army of the Amorites. As the story is told, the Master heard his caterwauling in the dark and followed the sound. Perhaps we can do the same, Madam! Perhaps he is even now yowling in some dark corner of this fortress. Is there a lower level? Beneath the kitchens and the cellar storehouse? Is there… dear Goddess, is there a labyrinth under the Fortress of the Wolf?"

Josepha's alarmed look brings Mochlos to his feet. He extends a hand to help her rise, thinks better of it, and waits for her to stumble to her feed on her own.

"No, you would not tell me if there was, and yet I see it in your face, my dear. The assassin has secrets beneath this monstrosity, secrets that none will live to tell, should they breach them. We cannot search the place ourselves and we will have no luck ordering his men to do so. And yet I will stake my head on it, this is where the boy has fled. He has fled down, down to the farthest corners of the deepest subterranean vault like the feral thing he is. A new dilemma," Mochlos strokes his newly shaven chin, "and yet do not despair, Madam, for though we cannot put our hands upon him, yet we now know where he has gone! He is not lost!"

"Not lost, Mochlos, but in terrible danger all the same!" squeaks Josepha, her hands over her heart. "Oh, he is in terrible danger," she whimpers, shaking her head. "And there is nothing anyone can do to save him!"

CHAPTER ELEVEN

The little settlement is engulfed in flame, the roar of it deafening. Starts Fire has left his team in trust of the saleable women and children and returned to the business of capturing the Father for later sport when he sees that Brown Wolf and the others have arrived. The raid leader leaps from his pony and sets to torching the last few unignited huts while the rest of the raiders begin their search for booty, slash the throats of the village men who are not on fire, and run at them helter-skelter with their primitive flint weapons. Starts Fire is pleased to step back and allow the favored nephew of Great Elk his due. He has already earned his glory, and Brown Wolf will recount the raid as it happened or be forever branded a liar amongst the men here today. The best of the booty is his, and already in the hands of Seven Foxes, Red Beaver and Storm Shadow. Let the others take what furs they can find. The sheep are penned and will have to be herded back to camp together. They will be distributed as Great Axe sees fit, most likely claiming the ewes for himself and offering his nephew the rest, a condolence for his loss of face.

Starts Fire is just turning to fetch his pony, which he had tethered in the trees, when the thing explodes from the fire.

It is half again as tall as any man standing, a great black corpse, its burial wraps singed by the flames, its bearlike chest crisscrossed with glittering bronze weaponry. The thing has no head, or so it seems to him, as it materializes out of the smoke and ash in the direction of the river. It is a pair of gargantuan arms wielding two ferocious crescent-shaped blades of silver that slice the air in all directions as it falls upon Brown Wolf, separating him from both of his arms at the shoulders as easily as a man scythes wheat.

Starts Fire turns and stumbles toward his pony, which rears and screams as he catches the rein, ripping its mouth on the heavy iron bit. Behind him he can feel the heat of the raging fire on his back, hear the snapping of timbers as the houses implode, smell the sizzling flesh of the village infants who are burning alive in their baskets. He makes a wild leap for the pony's back, but the animal swings its haunch just as his leg should find its home. An impact like the blow of a fire log cracks the back of his skull and he is airborne. The hand that held the pony's rein is hacked from his wrist before he can feel the pain. He watches that hand fly after the pony, still gripping the rein, as the animal flees into the forest.

He is shoved onto his back by a booted foot. Starts Fire stares up at the colossus in awe. How can this be, that this tiny village in the wood should have such a powerful shaman, who was able to conjure one of the twelve! For surely this is a guardian from Utgaror, the land of giants. The creature towers over him, wreathed by orange flames, and Starts Fire is struck with wonder, though his lopped arm spurts his life's blood and his vision blurs, that the monster does not melt in the heat. The twelve giants are of the far northern forests, where winter never loses its grip. Yet the thing seems to thrive in the heat of the inferno. Perhaps he is not from Utgaror but a fire Jötnar from the world of heat and fire. Perhaps he is Surtr himself! The black one, ruler of the fire giants, the one who comes to destroy the world on the last day!

The two moons of silver have disappeared and in their place a thick length of hemp is pulled across the wraiths great chest. Starts Fire stares up at the monstrosity, hoping that his end will be swift. But what is this? The rope is twisted around the stump of his right arm, yanked taught, tied off. He is flipped back onto his belly, and in less time than it takes the finest horseman to lasso a colt, his limbs are bound together behind his back. Then he is left on his face as the titan returns to the inferno.

Rush trusses the little barbarian with a length of his hanging rope, then turns to catch the rest of the cockroaches that are even now running for their ponies. They will have no luck. With two great strides he pounces on the two who came behind the one who had been about to torch the last of the houses before he was separated from his arms. He catches them by the hair, gritting his teeth against his own bile rising at the touch of the oily, lice-infested mops. He cracks their heads together at the temples and drops them, then slips the bridles off their ponies, allowing the beasts to flee into the forest. He turns to catch three more of the filthy fire maggots as they attempt to bolt past him, scooping two up in the span of his arms and catching the third by the seat of his pants in the same motion. They are not built for battle, but stout and spindle-legged. He carries them, kicking and squirming, to the nearest ignited hut and tossed them into it, then throws the still intact door shut and jams it closed with a nearby log. Four more raiders have made it to their ponies and are attempting to control them, but the animals have been tethered too near the village, which is now burning out of control. He approaches the two closest to him, snatches the reins of both simultaneously and pulls the men off by their pant legs, allowing the terrified animals to trample them before he looses their bridles and gives them their freedom. This is all that is needed to send the other ponies galloping after them through the thick trees, slamming their mounts into low branches and leaving them for Rush to mop up at his convenience.

Rush turns back to the inferno. The screams of men burning and the sad aria of infants roasting has died, and he hears only the soft mewling of a single babe, probably hidden by one of the women as the raiders attacked. He will not be able to find the child before it is smothered by the smoke, and his great heart burns with hatred. He picks up the bound thug on his way back to the women, thinks better of it, and drops him back on his face, instead bounding into the wood to finish off the raiders whose ponies have thrown them or knocked them off in their panicked flight from the massacre.

When he returns, his assassin's tunic and leggings are so soaked in human blood that they serve to keep him cool though the fire still rages. He takes up the trussed Starts Fire and drags him behind on his face.

He skirts the inferno, finding the women still huddled amid the bodies of their dead and shredded captors. The girl he gave the knife runs to him, throws her arms about his waist and buries her tear-streaked face in his chest. He drops the rope and the bandit. There is time for him later.

Rush gives the woman time to quiet, reluctantly allowing her to cuddle against him. Her hair smells of flowering herbs and her body is lean and strong. He finds himself relaxing in her embrace though several other women have rushed at him, all waiting their turn to embrace their savior.

Yet they know not who or what I am, thinks the assassin, nor what my motives are. How is it with the female of the species, that they have no fear of me, when I am peril itself?

"Enough," he grunts, as the last of them takes his left hand in both of hers and lifts it to kiss.

"I am no hero," he maneuvers his hand free and turns to pick up the rope. One of the women snatches it up, barks an order to another and in a moment he is presented with a donkey and a cart. The woman gestures. Put him here. Rush lifts the man by the rope and deposits him into the cart, reaches to take the donkeys lead, but the women surround him, patting his hands and stroking his arms, one even lifting his braid and caressing it as if it were a cat. Beautiful! she seems to say. The woman he trusted with the dagger has taken the donkey's lead, and to his astonishment, four other women have arrived with tiny babes in their arms. Relieved, Rush pulls the rough muslin wrap from one of the infants. The soft cap is white-blonde, and a jolt of sentiment jars him. The mother smiles up at him, takes his hand, sets it on the baby's scalp. You are his father now, she says with her eyes. Now that he has none.

"I cannot take you with me," Rush extracts his hand from the girl's grip. But she is like a kitten held out of a window, clinging with all of her strength to his solidity.

"You must find your kin in the next village." But she drops to her knees, pleading, her free arm clinging to his blood-drenched legs. The other women fall to their knees in unison, their hands uplifted, beseeching. Two of them, in their teens and childless, scamper off toward the livestock pens. Now they will bribe me, thinks Rush, bribe me with sheep that are already mine.

"No kin, then?" Rush sighs, "Will they make slaves of you as well? Woman, I am no babysitter." He makes an attempt to shake his leg free, but the girl holds fast. And has he not been a babysitter ever since he failed to slaughter the Rah? Indeed, he has had to babysit the boy ever since. And now he has come half way across the world, seeking justice for a gold-plated androgynous acrobat, who will hardly thank him, for no better purpose than to pick up more parasites, like

a dog with fleas.
"Leave me be!" he booms, which only serves to set the infants wailing, the women falling flat on their faces.
"Very well, have it your way!" he rumbles, pulling the girl on his leg to her feet and giving her a little shake. "They will be dead in two days!" he barks into her face. "This is no journey for infants!"
The two girls have returned from the livestock pens, not with sheep, but with a half dozen donkeys. The animals are saddled and carrying packs. Rush peers at the sight. The women with infants are already climbing onto the beasts. The others, whose babes perhaps perished in the fire, seem perfectly willing to walk behind.
"You were expecting these raiders, then," Rush nods. "And yet your men were ill prepare for war. A race of sheep," he shakes his head. "What good are you to me? I will not bring you to Amega to water the blood of my warriors! You are good stock for my enemies. I shall send you off to Babylon as soon as we cross the borders of my own country."
An hour later, having retrieved The Black on his way up the hillside, he finds Triggvi and the children where he left them on the crest. Before he has dismounted, Ilse and Ole are running toward him.
"Fenrir!" Ilse calls, hugging his legs as soon as his feet touch the ground. She smiles up at him. "Fenrir back!"
Ole has already taken possession of one of his hands.
"Just so," Rush is hard pressed to hold back his own smile. He pats the children on their dun-colored heads. "And I have brought your Triggvi presents."
The trader has also approached, though with some apprehension. He considers the scene mutely.
"The survivors, sir?" he remarks carefully. "Are we to take them with us to the Great Sea?"
"You, Triggvi, are in my employ," answers Rush, who has handed The Black to Ilse. "It occurs to me that you have not received your mark, that you may be protected, from now to eternity, by its authority."
"My mark, sir?" asks Triggvi warily.
"The Tear of the Bear, Triggvi, you recall that I have marked all who serve me with it. And yet, you do not wear the Tear," says Rush.
"I need no mark to serve you, Sir. I am well paid," answers Triggvi. "I am your servant until you chose to release me from your service."

"Yes, Triggvi, you are. And you are an excellent employee. And will continue to be one for as long as you are upright and breathing. But you need my mark, for I am sending these women and children to Babylon in your care, and without my mark the story you will tell will not serve you. Rather, it will be a death sentence for you."

"Mark me! Mark me!" cries Ilse then. She pulls at Rush's pant leg and hops excitedly, and the other Forest children have soon join her, though they do not know what the words they mimic mean.

"Mark me, Fenrir!" trills Ole, squeezing Rush's hand.

"Another time," answers Rush, chucking the boy under his chin. "Girls are not marked, Ilse, and I could not mark such a pretty face if they were," he gives her braid a tug. Ilse giggles.

"Now, Triggvi," Rush says in a more deliberate tone. "You will come with me, and in the morning I will send you ahead with plenty of money to buy these orphans clothing, food and lodging once you reach the Hatti Empire. You will only need speak my name, and show my mark, and you will be well cared for."

CHAPTER TWELVE

"Even his wife does not dare to enter his subterranean hoard," says Mochlos, who is mixing the second of the two elixirs he plans to take with him down into that very place. He wipes his hands on the apron he has tucked into his rope belt, then lifts the mortar and taps the contents out onto a parchment.

"No man in Amega will dare it." He curls the parchment and folds the ends, then takes a seal candle and drops a line of wax along the edge. "And the only man I know who would is stuck in Babylon babysitting infidels." He tucks the tube of medicine in his robe alongside the first, then turns to face Awiti. "But we must."

Awiti's ebony face is marble, her brows twisted with apprehension.

"How can we, sir? And if it is as strange a maze as we are told, how can we find the Rah before we lose our own way? We will be lost and when the Master finds us if we are still alive he will kill us for breaching his asylum." A bolt of shivers cascades down her spine, and she wraps her yellow robe more tightly about her, though it is a dead calm, hot day. Mochlos runs his glance down her form and frowns.

"You are too much girl for that, my dear. I put you in billowing robes for good reason." He waits for her to catch his meaning, then steps toward her and lays an arm about her shoulders, encouragingly.

"Do not underestimate your Mochlos. I have no wish to rattle that monster's cage. But think. What does he hate the most? Is it not cowardice? And what does he love, but bravery? I have here two concoctions. The one for Rah, to calm him, and this is why I bring you with me. He will not take it from me, but you, his Siriona, he will trust. The other, that one is for us. A hedge, let us say, against any....complications that might arise should that madman return before we find the Rah."

"But what does it do, sir? Is it a suicide drug?" asks Awiti, her soft voice warbling with fright.

"Hah, you think I would do his work for him, then? No, girl. It will make us invisible to him. Then we will follow the clues I leave as we descend, and find our way back to our beds, and he will be none the wiser. But we must not tarry. For surely if he returns home before we have recovered the Rah, he will find him himself. That man could find a tear in an ocean. And then what good are we to him? We must prove our value, by rescuing the Rah from his own folly, and bring him to his senses before the beast returns, so that all of Amega is witness to our worth."

"But the Master's men will not let us get past the kitchens, Sir! How will we descend into the labyrinth? I have heard that there is a watch set on the stairs above the food cellars, and that this is the only way down into the Master's treasury."

"Yesterday you did not know there *was* a treasury below the cellars, and today you wonder how we will pass the guard down the only stairs," chuckles Mochlos. "Ah, rumor is a wonderful thing. Most wonderful because it works both ways, Awiti, both backwards and forewards." He has finished packing his sack, which he has had Aros fit with two straps that he may hoist over Awiti's shoulders. "There, that is our food supply, and a few other items we will be glad to have if things take a turn for the worse. I trust it is not too encumbering?" Awiti hitches the sack more comfortably onto her back. "I have carried far heavier on my head," she says, biting her lip. "And for many miles."

"You must trust me now," says Mochlos, taking her shoulders and giving them a confident squeeze. "Must I remind you of your fate, had I not rescued you from the house of the Babylonian, Attaru?"

"No sir," answers Awiti, dropping her eyes, ashamed. "You saved me from stoning or worse, and my sisters from defilement, and I owe you my life. You will not hear me complain again. Forgive me."

"There now, girl," Mochlos lifts the girl's delicate, cat-like chin. "No one is going to take your life, and you needn't worry that you'll be fallen upon by that raging monster in the dark. This is 'not my first bull-jump', as they were fond of saying in Knossos. I have set another rumor going, and in an hour the way will be clear for us to descend into the bowels of this Tartarus. There are in fact two stairways down into the food cellars. This I learned from watching Brother Crispo, who has been given lone authority to use the second of these. That stair is the one we want, for that one is the one that leads to the Master's personal wine cellar. It is hidden behind the kitchens, and the doorway to the labyrinth must be beneath it, do you understand? He would not give the entire compound this information. Too many heads to lop should a theft be discovered. Nay, he has left it to one man, one too fat to run. And too frightened of the madman who owns him to borrow a fig from his own kitchen let alone steal a gem from that man's private horde. There will be no guard there, and the house will be absorbed with preparations for the Master's return and too distracted to notice the High Priest of the Moon and his Hermaphrodite wandering through the kitchens in search of the High Priest of the Sun, to discuss a duel ceremony, for the safety of the Rah!"

Mochlos allows himself a rare chuckle as Awiti's eyes widen with awe. "You started it?" she whispers behind her hands, looking about for spies. "You told them he was on his way?"

"I told no one, and so no one can fix the error on me. I did, however, mention his imminent return to the house man, Ham, based on my astronomical calculations, of course. I don't believe that last was in earshot of anyone of importance, but the first of it, well the two guards at the Lady's door certainly would have heard that part. And so you see, my girl, your Mochlos has not lost his touch. The kitchens will be so busy preparing a feast for their Master's return that there won't be a soul interested in our intrusion. And your veil will cover that pack nicely," he takes a moment to pull it over her head and adjust it about her shoulders, "Only let me set it lower. There!" And with a wink, Mochlos turns to the doorway and holds open the beaded curtain for her. As she passes in front of him he begins to hum a tune, and by the time they reach the catwalk over the lyceum he is singing it in a hushed whisper.

"Poor little cat has lost his way. But the devil will find him anyway."

The dragon's lair is pitch, the golden head of the Grain God, untouched by natural light, indistinguishable from the mound of jewels it rests upon. Rah has yowled himself hoarse, and lies still now, a jewel among jewels, hidden in a wealth of forgotten gains. He has lost his fragile connection with the present and has returned to the tomb of Lutarus to begin again what was never finished.

He is the Grain God of Knossos, and must be sacrificed on Mount Juktas, on the altar of his high priest, to save the world. He is here because they would have killed Ting Ya had he resisted. He is here because the world growls and snarls and opens its maw to consume him. He is here because the world belches fire and ash and he is here because the world sends plagues to kill and waves to drown those who have made him a god to be sacrificed. He is here because he resisted his vocation. He will not resist any longer. He will be what he was born to be.

But down a dark, wet corridor, and a further staircase that turns like a corkscrew well into the cold rock beneath the nest of mammon in which Rah sleeps, a monster wakes. It raises its great, deformed head and sniffs the stale air. It rubs its horn against the sharpening stone, for the horn is like a rhino's horn thrusting out from the center of its forehead and it loves the horn, which has made it beloved of the brother, a thing to be treasured beyond all treasure.

And the monster feels excitement, which it has not felt for a very long time, not since the brother brought it to war against the Greeks. It smells life, something sweet and young, fresh and sweating and beating with fear. Over the scent of this sweet young life another scent tickles its dog-smart nostrils. Delicious, delicate, sacred. It remembers these smells, hyssop, myrrh, it remembers a time when these smells surrounded it, when people brought it gifts of lambs and doves and gold and silver. It lived in a great pillared sanctuary then, made of polished stone and open to the sea air. It faced the sea and the morning sunlight poured into its temple. But then the darkness came, slowly, the horn continuing to grow as it aged, crushing its sight. And the brother saw that the sun pained it, how it fled the sun and shielded its head from the sun and bellowed with agony and raged against the morning, chasing its worshipers from its temple for the sun thrust great red-hot rods of fire into its eyes. And it learned to hate the sun, and to blame the sun, and it begged the brother to bury it, to hide it from the agony of the sun. Then the brother brought it here, where the sun could not reach it, buried it like a treasure, his greatest treasure. And the people forgot, but the brother did not forget, that it was a god, and that it was beloved.

Now a waft of cherries reaches the monster's nose. It lifts its head to better catch the scent, for its nose has replaced its eyes. And the cherries tickle it's long, eager tongue and it rises from its bed and it follows the scent. It needs no lamp, no torch, to navigate the channel upward, towards the fragrance that is Rah.

Crispo has left Mochlos and Awiti at the entrance of the stairwell behind the assassin's wine cellar.

The cook had just been returning from it, having deposited a roasted duck and a round of goat's cheese, a jar of olives, boiled and buttered turnips, as well as several loaves of barley bread and an amphora of good wine, at the bottom. Why he was ordered to waste good wine on a thing accursed by the gods was none of his affair, and he made a point of clearing his mind of such burdens of thought. He prepared a fowl each day, as well as an accompaniment of bread, cheese, fresh or dried fruit (depending on the season) and wine. Always the wine. And he left it, as ordered, at the base of the stairwell. In the morning he collected the basket and the tray and left a good breakfast of a half dozen boiled eggs, roast eel or smelt, bread and butter, cheese, fruit. There was a well down there, he had been told, and the monster drank from it. That was all he knew, and all he cared to know.

"He will eat as well as I do," he was told, "Or I will find a more accommodating cook, to cook the first, and feed my brother as I see fit."

Crispo never questioned the assassin. Who was he to say, "What, that? Your brother?" He'd have had a devil of a time finishing *those* words before his tongue was on the dinner plate. He kept his own council on the matter, understanding that he was chosen for his skill as a cook, but also for his discretion. Never mind why, he would do as he was told and never tell a living soul.

But then, today, Mochlos and his veiled apprentice had come upon him returning from that very assignment! He had only just deposited the meal at the bottom of the stairwell, when he heard voices in the wine cellar above! Shocked at first that anyone would dare enter the Master's private cellar, he quickly distinguished the High Priest's nasal pitch. Moon was brazen, and wily as a weasel. He would be searching for the Rah where no one else dare look, and taking advantage of all the confusion and rumor of the Wolf's return by nightfall.

Of course, he tried to hide from them the secret stairwell. What good could come of it? Surely the Rah could not be there, in that hole, even now, with the creature? But Mochlos would have none of it.

"Spare me your deceptions, Sun, this is no time for secrets! The return of the Rah is all that matters now, and you're more likely to keep your head if you help me find him. There is a second set of stairs behind this cellar, and I have good reason to believe that the Rah found them when the quake struck this morning. Everywhere else has been searched. He fled like a frightened animal down into the earth. Down! Down as he did in Cyrus, down into the Hall of the Kings. He is mad with fear and we have no time to lose. Lead me to them!"

Crispo took the pair through the maze of stacked amphora to the narrow stairwell at the back of the forty foot cavern. He lit the single torch there with his own rush light.

"I will go no further, Moon, and I advise you to do the same. That is more than the pit of darkness it appears to be. It is a pit of doom. A thing-" but he cut himself short. What? Tell the second confidence he has been given? No. Better the two never return, the secrets buried with them down there in that crypt of gold, than he should betray the Master twice.

Mochlos snatched the torch from the wall, gave him an offended look, and descended the stair.

"I am the brightest among you," Crispo heard him mutter on his way down the well. "And yet you speak to me as if I were a common fool." And then, "I shall save all our hides today!" he shouted up from the floor at the bottom. But Crispo made no answer. He could see the High Priest's narrow, high-cheeked face in the torchlight, his intelligent brow creased, his dark eyes intense with purpose. For a moment, the Sun priest felt a pang of sadness. Awiti's veiled head turned to look up at him from the bottom stair.

"Good fortune, Moon. Be blessed," was all he could say, before he turned and fled the wine cellar as quickly as he could carry himself without stumbling into a wall of precious Minoan wine.

CHAPTER THIRTEEN

The fire troll is unconscious. He lies like a sack of grain beside the fire, his stump still oozing. It has become infected, and soon the troll's arm will burn with such unquenchable agony that he will be of no value. The assassin has carried the man, strapped behind the cantle of his saddle, for two days. They are nearing the southern edge of the Lowlands, and Rush, unaccompanied, will soon make his way through the Pass to the Edge Of The Sea, and it is time for answers. He will not be taking this fire troll through Illyria, but he will need him alive and conscious if he is to find the answer he has come half way across the world to learn. Then he may roast with his brothers and when the smoke clears, feed the vultures of the plains.

Rush unpacks his water gourd and fills it at the river's edge. Then he returns to the fire and kneels beside the troll, lifting his louse-riddled head with one hand and trickling water into his open mouth with the other. The troll comes to, coughing and gagging on the stream.

"Where is your clan?" says Rush. The barbarian words Triggvi has given him are thick on his tongue, silly with Hittite trills and whispers.

"My clan," pants the delirious Starts Fire, "They are camped along the River in the Last Valley, before the Great Pass. Will you bring me to them?" He is thinking that the demon has felt compassion for him, and that he will be allowed to die among his tribe, set free on a great pyre, mourned by all, honored in the afterlife for all eternity for his great deeds.

But Rush can only understand 'River", 'Last Valley', and 'Great Pass'. These markers Triggvi taught him also, so that he could

decipher the barbarian's answer to his single question.
"Last Valley," he repeats, nodding. "Great Pass." He drops the trolls head onto the rocky shore. He is done with this pestilence. He rummages through his pack for a lye soap, returns to the water, scrubs his hands and arms.
"You will take me to them?" asks Starts Fire. The behemoth nods.
"You want to be in your homeland, little maggot?" Rush whispers in Hittite through his teeth. "Yes, you and all the children you have stolen and sold. I will grant your wish, for you will make an excellent torch."

Great Axe is enjoying his return home after a three moon interruption. He is lying with his favorite wife, Kolga, a girl he took from the Sun People two summers ago at the age of fourteen. She has blossomed since her capture, and like most women of the Nordic stock, she has become a fine acquisition. Tall and lean, strong and quick-witted, she is already pregnant with his second child. Best of all, she hates him with the passion of her kind, which is masked with such calculated craft that, had he not known she had tried to poison him at least three times now, he would believe she had somehow come to love him. Great Axe is not fazed by the attempted poisonings. He would want no less of the mother of his children. These children will be taller, fairer, and far more cunning than any he has produced with his barbarian wives. Great Axe sighs and rubs the girl's rounded belly. This one is surely a boy. He will teach it the ways of his clan, and the lad will be his successor one day. Such is his love for this woman.
Kolga pushes his hand away, frowning. He takes her chin and shakes it, attempting some discipline, but it is impossible. The girl is beauty itself. She has the face of a fox, all angles, brows and cheeks. Her eyes are the color of honey amber, and her teeth are straight and strong like a horse.
"He is mine, and you are mine, and I will make him Chieftain after me, Kolga. You are a slave girl. Can you not be happy that your son should rise to such a place?"
"It is a girl, Great Axe, I have dreamed of her many times. And she will be free, free of you and of the stink of this people and their fires."
"It is a son! I have too many daughters already. How many

daughters can one man sell? No. You will give me a son, tall and fair-skinned and amber-eyed like you, Kolga, and he will be my successor."

"Successor to what, Great Axe? Your people have no home. They wander and kill like jackals. What kind of life is that for a woman to wish on her children?"

Always she defies me, thinks Great Axe, who even now is excited by her insolence. Such strength! He should beat her, but he would not turn her into a cowering dog like all of the Fire People women, who were branded on the bottom upon marriage, and knew that to speak out of turn could cost them a brand on the face.

Great Axe has rolled over onto his Forest girl for another go at her innards, when the roar shatters the peaceful after-dinner time in the camp.

It is the roar of a mother bear, galloping out of a copse on the heels of a man who has injured her cub. A woman shrieks. Children are screaming.

Great Axe leaps from his wife's belly and ties a skin over his loins. He rushes out of his tent, his axe in one hand, a lit brand in the other. He will burn this bear! He will teach this beast a lesson it will not soon forget.

But what he sees when he throws open his tent flap is no bear. It is a terror wrapped in death rags, hideous and raging, riding a great black horse with blood red eyes and flailing hooves.

It is a fire giant from the fire world under the earth world! Perhaps Surtr himself! The black one, ruler of the Jötnar, who comes to destroy the world on the last day!

Great Axe falls back, his courage weakened by the sight of the supernatural monstrosity, a childhood demon, come to life, and seated atop his rearing black mount. But no! He must not show the clan his weakness! He must face this foe, however grim! He pushes himself off from his tent pole and stumbles forward, swinging his axe, poking his brand at the flailing animal.

Two things strike at once, the one, like a stone club, catches him in his jaw and splits it in twain. The other, slicing through the soft evening air like a silver bat, takes his head.

Rush turns the Black into a war spin, away from the troll and his lit brand. The animal pirouettes, sets its front feet, strikes out with its hind, and the satisfying snap of a man's jaw breaking sings in the assassin's fine ears. Before the horse has landed his hindquarters Rush has slashed down and back with a long Amorite sword, the reluctant gift of Samal-Etatani. He is fond of the sword for it is well-balanced and excellent for beheading on horseback, and he keeps it in a scabbard tied to the Black's cantle.

The fire troll's red braids fly about his loosed head, so that at the instant of death it has the look of a lass scampering playfully from her lover. Rush watches the man's body take a step, the blood fountain of his neck spouting merrily before the corpse pitches forward into the dirt.

The fire troll's brand tumbles away, dampened by the dusty earth.

From the tent flap comes a scream, a soprano aria of outrage and ferocity, and Rush turns the Black to face her as the honey-blonde maiden rushes at the fire troll's head, picks it up by one braid, and spinning round once pitches it up and over the tent. It lands with a thud on the other side.

Rush is on the girl in an instant. He whips her up and into his lap with his free arm just as the mob of fire trolls, who have witnessed the head of their leader fly over the chieftain tent and into the camp fire pit, come rushing at him like a swarm of angry bees. He holds the girl tight against his belly, clutching her just above the curve of her pregnancy, and swings the Black around, felling three of the trolls with one lethal war-kick. He spins the animal around in time to catch two more on the end of his sword, opening their faces into ear-to-ear grins before they drop to their knees. Another troll has made the impulsive error of taking hold of his left stirrup. Rush sheaths the Amorite blade and plunges a dagger from that boot into the man's right cheek, through his tongue, and down his throat. The blade sticks momentarily, but before the assassin can twist it free the girl in his lap has put her bare foot on the man's forehead and shoved it clean. Rush snatches the man's fire brand as he drops to the ground. He kicks the Black forward, losing the mob in a cloud of dust.

"Hang on to me girl, or become part of the blaze!" Rush rumbles into the maiden's ear. Though his speech is foreign to her, she turns and throws her arms about his torso when he lets her go to unsheathe the Amegan sword. He is as cold as the bottom of a lake, and it takes a moment for her to realize that he has deliberately immersed his fully-covered body in the river to thwart the fire he intends to set.

Rush growls as he sets to torching the line of tents that surround the camp with one hand, and cutting down the trolls who run at him with their own brands with the other.

"Let us give to them what they give to others," Rush barks over her head, which is now tucked into the cleft of his jaw, so that she can feel the vibration of his baritone in her temple.

The guard tents are blooming with flame like Cyrian poppies. They surround the troll camp with a ring of fire which is encouraged by a dry southern breeze and two weeks drought. Now Rush urges the Black back into the rivulet that he soaked in prior to his raid. When the animal is hock-deep, he slips from the saddle, leaving the girl mounted.

"Now you can take my horse and run, that I may hunt you down and make a fine sport of you when I find you, or you may wait for me here, and I will give you a life worth bringing that babe into." He moves to punch the Black on its haunch, but the girl slips off the saddle and into his arms before he can do so.

She looks up into his exposed eye with a wicked grin.

"You are a brazen one," he shakes his head, pleased. Then he hands her the Black's rein. "Stay here then," he stomps the earth to make his point. "I have some horses to loose, and a few more things to set right."

She smiles up at him, stamps one naked foot in agreement, and watches him slip away into the darkness toward the camp.

CHAPTER FOURTEEN

He knows his name because the one who loves him gave it to him. No one else has ever uttered it, but he has heard the brother hum it like a tune whenever he comes. He does not come often, but Minus listens all the day for that dark voice, for that dark hum. He listens and he waits. It is all he waits for. When the brother comes, he is complete.

Today there is no hum, but another noise, an eerie, deep vibration. It thrums in his maze of holes, and in the corridors between his sleeping place and the food. It is acute, like a drum on his skin, rising and falling. And it came while he was sleeping, after the earth shook him to sleep.

The monster's belly rumbles, as if in answer to the sound. He has had no time to eat his breakfast this morning. He had only just awakened to the lovely, smoky, sulfurous smell of eggs and grilled fish wafting down the corridors toward his sleeping place, when the tremors began. A quake. He had survived three when he lived in the light, when he was a god, being worshipped in the temple the brother had built for him. The last one had taken down the pillars, and had convinced the brother to agree to his wish to be buried where the light could not gouge his eyes. But he had never felt a quake here, under the world. It felt strangely calming, this rocking, rumbling sensation. Even when he felt the dust begin to fall from the ceiling onto his head, he felt no fear. Perhaps this time he would be sealed here in his sleeping place under the world, as in a womb.

And so he stayed in his sleeping place while the walls shook, waiting to be sealed in. And the quake rocked him to sleep like a mother.

But hunger woke him.

Now he rises, feels along the damp corridor walls to the bottom of the second stairwell where his tray waits, and finds the food cold but undamaged even by falling dust, for the cook always covers it with a linen. The smell of hyssop, cherry blossom and myrrh are fresh here, competing with the sulfurous eggs and the smoky fish. He brushes his palms along the bottom stair beside the tray, then the second step, the third. Curious. Had they brought incense? But there was nothing.

Minus stands at the foot of the stair and sniffs and listens. He paces back and forth, testing the air. The fragrance does not stretch down his own corridor toward his lair. It does not thicken if he climbed the stairs. But the sound rises and falls like the heartbeat of a whale.

Minus presses his hands against the wall of the stairwell. Extending past it is a corridor he is forbidden to enter. He lets his fingers creep toward the arch, and he waits. In his fingers he can feel the rise and fall of the heartbeat hum. It comes from the direction of the forbidden place.

He sniffs again, poking his head around the archway, and a jet of cool air from some internal depth rises and blows past him, lifting the end of his beard. There it is! Like fruit soaked in holy wine. Delicious, precious. It soothes his aching heart like a mother's hand.

Minus abandons his food at the bottom of the stair and creeps toward the blossoming smells of adulation, fear and love.

Rah is curled into an embryonic ball in the cool, jeweled dark of the assassin's lair. He has forgotten the world above. He has forgotten the light. He has forgotten what it is to be human, what it is to be god. He remembers only the ascent, great claws clasping his legs together, smoke choking his lungs, the wild ride through the air, and the density of blood collecting in his skull with the swing just as the world exploded.

He is an infant, lying alone in the dirt on his face, listening to the monster grunting, listening to his twin wailing in the basket above him, listening to his mother shriek in pain and horror.

It is only the warmth and the weight of flesh on his head that brings him forward and forward, into the present, into his body, and into the hole.

Minus has found a treasure. He has been here before, in the brother's vault. He has pawed through these jewels, weighed these gold bars, hung these pearl strands on his horn, as they did when he was a god. He has made piles of the gemstones, trading one shape for another like a merchant, a game to play with himself in his interminable loneliness. He has expected the brother's wrath, though it would not have changed him, nor discouraged him. Was not this treasure his treasure also? Had those who had adored him and worshiped him not brought *him* these offerings? But the brother never noticed, never quarreled with him. Perhaps he had hoped that he would. Anything. Any interaction at all would have been better than this unending isolation.

But now there was a real treasure in the brother's hoard! Flesh and blood and smells and breath and noise! Not just bobbles and bricks of gold. Could it be that the brother had left it here for him?

Minus knelt beside the whimpering, breathing smell. He could feel the heat of it push upward toward his nose. He could feel its breath on his fingers. Best of all he could smell the perfumes it was soaked in. His eyes, painful and crushed, watered as the delightful garland of odors tickled his sinuses. His stomach growled. He licked his bulbous lips. He leaned closer and for a time, simply breathed in the newness of the thing, the heat and the moisture of its aliveness. A treasure. One he would never, ever, release.

Rah feels the great, calloused paw on his forehead and bats at it with both fists, simultaneously springing like a jackrabbit from his nest in the pearl mountain. He throws himself backward in a frantic crabwalk, his arms flailing, and loses his footing on the slippery orbs. Now he is sprawled out on his back beneath the hulking presence that has been exploring his body with its nose and fingers. He cries out, snarls, snaps, all to no avail. The thing has caught his ankle and is pulling him out of the pile of pearls toward its maw.

Rah twists in its grasp, claws at the pearl mountain, kicks back with his free foot, catching his instep on the monster's bony horn. He yelps in pain. The thing snatches his free ankle and twists him back onto his rump, pulls him closer. Rah can smell the monster's hot breath on his skin as it pins his ankles together in one huge hand and sniffs at his legs, his thighs. The flat of its enormous palm smoothes across his belly, finds the gold belt. Thick fingers slip under it, follow it around his middle so that for one terrifying moment he is in its embrace. Rock hard knuckles rap on his hip bones, slide up to count his ribs, stopping to study the gold ring pierced onto his left nipple. Rah begins to warble. Knuckles turn into fingers to examine the ring. The fingers slide across his chest to find the matching ring. The thing grunts, then walks its fingers toward his chin, caresses his immature beard, follows his jawline to his neck, studies the thick golden collar.

Rah's warble deepens.

The monster releases a strangled chuckle. It takes Rah's head in its hands, tangles its fingers in his curls, unwittingly pulling a dozen strands free. Rah winces and spits. The monster pays him no mind. It draws his golden mane up to its nose and inhales, sighs.

Rah thrashes, pulls at the monster's hands, but he is unable to free himself. Finally he goes limp, offers a little cry of frustration. But the monster seems oblivious of his discomfort. It scoops him up out of the bed of pearls and lays him over its shoulder like a baby to be burped. It pats his skirted rump, adjusts his weight against its matted neck, rises to its feet. As it ambles up the corridor toward the stairwell it begins humming a tune.

Rah remains limp in the monsters embrace. He makes no attempt to scratch or bite the great, furry back he rests his head upon. This thing is half man, half animal. Perhaps he can reason with the animal half. He must not enrage the human side, better to ignore it entirely. But the animal side! He will befriend the animal.

At the foot of the stair leading up to the assassin's wine cellar the beast sets him gently down beside a tray covered with one of Crispo's linens. The glow of a torch at the top of the stairwell lights its face, and Rah sees Minus for the first time.

The horn that stabbed his foot is a rhino's horn, so thick at the base that it has closed the monster's eyes forever but for a tiny sliver. The thing is clearly blind, its face a misshapen gourd with bulbous nose, hare-split lips, permanently agape, protruding uneven teeth and a globular port-wine growth covering its entire left cheek, chin and ear. The right side is bearded unevenly, the beard covering its neck and running down its back into the curling fur that covers its upper torso. Its legs are long and well-shaped, and it wears leather sandals on its feet. Its lower body is covered by a short skirt not unlike Rah's. It wears a disk of gold suspended on a chain from its neck, and there is an inscription on it, a row of Egyptian hieroglyphs spinning round and round toward the center, in which is embedded a large emerald.

Minus points a thick finger at the food, then nudges Rah's ribs.

"You eat now," he says. His voice is the assassin's voice, pushed through the distorted lips and teeth of a freak of nature. The words hang in the air above Rah's head like a ghost.

"What name is?" Rah manages finally, swallowing the thing that fights to close his throat.

"My name," Minus points to himself, "Is Minus. I am the Horned God." His mouth stretches right, a half-grin.

The assassin's voice, greeting him from the monster's rabbit-mouth, has closed Rah's ears. He shakes his head, hard, as if he were under water.

"Why you sound like Wolf?" he squeaks.

"Wolf? Who is this wolf?" asks Minus, cocking his good ear toward Rah's mouth so that Rah can see into the furry channel of it.

"Is Wolf, he is Master here, Amega. He be master everywhere he want. Big, bad, bad. Want eat Rah. How you can be here, not know who Wolf is?"

"Ahhhh," sighs Minus, nodding. Another coughing chuckle. "Your wolf, little beauty, is Minus' brother." He picks up the tray, offers it to Rah. "His twin. Now you will eat for Minus. Minus will keep you now, keep you safe, forever."

"Wolf is twin?" Rah slides along the step away from the tray. "Is twin Minus? No can be twin of Minus. Not same."

But Minus only sighs, feels about to find a place to sit beside Rah on the bottom step, takes the tray and begins to feed himself.

After some time like this, Rah reaches toward the tray. He is wicked hungry, having sprung from his bed to flee from the trembling world before even he was expected in the kitchens for his morning meal.

"Rah can take?" Rah gingerly extends his fingers toward the food, waiting for the beast to feel them with whatever senses create his world.

"Ahhh, Rah," sighs the beast then. He bends toward the tray, sniffs at the Grain God's wrist. "You are Rah, also a god. This is good." He finds the fruit bowl, lifts it in Rah's direction. Rah snatches a handful of dates and pops them into his mouth.

"You speak as if someone has cut out your tongue, Rah," Minus nods, takes another bite out of a round of brown bread. Rah attempts to answer, but his tongue cannot find purchase for words in his date-filled mouth. Minus gives a half-smile with the human side of his face. He lifts a hand and pats Rah on his shoulder.

"Poor Rah. Poor boy. Does not know. Too young. They always kill their gods, Rah. They take all of our magic, and then they bury us, or cut out our tongues."

Rah chokes. "How you know this? How you know Rah story? Priest, he want to cut Rah open on mountain. Take heart. Wolf he stop him. Take Rah here, like pet," he spits the words. "Little Cat, he call Rah. Always Little Cat, like pet. Want to…." He trails off. "Maybe Minus want make Rah pet too. Or maybe… like Wolf…."

Minus has found a bit of grilled eel on his tray. He offers it to Rah.

"No can eat. Only eat what come from Rah, like grain, fruit, any vegetable, only milk and egg and cheese, have to be white chicken." As he speaks he reaches for an egg. "This from white chicken? You god, should be white chicken." He pops the egg in his mouth before Minus has answered him.

"White, red, maybe brown. Minus cannot see, so color does not matter, Rah. Color is for mortals."

"But Rah can see, Minus. Rah is god, too. You no believe?" Rah reaches for another egg. "Hungry. Too much scare. Heart race."

"Rah smells like a god," says Minus, taking another sniff of Rah's perfumed head. "Rah is bound in gold," he touches Rah's collar, the permanent ring of gold at his waist, "like Minus."

"Yah, and have emerald too," Rah takes Minus' hand and sets his fingers on the emerald in his crown. "Minus have emerald."

"Then Rah must be a god," says Minus, pushing the last of the eel past his skewed lips. "I will keep Rah here with me," he finishes.

Rah says nothing. He waits as Minus sets the tray down beside himself on the bottom stair and risesM to his feet.

"Come, Rah, come with Minus. I will show you my world." He moves to take Rah up and heft him over his shoulder.

But Rah slips out of his grasp.

"Rah can walk," says Rah, "No touch Rah."

Mochlos and Awiti stand in the alcove at the bottom of the steps. The high priest lifts his torch. There are two corridors, both narrow and low, barely large enough for two men to walk abreast, and even he who, though taller than most Minoans, is hardly the height of the Assassin, must hunch his shoulders to enter.

"I was never a fan of close spaces," he mutters, taking Awiti by the hand. "Nevertheless, we must do what we must do. What do you think, First Concubine of Rah, which way did the Grain God go?"

"Master, I can smell him," pipes Awiti. "I can smell him!" She sniffs beneath the left archway, then turns to take a step down the right corridor. "And something else." She sniffs again. "Fish!"

"It is not but the briny air of the sea, blowing up from some watery cave beneath." Mochlos wipes the crown of his head with a handkerchief. The enclosed space, the pitch dark, the stone hole and the thought of a pool of seawater waiting below for his lungs brings back the memory of his own drowning pool and the broad hand of the assassin on the back of his head. "If that one leads to a waterway," he says, nodding right, "I think I will explore this one first." He pulls Awiti back and begins down the opposite passageway.

Minutes later the two are standing at the door of an enormous cavern filled to the ceiling with gold and silver ingots, heaps of jewelry, bronze statuary, gems and pearls. There are bolts of fine silks, strangely shaped pottery from distant lands, and piles of exotic skins. Leopard, lion, antelope, bear. Some with heads still attached. In another corner a space is devoted solely to brilliantly colored, hand-knotted Hittite rugs.

Bracketing the entrance in which they stand are two large, unlit torches held by identical Minoan statues. Nude boys. Behind the one to the right is a niche fixed with a trough, and a running stream of fresh water which appears to be piped through the stone wall.

"I do believe I've seen these before," Mochlos swallows, recalling a soft spring day long ago, the long, open-air visiting room of Ananou the Sun Priest, a delicate white Minoan wine, the sweet fragrance of hibiscus blowing through on a sea breeze from the garden. Mochlos reaches to light the one nearest with his own torch. Seeing him do so, Awiti follows suit and lights the torch held by the bronze nude beside her.

"He will know, regardless of how we try to cover our tracks. No sense rummaging about in the dark with a single brand," says the priest.

"It is his treasure hoard," breathes Awiti, and Mochlos can feel through her hand that her whole body has begun to tremble. He allows himself a smile and looks over at his companion, who has lifted her veil off her face in order to better see in the dark.

"You surprise me, Awiti," he says, releasing her hand. "Women seem to have no fear of that blood-driven beast, and yet you do." He tilts his head, studying her face. "You very much do."

"Truly, Sir, he terrifies me," answers the girl, surveying the assassin's hoard of appropriated wealth as she speaks, her lips parted in awe. "He is like the jungle. Attractive from a distance, terrible and dangerous once you step under its canopy. Within it is every kind of death a man can conceive of, and some that he cannot." She looks up into the priest's eyes, the treasure forgotten. "He is like the jaguar in the tree above your head. You do not see him. You walk beneath his breath."

A chill straightens the high priest's shoulders. He tightens his lips. "Yes, well said. More words strung together from that ripe mouth than I have heard since the day I found it. I prefer less, I think," he swallows a second time, his throat dry as dust. "Come, let us poke about a bit, and see if we can find a sign that the boy was here."

"I cannot, Sir," Awiti is wagging her head back and forth, her attention returning to the treasure. "This you cannot make me do, though I owe you my very life. I will not touch his treasure."

Mochlos looks at her and frowns.

"Very well, I will do it myself. Here, hold my torch, and see to it that you do not set fire to a stack of silks with it. You are shaking like a cornered rabbit." He takes hold of her wrists and lifts them. "Like so, else we shall die of asphyxiation before we can find our way out."

Then, turning back to the immense fortune, he licks his lips and begins his search.

"Ah, now look here!" He has been walking through paths made in the bounty, which rises in some places over his head. Awiti can make out only the crown of his shining pate when he calls to her.

"What is it, Master? Have you found him?" she calls, taking several steps forward in her excitement.

"Not exactly, my girl. But evidence enough that he has been here. A clump of golden strands, just here atop these pearls. As if they had been pulled out purposefully. What the devil…"

He returns to Awiti. The clump of strands lay in his extended palm, cling to his fingers.

"Master, it is as if they had been pulled together from his head!" laments Awiti.
"Indeed it is, child. And so we have two answers. The first, he was here. The second, he was taken elsewhere. Apparently by force."
"Taken down the other corridor! But by whom?"
Mochlos has relieved Awiti of his torch.
"Douse those there in that trough."
When she has done so, and replaced the two torches into the hands of the nudes, he continues. "Do you not recall what Brother Sun said to us as we descended the stair? That it was a pit of doom? And then, 'a thing', he said. A thing. Before he cut himself short. Well I am not an imbecile. What thing? A pit is a pit. But a thing….what? Lurks within it? Do you believe that the Wolf of Amega, the Terror of the Aegean, would leave his hoard unguarded? I for one do not. And so now we know. There is your proof." He holds the golden curls up to Awiti's nose in the light of her torch.
"That *thing* has taken our Rah!"

CHAPTER FIFTEEN

The troll camp is a ring of fire, like the head of a volcano, shooting happy flames up into the starry night sky. Rush has released the camp ponies from their brush corral and set it aflame as well. The animals stampede north, away from the blaze. North to the steppes, to their homeland for they too were taken and enslaved. Now the assassin slips inside the inferno at the only portal, which is the river itself. He emerges, his muslin leggings soaked and cooling on his skin as he leaps up the bank into the village center to deposit the dying fire troll hanging from his shoulder, into his own fire pit.

"You may all roast like piglets, man and woman and child alike. For you are a breed of viper that does the world no good," he grunts, heaving the man's unconscious body into the flames. "Go to Tartarus and burn forever, fire-lover."

The girl, Kolga, is still waiting at the bank of the river, half a mile south of the camp when he returns. She has ripped the hem of her tunic to sponge down The Black, and he is cool and blowing contentedly, foraging in a patch of duckweed when Rush emerges from the dark. Rush gives her a curious look, then nods his approval and moves past her to untie his sack from the back of his saddle, which she has removed from the beast and placed on a dry rock. He fishes out his sleeping leather and his bar of soap, finds a suitable place on the shore and lays the leather flat. Then he tosses her the bar, which she catches in mid-air. He nods to the river.

"That should take the lice off you," he pulls his hood free and takes hold of his own braid, pretends to wash it. "You understand?"

The girl nods aggressively and heads for the river.

When she returns her hair is unplaited, falling around her shoulders and down her back in thick wet locks. She looks about for a place to settle herself for the night, but Rush pats the leather beside himself.

"I won't have you freezing all night in this northern air," he says gruffly. As she stands in her wet clothes he rises, paws about in his sack, and pulls from it a simple white robe.

"Tonight you may dress as a Minoan Priest of the Dead." He hands her the robe. "Take those wet things off." He tugs the sleeve of her tunic. With a gracious smile, Kolga offers the assassin a Nordic curtsy and snatches the robe. Then she slips behind a tree and changes into it.

"Pah, as if I would have you," Rush frowns. "Pregnant with a barbarian no less." He lies back down on his leather, making a pillow of his own hood and tunic. "That'll be the day," he mutters. But he is smiling to himself when the girl slips beneath his left arm and cuddles against him.

In the morning he is gone when she awakens. There is a fire, and a brace upon which a small pot steams. The smell of nettles and some exotic leaves brewing brings her to her feet. She looks about for the Black, sees that he has been tethered further up the bank to graze on wild grasses and weeds. His pitch coat is shining in the dawn light like polished coal. His mane, which has been left to grow out from a war horse roach during the months of the assassin's travels, is twisted in knotted clumps and his tail is thick with burs and nettle. Kolga looks about for some means of remedying this. She walks along the river's edge, away from the troll camp, which smolders half a mile up river, dirty clouds of its remains tinging the sky above the treeline. She takes a moment to hold a cupped hand over her belly. Perhaps the child is not the barbarians. Perhaps it is Lars child. It would not be impossible, however unlikely. It was the proper time in her cycle, and the moon had blessed them with its fullness that night, a good sign from the goddess, Frya.

He had been brought back to camp with five other men. The strongest. He would not last long, given little to eat and worked from dawn to dusk. But he was still strong that night. Perhaps strong enough that his seed might do battle with that of a barbarian and take up purchase in her womb.

She had been watching him for weeks. He was tall, like her own people, though not from her tribe. They had kept him alive for that reason, for his height, and for his strength. He was young, perhaps only a few summers older than she, but he had a man's beard and a man's back, strapped with muscle, wide at the shoulder, tapered at the waist. Despite Great Elk's feeble poking every night, she knew she was not yet with child from the barbarian, and she did not intend to be. Whenever she could, she watched Lars, moved past him slowly on her way to the river to wash the barbarian's clothing, stopped and waited to catch his eye as he lifted the axe and brought it down on the logs. When he did meet her gaze she did not drop it, but lifted her chin, to show him that she still had her will, that the barbarian had not broken her, and that she would take risks to remain true to her own blood. He understood her well enough though he did not allow himself to acknowledge her impertinence. He simply stared back at her, then returned to his work.

That day he had been gathering deadfall, wood for the camp fire, shackled loosely. The war party had been gone three days, and the old men left on guard were snoring in their tents. The camp women were enjoying their own freedom from their men, relaxing in a group in the center of the settlement while their children played a game with a skull and a stick. No one was watching her.

When she saw him lay down his burden and head for the bank of the river for a drink, she went to him. No words had been spoken. She took his hand and led him a little way into the duckweed, out of sight of the camp, and she felt the strength and stamina of a real man for the first time since she was taken. Her own husband was dead, clubbed by a barbarian brute on horseback and set afire while he lay unconscious. They had been married seven days.

Kolga prayed to the goddess of her people that his seed would take as they coupled. When it was finished, she felt her womb smiling, a ping in her left side, as if the seed had taken root already. She took his face in her hands and kissed his forehead.

"You will perish, but your son will survive. I will make you this promise. He will survive like a falcon chick laid among the eggs in the hen house. He will grow strong on their lambs, and one day he will kill the one he must call father." And Lars nodded. "I believe you, Kolga," he said, and rose and returned to his labor.

Great Elk worked him to death, as she expected. But the child within her grew. She was only six months pregnant, but the child was heavy and sat low in her belly. It would be a boy.

Kolga's eyes lite upon what she has been looking for. A parched fish bone, several of the spines of the ribs still attached. It was a large fish, and would do nicely for a comb. She picks up the relic, rinses the sand and weed off it in the river, dries it on her skirt and begins to untangle her own locks. The device works nicely. She continues to comb her own hair as she returns to the fire, and is surprised by her leaping heart when she sees the man is crossing the river toward her, holding the hind paws of a dead rabbit in his left hand.

He raises the trophy.

"Breakfast!" He is smiling. It is not an unpleasant smile, though the blue-black eyes are without light. She returns his grin, runs to him, shows him the fish bone comb and then points to the Black and then herself. He regards her with amusement. She curtsies, takes the rabbit and the dagger he offers her, and brings it to the fire to dress and roast.

"Not to well done, now," Rush purses his lips, realizing too late that he would eat it her way in the end. He returns to the river to bathe while she cooks.

After their meal she combs out the warhorse's tail and mane while Rush packs his gear. Then he mounts the animal, pulls her up behind him, so that she is sitting on his pack behind the cantle of the saddle, and heads south toward the pass. They ride all day until dusk, stopping only to water and graze the horse and to take a meal themselves, sharing a loaf of barley bread and some dried deer meat Rush has confiscated from a prior host. When they remount, Kolga puts her arms about the assassin's waist, braids her fingers together, and lays her head on his shoulder to nap. When her lips part and moisten his nape Rush slows to a walk, assuming she has fallen asleep. He shakes his head at his own thoughtfulness, and faults the Rah.

At sunset Crispo leaves Minus his evening meal. He considers leaving a second tray for Rah, a tray of boiled eggs and hummus, fresh peaches and perhaps a batch of Ting Ya's cakes, but he thinks better of it. If the freak has not found Rah, he may well suspect that the second meal is for another, and search him out. Crispo has shirked his duties in the kitchen today and remained at the foot of his altar, praying to the Sun, that it might shed its light on Rah, protect him, and lead him safely home. Enenoch and Tyrus also pray before the altars of their gods, but it is Cara who draws the biggest crowd.

"We must pray to the Goddess, his mother, that she might have compassion on us and bring her son back to us whole and unharmed," she announces, "We must give her offerings that we know to be pleasing to her, that which is born of the sea and of the field, that which is born of the night and of the stars." Her afternoon is spent accepting a procession of gifts: rare shells of abalone, Chinese incense and Egyptian honey, all manner of shorebird eggs and feathers, raw silks and virgin wool.

But beneath the fortress, deep in the heart of the cliff upon which they pray, Minus has led Rah not upward, toward his Amegan bed, but further down, into the bowels of the mountain.

"Can smell water," says Rah, sensing a cool draft to his right where the corridor has opened up. "We go this way." And he has disappeared through the aperture.

"Wait, little god!" cries Minus, pursuing him. "The rocks are slippery! You must wait for Minus!"

Rah follows the sound of water lapping against rock to the stony edge of a hidden lagoon. He kneels and dips his fingers into the pool. He brings his fingers to his lips and tastes. "Is salt water. This take Rah out to big water!" And before Minus can catch hold of him, Rah slips into the pool. Eel-like, he stays underwater, following the bottom until he is out of breath and comes up splashing.

"Is salt! Can swim to Knossos from here!" Rah sputters, excited.

"Yes, Rah. You can swim all the way to Egypt from here, if you are a mullet. A man, though, would need a boat."

"Minus, you can get Rah boat? Rah is go back Knossos. This where Rah be god. This where Rah dance for king, bring good crop, bring rain. Minus take Rah to Knossos, Rah and Minus both be god there. Knossos where Rah belong!"

Rah is panting with exhilaration. He has backstroked out into the middle of the pool, far from Minus' reach. Beneath him he feels the slip and stroke of fish against his bare skin. He will not release the freedom of water, now that he has found it.

"Rah is a good swimmer?" Minus chuckles, unconcerned that Rah's voice has retreated. There is nowhere to go from here but back up onto the stone ledge where Minus sits on his haunches, or else out to sea, to be battered by the rip tides upon the rocks.

"Rah can swim," answers Rah. "But maybe no can swim to Knossos. Minus get Rah boat, we go! Take horse-"
"Whoa, little beauty! Minus has no boat. Minus has no horse."
"Rah has many horse. Can get boat. Only need to take some good pearl, emerald too maybe, swim out to big water, find men fish, they take Minus and Rah. You see."
"You would steal then? From your Wolf? Not a good idea, little Rah. Even if I let you do it, and I will not, it would be your death warrant." Minus chuckles again. "You cannot swim out past the lagoon, Rah, even a god would be crushed by the waves on the rock. And what fisherman would look upon Minus and be willing to take him into his boat, and sail him to the lost Minoan island?"
But Rah makes no answer. He is underwater. And finding the shallow bottom, he is soon surrounded by a glittering school of goatfish, which he follows out of the cave around an outcropping of underwater rock. The goatfish disperse as the cave mouth opens onto a sunlit lagoon. Rah pops his head out of the water. Around him is a paradise of aquamarine stillness, broken only by the height-softened calls of cliff-dwelling shorebirds. The lagoon is hidden under the cliffs beneath the fortress walls, and surely guards are posted above along the ledges and parapets. Rah breast-strokes out to the horn, pulls himself up onto the shore and lies flat on the sand and shell beach. He is a beached starfish, legs and arms akimbo. He breathes in the sea air, filling his lungs, exhaling slowly. He digs his shoulder blades into the comforting constancy and strength of the shingle, he digs his fingers and toes into the pebbles, content to be held by the beach like an egg in the palm of a hand. He feels his body sink deep into the seashore, his soul lift like a gull into the crisp assure sky above. Both are loved.
He is part of the earth. He is part of the sky. He is part of the sea, and loved by the sun. He is the Rah.

The boat sits low in the water, two squat, narrow decks at bow and stern, each barely large enough for one man to sit upon, feet dangling into the hull. A single mast rises from the center, along which is hitched a square sail.
Today there is barely enough of a breeze to account for its unfurling. But Kleitos and Thymus are not interested in sailing. They have paid a good sum for the use of the craft for the day, having left the stable

shortly after the last of the horses were caught and returned to their stalls. It had been their day off, but the quake had already stolen several hours of their drinking and in Kleitos' mind, at least, there was some catching up to do. He has already polished off a half skin of bad wine and has lost his side of the net twice, allowing a half dozen undersized mullet their freedom, before his drinking partner has popped the cork on his own jug.

"Are you stupid?" Thymus barks. "Are we out here for fish? Or are we renting a boat so's we can piss over the sides all day?"

"Either way's fine, y'ask me," answers Kleitos, belching as he rummages about in his lunch sack with his free hand. "Where's those loaves? You got'em over there by you? All's I got's this wedge o'cheese and a knife to cut 'er with. Oh, here's a pot a honey too. And one o'butter. Good wife, she is."

"Last night you was planin' to slit her throat as she slept, I recall," grumbles Thymus, watching his mate's unsteady grip on his end of the net. "Didn' I tell you you shouldn'a married an Amegan woman? You ever do decide to do her in, she'll slit yer throat before you get yer knife outta yer belt. Loave's in my sack over here. And yer not gettin' one 'til we catch us a net of fish."

"You're an old hen," chuckles Kleitos. But he returns the cheese and spreads to his sack and dutifully takes up the netting with both hands. "Fair enough, then. A dozen of anything, and we eats."

A half hour later, and a bushel's worth of sardines, Thymus has caught up to his drinking partner and is in better spirits.

"Shall we lay those octopus pots then?" he burps. They are out past the peak of the horn, burning in the quiet stillness of teal water.

"I s'pose," answers Kleitos, scratching his sunburned chest. "I'm gettin' all itchy out here. 'Bout to roast. Don't care for the stinkin' things myself, but they'll pay for the boat."

The two had retreated from the hubbub at the fortress and wandered into town shortly after midday. They had been out on the boat for several hours, and the sun was hanging low in the west. They had not heard of the Rah's disappearance, and unbeknownst to them, they had avoided being pressed into service to find him. Indeed, they had, in all Amega, enjoyed the most pleasant afternoon of any, save perhaps Minus himself.

"Could come pull 'em tomorrow evenin'. After dinner," Thymus muses. He has set his empty jug down and now tugs the aft end of the net out of Kleitos' hands. "Let's be getting' back then, 'fore these sardines spoil."

Kleitos has let go the net. And for a moment Thymus thinks that it has somehow become tangled in another man's pot, when a set of pale fingers come up with the netting to grasp the port gunwale. Kleitos lets go a grunt of alarm. But Thymus has seen the glint of the golden bracelets. He scrambles to pull the net up off the boy, then reaches to pull Rah from the water.

Rah heaves himself over the deck, knocking into the pail of sardines. The fish have been gasping the last of the oxygen in the bit of water the two drunkards left them in to keep them from spoiling. Rah throws the pail overboard, fish and all.

"Thymus! You have boat! Can take Rah to Knossos!" cries Rah, standing between the two men in naught but a soaked Minoan skirt and his eternal gold.

"You've just tossed a day's labor, you feather-headed toff! Them fish were to pay for the day's rent of this craft!" Kleitos bellows, standing as well. But Kleitos does not have Rah's balance. He takes a step forward, wabbles, tips backward on a light wave, and pitches over the stern.

"Kleitos can swim?" Rah looks at Thymus with concern.

"We'll know any minute," answers Thymus, shaking his head and reaching for the pail, which is sinking out of sight under the vessel.

"He wasn't the Murdering Devil's favorite I'd fillet him," spouts Kleitos, who has come up on the starboard side of the little boat and is attempting to pull himself in.

"Put leg over, Kleitos, Rah will help," says Rah, kneeling in the hull beside Kleitos. His face is a theater of compassion, golden brows peaked, wide-eyed.

"You are a pox," grumbles Kleitos, hefting one leg over the side. "A pretty pox, what needs a good thrashing, you do." Rah catches his ankle and yanks it toward the interior of the boat.

"Aaugh! My friggin' balls!" Kleito yelps. Rah stands, takes hold of the man's belt, and throws his weight against it. Kleitos flops into the hull, puffing and red-faced. "Day that man's had enough of ye there'll be a line up to Hattusha, men arguin' over who's gonna get to cut yer throat."

"And another line of men down to Babylon wantin' him fer themselves," comments Thymus, tipping the last few sardines out of the pail into the water. "Now what's this about us takin' ye to the doomed island, boy? This here is a fishin' boat. Not a shippin' vessel. Only a couple of idiots would try and sail it to that charred rock. And then what? What'd you think is left of it? You think you'll just walk up the Bridge Road to the Palace and take yer pick o' dancing girls? They's nothing left. Place is a smolderin' pit o' death."

"How you know, Thymus? You go already? You talk to somebody go?" Rah has slipped down into the hull of the boat to sit, cross-legged, among the nets and traps. He notices a tiny sardine still wriggling in a pool of water and picks it up by the tail, leans over the gunwale, gentles it into the water. "Ah, you see? He is okay. Can swim. Good thing Rah come."

"Bloody hell, good thing. Not a single sardine left of all a day's work out here in this boiling sun," gruffs Kleitos miserably. He picks up his empty wineskin, turns the spout into his mouth and lifts it full over his head. Several sour drops wet his lips. "I could cry, I could," he whimpers.

"What this for?" Rah has lifted an octopus trap off a stack. It is a cone-shaped basket with a wide lip. A pile of hemp roping lies beside the stack of traps. The baskets are as long as a man's arm.

"S'fer the octopuses," answers Thymus carelessly. The sea is dead calm and he is reaching for an oar. He has not finished his words and the basket is flying over his head.

"Wait ye damned fool! We've not tied the lines!" Thymus cries, reaching for the sinking basket. Rah has tossed the remaining stack of baskets off the starboard side in the meantime.

"Octopus nice animal," Rah pouts. "So beautiful in water, move like dancer. Very smart too. What you want octopus for? Why you want to kill? Stupid. Rah make you rich. No need kill octopus. No need baskets."

Thymus has risen to his feet to catch the coiled ropes Rah holds over his head, but he manages only to rock the boat, loose his footing, and pitch over the side. Rah hops onto the half-deck upon which he had been sitting. He casually tosses the ropes off the prow, balancing on a gunwale. He looks back as Kleitos, who is sitting with his head in his hands, muttering.

"Maybe better help Thymus, I think Thymus he can no swim," remarks Rah, making no effort to offer his assistance.

Kleitos catches Thymus wrist as he sinks, pulls him back over the side and into the bottom of the boat.

"By the gods I'll teach you-!" cries Thymus, but Rah has already dived off the stern of the fishing boat, using the higher platform to launch himself from a backward handstand into a pike and a twist, and he is gone. When the two disgruntled fishermen see him again he is a furlong inland, his mane of curls flattened against his head, his emerald gleaming like green fire in the fading sun. He raises a hand, a sociable wave to his friends, then cups them at his mouth to amplify his call.

"Rah is make you rich men, Kleitos and Thymus! We meet tomorrow! First thing! Rah is be back, lot of gold. You bring boat and we go! Go back to Knossos!" And he turns and disappears underwater to find the safe spot in the channel, which he discovered swimming with the goatfish beneath the waves.

CHAPTER SIXTEEN

Three weeks after the massacre of the camp of the Fire Trolls, Rush and his pregnant companion are safely inside the formidable walls of the city of Hattusha.

The Assassin approaches the city from the north in full daylight and makes his introductions at the gate dressed as a merchant. He is not the notorious Ameg, but his brother, a slender, and therefore seemingly taller version of that man, the less known Markas, who deals in amber and fur, wolf pelt most especially, and trades as far south as Koptos on the Nile, west to the hills of Mycenae, east to Susa. Markas is newly married to a northern slave girl that he is clearly infatuated with. The girl, who cannot be more than half his age, is quite beautiful, and has learned a few dozen Hittite phrases, sufficient to keep her doting husband on his toes.

Markas stables his high-spirited Amegan warhorse in the north quarter, then rents a litter to take him and his wife to the Palace. As the brother of a close associate of the Wolf of Amega he is welcomed enthusiastically, so much so that he must beg off a formal dinner in his honor. His new wife is installed in her own suite of rooms and immediately assigned six ladies and two dressmakers by the Steward of Royal Guests. Markas himself, keen on giving his bride all of the privacy and peace a woman in her condition might need, takes a smaller set of rooms just down the hall from the King, ousting of the former tenant, the royal Tailor, and his wife and two children.

Markas allows himself to be amused by the Palace Minister of Entertainment by day. But at sundown he retires to his private chambers, dons his assassin's garb, and when the moon rises he slips out the window of his sitting room and descends via a series of well-guarded parapets to the street and the city.

On the streets he discovers that there has been a quake in Amega, that the Rah has vanished and is suspected to be lost in the Master's labyrinth of mystery below, the Master's wife is gone mad with grief and fear, and the High Priest of the Rah, having defied the Master's order to remain in Babylon has returned to his former rooms in the fortress, and has, along with his hermaphrodite, descended into the bowels of the citadel determined to recover the lost Rah.

Gossip is the common fodder of the fool, the rare indulgence of the wise. Rush gives little heed to the reports of his wife's madness. Josepha has never shown an inclination for drama, nor for a weak mind. He is sure that these rumors are exaggerated, however, the tales of Mochlos' decent into his lair are less easily dismissed. There would be no reason for the High Priest to be included in the gossip at all, since he is known in Hattusha as the biggest fool in creation, a meddling cleric who traded the Rah for the King and then ran off with bandits to Babylon, thinking he would outrun the Wolf of the Hatti. Why he is still alive at all is anybody's guess. And this story paints him as some sort of hero.

But the most disturbing part of the story is the priest's decent into the labyrinth beneath the citadel. No one but his most trusted men know of the maze of corridors beneath the wine cellars, and now the secret lair of the Assassin is common knowledge! Worse still, the priest has taken the "hermaphrodite", Awiti. Rush has no desire to cut that pretty little throat, and can rather think of several other alternatives to keep her quiet. But the priest! He has taken his 'authority' as the author and protector of the Rah too far. He will have to be sent to the land of the dead.

Rush spends two days in Hattusha. During that time his old friend, Tryggvi, arrives with the children and the other freed northern women. He arranges for their care, purchases the trader a reliable horse and packs for the last leg of his journey home. When Kolga meets him at the stable on the morning of his departure, dressed in new Hatti traveling clothes and looking more pregnant than ever, he dismisses her.

"I will not take a pregnant woman on a journey I intend to cover in half the time it should take me. You will stay here and be well cared for. When the babe comes, I will consider what to do with you."

But Kolga is not so easily gotten rid of. She narrows her eyes at him, hands on her hips. She has understood enough of his Hittite to know she is not going with him. She stamps her foot, looks about the stable, finds a small, dun mare and pulls her out of her stall.

"Her!" she says, swatting the mare on the shoulder to prove she has chosen well. The animal is dull as a tree, and swats its tail at a fly before lowering its head to search the aisle for dropped grain.

"Good! Safe!" says Kolga. "Me go you!" She smiles and curtseys at Rush.

"Doesn't understand a word of it," grumbles Rush, turning to lead the Black out into the morning.

"You cannot come, miss," Triggvi scolds Kolga in her own tongue. "He will not have a woman in child harmed by a rough journey. Now grow a brain and stay here where he has seen to your comfort. There is not a man nor monkey in this city will pull a hair from your head with this man's name behind you. Think of the child," he adds vainly, taking his own mount by the reins and turning him toward the door.

"Triggvi!" Rush barks from his mount, already out the door and trotting down the street toward the south gate.

"Be smart, girl," says Triggvi to the woman, who stands in the aisle, fists clenched, beside the docile mare. "Take what this man has given you, gratefully. And do not steal what he has not. I have seen his temper."

"As have I!" shouts Kolga at the receding rump of Triggvi's pony. As their retreating hooves clatter down the stone street, she turns to lead the mare back into her stall.

"I will see you again, Markas the Merchant," she mutters. "And when I do, I will not sound like an idiot. I will speak for myself, in your own tongue." She latches the stall door. "And I will show you that I am no brood wife for barbarian filth," she spits, raising her skirt to waddle toward the doorway and her waiting litter, "For if this child is barbarian, I swear I will kill it myself."

Mochlos and Awiti have passed the foot of the stone staircase at the bottom of the wine cellar and continued down the opposite corridor. They are nearing the aperture where Rah slipped away from Minus when the Grain God's dusky voice, echoing over the underground lagoon, reaches their ears.

"It is him!" Mochlos hisses, his free hand striking out to snatch Awiti's arm. "Hush! Listen!"

"Minus take Rah back to treasure now. We take enough gold and pearl to buy this boat tomorrow," says Rah, breathless.

"Little god of Minoa," answers the voice of the assassin, driving a hot thrill through the high priest's innards. "Do not leave me, and all of my brother's gold is yours to keep."

"This no your treasure, Minus," answers Rah, and Mochlos must peak around the edge of the rock wall to steal a glimpse of the Grain God. What he sees takes his breath. He falls back against Awiti, blinking as if to clear the image from his eyes.

"Brother?" he whispers to himself. "I am gone mad." But he presses himself again to the edge of the opening, holding his breath to listen more intently.

"This Wolf treasure, no Minus treasure. Cannot give what is no yours to give. But Rah is take. Tomorrow Rah give to Kleitos, Thymus, and they take Rah to Knossos. Give man enough money, do anything. Man think money everything. But is nothing if no crop, no rain, no dance. No King. Now you take Rah back, Minus. No waste time."

"Quick!" hisses Mochlos, grabbing Awiti's wrist and pulling her past the opening leading to the pool. "We must hide further down this corridor and let them pass."

"Only take little bit," says Rah, stuffing a handful of pearls into the hem and pockets of his skirt. "Wolf is no even notice. Be okay."

"Your wolf notices the twig that is bent, little beauty. He will smell that you have been here, for you smell like a temple. He will know you have taken his treasures."

Minus had been waiting at the edge of the water for some time, calling out to Rah, listening to the echo of his own solitary voice. After a time his heart sank. He should never have brought the boy to the water, but it was not so much his leading as Rah's urging that had changed his course and brought him there. Somehow the little god had tricked him into allowing him to escape. Now he had disappeared like a slippery fish under the glass of the underground pool, and he was gone forever. And Minus was overwhelmed by the weight of his own loneliness.

Minus sat hunched, rocking on his haunches, at the edge of the pool and considered his folly. Had he not tried to trap a god? Did he not know better? No god could be trapped and kept. Not even by another god. He had disrespected the little deity, and he deserved his fate. He had been given a gift, and he had lost it to greed and foolishness.

And then the splash, and the thump of a wet body slapping the rock ledge beside him. Minus was overwhelmed with relief and gratitude. I will not be so foolish again! He thought. I will be your servant. I will submit to your will. More than that, I will be your champion! Thus, he quickly agreed to lead Rah back through the maze of passages to the hoard of the assassin.

"Maybe notice. No matter. No catch Rah. We go morning. Minus follow Rah, under bad water. Swim to boat. Go to Knossos. Be god again."

"Minus cannot swim, little beauty. Minus cannot see, cannot breath underwater like a fish. Like Rah."

"Minus hold rope. No problem. Hold breath underwater. Follow fish. Easy." Rah has stuffed his pockets full. "We go where Minus sleep. Tie up all this gem piece of linen. Tie to belt," Rah lifts his golden waistlet with one thumb. "Plenty money, no?" He recovers a few enormous rubies from his left pocket to show the blind Minus.

"No doubt, little Rah. Enough to buy a dozen boats. But Minus cannot come."

"Maybe Minus come later, come with Wolf," Rah grabs Minus' wrist.

"Maybe. Rah go first. Is better. Then Minus come. Knossos need new god after…" but he trails off, as if visiting a distant mountain.

"First Rah, then priest. Then wolf he come, come with Minus, is Horn God, yes?"

"Minus is the Horned God, yes, Rah," answers Minus obediently. Seeing that Rah is ready to return to the bedchamber, he leads the way. Rah snatches a torch from one of the nudes and follows.

"Is good, Horn God. Like bull, king keep under palace. Maybe Minus want to live there. When Wolf is King."

"When Wolf is King," repeats Minus, breathing deeply the sea-salted sweetness of Rah's unquenchable perfumes.

"They will return in the morning. The boy has found a waterway out of this hole, right here beneath this pond, leading to the sea. He must have given that *thing* the slip. He is an eel in the water. He will have swum out past the breakers, found those two oafs loafing on the bay in a fishing boat, and bribed them into meeting him in the morning. Now he will steal the assassin's gold and jewels and sail with them to Crete!"

Mochlos is pacing like a caged tiger at the edge of the underground pond. Awiti has relieved him of his torch, which is nearing extinction.

"Master, how will we bring him back to the surface? He is in the hands of a monster, a monster who claims to be the assassin's brother! Do not ask me to attempt to seduce him away from that….that thing!"

"No, no we cannot allow that freak of nature to know we are here in his miserable hole. We must," Mochlos looks about, sliding the palm of his hand over his pate nervously. "We must return to the surface unnoticed, and tonight we must exit the fortress and follow the coast east, crawling along under the cliffs until we are past the guards. Then we will find those two buffoons, Kleitos and Thymus, on the beach preparing to launch a two man fishing boat into the Great Sea and sail that golden imbecil's precious bum to the no-doubt-Greek-infested lost island of the Minoans. We will simply bribe them to take us with them. If they are dumb enough to risk their lives to take the Assassin's jewels once, they will do it twice."

"Bribe them, Master? W-with-" but Mochlos has taken the torch from her and doused it in the pool.

"Come now. We must find our way back in the dark to the assassin's treasure and fill our pockets. It is the only way."

"Steal from him?" Awiti squeaks. "Steal from *him*?"

"Remember what we are sworn to do girl. We are not taking anything for ourselves but utilizing what is presented to us to continue our sole burden, that is securing the safety of the Grain God. We are without a choice. He will kill us if we fail in this. And by now everyone in Amega and half of Hattusha know that we have descended into the bowels of this foul hole to find him. Shall we return empty-handed? No, we must disappear, as he has done. Go with him, to Crete," Mochlos takes Awiti's arm once more and propels her toward the aperture and into the tunnel. "Even if we have to do it on the back of a whale."

"Why was I not sent for sooner?" Rush has returned to Amega in his usual fashion, unannounced, unseen, unheard, evaporating like mist up into the fortress from his own secret passages, and in the morning a thing you roll into in bed, all muscle and strength, a thing that could perhaps unhinge its jaw and swallow a bull.

His wife had not recognize him.

She, upon waking to his enormity against her, flung herself from his side and cowered in a far corner of their matrimonial chamber. This unusual behavior was not the first peculiarity Rush noticed.

Even in the dark, while still sleeping, a fool could tell that Josepha was no longer his plump little wife. Josepha was half her own breadth. Her luxurious brown hair was gone. She was as bald as a peach. And her normally manicured nails were chewed to the quick.

Now, whimpering at the sight of him, shrunk into a corner of their bedroom, she looked at her husband as he lay in their bed, rising on one elbow like a man who thinks he may still be dreaming. And then she screamed.

"What in Tartarus," asked Rush, peering at the thing that had taken the place of his beloved wife, "Have you done to yourself, woman?"

But Josepha made no reply. She followed her scream with a tortured wail, and then began mumbling what at first to his ear seemed an incantation.

"No," said Rush, more to himself than to the lunatic on the floor. "No, you are not my Josepha. This is a spell, this is magic. Someone has changed my wife into a … into this. You will not occupy her place in my house. Until she is recovered, you will be kept from me. Babylon, yes. A problem for Niki to solve. He may start by cutting the heads off all of the priests of Marduk and Ishtar and Baal. If that doesn't work, we'll decapitate the rest of them. This is a magician's work. But the sword is the best magician of all."

With that he dressed, left his chamber, and called the commanders together in the War Room.

"Why was I not summoned?" he repeats, for not a man among them has opened his mouth. Who had the balls to say, "Sir, we did not know where you were," or "Master, no one wanted to bring you bad news, as it does not end well for that man." In the end, he turns his back to them and waves his hand over his head, a dismissal. "Send me Ham. He knows more of what goes on here when I am gone than my entire army. And bring me the family guards. The two assigned to Josepha. I will start there."

When Ham arrives with the trembling guards, the assassin is skinning a goat.

"You sent for me, Sir," says Ham from the doorway. It is not often that his master takes to butchering on the war room desk. This goat is filleted nicely, the head and feet in a pot on the floor, the body eviscerated and deboned in one piece on the desk. It is quite a piece of butchering mastery, but not one a simple servant likes to see on his Master's war-room desk, after being summoned by a shaking left-flank commander in that man's army.

"It calms me, Ham. Like weaving did my wife," the assassin looks up from his work, his hands covered in blood gloves. There is a pout on his lip. Also a glob of gut in his beard, as if he had, like a hunger-mad wolf, taken a bite out of the carcass' heart as he gutted it.

"Yes, Master," answers Ham calmly. "Weaving was her solace."

"Surely you do not mean to suggest that she required solace, Ham? Did I make her unhappy? So unhappy that I drove her mad?" asks the assassin, his favorite dagger yanked out of the carcass so swiftly that it makes a sucking sound.

"All of us require solace, Master, regardless of our station. And even the best and fiercest amongst us cannot save our loved ones from life's arrows."

The assassin sighs, releases his blade, picks the carcass up by the hind legs and drops it into the bucket with the head.

"He had something to do with this, didn't he, Ham," he sighed again. "I should have put a stop to him. I saw what he was. I saw-"

"Gods are greater than men, Sir," whispers Ham. And it is said. The two men look at each other across the room. The older, grey-bearded, holds his body erect in an attitude of military respect, subordination. The taller, black-bearded but for the blood of the goat dripping from his moustache, lifts his chin with certainty.

"He goads me, Ham. He takes my hand and draws my blade against his own throat against my will. What, who is he, Ham? *Who* is he?" A dull thud, and the dagger is stuck in the table, so that even the one who put it there cannot now pull it out again.

Ham regards the blade.

"She blamed herself, My King. For something that had passed between her and the boy. She was heard to say, 'What have I done?' and 'Oh, my darlings.' Darlings. Your sons are well, were sent away to train in Aleppo before her condition became apparent. What darlings did she speak of? If not her husband, and the Rah."

"He has lain with my wife," says Rush, the words pushed from his lips like clods of earth. "And the guilt of it has driven her mad." He makes a weak attempt to pull the dagger from the table, then sits down in the chair behind it with a dull thud.

Ham is silent. He waits, his arms hanging, his hands folded in front of his groin.

Rush looks up at his servant.

"My instincts warned me," he murmurs, his black eyes warmed by the rim of red around them.

Is it anger, thinks Ham, or sadness? Or something altogether else? Is he angry at the boy, as he should be…or at the woman, whose life he saved the day he stole her from her slavery and from her people's fate?

Ham clears his throat, which is clenched in a knot. Who will die today, he thinks to himself, the boy or the woman, or both? For there is no place deep enough for either to escape from the sad wrath of this man.

"Send her to Babylon," Rush is running the tip of his finger along the exposed blade that stands like a drunken soldier before him on his desk. Ham waits for the blood to spurt, but there is none. Bloodless man, he thinks.

"Yes, Lord," answers the servant.

"Put her in the Tower of the Rah and keep her from the sight of the people. She will be safe there, as safe as any madwoman can be."

"Master," responds Ham, bowing his head. Thank you, gods, for this mercy, he thinks.

"I will find the Grain God myself. And the priest who made him."

It is dawn when Rah swims out to meet Kleitos and Thymus on the little two man skiff. The boy empties his pockets without ceremony, dropping handfuls of precious emeralds, pearls and rubies on the bottom of the boat among the nets.

"What you think, Thymus? Enough get Rah to Knossos?" Rah smiles, watching the two thieves scramble to collect the jewels and stuff their own pockets.

"Enough to buy a warship," answers Thymus, "and a navy to man it."

"Now you take Rah to Crete. You be safe. Nobody know who take Rah. Come back plenty fish, nobody know," he nods at the handful of gold pieces he has found in another pocket of his skirt. "Can have this too," he hands the gold to Thymus.

"There's no comin' back for us, boy," answers Thymus, reaching for the gold. "Best for us to sail on to Mycenae."

"He'll put two and two together soon enough," adds Kleitos. "Best for us to disappear altogether once you're on the island. He'll come to find you there. You been spout'n off about how you're goin' back since you got to Amega."

"Ya, Wolf is come," nods Rah soberly. "How long it take get Knossos?"

"Day and a half, if we sail all night. Calm day like this, maybe faster," answers Kleitos, tacking out into the great blue plain of the sea. Rah leans over the gunwale, running his hand over the warm water as the tranquil aquamarine of the shallows turns azure and the bottom of the sea drops from beneath them. A school of silver bream dart beneath the vessel, and Rah reaches to stroke the dorsal fin of a straggler.

"Good eatin', those," mutters Thymus. "Been a good catch, we'd had our nets lowered."

"'Stead of runnin' for our lives," says Kleitos as he pulls Rah back into the hull of the boat roughly. "You sit there on the nets. I've a better chance of living to spend this if I don't lose you in the middle of the bay."

CHAPTER SEVENTEEN

Knossos harbor is a mass of rubble. Collapsed villas and storage buildings along the coast have formed a wall of white boulders where the beach once greeted the softly lapping waves. The harbor itself is now a nautical graveyard, the surface calm and inviting, while beneath the water the sharp edges of architectural debris claw toward the surface, a submerged lion, waiting to tear the hulls of unsuspecting Greek ships.

Ganus the Destroyer is not the first to look upon the upturned harbor of the greatest sailing nation the world has ever known, and there are seven earlier Greek warships sunk in the bay to prove it. But he is the first to deny the Minoan lion his hulls. He has anchored a good half mile off the shore, and watches now as his men disembark in groups of ten onto smaller boats to paddle across the bay. Once established onshore, the boats return to the warships to ferry another group across. In this way, all but a detachment of six men remain on the ships to defend them.

Not that there is a likelihood of the need of defense. The island is a desolate moonscape, most of the vegetation on the north side having been ripped up by the roots and burned by the fires created by Thera's ash cloud. New growth, mostly maquis and pine stubble, offer some greenery where once prehistoric forests loomed like gods over the bay.

Ganus the Destroyer surveys the broken city from his perch on the bow of his warship. The Great Bridge is collapsed, dead center, and beneath it a pile of rubble fills the narrow channel that was the river. There has been drought here for some months, he can see by the tide lines along the basin. The Bridge Road remains intact beyond the collapse, and his men can use it to gain the city and the palace, which, from the bay, appears to be partially undamaged. He will make the palace his war room, and send his men out in groups to explore the hills. He is not used to finding destruction, but making it. How is a conqueror expected to take such a place, he thinks. There is no sign of life. No tilled fields, no oxen or sheep or chickens to eat. Only fish. Are we to become an army of fishermen? Perhaps the south side of the island, protected from the catastrophic eruption to some degree by the height of the mountains, is still populated. Perhaps they fled in boats, leaving their livestock. Optimism is the meat and drink of the conqueror. Fear is the poison. He would not allow himself to think, even briefly, that he had been sent here to be rid of. That his King, who had promised him his own niece and a territory of his own to go with her, might in fact have sent him to this burnt hell in exile, preferring in secret to marry the girl to his brother's son, an official, and Ganus' enemy, is not a thought that he will allow himself to think. I will, as I have always done, fulfill his commands to such a degree as to make them pale in comparison to my achievements.

Ganus turns to his second-in-command and nods his farewell as the rowboat comes up to flank his warship and take him to shore. He has given orders for the men remaining in the bay to shoot flaming arrows into the sky, in the unlikely event that they find themselves under attack.

"Good fortune, Sir," says his lieutenant, saluting. "And happy hunting," he adds with a wink. It is no secret that the Minoan Empire is like a dead dragon, floating in the crystal blue sea, no longer capable of defending the inconceivable treasure it has nestled for a thousand years.

In two days' time, Rah and the two thieves have sailed on the currents west, parallel to the Anatolian coastline, and then east and south again to the Bay of Gournia. Now the little two man fishing boat sits calmly in a shallow, azure sea, two hundred meters north of the cove. Behind them the southern tip of Dragon Island points like an arrow toward the once lively city.

"Look dead," says Rah, standing on the forward seat beside an exhausted Kleitos, who has been rowing against the bay current for an hour.

"Ye' were expectin' a damned welcomin' party? Ye'll find nothin' but bone and ash boy. Ye may as well give this up now and come along with us to Mycenae."

"No want to go Mycenae," pouts Rah. Want to go home, Knossos. Why you take Rah here? This no Knossos. This Gournia. Next town," he points to the northwest, where the coast juts into the sea and then falls back toward Knossos. "That be Malia, this where Wolf he find Cara. That bad place. Lot of thief and slave trader they live there. This why Marta she have no thumb," Rah puts a thumb up, like a sextant, at arms' length before him. Then he swings it west, following the Cretan coast.

"Maybe like," he pauses, peering over his thumb, "Forty mile maybe," he murmurs. He looks down at the top of Kleitos' sunburned head. "Ya, Rah can do this. No problem. Can find water. Still be cistern. Still be some fruit tree, some crop. Nothing can kill everything." He turns to find the goatskin sack Minus packed for him from his own breakfast. Dried plums and apricots, a few handfuls of shelled nuts, a string of figs, a half dozen boiled eggs. Rah has kept the pouch under the forward seat lying on top of a bucket of cold seawater. "This enough go forty mile. Find people still here. No everybody can get on boat. But maybe other side mountains, no everybody die. Some still be here. Some still remember Rah."

Thymus must swallow the lump that has risen in his throat. He blows air into the goatskin sack, then ties it tight and attaches it to Rah's golden collar, where it will float behind him until he reaches the shore.

"Two miles, maybe," says Thymus, unconsciously laying a hand on Rah's shoulder. "Sure you don't want us to wait a day or so for ye? Case maybe somethin' goes wrong? We could haul 'er up here on the beach," he cocks his head at Dragon Island. "Live on the fishin'."

Rah looks up at Thymus, and Thymus blinks away the blur of tears in his eyes, only to notice that the boy's irises are the exact color of the bay.

"Ye got eyes like a witch, boy," he mutters. "Pick up color better'n a paint brush."

"We'll wait 'til yer safe on shore," says Kleitos who has come to stand beside Thymus on the floor of the boat. "We'll be right here on the Dragon, the spit," he nods to the point, which is little more than a bar of sand jutting into the bay. "We can live on fish," he chuckles miserably, "And there's got to be a few unbroken amphora of wine left in those storehouses. The Terror himself had a storehouse on the east side o' the harbor. Built into the hill. Maybe worth a tour," he drifts off, but over Rah's head, winks at his mate.

But Rah has turned about to study the pair one final time before parting from them. He looks into Thymus' eyes, reading him, then Kleitos'. Impulsively he takes Thymus head in both hands, raising himself on the balls of his feet, and kisses him sound on the mouth. Thymus is too stunned to protest. Kleitos is next, and the Aegean breeze hasn't lifted the silk from his lips before Rah has plunged into the water.

"He'll make me sick with worry," mumbles Thymus, watching the platinum head surface several yards from the boat. Rah is a streak in the water, a silver dolphin shooting toward the Cretan shore with the sureness of a migratory bird.

"I am sixteen, Lord," says Kolga. She stands before Mursilis in the throne room.

"And how am I to judge whose child this is?" asks the King. He looks to his advisors, packed together at the right of the dais, clucking like hens. This woman came into Hattusha with the brother of Ameg the Merchant, friend and business partner of the Wolf of Amega, who claimed her as his wife. In their eyes, there is no reason to doubt her story, that the child she carries is her husbands. Nor do they have the courage to ask the King for his reason for doubting her. But Mursilis has his reasons. Something in that man's manner, something in his speech. He was not who he said he was, though he was surely tied to the assassin as an apron is tied to a chef.

"He is my husband's child, my King, he is the son of Marcas," answers Kolga. Her Hittite is vastly improved since her arrival here in Hattusha.

"You know his sex then? Are you a witch?" asks the King. Mursilis strokes his chin. His beard is coming nicely. He will have a beard as full and dashing as this Marcas one day, he is sure of it.

"You think I am a witch?" asks the girl. Her foxy face tilts at him, her honey amber eyes flicker up to catch his own, then drop to her toes like stones.

I think you are a queen, if ever a queen walked the earth, Mursilis hears himself thinking, holding back a mighty grin. You are a fox and a tiger. Beautiful and brave beyond reason. And smart! Did you not just come from the land of the Sun People? You speak Hittite better than some who have lived here all of their lives.

"Girl," says Mursilis, "You answer questions with questions. You compound lies with lies. I could have your head."

Kolga's eyes flash up at him again, and this time, the gaggle of advisors see the impropriety and gasps.

"Two, Lord, you could have both our heads, but what good would it do the King? Would you not rather send me to be with my husband? A gift of heads?"

"I suspect he would have taken you with him, had he wanted either," snaps Mursilis. Who spoke to him this way? This was an experience he had never had, like playing a game of Twenty Squares with a boy his own age, one who would not give the game away because he was the King.

But his harsh words have drawn her up. He watches the fox-sharp jaw clench. He waits. This is a fine cat-and-mouse and he would not have it end so quickly.

Suddenly she lifts her chin, high and stubborn. She meets his eye directly, and the advisors make a unanimous "huff" at her insolence. But Mursilis can only bite his lip to keep from laughing. How pretty she is angry! Her breast heaves over her pregnancy. She is like a swallow, its nest robbed, flitting furiously with feeble pecks at the raven who has her chick in its beak.

"If he fled from us, he only did so to protect us, for he planned to ride hard from here, straight into the jaws of the one you call the Assassin!" she spits.

"Indeed," smiles Mursilis. "He did indeed. And so they shall in all likelihood be sitting together at table breaking bread when my message arrives. How delightful!" He looks to his advisors, one brow raised. "Don't you think?"

The popinjays nod and bow agreeably, though utterly befuddled by his comment.

"And so now, gentlemen, you will send this message immediately to the Master of Amega. Sir, Your King requests your permission to take this Kolga, who is the property of your friend, Marcas the Trader, for a wife. Your King will pay this Marcas whatever he deems a fit sum, whether it be in land, in gold, or in men. Your King has found no woman as desirable in all of his kingdom as this Nordic she-wolf. She is both ice and fire, and she speaks to the King as if she were his equal, a pretty kitten arching and spitting at a bear in his own den. Do not think that We are not aware of your service to Us. And to you we are forever indebted. Like a father, you have given Us what we are, and so as unto a father, we dare to ask for more. It is your own hand we seek to empty, for in truth this woman is yours. Therefore, whatever it may be, We await your answer eagerly."

A scribe has been pressing the end of his reed into a soft cast frantically to keep up with the King. Now he lifts his head, awaiting further instruction. Mursilis flicks his eyes at him, nods at the door, and the man rushes off to hand deliver the cast to a messenger. That man will be one of two, always at hand, quartered near the stable and in the best shape to ride the King's fastest horse wherever it is sent. Today, that man will be riding Reh-kabil's racer.

"Damned him!" Mochlos has fallen to his knees in the pebbles. His pockets are filled with the Assassin's jewels. His bag is stuffed with provisions he has stolen from Crispo's kitchen. His 'hermaphrodite' stands by his side, her yellow robe billowing like a blond fire beside him in the gentle Mediterranean breeze. The high priest pounds his fists into the beach, cutting the pad of his left hand on a shard of pottery. Here the fishermen from the village cook their evening meals, discarding whatever clay pot or trap is broken that day on the seaside. His hand begins to pound from the stab, and he lifts it, allowing the blood to run down his forearm. He stares at it, mesmerized. "Blood," he coughs. "He brings me blood."

"All is not lost, Master," Awiti's soft, rich voice is a cloud of kindness over his naked scalp. "There are other fishermen, look there, up the beach along that spit! There comes a threesome now, look how their clothes are but rags and their hair long and unkept. These men will take your money, and us to Crete."

"Ah, girl," sighs the priest, looking past the rivulet of his own blood down the beach. "It may be so. But do you not read the signs?" He holds up his wound for her to see. "The boy, he brings me my own blood, girl. He is the death of me. Here I have stolen from the man to save him, and yet he escapes me! How early did they leave? Was the sun even up in his heaven? Had he peered over the plains of

Syria? But you are right. We must pick ourselves up," and with this, and a grand heave, he rises from the beach, his forearms stuck with sand and fragments of shell that make them glisten and shimmer.
"Very well," he nods toward the vagabonds launching their small vessel into the water. "Go and stop them. Pull off your vail and wave your arms and make a flag of your robe. They will stop when they see you coming, you are a vision with your black skin and yellow silks. They will think Ishara has escaped her temple to join them."

"And to think it took a volcano to bring down Crete," sighs Ganus to his second lieutenant. "When an army of Greeks with half our experience took Troy. Had I been given the go ahead, I would have had this island ten years sooner."
"And it would be us fleeing to the boats," laughs the Lieutenant, who is standing several yards from Ganus, marveling at a near-intact fresco on the upper-story eastern wall of the palace. "How great there art," he muses, running his gaze over the image of an acrobat leaping a bull. The thing is made on relief plaster, painted in white, red, light blue and black. "Besides that," he continues, casting a rye look at his commander, "I recall that the boys who seized Troy gave it back in less time than it took this colossus to destroy Minoa," he waves a hand past the flattened north wall, indicating Thera.
"Give, take," snuffs Ganus. "War is war. We would have had it again, if it hadn't been for that monstrosity, Antares. Eater of Heads, they call him. Taker of Souls. Why, do you know that they say he has built a wall of Amorite skulls along his eastern border? Hatti Demon! To remind his enemy what they may expect of their afterlife. Well, I'd have given him something more than my back, I can tell you. I'd have showed him what his mother forgot to tell him about her countrymen! He's half Greek you know."
"So they say," answers the lieutenant wistfully.
"What, Marius, are you another Greek lad, starry-eyed over that Hatti Devil? Let me tell you this. He was a boy himself when he took Troy back, and he did it with half the men we had and no resources. They were starving in the fields we'd burned," he nods to himself, remembering. "We were over confident, that's what did us in. They came in over the walls at night, like rats. Like thieves. They killed without exception, every man, armed or not. Every soldier, every officer. When his own commander bade him spare the lives of those

who could be pressed into Hatti service, well, that man's head was never found. But the skin of the corpse made a dandy Trojan flag while he was occupying the city. So you can admire him as a conqueror if you like, but don't ever hope to meet him."

"They say he owned land here on Crete. Had a wife living here too, and two sons," Marius has turned from the fresco to push rubble about with his drawn sword. "Perhaps he died in the cataclysm," he looks up at Ganus, one brow cocked.

"Pah," snorts Ganus, "That one saw it coming before all others, for he owned half the storehouses on Thera. He would have shipped his wares off-island long before the eruption, and anything he loved of Minoa."

"The wife and sons, then," nods Marius. "His house, though, must be destroyed. Did he have only the one?"

"I'm told he had a home on the far side of the city, and further south, not a villa on the water but a small fortress, walled and fortified, north and west of the palace. It may still stand. Leave it to that devil to have had the foresight to build inland." He shakes his head, wondering. "If it *does* stand, I wonder, did he strip it bare? Or is there treasure there still? He would have believed he would be first back. First to claim Crete once it had cooled and settled. Ah, Marius, there is a reason I keep you around. You have given me an idea. I will find his house, and I will occupy it! I, Ganus the Destroyer, will occupy the Minoan home of the Terror of the Aegean! What will the King think of that, eh? Will he then have the face to give his niece to that coward, Democritus? He will give me the island for as long as I can hold it, and his niece as my reward! He cannot deny the man who dares take the home of Antares, Eater of Heads. Come, enough with this blasted palace. There is nothing left here but broken pottery. We will find that black-eyed bastard's estate."

CHAPTER EIGHTEEN

The coach is bolstered and enclosed in thatch. The seat Josepha occupies is made of fine brocade silk, red and gold, and is as deep as a couch. Behind her, her things, a box of jewelry making devices and stones, a truck of simple clothes, a small loom and a child's harp, rattle with the rhythm of the wheels along the dusty path that snakes through the Table of the Gods and on along the river to Babylon.

He cannot know, else he would have said it, thinks the assassin's wife. He thinks me mad, but I am not mad. Only infected. I did what I could to protect them both, one from the other. In doing so, I have been stung by a scorpion, and I am poisoned. For nothing can be the same now, not now, not after …

The dust has filtered through the thatch sides and roof of the wagon, and Josepha coughs, loud and long. The steward sitting with the driver draws back the flap to check on his mistress. He is a slender youth, too frail for swords, too poorly sighted for arrows. He is good with a needle and thread and he can fix a loom, for his father builds them. It was Ham's idea to send him with the assassin's wife.

"Are you well, madam?" he asks, his voice cracking along with his lips, for the land is parched limestone. His lashes are white with it.

"Not well, no, Hassin. I am a broken thing," answers Josepha, pulling at her haphazard locks under her veil. She will keep up her show of madness even now, for she trusts no one. I have removed myself, she thinks, and used my husband's hand to do it. I am safe from him, and he is safe from me. But the thought brings no comfort.

His kiss was like the breast of a dove, soft and trembling.

It was all it took.
Who do I love?
What are you? What are you? What are you?

In Amega, the ship builders are working day and night. The fleet must be refitted, and must carry more men and horses, livestock and food stuffs, than it has ever needed to transport. The Master has given his boat builders five days. After that, heads begin falling into the sea.

Crispo has been given charge of choosing and sorting foods and food animals. And this morning he is hard at work choosing chickens and geese, goats and sheep for the New Kingdom. Tyrus has been given the responsibility to negotiate the purchase of proper grain and vegetable seeds and fruit and nut tree saplings, while Enenoch is charged with the overseeing of the packing and transport of the four holy houses. A messenger has been sent to the twins, charging them with the care and safety of their mother in Babylon. Nikolaos has been instructed, in the same way, of the goings on in Amega: the disappearance of the Rah and his priest, the condition of the Assassin's wife, the disposal of those suspected of witchery in Babylon, the departure of the Master and the Four Houses of the Rah for Crete.

On the third day Rush sends for his commanders to give them their orders. There are twenty seven vessels, four of them carrying only his best, the elite fighters that took Babylon from the river. The fleet will dock in Gornia and set to rebuilding the city. When the time is right the four commando vessels will sail into Knossos at night and set fire to the Greek ships. But nothing is to be done until Rush give the word.

It is not until the fourth day that Rush descends to his hoard. Even four days after his disappearance, Rah's hyssop and myrrh betray his presence at the base of the stairs, and Rush raises his muzzle and sniffs. The peculiar mixture of holy perfumes lingers in the still, damp air, and continues down either hall, left and right. Rush heads for the treasury first. There is evidence that the torches have been lit, removed and replaced, that a boy-sized cherry-blossom slept in the pile of pearls directly in front of the entrance, and that handfuls of gems and gold are missing. He snorts. This thievery suggests the priest, but the rank scent of his brother is here also. Minus would not have let the priest live past the stairwell, and would have left the body at the bottom. He would have tripped over it. So Minus was not aware that the priest was here. There was only one way that would have been possible. He would have been distracted by the Grain God. And as neither were in evidence, he did not kill the lad, but took him away alive. The priest must have come afterward, hoping to rescue the Rah in order to maintain his usefulness to the assassin, but he could not resist helping himself to some gold and gems, before continuing his pursuit of the greater treasure.

The question was, what had become of them? There was no way out of this labyrinth but back up into the fortress via the wine cellar, or further down, to Minus' personal hole. There was the underground pool, of course, but none but an expert swimmer could negotiate the channel beneath out into the cove, and then swim beyond the rip current. Rah could have done it, or might be dashed upon the rocks, a bloated, fish-eyed corpse looking now more like a dead goatfish than a god, his lungs filled with sand and that blonde mop tangled in seaweed and shells….

No. Not that little athlete. Did he ever attempt a physical act he did not know he could accomplish? He was fond of life, and full of purpose. He would have slipped away from Minus, and escaped by way of the underground lagoon.

But what of Minus? And the priest?

Rush sniffs the dank cave air again, and this time picks up a new scent. Yes, the little concubine. A frightened girl.

Rush pulls his crescent blades from their holsters at his sides. There is one foe he never meets without them at the ready. He takes a deep breath of the fouled cellar air, and lightless, begins to make his way to his brother's nest.

At the fork in the tunnel he holds to the right, now feeling the wall for the natural hole that opens to the underground spring. Finding it, he eases in, his bulk barely able to fit through the gap sideways. Rah would have slipped through this hole like an eel slips through water, he thinks, unable to avoid a picture of the boys narrow hips doing just that. I will grind him to powder, thinks the assassin. He feels along the inside wall, finds a small torch, and replaces his blades in their holsters to light it with the flint that is forever on his person. The fire sparks and glows, and he holds up his light source, expecting to find Minus crouched at the pool rim even now, perhaps weeping into his hands.

Instead, he finds his brother sleeping on a pile of wolf skins against the opposite wall.

"Minus!" Rush presses the torch back into the crevice he took it from in the wall. Minus rises, slaps the human side of his face with his right hand.

"It is your brother."

Minus lifts himself onto his feet, shielding his eyes with his left hand. He is weaponless, thinks Rush, but that is hardly a comfort. His brother has lost and found the Grain God in a day, and will be formidable in his new agony, if not handled skillfully.

"Do I not know my own voice?" asks the Horned God. He scratches his beard, lowering his head against the uncommon light. "You come for your Treasure, do you not, brother? He is not here. He has returned to his kingdom. Gone from Minus."

"You let him go," answers Rush. It is a statement. He lifts the torch again to better see his brother's face. But Minus turns away, shielding his eyes. "He has stolen from me?" His voice is flat.

"You know that better than I, brother," answers Minus.

"You could not resist him," says Rush. Another statement.

"Who can resist a god, brother," the words are followed by a choked sob. "Take me to him, Maxus!" he cries suddenly, and he is on his knees, his hands folded above his head in supplication. Rush, startled by the sudden movement, steps away.

"Oh, where did my brother find such a delight," weeps Minus, sitting back on his haunches, his hands now covering his two faces.

"I fear he found me, brother, and not the other way around," Rush answers. "I have been chasing him ever since, and now, it seems, I am to chase him to where it all began." He pauses. "And you would have me take you with me there."

"I would!" cries Minus, rising to his feet. Rush instantly recovers his blades from their holsters. "Take me, Maxus, take me to Knossos. He tells of a labyrinth there, beneath the palace. I will be the Horned God of Knossos. When you are king. I will be the-"

"Horned God of Minoa," finishes Rush. "The Mino-taurus."

The thriving city of Gornia has vanished.

Rah walks among the ruins on a pair of Minoan sandals he has found in a home near the beach. The town itself has already begun to become partially buried by the sand, ash and decay that has blown over it by soft sea winds, a place for the indigenous vegetation to take hold. The house he discovers, quite by accident, is built of stone, a kind of man made cave backed against the shore breezes. Inside a low flat rock in the center serves as a table. A cooking surface below a chimney is built into a southern wall, and two long foundation stones jutting out from opposing walls serve as beds. A few personal items remain, somehow having escaped the pull of the wave that otherwise emptied the little dwelling. A pair of sandals made of leather, the sole stuffed with horse hair, hang from the low ceiling by their ties, and are a perfect match for Rah's small feet. He finds a wooden spoon, a jug for spring water, and a double-bladed fish knife, behind a loose brick in the wall beside the chimney. A fisherman's house, emptied of all life save the sand crabs that scuttle toward the walls at Rah's entry. Rah wonders if the man and his family that once occupied it managed to escape, fleeing into the hills, or was his fishing dinghy sufficient to take them to Canaan. Or perhaps they were swept out into the sea, to be dined on by those creatures upon whom they had once dined.

Rah tucks the knife, the spoon and the jug into his sack and follows the coast west, where what remains of the Palace of Gornia, much smaller than that of Knossos or Cyrus, sits on the rise of a hill. The two bottom levels still stand, though the uppermost and third floor has caved in, the jagged brick walls now overrun with weeds and vine. Behind it, an azure sky is high and clear, and a dozen goats speckle the hills to the south, grazing on the rich vegetation that has taken advantage of the ash fallout from Thera.

Rah enters through a wide doorway on the western side. The first floor, made up of a maze of storerooms, has been looted clean, and only a few broken amphora remain. Rah climbs an interior staircase to the second floor, which has also been ransacked. He crosses a light well to a lustral basin, now filled with fresh rain water, where he fills his jug.

"Where theater is," murmurs Rah, looking about at what once was the Queen's private rooms. The brilliant red, blue and black frescos of a lost people cover every interior wall: dancing boys and girls, leaping dolphins, irises and lilies. One fresco stands out among the rest. It is a profile of the queen herself, seated on the throne, her elaborate hair rising like a tower from her crown, while behind her two tall slaves fan her with great colored fronds. A tiger rests at her feet.

"Pah," frowns Rah, "King Knossos, he have no tiger. Why little queen of Gornia have tiger, and Knossos no have. Stupid."

Rah follows a hall back outdoors to the central court, and finds himself looking down on a stage.

"This theater!" says Rah, dropping his jug and untying his pack from his collar. "No like Knossos. No great hall. Palace so small, have to dance here." He turns to hop down a set of steps to the court floor nearly tripping over the sacrificial stone imbedded there.

"Make sacrifice here, maybe," he kneels to run his fingers over the smooth surface.

"No like Knossos. Sacrifice right here, right in theater. This better. This how we do."

Rah brushes his fingers gingerly across the cool slab, which is polished to a luster beneath the dust. An idea strikes him, and he sweeps off the ash and dust with both hands. Then he wipes his face with his dust-caked palms.

"First have to put make-up."

When his face is yellow-grey and his brows and lashes heavy with soot, he stands up, opens his arms and takes in several long breaths. Then he steps onto the sacrificial stone, shifting his weight onto the balls of his feet. He lifts his chin, and his damp curls fall back over his shoulders. He draws his hands up over his head in supplication.

"Now is Rah be make Crete beautiful again," he says in Minoan. "Now is Rah be come home be sacrifice. Bring rain, bring crop, bring man and woman to make lot of baby. People dance in street. Bring joy. Now all good thing come back to Crete, because Crete make Rah god."

He falls in slow motion to one knee, his arms still raised like a crane's wings from his sides, elbows high, wrists bent, fingers collected and down, then launches from the stone slab into an aerial twist, pike, and somersault. The pads of his feet hit the thick dust on the court floor soft as panther paws, and he is in full costume, Aros' glittering wings made of the finest silks billowing from his golden collar and cuffs. He is Rah, the Grain God, performing The Tears of the Moon to the Court of Knossos, a golden boy who would cause a goddess to weep doves, and break a great wolf's heart.

When his dance is finished, there is only the lapping of the sea against the shingle that was once the Gornian harbor for applause. Rah bows to the sea, his body shimmering with sweat. Then he turns his back on the drowned city of Gornia, and heads for home.

CHAPTER NINETEEN

"I will go with you, Sir," bows Triggvi, who has been summoned from his new accommodations in the military wing to stand before the Master of Amega in the war room. His life has much improved since he trotted into Amega on a pony with this bear of a man. He has seen the extinction of the Fire Trolls, has rescued five babes that may have been his own, has been offered his choice of a wife, and as he is, though in his fortieth summer now, still a pleasant enough looking man, kind-eyed and a favorite of the Master, there will be no twisting of her arm when he chooses one. For now, a widower these six years, his own sweet wife having died in labor with their last child, he is content to be single, at liberty to take his pleasures at the military brothel. One day he will send for his sister, who cares for his own brood. But for now it is best for him to 'gather fish while they run' as they say in the north, and he is set to put himself fully at the disposal of this man.

"Yes, you will come with me, as that mark on your cheek tells me you must. For I need you to get inside that corn silk head, and I need you to do it in the boy's own language. I need to know what happened to him, why he is as he is, and why he wants to sacrifice himself on a mountain when I moved heaven and earth to keep that from happening."

"I have not met this Rah, Sir," answers Triggvi carefully. "But if he is the last living member of the White Elves Clan, I am as eager to save him, and to learn what he has suffered, as you. My heart is in it, Sir."

"We will travel together, apart from my army. We will be Greek, and sail into Knossos on a Greek vessel, painted in the fashion of a service ship. You speak Greek? I am Kapnos the Importer, you are my steward. You can keep your own name. There is no masking your northern race."

"Are there Greek armies on the island, Sir?" asks Triggvi, swallowing a bit of bile.

"Be prepared, Triggvi," Rush smiles. It is an evil grin, extending his cheeks sideways, offering no humor from the eyes, which only glitter with a curious hate. "Always expect the expected, know your enemies as you know yourself, and take advantage of every disadvantage." He slaps Triggvi on the back, pitching the man forward onto his knees.

"Good man," he rumbles, then turns to take a draught from the wine cup on his desk. "Another gem I have collected from the north."

And Triggvi blinks at him from his knees as the assassin turns to choose a short, double-edged Grecian sword from his armory on the wall, then slip it into a sheath on his right hip. He finds another, lighter Grecian weapon for Triggvi and hands it to him.

"Keep it on your belt," he advises, "And put your hand on the hilt when you approach a Greek. This is how they salute a countryman at arms."

"But we are to be importers, not soldiers, yes?" asks Triggvi, rising to accept the weapon and secure it on his belt.

"For the invading army, yes. They will expect stores shipped to them from Mycenae periodically. Kapnos the Importer is already well known in Mycenae. He is shorter than I, and wears no beard. Pity. He has a limp, brought about by his penchant for eating raw meats. He will be recognized and accepted on Greek soil. We will stop there, for he has a wife and two grown daughters in Mycenae and has not seen them for some time. Kapnos will be paid well by the king to sail in to the Minoan harbor, in waters known to be infested by the pirate fleet of the Terror of the Aegean, to bring supplies to his invading forces. In this way, we will learn all there is to learn. Who has been given the job of securing the island? Once we know who, we know how. We load the ship, and sail to Knossos."

"You are sure there are Greek forces already on the island, Master? Or do we make these preparations perhaps as a precaution?"

"No preparation is in vain, Triggvi," answers Rush. "I would make the same preparations whether or not the Greeks are on the island. I need information. I will get it in Mycenae."

"And this 'Terror', Sir? Who pirates the Aegean? Do we prepare for him also?" gulps Triggvi.

A glint in the assassin's cobalt black eyes sends a chill through the trader's innards. I am a fool to ask, he thinks.

"He, we cannot prepare for. For he is like thunder, that comes from the west and sweeps the plains of Troy before the boats are launched. I fear him most of all, my friend," answers Rush. "Listen," he clears his throat and steps away from the desk.

"'A sharp ridge rises out in front of Troy,
All on its own and far across the plain
With running-room all around it, all sides clear.
Men call it Thicket Ridge, and there
The Troyans and allies ranged their troops for battle.'

This is a Greek poem. But it was a Hittite, composed it. A young captain, barely twenty-five summers. He took Thicket Ridge, but the Greeks burned the fields ahead of him, and his men and animals had no food. They starved, but he would not give back the Ridge. He devised a plan, and took a handful of his best. He scaled the walls and entered the city in the dead of night. And he slaughtered them. Silent slaughter. In the morning there were no generals, no lieutenants to give orders, none but he and his men. None dared defy him, for he could fell five and seven at a time. That is your Terror. That is the one the Greeks fear."

Triggvi peers at Rush, whose oddly pale skin has flushed, whether from the wine or from the story he recounts, and he thinks he begins to understand. "You were with him," he whispers. "You were one of his elite fighters."

"Make yourself ready, Triggvi. We sail tomorrow at dawn," Rush sets one great paw on the trader's shoulder and squeezes it gently. "And do not concern yourself about the Terror of the Aegean. For he is our ally."

Mochlos and Awiti sleep in the hull of the little fishing boat. Overhead, cumulus clouds are stacked in the brilliant blue afternoon sky. The fishermen have taken turns sailing the vessel along the Anatolian coast with the currents, then south along the Cretan Passage and again west along the coast of Crete. They have passed Dragon Island, and had they known it, have passed The Grain God, who at the time of their passage was performing his Dance of Tears in the Courtyard of the Queen in Gornia. They have continued up the coast, past Malia, to the harbor of Knossos, where they now sit, adrift in the still waters, as yet unseen by the few who occupy the Greek warships resting in the bay. One of the fisherman, the eldest of the three, now nods to his younger brother.

"Best we wake them," he hisses above the pair who lie back to back on a spare sail at their feet. "These are Greek ships. I'll warrant the priest here didn't expect Greeks."

"Will they kill us?" asks his brother anxiously.

"What for?" says the third, picking his teeth with a fish bone. "We aren't the first fisherman have come here to drop our nets. Bass, bream, shrimp..."

"I saw two boats up in Malia," says the younger hopefully.

"Yes, squid trawlers," answers the oldest. "Best squid in the Great Sea, off Dragon Island. But here now, the priest awakens."

Mochlos has come to his senses and is shading his eyes from the bright Aegean sun. He has heard most of the conversation, but he will pretend he has not. He lifts himself up onto his elbows, flinching as the muscles in his neck spasm into a cramp, the result of his awkward sleeping position.

"Well, my friends. Have we reached Knossos?" he forces an uneven smile.

"We have, Sir. But there are Greeks in the harbor. See for yourself," answers the oldest brother.

"Indeed," answers Mochlos, peering over the gunwale of the little fishing boat. "And I don't suppose you, being Hittite, care to run into them. Very well, deposit us further down the coast. Just there. You see that spit? Round it. We will take the old Bridge Road back. I have a plan."

"And our silver?" asks the second eldest brother, who of the three is a bit hot headed and already anticipating a trick.

"You saw your silver, did you not?" answers Mochlos evenly. "If I denied you now, would you not take it anyway? Regardless of my priestly curses?" His eyes narrow, glinting.

"He'd do no such thing," responds the elder quickly, helping the priest to his feet, then reaching down to offer Awiti the same hand. "We've no desire to incur the wrath of Ishara."

"Instead, be swift, and incur her blessing," Mochlos offers the elder a brittle smile. "I must make the Bridge before sundown, or else we will be sleeping in the brush like pigs."

The boat is paddled back into the current, the sail set, and tacked around the spit. On the far side is a cove, so shallow that the priest and his hermaphrodite must wade in to shore. Before they have reached it, the fishing boat has disappeared.

"Master," pants Awiti, dragging her sodden robe onto the beach and collapsing there. "The bridge has collapsed. You have given them all of our money. What are we to do?"

"Silly child," answers Mochlos, collapsing beside her. "I speak fluent Greek. And Minoan of course. And I gave them all the silver, yes, but I still have all of the gold, also rubies, emeralds, pearls… sewn into the hem of my garment," he lifts his robe to show her the heaviness there, "and in yours, by the way. Now forget who you have been, for the time being. We must create a new history. The Greeks are not so fond of sexual freaks." He rubs his chin, which is beginning to itch, for he has not been able to shave in three days. "You are a Nubian princess, the daughter of a king. The Egyptians took you as a slave girl when you were only an infant, and I, being a refined Minoan priest, saw your value and purchased you to serve my god, the son of the Moon Goddess, the Rah."

"That is not so far from the truth, Master," smiles Awiti. "I can remember it easily enough. I have a little Egyptian, you know. Our mother was purchased with me, and the master's mother-in-law was Egyptian born. She took my mother for her own handmaid and taught her the language. My mother, in turn, taught me, before she died. We used to converse in Egyptian in order to keep our conversations from the other servants," she laughs. "They could not keep theirs from us, though, for she also knew some Greek, and several of them were Trojan war prizes. They spoke thinking we could not-"

"Perfect!" Mochlos cuts her off. "Then we will speak in the tongue of the Pharaohs, you and I. For I am fluent in that language as well." Mochlos rises and takes up his pack. "But be careful!" he takes her shoulder and squeezes it. "You must not let them know you can understand them, else they'll want to know how a Nubian Egyptian slave-"

"No, of course, Father," Awiti assures him.

The two begin climbing the dunes toward the Bridge Road.

"Your two younger sisters, they were not of the same father then?"

asks Mochlos after a time.

"You know how masters are around beautiful slaves, Sir," murmurs Awiti, then gives the priest a look of chagrin, clapping her hands over her mouth. "I'm sorry."

"Quite right, girl," responds Mochlos, frowning. "I do indeed. Say no more."

CHAPTER TWENTY

The assassin's apartments are intact.

The tall white walls that surround the compound are unblemished, though great trees have been uprooted and tossed across the road leading to it, prohibiting the soldiers from carrying Ganus' personal belongings up to the gates. The gates themselves are chained closed, and it is with unwholesome delight that the man who calls himself The Destroyer takes his heaviest sword to them, pushing the point into a link and twisting the degraded metal apart. He has had to leave his horse behind as well, triggering in him a sense of nakedness as he pulls off the broken chain, reaches in to throw the inside bolt back (an act that would have cost him both his hands and most of his forearms in the days before Thera) and thrusts open the iron portal into the assassin's private domain.

"Do you feel it, Marius?" he groans, looking up at the threatening facade of the house. Two enormous stone dogs flank the steps leading up to an elaborately carved front door. Honeysuckle has claimed most of the compounds interior walls but the house itself is drowning in clematis and wisteria, covering the porticos and arches as if planned so.

"I feel nothing but dread, to be honest," answers Marius, kicking at a broken bit of paving stone, pushed up by vegetation. The pavers lead to the front door in a broad arc.

"That is precisely it," grunts Ganus. And sheathing his sword he lifts his chest, draws in a warrior's fighting breath, and marches up the walk, but slows approaching the door, upon which hangs a bull's head as big as his own. The beast is golden-horned, made of black obsidian, and inlaid with jasper eyes and mother-of-pearl snout. Two holes in the nostrils suggest that it had originally been a priest's rhyton, designed for pouring out the blood of a sacrificed bull.

"Man of blood," he spits in the bulls face and pushes open the door.

Inside the house is alive with the chirping of sparrows and swifts, and above nests spill from every crevice where stone wall meets wood roof. They move down a dim corridor into a front hall lit by a large light well in the center of the room, beneath which sits a giant cistern meant to catch the rain but filled now with green slime and leafy debris. As their eyes adjust to the dim light, they see that the walls are blank, the home empty of furnishings and the floors are heavy with soot and ash which has found its way in through the battened windows.

"I wonder, you monster," muses Ganus, crossing the room and turning to approach the stair, "Where do you sleep?"

"Could there be traps set yet, Sir?" asks Marius, hesitating.

Ganus looks down at his second-lieutenant from the third stair. "It could. A snare, setting off an arrow. A blade meant to slice from above upon the opening of a door. Would he not have set it at the entrance door? Perhaps not. He could catch only one thief that way. He would have set them all over the interior, the more likelihood that he should kill several. Certainly his bedroom, his inner sanctum. Good thinking, Marius. Open the shutters," he nods at the windows, "Carefully."

At the top of the stairs Ganus stops to consider which direction to take. A hall leads left and right, but a wider hall continues in the direction of the stairs, south. He recalls that the palaces of the Minoans were said to always be built around a central courtyard, storehouses and servants on the west wing, royalty and workrooms on the east. Kitchens would be in the back of the home, and naturally on the first floor. So the assassin's own rooms, and those of his family, should be along the upper eastern wing. Ganus turns left to explore the family apartments.

Below Marius has crossed the front room to make his way toward the back of the house. He finds his way down a corridor which opens onto a portico and the courtyard. The walls surrounding the yard are overgrown with climbing roses of every variety and color. The paving stones leading through the gardens are thick with ash and debris and hard to find in any event, for the deadfall from lilies and hyacinths, their bulbs delighted with the nutrients provided by Thera's fallout, cover the paths. There are no statues, but stone benches and fountains, neatly placed beneath fruit trees, suggest that the lady of the house may have enjoyed entertaining here. Two multi-leveled dove cotes stand on poles in the center of the courtyard between which has been built a low stone pool, perfectly square and big enough for a man to bathe in. He sits gingerly on the edge and sets his cupped hand in the water for a drink. To his surprise, a carp splashes away and darts under a lily pad.

"Doves, fishes," says Marius aloud, shaking his head. "These are the pastimes of the wife of the assassin? I should think she would have preferred baking poisoned pies."

A thump overhead, followed by a cry of pain, brings him to his feet.

"General? Are you hurt?" he shouts toward the east wing. When there is no answer he rushes back inside and up the stairs. The noise came from the second story.

"General? Are you hurt?" he barks again, making his way more cautiously down the upper east wing hall.

"Damned him and his three-headed dog!" hisses Ganus behind a partially opened double door.

"General," answers Marius between gritted teeth. "Are you hurt? Can I enter?"

"It is no wonder he still lives," answers Ganus grimly. "For Hades himself will not share his kingdom with the brute. He has pinned me to a wall, Marius. My left shoulder is pinned, through the fat and muscle, the gods be praises. Yet if I pull this arrow out, there is another poised to take my heart."

"How so, Sir? How can one arrow know the placement of another?" Marius peeps through the opening in the doors.

"Stand fast, man!" Ganus cries through clenched jaws. "If you so much as touch that door, the next arrows are in you! He has them in the ceiling, crossbows. Four. I discharged this first when I lifted this spear, which was fixed in that hole by the head of the bed. But the next three know that I have cried out in pain, and called for help, and they will fly when the double door is flung wide."

"What can I do, Sir?" asks Marius, looking up through the doors. "I see nothing."

"The bows are behind the doors. You must enter through the next room, his wife's chamber. See there? To my left. There is a passageway."

"But that room is no doubt also baited and snared, Sir," considers Marius. "If I am felled there, I cannot save you," he adds judiciously.

"Then call up a foot soldier, for the love of Zeus!" snaps Ganus. "Send him in through her chamber. And if he falls, call another, until I am unleashed from this fiend's claws!"

Outside, Marius choses his least favorite lackey, a big man with a barrel chest, rotten teeth and a foul breath. He has lost to the brute once too many times arm wrestling, and he owes him a debt of two cows and an ass. The man follows him inside, unaware of the dangers that await him. Upstairs Marius deliberately passes the assassin's chamber without comment, and Ganus remains silent within.

"This one I have searched, and there is nothing of value there. Perhaps it was the servant's chamber. You take the door ahead, and I will search the next. And mark me, Pithius, do not attempt to steal for yourself what is the General's due. The dust is heavy and he will see what has been moved and missing, even to the smallest trinket."

"A decent trinket could settle our debt, though, Lieutenant," smiles Pithius, exposing a row of broken, black teeth.

"No, I will keep my hands, thank you. We will settle between us soon enough," answers Marius, nodding again at the second door and making as if to continue down the hall.

But there is no time to take a step. For just as Pithius opens the carved double door, an axe has cleft his head in two. The man's skull is hung up on it, his big body suspended and limp. Marius has seen much in battle, but the sight of the man he hated moments before, done in by an assassin's vicious humor concocted more than two years earlier, just waiting there for his death, causes him to double over and wretch. Ganus, hearing the sound, cries out to his lieutenant.

"For the love of Venus, man, what is it? Are you down?"

Marius stares at the contents of his stomach on the ash-caked Minoan tile.

"Be still, Sir. The man I sent, his head was axed at the doorway. He hangs from the head there, and surely I cannot pass him without releasing another trap. Nor can I in good conscience send another

Greek to his death by the stealthy hand of the Terror, who is as much alive in these walls as we are."

"You will send another, Marius, or be skinned alive and burned in the Bull Cauldron," snarls Ganus, whose vision is beginning to blur, despite no loss of blood.

Marius pushes himself to his feet.

"Not from this room, General. This is the wife's room, and better guarded by that demon's forethought than an emperor's wedding chamber. I will send not one but three men through the door of the room you are trapped in. Surely one of them will survive to unpin you."

"Do it quickly, Marius," answers Ganus, who feels his knees buckling beneath him. "I fear what should come next, should I fall here."

True to his word, Marius returns with three men. Two are youths, slim and agile. The third is as big as Pithius. Marius is hopeful that the larger man will catch the better part of the assassin's handiwork, sparing the other two. He is not disappointed. For as the bigger man pushes the doors full open, three arrows are buried in his flesh, keenly placed so that one splits his nose, one his larynx, one his femoral artery.

But the boys have escaped harm. They quickly recover their senses and rush to their General, who is slumped now over the arrow in his shoulder.

"We must break off the tip," Marius cautions his commander. "You may well faint from pain," he adds, then nods at the two young soldiers to hold the general upright.

"No, Marius. Let them stand guard," Ganus gasps, "there at the wife's door." He tilts his head toward the beaded curtain leading into Josepha's chamber. Marius raises his brows, looks over his shoulder. He sees what his commander has had time, pinned by the shoulder to the wall, to observe. There is a spring loaded brace of daggers imbedded in the header over the archway. A near-invisible horsehair line attaches it to the axe hanging on the wall behind the assassin's headboard. When the axe is lifted, the daggers are released in the direction of the lifter, who, because the axe is hung askance, must be standing precisely where Ganus is pinned.

"The fewer bodies in my vicinity, should that axe fall from the sheer vibration you make when you break the arrow, Marius, the better."

Marius swallows. He nods to the men to retreat beneath the

archway. Then he whispers to Ganus, "Is there no way we can disarm it before we attempt this, Sir?"
"Not without risking that we set it off in trying. Have you a file, Marius? The arrow is wood."
"I do not carry one on my person, Sir. But here, this may do." He pulls a rough edged blade from his boot. And carefully, barely breathing, he begins the task of filing through the arrow without becoming the assassin's next victim.

CHAPTER TWENTY ONE

Rah has reached the house of Ananou, the House of the Sun. It is noon on the second day of his hike to Knossos, and the sun is high and white, the sky a dome of radiance above a tranquil deep blue sea. Rah travels the old North Road, strewn now with rock and debris, the ever abundant ash, and also the tracks of a profusion of animals, both domestic and wild, that have not only escaped annihilation by the catastrophe of Thera, but have thrived as a result of it. Sheep and goats, traveling down the road in shepherdless flocks, have stamped their identity into the ash and mud, and in some places the road is as hard as paving stones. Donkeys and pigs, kri-kri, quail and pheasant in smaller numbers, as well as the occasional hare, badger and weasel have left their print in the dust, and in the many cisterns he has passed along the way, frogs peep, while green lizards and geckos creep along the damp walls. A plethora of cat snakes curl in the bows of trees, and within the ruins of the once fine inns along the road, rats, mice and bats nest.

Entering the eastern boarders of Knossos, Rah recognizes the high walls of the Sun Priest's villa overlooking the road to the north. The House of the Sun God, the Villa of Ananou, is on the dark side of town. Half the size of Mochlos' Villa, Ananou's house was built on a sun-bleached outcropping on the east end of Knossos, past the poorer neighborhoods where houses were low mud-brick, single-roomed and dirt-floored, on the road to Gournia. There is little but rubble left of these now. But the Villa itself, which sits behind an eight foot wall of brick and marble, is visible up an embankment. Rah wonders, is the House of the Sun still full of light, open and spacious? Does gold leaf still gild the interior walls? Are the bronzes of beautiful youths with broad shoulders and nipped waists, bringing saffron offerings to the Sun God, still festooning the walls and courtyards?

Rah cuts into the brush, ignoring the stinging nettle and the prickling spines of juniper bushes and weaver's broom, and hikes up the hill to the villa's west gate. The great doors are missing, no doubt pulled away by the wave, perhaps lying beneath debris along the shoreline. Orchids bloom in profusion along the wall in either direction. But Ananou's entry garden is a battered jungle of broken bronze statuary lying about beneath weeds so thick that Rah can barely find the stone paths beneath. Still, flowering almonds and fruit trees gone wild burst with pink, rose and salmon blooms. Half a dozen feral cats, all white and golden-eyed, explode from their hiding places in the weeds, some heading for the house, as if the old priest might still be within to welcome them with saucers of goat's milk and fresh sardines.

Rah drops his pack and follows the main path through the garden where once an assassin advanced like a ghost upon the cowering Sun Priest, Ananou, who had put out a contract to kill the Grain God of Knossos, and bartering boy for boy, head for head, had ultimately saved both.

In the stillness of the empty garden, Rah hears with the ears of the clairvoyant, the echo still. "Your dogs are dead, old man. I am the wolf who killed them."

"Wolf he find Ananou here," says Rah to himself. "Kill him later, Cyrus. Save Tiko, save Rah. Kill everybody else. Crazy wolf." He shakes his dazzling head. "Why this wolf be so crazy, heh? Something bad maybe happen when he is baby. Maybe somebody drop him on head." But realizing that this in fact was the impetus for his own condition, he pushes the thought out of his head.

"Now Crispo is Sun Priest. Maybe he live here one day."

Rah wanders through the vacant villa, his mouth watering with the thought of Crispo and his kitchen installed here for him to pilfer at will. White cats skulk past, or shoot from empty rooms toward the open front door. Most of Ananou's belongings have been removed, but the carpets remain, barely recognizable under the layer of dust and ash. The interior statuary is gone, and Rah wonders who might have seen fit to clear the old priest's house. No one in Knossos would have known of Ananou's fate in Cyrus, and the household would have assumed that he would be returning. Probably his acolytes had hired a ship, paid with Ananou's bronze and gold, and left with the rest of the rich for the coast of Canaan. Where were they now, the deserters? Rah had never considered it before now. It had not been only Rush and the House of the Moon, the Bull God, and the Sky, but all of the other kings and queens, all of the priests of the cities of Crete, as well as the richer merchants. They would have fled at some point during the days before the cataclysm, leaving behind servants, livestock and the poor. Rah glides his palm across the face of a dented bronze mirror that has been left on a wall in the old priest's west-facing chamber. The mirror is a sun, and bronze rays radiate out from the once polished center. The dent may have been made while the furniture was being taken apart and rushed down the beach to a waiting shipping vessel. Someone had decided it was useless, but wiping away the dust with his forearm, the Grain God of Knossos sees his own reflection mirrored in it. His leonine mane has sprung up about his head like the rays of the bronze mirror. His face is caked with white ash, making his brilliant sea-green eyes all the more intense. His gold collar, polished by his swim to shore, gleams in the noonday sunlight shining through the open air windows.

"Maybe Rah live here now, House of Sun. Wait for priest come, can take to Mountain and send home to Rah. Be one with Rah. No like here, half man, half god. Now Rah return to sky, return to place he is born. Then Crete be safe. Crop return. King and queen, all people love Rah, they come back. Wolf is make sure. Wolf is love Rah. Honor Rah. But Rah is love Crete. Must die for Crete, what make Rah God."

Rah follows his own footsteps back out into the overgrown garden. He had spotted a kind of hammock tied between two trees. The hammock is filled with almond blossoms and nut shells. He flips it, shakes it out, and finds that it is made of a dense, double woven sail cloth, like the kind used to make palanquin drapes and imperial sails. It is stained with nut rot and smells faintly of urine. Chipmunks and squirrels have used the canvas to nest in. But this is nothing to a boy who was kenneled with dogs. Rah climbs into the swing and curls his body into a ball. He is soon fast asleep, and dreaming of a calm sea, a soft breeze, and a bridge road to nowhere.

Across the city, Mochlos and Awiti are climbing down the rock strewn south western side of the collapsed Bridge Road. It is high noon and as the sun bakes the seawater from their robes a chill tightens the high priest's shoulders, reminding him of his stiff neck. The pair are damp, they are tired and hungry, and before them is a strenuous hike up the ridge to the eastern side of the bridge and the city.

"When we enter the town we will be accosted by Greek soldiers. I will engage them in Minoan. Remember, we were displaced from our temple. The city was in a panic, and thieves broke in and robbed us, made away with our vessels, leaving us to die here. But we were smart. We travelled south. We survived the cataclysm in hidden caves on the south side of the mountain. I have a temple there, in fact. A place of preparation for the holy sacrifices. We have no time to discover what has become of it. But neither will they have had time to find it. Let them assume we have holed up there until now. Some colonies must have survived on the southern coast. I will tell them that I bartered my magic for goats milk and fish. They will listen to gold and rubies, if not to my story."

"Are we to become the property of the Greeks then, Father?" asks Awiti. It is the first time she has used this term of endearment on the priest.

Mochlos' lips pull back in a narrow grin. "The property of the Terror is always the property of the Terror, regardless of who thinks otherwise. It is only a matter of time, daughter. For now we must do what we must to find and protect the Rah, until our true master arrives and settles things his way."

They have waded across the river and climbed half way to the top of the eastern embankment of the Bridge Road when a guard spots them and sounds a ram's horn. Mochlos takes Awiti's arm and holds her back.

"Here, they have spotted us. Let us rest and allow them to come get us. Remember we have travelled down a mountain. We are hungry and tired. Our cave has been looted and we have only the clothes on our backs and a few coins."

"Your story lengthens, Father," pants Awiti, glad to be allowed to settle herself on a pile of rubble that was once part of the side wall of the collapsed bridge.

"No more Hittite now. A few words in Egyptian is all you may allow yourself in their hearing. Let me do the talking, no matter what."

The guards, three of them, have made their way down the steep, rock strewn slope. Mochlos makes no effort to rise from his perch beside Awiti. He raises his eyes wearily to the largest guard and sighs a sigh of relief, then says in Greek, "Thank Hera you have come. The gods be praised! This is the day of our salvation. Mycenae has arrived to claim this devastated country, and we are saved."

"You are Greek then?" asks the guard, who has a hoarse, breathy voice for a man his size. Mochlos notices a deep scar running across his throat.

"My mother, by birth. I am a Minoan priest, Priest of the highest of the houses of Knossos, priest of the Rah. And this is all that is left of my house, first concubine to Rah, Awiti of Nubia."

The guard looks over the ash-dusted ebony face of the concubine.

"Well, priest of Rah, you are now the property of the Empire of Greece, and the charge of the King of Mycenae, under the command of Ganus the Destroyer, who has come to reclaim Crete for his country." He nods at his men to take hold of the priest and his concubine and guide them up the remaining hundred meters to what is left of the street above.

"Was Crete ever Greek then?" asks Mochlos innocently, readjusting his pack over his shoulders.

"You will lose your tongue with words such as these," responds the guard, "No matter how fair your dialect."

"But the Minoans have been here for a thousand years," Mochlos continues. "I have never heard any such legend, that the place was once Greek."

"You would be best to assume that everything was once Greek, man," says the guard, pursing his lips and giving Mochlos a sidelong glance that is a mixture of both compassion and fear. "For might is right in the Greek world, and anything and anyone that can be taken, becomes wholly Greek, even his history."

He is Ionian, thinks Mochlos, but only nods at the man. "I see. I am well advised, Sir, I thank you."

At the top of the embankment Mochlos finds himself dumbstruck by the landscape of the once glorious city of Knossos. The Bridge Road is strewn with deadfall and vegetation, the broken walls of the villas that lined it, boulders washed up from the sea, even the remains of a shattered Minoan ship. The vessel's sail is no longer the great gold and red rectangle it was, but a frazzle of burned shreds blowing in the warm summer breeze. Not far from the bridge, his own villa is almost entirely gone, a pile of rubble falling into the street on one side, into the water on the other. The high priest closes his eyes, brings his hands together at his chest, composes himself. Still, it is with the sting of tears in his eyes that he turns to the First Concubine of the Rah. He points to the demolished villa, clears his throat.

"That was the House of the Moon, my dear. That was our home."

Awiti looks past him to where he points, then at the three guards, who are watching them with renewed interest. She brings her palms together at her breast as well, mimicking the high priest, and murmurs a prayer in her mother's tongue.

When she looks up, Mochlos has turned back to the wreckage, his eyes empty of emotion.

"We will rebuild it, Sir. The Wolf will have his Rah in a proper temple," says the girl.

"Perhaps," answers Mochos, "But what is lost is lost forever. He can rebuild, but even he cannot bring back the Empire of the Sea People. It is lost for all eternity."

This exchange has been in Egyptian. Now Mocklos nods toward the rubble of the House of the Moon and speaks directly to the big Ionian. "It was the temple of the Rah. It was our home. We grieve."

"There is much to grieve," nods the guard. "The Palace of the King is destroyed. And much of the old city. But there is a house perched on a rise to the west, one they say was occupied by the Terror of the Aegean. That house is intact, and that is where Ganus the Destroyer intends to take up headquarters."

"The Assassin's compound? Intact?" Mochlos wrenches about to regard the Ionian, causing himself a wretched spasm. "That fiend," he snarls, kneading his trapezius, then congratulates himself inwardly for his outburst. His hatred of the assassin will only serve to convince these Greeks of the sincerity of his story. "Leave it to that monster to build a house that even the likes of Thera could not blow down."

"You know him then?" asks the big man, pulling Mochlos to face him by one arm. "Ah, yes. There is his mark on your cheek. The Tear Of The Bull."

"Easy man," pants the priest. "I have sprained my neck in a fall on the rocks. Have mercy."

"Answer me," returns the Ionian.

"He came and went as the Merchant, Ameg. A man so wealthy he might have built a palace to rival that of the King, had he chosen to do so. I only learned who he was at the end, when he made no effort to hide behind a disguise. He made me his then, but spared my life in order that he might utilize my magic to safeguard the Rah, whom he coveted beyond all else. By that time the royals had fled, and anarchy reigned. My villa was plundered by palace guards from the southern kingdom of Cyrus who had gone renegade, my own ships were out to sea. We had no choice but to flee to our sacred temple in the mountains to save our lives."

"And this is all that is left of your house, you and the girl?"

"The others were killed defending us. The Rah was already in the clutches of the one you call the Terror. He was in fact stolen from our house by the beast, who intended to take us all to his fortress in the kingdom of the Hatti. But Thera herself prevented it. Whether or not he survived the cataclysm, we do not know. But I can assure you this, if the Rah lives, he will return to Crete, for he was made a god-slave here, this is his kingdom, and he is driven by the god within him to restore it. And when he returns, the Assassin will follow him."

"And how will your Rah return, priest? Does he fly?" the Ionian scoffs. "And what would the Terror of the Aegean care about a Minoan god. He has his own Hatti gods to please."

Mochlos can only shake his head at the man's amusement. "Perhaps you will meet the Rah yourself one day, Sir. One look, one glance, and all of your questions will be answered."

The group has passed the remains of the palace, and Mochlos is struck momentarily dumb by the devastation.

"There's very little left, is there," he swallows, for other than the great, blood-red pillars holding what was once the grand colonnade, there is little intact of the front of the palace, which the Great Wave would have struck with the force of a falling mountain. Rubble is strewn everywhere, and the streets are blocked with debris. The finely paved Thoroughfare of Knossos is buried beneath it.

"Was it as beautiful as I was told?" asks the guard, looking over the ruined palace. "I've only stories to compare what remains," he murmurs.

"More beautiful than you can imagine," responds Mochlos with an edge of arrogance. "The Jewel of the Sea," he adds, turning away. "No matter. What is a palace without a King and Queen? Your military will rebuild as you see fit. We now stand on a Greek colony." He nods to himself, pursing his lips against an unexpected pain in his breast.

"Yes," answers the guard. "Wherever the Greek army sets foot is a Greek colony in the making." But as he moves on past the broken palace, his face belies his boast.

CHAPTER TWENTY TWO

Kapnos the Importer has landed on the coast of Mycenae. His ship is empty, ready for cargo. His crew consists of two dozen brutes capable of handling the oars and loading and unloading the vessel. Their Hittite locks have been clipped near to the skull, their beards shaved, in the fashion of the Greek soldier, who considers long hair and beards the foolish conceit of the Hatti warrior.

Kapnos the Importer paces at the helm of his ship. He is dressed in a short tunic and open robe, his exposed thighs betraying years of hard work. He strides with feet splayed, giving him an arrogant, bow-legged gait. As a result, he is shorter than the assassin, a bit bullish, and he advances with a decided limp, which he attributes to a wound he received in the Seven Day Battle of Troy against the Hatti. He wears no beard, and a blood red merchant's cap hides his waist-long black hair.

Beside him Triggvi stands resting his hands upon the gunwale. His ice-blue eyes regard the craggy coast, the steep rise to the cultivated hillsides, the fortified walls of the citadel overlooking the sea from the highest point.

"I have never seen such a place as this," he shudders. "This is a city of warriors, built for defense."

"A city of cowards, for what is the purpose of a wall? They go out from it to take what has never been theirs, and returning home ever looking over their shoulders for retribution to come find them."

"You have a wife here, and two daughters," Triggvi looks up at Rush carefully. Does that not make you a citizen also?"

"If I were not, would she still stand?" Rush smiles ruefully toward the citadel. "My wife sleeps here, yes, and my daughters," he casts a quick glance down at the trader, a cold fire burning in his obsidian eyes. "My enemies also."

"Will we stay aboard the ship, Master? Or in your house?" asks Triggvi, following Rush amidships, where a smaller boat has come along side to take him to shore.

"You will remain with the ship, Triggvi. I will tend to business in the city on my own." He begins descending into the rowboat when a man above tosses him his pack.

"Tomorrow we will receive our cargo, and you will meet your first Greeks. Remember what I have told you. Salute with your hand on your sword, and make a careful account of all that is loaded on board. Look the part I have given you. I will return tomorrow evening."

That day Rush spends his time in the streets, brothels and wine dens of Mycenae. He is well known and welcomed by most in this city, though there is one place that shuts and bolts its doors when the man at the door sees him coming. That place burned to the ground after an altercation with the Importer, in which a woman of the street was pulled into the place by an oarsman and his cronies and manhandled. Then Kapnos barked an oddly foreign phrase, someone later said it meant "obey the master" in Hittite, and in the next instant a table broke in half on a man's back, and the leader of the pack of ruffians' throat was sliced so neatly in half one would have thought a scythe had done it. No weapon was found on anyone, and there was no evidence of Kapnos when the city guards arrived. He had evaporated, like the smoke his name suggested. But five days later a fire took the place to the ground and it was only his wife's pleading that ultimately caused the owner to rebuild, against his better judgement.

Through his reconnaissance Rush learns of Ganus the Destroyer's mission to 'reclaim' Crete. He is put in touch with the man in charge of supplying the operation with food stuffs and building materials, and he arranges for an enormous shipment to be loaded onto his vessel the next morning. Kapnos receives half his wages for the dangerous task. He will receive the remainder when he returns.

That night Rush spends in the house he has provided for his Greek wife. It is a Minoan styled villa on the eastern side of town, still high enough on the hillside of the city to overlook the city walls and provide a magnificent view of the sea. He has heard that his wife, ten years older than he, has been ill for some time, and seems to have been clinging to life out of sheer determination to see him again. When he arrives, his two daughters are at her bedside. They have not seen their father for two years and fall to their knees at the sight of him.

"Father! You have survived! We thought you might be dead, killed in the cataclysm on Crete, and that we were to become paupers!" says the more talkative twin. Her sister quickly grabs her arm to silence her.

"How can you say such a thing?" she hisses at her sister. "Can you think of nothing but yourself and your luxuries? Our father has always provided for us, and he will do so in death as in life."

Rush smiles inwardly. His daughters are vipers, and half Greek. He has spoilt them as he has his Greek wife, but has kept the best jewel, his true identity, from them. They know he is a rich man, but they do not know they are the spawn of their country's mortal enemy.

"Daughters, give me time now with your mother, for though she sleeps, we must believe that her spirit knows and hears us. I would ask for her blessing when she comes to her rest in the land of the kings."

"She has always been devoted to Diwia and to the Lady of the Labyrinth, and has given alms freely. She prayed always for your safety father, and gave much to the priests of Poseidon to keep you safe on the sea, that you may never be harassed by the Terror."

"No money is wasted on prayer in my behalf," says Rush, careful not to allow himself a disparaging snort. "Go now, I would speak to your mother."

When the daughters are out of earshot, Rush bolts the door, then carefully pushes his cataleptic wife's bed from the wall. Behind it a hole has been chiseled into the stone foundation. It appears to be empty but for the clean beach sand filling it. He presses his fingers into the sand and removes a wooden key. The key is Egyptian, and made to be inserted into a lock and then lifted upwards, displacing falling pins that are held down by gravity. He will need it to recover an item that is secured in the Queen's Quarters in the Palace of Knossos, without which his meeting with Ganus will give little personal satisfaction.

Pushing the sickbed back in place, Rush kneels at his wife's side, whispers a few words in her ear, and holds back a grin when her body convulses as if to respond. Then he removes the silk pillow from behind her head and places it over her nose and mouth. It is only a matter of a minutes before she is dead.

CHAPTER TWENTY THREE

Ganus The Destroyer has been unpinned from the Assassin's wall. He has returned, embarrassed, and bleeding profusely now that the arrow has been plucked, to the Palace of Knossos, where he has taken up residence in the Queen's wing, the only section of the once magnificent edifice still in possession of all four outer walls, running water and a roof. It is a big enough area for his command. Much of the Minoan plumbing is still intact, and a cistern in the Queen's courtyard, cleaned of debris and drowned pigeons, provides water, running from a pipe that has its beginnings two miles from the palace in a cave on Mount Juktas. The clear spring water tastes like hibiscus and lilies, and as the Destroyer is ministered to by the military surgeon he wonders if it does not have some sort of healing properties. He wonders also how it can be that a man he has never met has wounded him, indeed, from a span of not just hundreds of nautical miles, but two years time. Had I met you on the battlefield, thinks Ganus, I would have given you equal mark for mark. But coward that you are, thief and liar, fraud and deceiver, you hit me from the shadows.

Ganus reflects on his great deeds in battle as the surgeon stitches his wound. There was the Seven Day Battle of Troy. He lost his left ring and pinky fingers in that one, and the ring he received from the King for his first ten years of service. The beast who took it was a Hittite giant with legs like tree trunks and the shoulders of a brown bear. Ganus lived only because his archer put an arrow in the man's back, which curtailed his onslaught, though it did not stop him from turning and hurling his axe into the archer's chest before he could nock another arrow, and then take the Destroyer's fingers and ring as a souvenir.

Ganus groans as the surgeon tugs the last stitch through his flesh, then wraps it in a poultice. The wound is throbbing and he worries about infection. The beast must have treated the arrow with something evil, a poison that could last two years. It is as if the man is spitting in his face from the moon.

"We will meet, you and I," grumbles the great general, shoving the surgeon away as the man ties off the cat gut suture. "Enough, get out all of you. We will make our headquarters here, in the ruins of the palace. When the construction battalion and engineers arrive we will rebuild in the Greek fashion, a proper military citadel. I will not command from a Minoan bordello."

A young boot has entered the Queen's chamber with a crate covered in ash.

"General, we found these in the chambers under the kitchens. It is good Minoan wine, Sir. In your condition, I thought you might enjoy-"

Ganus purses his lips in irritation, then, thirsty from his loss of blood, and defeated, licks them. "Yes, very well. Leave it there, boy. The only good thing to come out of Crete is the wine."

The youngster sets the crate on the cracked marble tiles, then uses a short fillet knife from his belt to pry open the lid. Twelve amphora are nestled within in a bed of straw. He chooses one, then uses the tip of the same knife to dig through the wax stopper, offering the general the jug.

Ganus takes the amphora, wipes the neck on his clean sleeve, sniffs the wine.

"Hmfh," he begrudgingly takes a draught. He gives the lad a look-over. "What is your name, boy?"

"I am Clovis, Sir," answers the boy.

"You cannot be old enough to serve, and if your birth name was Clovis, I am an antelope. Yet you have weaseled your way down into the labyrinth of Knossos ahead of my more…ambitious…men, found a crate of good wine that has not been taken in two years of locals thieving, and have the good sense to bring it to your commander. What is your rank?"

"I am a cabin boy, Sir. Ship steward. Not in the service." He raises his gaze hopefully, with a wry smile creasing the corners of his hazel

eyes. "It was hidden in a pile of rubble, right in the kitchens."
"You are in service now, Clovis, to me. You have just enlisted and skipped five grades. You are my steward. Go find yourself the acquisitions man and get a proper tunic and boots. You've no need for a weapons belt. I've cooks who can clean a fish."
As the boy dashes off, leaving the case of wine, Marius enters. He has put a guard around the Terror's compound on Ganus' orders. Twelve good men, he thinks to himself, as good as dead should the man return in the night to take up residence there.
"A guard is set, General," he stands at attention at the doorway, flicking his eyes around the Queen's apartment. The place was flooded, and there is a film of sand on the floor, but except for the extensive looting, it is much as it was in the Queen's day. The great platform bed dominates the middle of the room. The bolsters and linens and pillows are gone as well as the drapes, but the bed is too heavy to have been moved. It is a wood platform built over a clay foundation heated by a flue from a brazier behind the headboard. Servants would have been posted through the night in winter months to adjust the fire. Now the inlay of silver, mother-of-pearl and ivory is missing, most of the gilding peeled off the headboard and legs, but the original design is evident by the indentations along the wood flanks. Fish jump and spray in the Aegean Sea on the headboard, while a fleet of Minoan ships sail to distant lands along the sides. The General has covered the top with several woolen blankets and a few coarse pillows.
"Sit, Marius, and join me. My new steward has found me some excellent Minoan wine and I am not in a mood to drink alone," says the General, who is seated on the Queen's bed, his wounded arm hanging limply in his lap.
"Thank you, Sir," Marius takes his place beside his commander, who offers him the amphora. After the jug is empty, Marius rises to pull another from the casket.
"He will not be long," says Ganus from the bed.
Marius straightens.
"The Terror, Sir?" he turns his head to see that Ganus has plucked the wrapping back from his shoulder to examine his wound.
"I have waited for this hour, Marius. Long have I waited. Now it is here…" he trails off.
"It is the fortune of a soldier to die in battle, General," says Marius

after a moment. "There is no other."
"I wonder," answers the General. "Whose fortune will be first then? His or mine?"

In a week's time the rubble that blocked the Thoroughfare of Knossos has been cleared away, the flagstone surface exposed, and side drains and shoulders cleaned of debris. A shipload of timber, as well as a forge and a bellows has been unloaded and carried by oxcart up to the palace to begin the repair of the storerooms and barracks. The Great Hall upon which the Rah of Knossos once danced has also been unburdened of wreckage and the floor swept. The stone seats that once made up the lower gallery for the audience are for the most part still intact, and Ganus has transformed the space into a military staging area. The stone thrones of the King and Queen are also undamaged, and these he has assigned to himself and his aid. The Queen's quarters has been swept clean of ash and dust and is now a proper Mycenaean command. On one wall the decadent murals have been scrubbed off and maps, carefully patch-worked together as the result of Greek reconnaissance that is spreading out like the tentacles of an octopus from Knossos, are replacing the Minoan art. Ganus must content himself otherwise to sleep beneath the dancing dolphins and Minoan scrolls, the deep reds, blues and gold, that remind him from sunrise to sunset of the great Queen in whose chamber he rests. He is grateful only to the private bathroom behind a half wall at one end of the chamber, and to the ingenuity of Minoan plumbing.
There has been no sign of the peoples who once inhabited this place. No bodies, neither human nor animal, have been discovered beneath the rubble in the streets and villas. But neither has anything of value been discovered. Signs of plunder are everywhere. The gold, and silver, jewels, weaponry that would have crowded the palace storerooms are gone, and foodstuffs that would have been stored in hundreds of man-sized amphora beneath the palace seem never to have existed.
"They would have needed carts and oxen to remove them. There must be colonies thriving beyond the mountain," grumbles Ganus to Marius as the two stroll down the secured streets of what once was the seedier side of town. "Colonies of thieves," he adds, rubbing at his beard. "Gods what I would do for a proper shave," he allows

himself a good scratch now that they are out of view of his men, as they have turned off the Thoroughfare to march toward the last of the priestly villas, the one the Minoan cleric called The House of the Sun.

"That priest claims that palace guards from Cyrus were looting the place even before the wave came. Would they not have returned, assuming they survived, once the dust had settled? Perhaps they have established an army, taking on local men. Perhaps there is a war to fight here after all," puffs Marius, for the hill is steep.

"What sort of 'high priest' lives out here on the outskirts of the city, eh? I suppose Knossos didn't have much use for his magic once that oily fellow, Mochlos, made his own Ra," snorts Ganus, nodding toward the House of the Sun.

"This is not the Egyptian Ra, Sir. This Rah is a child of the Minoan Moon Goddess. He is the god of harvest, abundance, sex. These Minoan's seem to have thought of nothing else," Marius stops to catch his breath.

"Same thing," grunts Ganus, "A creator god, yes? Sailing across the sky by day in a boat, journeying through the underworld by night, reborn in the east every morning? 'And Ra wept, and from his tears came man,' and everything else thereafter: the wind and rain, the months and years, all that is living."

"According to the priest, this Rah was responsible for great magic here before the eruption and the wave. Cities thrived, crops flourished, where there was drought, rain."

"Didn't take long for his magic to blow the whole thing to smithereens," Ganus turns to wait for Marius to catch up. They have reached the eight foot wall of brick and marble at the top of the embankment. Marius' calves are scratched and bleeding. He stoops to pull a stinging nettle vine away from his ankle. When he raises his eyes he is looking over Ganus' shoulder at the villa's west gate. The gate is nothing more than an archway now, but it is clear that a pair of enormous doors once opened onto a wide garden leading to the front colonnade of the house. Orchids bloom in profusion along the wall, beyond which is a battered jungle of flowering almond and fruit trees. Broken statuary lies about nearly enveloped by weeds. As the two men pass under the archway, a dozen feral cats, all white and golden-eyed, explode from their hiding places.

The two had come to survey for themselves the remains of the

House of the Sun which, being on the outskirts of the city, had not been considered as a military post, but was now under consideration as a replacement for the Villa of the High Priest of the Moon. It was not that Ganus the Destroyer had developed an affection for the man since their introduction two weeks ago. On the contrary he sensed a duality in that Minoan face that caused his bowels to twist whenever he thought of him. He claimed to be a victim and an enemy of the Terror, the Assassin as he named him, but did he not sport the Tear of the Bull? And did he not live? He advised that the Rah must be on the island by now, and that he must be found and held as a hostage against the man, who would surely come to claim him, and Crete. The only hope of Greek survival on the Minoan island was a truce, a plan, a stratagem, that would placate the Rah and the Terror with one agreeable design, and that design incorporated the priest at its center. To do this, the cleric insisted, the Rah must have a House, and the priest who made him must oversee it.

That was all well and good, for Ganus had no interest in this 'Rah" character and wanted no part in a tug of war for a god-slave. It was the island he was after, and he was not so vain as to believe that he and his band of raiders could stand up to a full scale war with the man who put kings on Hatti thrones.

Still, if the boy were that precious to the monster, perhaps some sort of snarling truce could be reached. Perhaps Mycenae could be placated with a western settlement, leaving the east (east of Knossos, that is) to the Hatti prince. Perhaps the island could be divided, on the premise that, finders being keepers, once this 'Rah' was re-established on the island with his maker and in Greek hands (and sustained by Greek worship) he would chose to continue as such.

Thus the priest's plan was for Ganus to send for a proper household for the Rah, an environment pleasing to the god, including six concubine, an excellent dance troop and a good cook.

The boy, Mochlos had insured him, had no prejudice when it came to women, dancers or cooks, whether they were Minoan, Greek, Hittite, brown, red or black. He was entirely color and country blind. Your first order of business must be to find and please the Rah, for the Rah was the key to the Assassin. Yes, Mochlos insisted, the only way to survive the fact that you have had the unmitigated gall to lay one single Mycenaean boot print on this island, which the Terror knows to be his own, is to recover the Rah of Knossos before the Terror finds him himself. Capture and content the Rah, and you paralyze the Assassin.

At first, Ganus' Greek pride nearly cost the priest his head. But Ganus the Destroyer was not alive, nor in leadership of a battalion of colonizers, because he made rash decisions. He slept on the priest's advice. And tossing and turning on the platform that was once Queen Nanaea's love nest and had, in fact, once supported the weight of the very monstrosity that he wrangled with now, he considered his other options. His brush with the long fingers of the Terror at his Minoan retreat had taught him something about the man he had not considered until then, that is, what he claimed for himself was and would always be his. He had heard enough stories, indeed, stories of his escapades at Troy for one, to know that the man could slip like a shade into any castle and gut the very devil if he chose, whether an army of Herakles stood in the halls to defend him or not. Beyond this, Ganus liked the idea of a kind of "got you by the balls" stratagem against the Terror. Could the Grain God of Knossos really be the monster's Achilles Heel? It was doubtful, but what else did he have? The day he had walked away from the man's house thanking Zeus for his protection a seed of doubt had entered his blood, infecting him, like a poison from the tip of the devil's arrow, and he no longer believed that he could sustain an attack, let alone maintain the island for Greece, against such a beast. Ganus believed that the Priest's arrival was not an accident, but serendipitous. He was being guided by the gods, given a weapon against his enemy. He would not turn a deaf ear. He would see this thing through. And really, what other options were there?

Ganus and Marius have entered the front garden of the villa. A light rain has begun to fall despite a fiercely bright sun. Another omen, thinks the Destroyer. A rain shower. He considers the child's cradlesong, 'When the rain falls while the sun shines, the fox weds and the wolf dines.' Pondering only the first half of the tune, the Destroyer smiles to himself. "Foxes will be lucky today," he puffs his chest, gesturing at the cloudless sky. "A good day for a clever man."

Marius shoots him a puzzled look.

At the doors, which are ajar, the two give each other a wary glance.

"The priest says it is the house of another priest, Sir," remarks Marius. "Have we any reason to doubt him?"

"His fate is in our hands," asserts the Destroyer. "If we are harmed on his advice, he will not live to see the sun rise. He is in the hands of the Greeks now, and well he knows it." He thrusts the thumb of his good hand into his weapons belt importantly and struts throws open the doors.

Inside golden light illuminates the white walls, high ceilings, and swept floor of the villa entry room. Several white hens are strutting about the room, and a nest of dried seaweed rests in one corner where two more birds appear to be laying. Another nest, this one made of feather reed grass, dominates the center of the room. Two small white goats are munching greens in the opposite corner.

"What is going on here?" hisses Ganus, his good hand finding the hilt of his sword. Marius has pulled his from his hip and now welds it, stepping in front of his General and moving toward the hall.

"Who lives here?" he shouts in Greek, and then Minoan. A pigeon dives from a window ledge above and whistles out the open doors. Two more follow, one defecating on the general in its panicked flight.

"What the devil?" Ganus wipes the guano from his scalp. "Squatters?"

Marius has returned from the hall.

"Sir, I think you should see this." He nods toward the archway. Ganus pulls his sword and follows him into the main hall. Marius turns left, leading him into the High Priest's bedchamber.

A nest of feather grass under a window, a jug of fresh water, a fisherman's scaling knife and a spoon. A pair of worn peasant sandals. On the wall, a polished bronze mirror in the shape of a sun. On the window ledge is another, diminutive feather grass nest, this one woven with greater care, and a white dove is burrowing into it at their approach, as if it cannot fly.

"What the devil," murmurs Ganus for the second time. Still, his voice is gentled. He moves across the room to the mirror, examining the polish, in which his face reminds him of his years and the stress of his mission.

"It has been polished," remarks Marius. "And the floors swept. And yet…" he picks up a sandal. "Small feet, but not a woman's," he holds the sandal out for Ganus to examine.

"A child?" Ganus looks about at the strange décor. "Alone here? Preposterous." He slips his sword back into his belt. Marius does the same.

"Too big for a child," remarks Marius, tossing the sandal beside its mate. "Whoever has been squatting here knows how to survive, and has knowledge of animal husbandry. They are living on eggs, goat's milk, fruit, nuts, possibly fish," he bends to pick up the scaling knife. "That dove, it has broken its wing, or it would have taken off when we approached." He moves slowly toward the window and the bird. "Easy, little one," he puts out a hand, but the bird only cowers further into its nest. "They are providing it food and shelter until it mends, rather than enjoying its meat. This person has the tender heart of a maiden." He catches himself and clears his throat, glances back at Ganus.

"A woman alone here?" Ganus frowns, "Preposterous. When we landed, and you know it as well as I, I had my men scour this town for inhabitants. This-" he lifts a hand to wave at the room, "Person has only just taken up residence here in the last two weeks."

"Who then?" asks Marius, turning to the polished mirror. "Who would polish a mirror to look into, but a person used to being admired? Is it possible, Sir? Could what the priest-"

"Could what the priest told us be true?" finishes Ganus. "That this Minoan god-slave, this 'Rah', this pet that the Terror of the Aegean so loves, might somehow have returned to his island, and is living right under our noses?" He shoves his thumbs into his weapon's belt and lifts his chin, satisfied. "I saw it in the sun shower, Marius! A good omen for a clever man!" He lifts his good arm to tap his temple and wink.

"What I don't understand, Sir, if I may be so bold," cautions Marius, stepping clear of the debris on the floor to stand beside his superior, "Is how we are to keep the Assassin, once he discovers that his treasure is here in Knossos, from taking the Grain God for himself. History if nothing else tells us that the man can walk through walls and kill men like plague, leaving no sign of himself save the mark on their cheeks."

"The Tear of the Bull, yes. But this is not war, Marius, this is a game of Twenty Squares. If the man loves this god of Knossos, and this god of Knossos is happy with Greece, then the Terror must tolerate Greece. That is the priest's stratagem. I think it sound."

But the Terror can still make you disappear and cut your throat where no one can see him do it, thinks Marius, biting his lip. Or mine, for that matter. Anyone this god finds displeasing. Anyone not up to his standards. And what are his standards? How should anyone know? Perhaps he will lay eyes on me and hate me at once. Perhaps the Terror will bash my skull in with my own-

"You are musing, Marius. Leave it be. Leave it to better minds. Come now, we must set a guard on this house so as to capture the god-slave."

CHAPTER TWENTY FOUR

Rah has returned to the house of Ting Ya.

The road to the Burial Mounds of the Ancients runs along the coast. But unchained, the Grain God of Knossos can now visit his friend at night, easily skirting the Greek soldiers whose posts are along the Thoroughfare. He stays in the shadows, skirting the city by hugging the hills to the south, then navigating the slippery boulders beneath the demolished bridge to the far side and climbing the embankment to the road. The pavement is buried beneath sand and ash, but in half a kilometer it curves south into the hills and slowly the familiar brick appears. As the land rises the road becomes less a road and more a wide path through grass and brush, and then meadow and wood. A few stray sheep and goats still dot the meadows, which are overgrown now with fragrant wildflowers: poppies and anemones, rock rose and sage, campanula and on the higher plateaus, crowns of purple orchids. The mounds are on the north face of the mountain, a nest of man-made caves with faces of squared stones. A cluster of more recent burials, the City Of The Dead, tumble down the side of the mountain where a commune of priests once lived to tend to them properly, exhuming and cleaning bones buried for one season of rest before being transferred to their family tombs.

Ting Ya had tended the ancients alone, further up the mountain. Those bones were already cleaned by time and considered too sacred to move or to rearrange. Ting Ya had lived in the small mud brick building near the stone entrance to the mounds, and Rah makes his way there. He will sleep there tonight, and perhaps he will dream of Ting Ya.

The little hut is undamaged. Rah ducks through the doorway to find the place much as he last saw it. A cooking pot is lying in two halves in front of the hearth in the center of the tiny space. Cobwebs cover the window opposite the door. Ting Ya's woven bed mat lies in the corner under a layer of dust and mouse droppings, and a moth eaten woolen blanket. Rah, suddenly sleepy, pulls the mat and blanket outside. He shakes them off under a sliver of moon, then returns them to their spot in the corner and curls up on the mat, pulling the old blanket over his shoulders. But sleep will not come. His mind wanders back down the mountain, searching for what is lost. A path, a trail never taken. Once he was a slave, nameless, unacknowledged. What then? A hijacking, a break in the course of his original journey. A boat, a priest, a dance, a monster. And then the self he had never fully owned was lost forever, and he was Rah.

The sun was high and hot, the sky an opalescent blue as the procession began its ascent up the mountain. He had been overtaken by the drug and was paralyzed. He lay on a kind of stretcher, carried by two priests. He was being carried up the mountain, surrounded by the Two Houses, and the Eleven.

The group reaches the gates of the ancient cemetery where Ting Ya meets them, wearing a thin white veil that covers her entire head and face and disappears into the folds of her white robe. Ting Ya opens the gate, steps aside for the two high priests, then comes beside the pallet. She quietly slips one small hand out of her robe and rests it on Rah's arm.

The procession comes to a halt in an open area surrounded by burial mounds. Inside a circle of shallow stone steps is an altar also made of stone. The pallet is lifted and placed on the altar, then the pallet-bearers step away from it. Torches have been lit in a ring around the congregation. Ting Ya lights votive candles around the base of the altar and steps away from it. The priests and the Eleven Watchers arrange themselves on the steps, kneeling around Rah while Mochlos and Ananou loosen the trusses that strap him to his stretcher. Mochlos passes his hand over Rah's paralyzed form, sprinkling grain from his fingers. Then the high priest backs away and kneels.

The priests begin to murmur, at first incoherently, then in rhythm. It is a chant, a call for The Grain God, Rah, to come and inhabit the body they have prepared for him.

The congregation waits for the boy to stir, chanting as the sun begins to drop in the western sky.

And suddenly, high above the chanting voices is the flapping of wings. Several of the Watches lift their cowls to see a flight of doves descend to settle about Rah's limbs. Six of them, the holy number of Rah.

The birds alight on the shroud one at a time, cooing softly and walking back and forth, pecking at the seed and corn that the priest has surreptitiously dropped into the folds of the boy's shroud. The chanting stops. Mochlos rises from his knees.

He raises his arms out to his sides, his robes making wings. He is a great white bird.

Then he says the words that make a slave boy a god: "See the purest spirits of the earth come to worship him! It is the Rah!"

And the god enters him. He can move again, for the god has restored him.

He sits up, dismisses the doves, and he is on his feet on the altar, and the shroud has fallen in loose coils about his body. It is no impediment to one who danced in a cloud of colorful silks in the Great Hall before a king. He hops off the slab.

About him are a circle of spectators, priests, black-robed Watchers and bare breasted virgins, kneeling around his altar on the stone steps. What is expected? He considers the priest, the pain-maker. He can still hurt me. He gentles into his humblest bow.

A murmur runs through the Eleven. One steps forward and pronounces:

"Blessed be Rah, son of Moon and Sun. Praise to Rah, for he has accepted the offering and has come to inhabit the body of this Grain Dancer."

"You have heard the verdict of the Watchers," pronounces the High Priest of the Rah. "We must now celebrate, for Rah has found favor with this human vessel!"

"You remember, Jin yu," smiles Ting Ya from the doorway of the little hut. She is wearing the white veil and robe she wore the day he was made a god. Behind her, through her gossamer form, he can see the dawn breaking in the salmon sky. He rises to his feet, tossing away the moth eaten blanket.

"Ya, Rah remember," he nods, careful to deny his body what it wants, which is to rush the dream and take her in his arms, for she is as ethereal as the smoke that once ascended from her chimney. "You are dream, Ting Ya, no here. Rah here. Ting Ya, no here."

"Jin yu, remember what I say," says Ting Ya, whose voice is in Rah's right ear, though the apparition remains in the doorway. "Bad day, Jin yu. Bad day." Now Rah is all ears and eyes. When Ting Ya steps out of the house she gives her head a little shake. "Bad day, Jin yu. Remember what I say."

His heart is pounding now, full of fear, not for her for she is a phantom, but for himself. His body is electrified with panic. He begins to move toward her, remembering that the wall along the western edge of the cemetery is broken and he can scale it quickly and leave danger behind.

But as he passes through the doorway a man dressed in Greek battle gear steps away from the brush behind Ting Ya's door. He leaps at Rah, shoves him against the wall of the hut and puts a knife to his throat.

Three more men step out of the shadow behind the house, then two more approaches from the gate, all dressed as the first man is dressed, in the uniform of the Mycenaean soldier.

Rah takes no notice of the knife, wrenching away from the man who holds him, and causing the blade to slice across his golden collar and open a gash under his chin. He springs away toward the south wall, but before he can clear it two of the men jump him and take him to the ground, face first. One attempts to grab his wrists to bind together, but Rah manages to spin onto his back, and twisting his hands free, he strikes out, clawing at the man's face. The soldier instinctively releases him to shield his eyes. Rah bares his teeth, snarls a warning. The other man reaches for his wrists and Rah lands a powerful bite on the man's cheek.

"Agh! He's bit me! Clear to the bone!" the man rolls off Rah clutching his face.

"That's enough of that, you!" A third man comes behind Rah and grabs him by the scruff. He pulls him roughly to his feet in time for the man who has been bitten to rise and swing, punching Rah square in the left eye. Dazed, Rah crumples to his knees.

"Rah of Knossos!" barks the leader, who has replaced his dagger in his belt and now steps over the man with the clawed face. He stands over Rah, legs apart, hands on hips. The two uninjured soldiers take

Rah by either arm, holding him fast.

"You are the property of Greece! Your high priest and first concubine is in our hands. Give yourself over and they live. Fight and flee, and they die."

Rah looks up at the man, panting. His left eye has filled with blood. He hangs limply in the soldiers' grip. He flicks his eyes toward Ting Ya's doorway, where the little priestess still stands watching the scene. She nods, a single slow nod.

Rah turns his gaze at the leader, drops his head. "Rah come," he says in Greek.

The man squints at him.

"Speaks Greek," says the soldier on Rah's right. He is staring at Rah, blinking. The man behind Rah releases his scruff, and Rah's head lolls onto his chest.

"What the hell is he," says one finally.

"Jin yu," says Ting Ya from the doorway. But only Rah can hear her. Jin yu. Gold in abundance.

Rah lifts his head. Ting Ya is smiling at him. She makes a fist, bumps her chest with it, extends her hand to him, fingers opening. Many lifetimes, always friends.

Then she is gone.

"Bind him, damn it!" snaps the leader, finding his voice.

The man to Rah's left grabs his wrists and trusses the Grain God's hands together with a rough rope.

"No," Rah pants, "No touch Rah."

"Something wrong with his tongue," says the man to his right, "But that's Greek."

"Let us get off this damned mountain," says the leader. He takes the end of the rope that binds Rah's hands and yanks him forward.

Half an hour later a great breathing mass of black wrapped fury arrives at the gate. By then the cemetery is empty but for the souls of the ancients, the bees, and the whisper of hummingbird's wings hovering in the purple clematis that tumble over the cemetery walls.

Rush has followed the boy as far as the field where the King's horses once grazed in a stone enclosure on emerald summer grass. He stops there and watches as Rah, having leapt the fence like a bobcat, runs at top speed into the center of the field.

You run like a spring colt, though your memory of this place should bring you to your knees, thinks Rush. Do you not remember your cur dog? That terrible day when you watched them cut his throat? Where does your joy come from, Rah? Rush sets his chin on the stone wall, watching to see what the boy will do next.

In the crescent-moon light, Rah drops to his knees, then sits back on his haunches. He lifts his arms, and Rush can see them, the six doves, sitting like clay pigeons on his wrists, forearms and biceps. Rah nuzzles the closest invisible dove. Now he rises like a spirit from his ankles, with all the grace and balance that has made him a superstar in Knossos. He rises to his toes, lifting his arms up with eerie slowness until his wrists are above the height of his shoulders. He holds that position, then bends his knees until he is half that height.

And his next movement is so fast that Rush cannot follow it. It starts with a leap and a spin in reverse, at the top of which the boy extends one perfectly straight and vertical leg in an arch over his head. And Rush finds himself searching the sky for the invisible doves, which must have flown off in six different directions. When his eyes return to Rah the boy is folded in on himself and from an impossible height has landed with no more percussion than a feather. Rush shakes his head, mumbles to himself, "This is how it began," but he knows it is not true. Nor did it begin on the Bridge Road, the day he could not take the boy's head for King Cyrus.

It began in the Great Hall of Knossos, the first time he watched the ethereal slave-god dance for the House of the Moon and for a king.

"And I will see you dance again on that very floor. And you will dance for me," growls the wolf, turning to rest his back against the cool stone wall. From here his keen eyes can see the black bay beyond the broken bridge. He can also make out the silhouettes of Greek soldiers walking along the Thoroughfare. In the morning, Mycenaean stone smiths and laborers will fill the streets with activity, rebuilding the front walls of the Palace, and on the cliff where once stood the House of the Moon, the war-slaves that he himself transported from Greece just last week will continue removing debris and salvaging what can be reused in preparation for the reconstruction of the villa. But why? How has Mochlos endeared himself to Ganus the Destroyer to such a degree that his villa is being rebuilt for him by the Greek invaders? This information Rush has not discovered on the streets, for the streets are infested with Greek soldiers. No civilians mill about in front of shops nor hawk their wares in the market. The place is a military stronghold now, and the foot soldier does not know what the head man is planning. He could not obtain his enemy's strategy from them with both blades drawn, for they do not have it.

He has known for two days of the boy's nest in old Ananou's villa. It had been his plan to snatch the boy as he slept, coming upon him silently and wrapping him in a woven rug to avoid the bites and scratches, as well as the noise that would surely come. The plan was a good one, for though the streets of Knossos were swarming with Greeks during the daylight hours there were only a string of sentries watching the Thoroughfare during the night. Under cover of darkness it would also be much easier to carry Rah away. But the past two nights the boy had not returned to the villa after scavenging for food all day on the hillsides beyond the city. Rush spotted him only by chance on the second evening when, having searched the house room by room up to the rooftop, he took a moment to scan the beach from there. And there he was, a pale figure coalescing on the shoreline, caught in the light of the last sliver of the moon before the new. A ghost appearing out of nothing on a silver shingle, rising from the faintly lapping water, golden curls hanging in ringlets to his shoulders, his body as taut and fine as ever. He was naked, and the thatch of golden hair at his groin gave Rush a shock of surprise, as he realized that though he had owned the boy for two years now, he had never seen the whole of him. But had he been covered from head to toe in in a priest's robes, Rush would have recognized that otherworldly grace, that airy ease of movement that was Rah's alone.

Rush watched as the boy rose from the water, shook himself like a dog, and started up the beach. He had been swimming in the dark: a leopard, a predator cat, patient and diligent, and his patience had paid off. In either hand he held a still wriggling fish.

Then bending to snatch up a stick from the sand, one he had no doubt sharpened for the purpose, he quickly spiked them both, walked a few yards further up the shingle and laid the stick between the yokes of two branches stuck in the sand on either side of a snapping beach fire. He crouched there, still naked, watching the fish sizzle and smoke over the coals, and testing them now and again and snatching his hand back sharply when the flames licked at his anxious fingers.

"You are hungry, little cat," said Rush aloud. "Come to papa and you will be satisfied." But the boy did not return to the villa. He made his bed that night on the beach beside his fire, and Rush returned to his own roost at the Palace, on the roof above the Queen's chamber. Ganus had set guards all around the city, but he had failed to put one above his own head, and it was no great feat for the Assassin to scale the Palace Garden wall, set to the east as all Minoan gardens were, for that wall was so overcome with the flowering and fruiting vines once planted there as ornamentals that the wall itself could not be seen through it.

Rush turns to find that Rah has quit the field. But he knows where to find him, and find him he will. Then he will take him back to Gornia, where, unbeknownst to the Destroyer, there are twenty-seven Amegan vessels, four of them carrying only his best elite fighters, docked in the harbor, and Rush's own builders and homesteaders are converting a flattened Minoan town into a Hittite stronghold.

He hops over the ancient stone wall, crosses the field, stopping to kneel where the boy had been. Barely a blade is bent, but the scent of the boy remains, that unusual combination of cherries and myrrh even now, when he has been on the island for a week or more, living like a dog in the old man's washed out villa with goats. Where did he obtain the perfumes? Surely the House of the Sun was sacked, no stone unturned, in the days that followed the volcano and the floods. Perhaps he had found a hiding place, a safe, that none had seen, full of the priest's potions. Or perhaps he had always smelled like that, with or without perfumes. A god, emanating essences from his heavenly home.

Rush rises to his full height. He is dressed as the Assassin and he is a shadow. He strides up the grade to the opposite wall and hops over it, then continues up the trail to the fork toward the City of the Dead, where he makes a detour. When last he saw it, it was on fire, a smoking colony of huts, the bodies of those who tended the dead roasting on the trampled clay earth like holocausts. Now the whole of the island was a holocaust, much burnt, much destroyed by wind and water. A holocaust to who? What god demanded this?

Rush follows the rough trail into the City Of The Dead to find little more than lumps of ash and mounds of rubble. Only the bigger family tombs still stand, the smaller tombs caved in and filled with vegetation. A few indigenous goats dot a field to his left, one bleating out a warning at his appearance.

Rush pauses, imagining Rah the night he made love to Cara here, right under the assassin's sleeping nose.

He had approached the courtyard of burned out huts from the east when he spotted Rah and Brother Crispo rounding the barns on the southwest end of the colony. He was already annoyed that Rah has disobeyed him and wandered, doubly annoyed that the boy has copulated with a woman he had every reason to believe was the assassin's wife, or at least his property. Now he watched as the boy entertained the attentions of the fat, fool priest, who had fallen, much against his own wishes, into the sad position of Head priest of the City of the Dead.

"Oh dear, oh dear. If it isn't the devil himself," the priest had cringed, while the boy dropped like a tassel of corn silk to a full bow, his face hidden as his curls fell into the dirt.

Rush sighs. "I am in love with your ghost," he says aloud, and turning from the image, he heads toward the road to Ting Ya's. But as he rounds a tomb he is surprised by the flash of a fox's bright brush.

Curious, he follows the tail around the tomb. Another flash of the brush at the end of an alley between two larger tombs leads him into a crevice of rock he can barely squeeze through. He rummages in his sack, removes a flint, and lights a rush. Holding it at eye level he peers into the crevice to find two amber eyes regarding him. It is an immature fox, rather scrawny, its ears tipped with crust. It smiles at him, lies down and digs at its left ear with a back paw.

"Mite," mutters Rush, setting down his pack and rummaging through it. He finds what he is looking for, tosses it at the fox. The animal hops to its feet and snaps up the scrap of dried meat greedily. Rush crouches, fishes another bit of jerky from his bag, holds it out to the kit. The animal trots forward, sniffs at the offering, nibbles at it as Rush holds it tightly and skims over the beast with his rush-light.

"Not bad, just the tips of your ears." He paws through his sack once more, this time fishing out a waxed tub of honey. Breaking the seal, he snatches the fox by the scruff and presses it into the ground, rendering it helpless. He dips his fingers into the honey and coats the mangy scabs, then lets the beast go. But the fox only creeps forward to lick his honey'ed fingers.

Intrigued, Rush moves to ruffle the kit's scruff. Still mawing at his fingers, the animal squirms onto its back, curls its brush up between its hind legs and expels a series of whimpers, purrs and laughs.

"Little orphan, eh?" Rush finds another strip of jerky in his sack and offers it to the kit. It licks his hand first, then squirms between his knees, pressing itself into his thighs, and snaps up the meat.

"Another pretty little orphan," sighs the assassin, rising to his feet. He is suddenly overcome with fatigue. He has been gathering information for days, watching Greek soldiers patrol his own compound as if it were in their possession, following Rah at night, and waiting to find the priest on open ground in daylight. He is certain the priest is here, though he has yet to spot him. He has no doubt that he is being kept within the Palace and that he has made some claim of his crucial importance to Greece, though what that claim could be, he cannot imagine. What good is a Minoan High Priest to a Greek conqueror? He could snatch the priest under cover of darkness, but it would take the deaths of a dozen or so Greek soldiers, and it is not his intention to expose his existence to the Destroyer, not yet.

"I will leave him to his wanderings tonight," decides Rush, pulling his soldier's leather from his sack and spreading it on the ground at his feet. It is as good a spot as any to get some rest, protected on all sides and hidden from view. He lies down on his back, the fox kit tucking itself under his right arm against his ribs. The last slice of the moon has risen to the crown of the heavens and offers him the advantage of seeing anything that might come upon him from above before they see him. In moments, he is asleep.

It is the fox, licking his cheek, which awakens him. The moon is gone, and dawn has broken. Annoyed at himself for sleeping this long Rush jumps to his feet, gathers his leather and sack and strides through the burned out courtyard of the City of the Dead. He has begun the climb up to the Burial Mounds of the Ancients when it hits him. Did the priest promise them the Rah?

The boy hasdkept himself a secret, staying out of sight in daylight, skirting the city at night. No one would be aware of his existence unless the priest…

Rush begins sprinting up the path, the kit bounding after him. His guts have filled with black dread, his mind with red rage. These Greeks had their own gods and made no use of god-slaves as the Minoans did. Even if they had spotted him, unless the priest told them of his value, Rah would appear to Greek invaders nothing more than a strange albino native, of no use and little interest other than as a thing to make sport of. It is unlikely they would waste effort to catch him for that, although as time went on, this too was a possibility. But what if the priest *had* told them? What if he had used this bartering chip to prove his value to the enemy, saving his head and feathering his bed at the same time? Look here! There is a Minoan god-slave wandering around on this blasted rock who could make your lives a good deal easier. With him in your possession, coddled and preened as he expects to be, you could contrive a truce, for the Terror holds him dear! And look what convenience for you! Here I am, his priest and maker, at your service to keep the god bound within him.

Rush's gut twists as his anger curls and turns against him. He allowed himself to lose track of Rah hours ago. What if the Greeks had spotted that golden head on its way up the mountain, and had also following him? He had been asleep for hours. They would have had time to reach Knossos and the safety of their stronghold! But he had heard nothing, no animal yowls of fear and rage, not so much as a housecat's warble. They could not have found Rah. The boy would have never allowed himself to be taken without a racket. And there would have been a good bit of noise from the men as well, for he was far stronger than he appeared, and could deliver a vicious bite. Unless the crevice of rock he'd made his bed in had muted the noise! No, the boy must still be in Ting Ya's cemetery, perhaps hiding among the tombs, perhaps over the south wall and on toward the hole in the earth that once was Cyrus, having spotted the soldiers coming for him.

Rush reaches Ting Ya's hut as day breaks. The patch of dirt at the gate tells him all he has feared has come true. There are the fresh prints of near a dozen feet, all but one pair booted.

The agonizing imagine of Rah in the hands of his enemy hits him like the head of a mace. All because of his own carelessness overconfidence! Rah, bound and gagged and being made sport of by a pack of Greek half-wits who were known for the delight they took in molesting their prisoners!

Rush lets out a bellowing roar to make a mother bear blush, pulls both crescent blades from their holsters, and bounds down the mountain trail toward Knossos.

CHAPTER TWENTY FIVE

"It will be a replica of its earlier self," smiles Mochlos, who has come down to the site of his former home to see what progress has been made. "But finer. The gymnasium will be twice the size, large enough for a city audience. My creation will not be hauled to the Palace in the back of an oxcart to perform. No! They will have to come to us, Awiti. The great and the small. His temple shall be here, and here he shall stay, under guard and content with his troupe and his concubines and his doves."

Mochlos dabs his lips with a handkerchief. He has been munching on a pear plucked from his only surviving tree. The tree had been planted on the south side of the villa by his acolytes, too close to the wall, in his opinion, and a bit of a burr in his loincloth for that reason, though it bore delicious fruit. Its proximity to that southern wall had in fact saved it. Just as I, thinks the high priest, have been spared by the thing that has goaded me for so long. The boy, the beautiful boy, has shielded me from that volcano that is Rush. And now he will bear me sweet fruit indeed, on both sides of this equation.

"But what of his horses, Father?" asks Awiti, who is nibbling on a pear which has fallen to the ground.

That is just like you, thinks Mochlos. Taking only what is given, yet sometimes that which has fallen to earth is indeed the sweetest.

"There will be a stable," he points southeast, "There, on that flat. He can play with his horses to his heart's content." The ground he refers to is being cleared of rock and rubble. "It is perfect for him. Thera has made him an arena of sand. All that is needed is for the debris to be cleared and the sand mixed with the loam beneath. The drainage is excellent on this hill."

"You have thought of everything, Father." Awiti signs, pushing back her veil and turning a dozen Greek heads in doing so. "But where is he? What if he has drowned, trying to swim back to the island, or been caught and killed by surviving natives, who will have blamed him for their plight?"

"If any Knosson is so foolish as to harm a hair on that golden head and has also had the sense to survive on this island, I will eat my sandals," scoffs Mochlos. "He is priceless, and well they know it. Though I cannot speak for the outlanders. But he will have headed for Knossos, certainly. He will have headed home."

"Truly," answers Awiti, nodding with feigned certainty. "But," she peers down the shoreline to the east, shading her eyes with a long-fingered hand. "Where is he?"

A commotion on the Thoroughfare beyond the rise Mochlos has been pointing to takes their attention. Several soldiers, shoving anyone in their way to their knees, are hurrying toward the villa.

"Ah," smiles the priest. "I think I know." He takes Awiti's hand and, skirting the laborers and their equipment, he casually heads for the street in front of his home. "Of course it will be a few more weeks before it is livable, during which time we will have to make due at the palace, but by then the importer will have returned with all that I have asked for. The interior will be much the same as it was, except for the murals of course. There is no leeway on that I'm afraid. These Greeks are devilish prudes when it comes to art. No matter, a white wall is a light giver."

His head springs up from his conversation as the soldiers descend upon him. They swiftly surround the pair and begin herding them toward the palace.

"Might I ask?" is all Mochlos can say before the man he recognizes as the Ionian who brought him to Ganus that first day flashes him a dangerous look.

"Your god-slave, priest," says the man tersely, "We have found him."

"Rah!" cries Awiti, in her delight forgetting that she should not have understood their Greek. "Rah?" she looks at Mochlos for help.

Mochlos looks at the Ionian apologetically. "He is all she thinks of." He turns deliberately to Awiti and says in Egyptian, "They have found our Rah."

Awiti bursts into tears, slipping out of the grasp of the soldier who is steering her toward the palace and falling to her knees. She lifts her hands heavenward. "Praise him! Praise him!" she sings in Egyptian.

"Give her a moment, would you?" Mochlos stops to whisper in Awiti's ear, "Good girl." She allows him to raise her to her feet, and, falling against the arm of the nearest soldier, she dries her 'tears' on his tunic. The soldier blinks, looks helplessly at the Ionian, puts an arm around her waist and guides her forward.

Half way up the Thoroughfare Mochlos dares, "Sir, might I know your name? Were you not the man who rescued us?"

The Ionian continues on silently. At the entrance of the palace, the soldiers guarding the door step forward to take Mochlos and Awiti.

"Are we under guard, then?" asks Mochlos.

"Be silent," barks one, shoving Mochlos forward through the door.

"Idiots!" shouts a tall young man marching toward them from the Queen's wing. He wears a short, sky blue cape and an officer's weapon's belt.

"Ah, Lieutenant Commander!" Mochlos breaths with relief. "I was beginning to think we had been charged with some capital crime."

Marius, ignoring the Priest's puffery, turns on his men.

"Is it not enough your comrades have battered the boy so badly he can barely see? Would you now have me answer to the Assassin for his priest's injuries as well?" He lifts the hilt of his sword and smashes it across the Ionian's face. The man, bigger and broader than Marius by half, falls to one knee.

"Mother of the gods, no!" cries the priest. "You have not injured him? You have not scarred him in any way? No, no! Did I not tell you-"

"Be careful, priest," Marius pulls in a long breath. "Do not question the Destroyer thus."

"Do you think your commander can frighten me?" Mochlos yelps, pointing to the mark on his cheek. "I have had that beast on my breast in the middle of the night! I have heard his bellow in my ear when I thought he was in another country! I have been drowned by him, beaten by him, scarred by him, all for making the thing he loves the most! Do you think I can be frightened by some self-important Greek windbag with no idea what this man is capable of?"

"You told us to capture the boy, and so we have." Responds Marius, wearily. "Our troops are used to doing as they please with prisoners.

That 'wind-bag' you speak of left it to me to instruct the men who were sent to find him, and it was I who failed to anticipate their…immoderate…astonishment… at the appearance of this 'god-slave' of Crete. They took some sport with him, and he, being apparently wholly without common sense, made no effort to mollify them but instead escalated the abuse by spitting and scratching and biting like a wild animal. He is a sore sight indeed at the moment. But he will heal."

He may, thinks Mochlos, but you and that gasbag, Ganus, will not.

"Show me him," says the priest, stepping past Marius toward the Queen's wing in frustration. "He needs me now."

Marius puts a hand on the high priest's shoulder. He turns him toward the great hall. "He is in the dungeon."

"Heavens mercy," Mochlos closes his eye and shakes his head. "You mean the bull pit? It is no wonder you cannot keep Troy more than a day." Without waiting for Marius, he takes Awiti's hand and leads her across the expanse of what was once the Great Hall to a yawning black hole two levels deep. At the bottom, a pale figure lies on a soldier's pallet.

"A lantern!" Mochlos snaps his fingers over his head as he looks about for a ladder. Marius snatches a lantern from a soldier, hands it to Mochlos, then orders another to lower a ladder down into the pit. Holding the lantern out to illuminate Rah, Mochlos starts down the rungs.

He is half way down the ladder when a burley soldier begins climbing down after him, his torch held over his head.

"You?" Mochlos screeches up at the man's rump. "You think he needs another beating, do you?"

"For your protection, priest," Marius shouts down from the floor of the hall. "He is quite wild-"

"You think I do not know that he is wild?" Mochlos shouts back. "Get that ape off this ladder, man. The Rah needs his priest, now. And bring me some warm goat's milk, and some cheese if you have it. Have your steward boil a few eggs. Have you fed him? No, I thought not."

Mochlos is nearing the bottom of the ladder of the pit when Rah groans.

"I am coming, pet," coos the priest. He steps onto the floor of the pit, which has been emptied of the fetid soup of dried animal dung and fodder that had been occupying it for nearly two years. But the place still smells of bull dung and death. "Do you expect him to lie in his own filth, you idiots?" he shouts up to Marius. For there is no provision for a latrine in the space, though a pipe conveys a constant stream of fresh mountain water through a trough in one wall. "Or should he shit here, where he drinks."

"It was only a temporary arrangement, Priest," comes the voice of Ganus the Destroyer, now standing with self-important pomp beside Marius above. "The creature is near impossible to contain. My men had him in the soldier's brig in the west wing, but he leapt to a two story window and nearly escaped, and thus you see his condition as a result. My men are trained to keep their prisoners at any cost." He gives a sniff.

"Yes I see," spits Mochlos. "However you might have instructed them that this particular 'prisoner' is beloved of the Terror of the Aegean. He was to be treated as an honored guest, the living house of a deity."

"You ought to curb that sharp tongue," Marius lifts his chin with attempted indignity now that his commander is beside him, "If you are addressing the General, priest. Do not forget that you, too, are a guest of Greece."

"My arse," scoffs Mochlos under his breath. "Come down to me, child," he gestures to Awiti. Then, recalling that she should not understand Greek, he repeats the phrase in Egyptian. Awiti nods, lifts her gown and starts down the ladder.

"Gaaaah?" Rah croaks from the pallet.

Mochlos turns to the crumpled figure, his lantern at his side. Rah is lying on his back on a bed made of coarse burlap stuffed with straw. He has been stripped of his Minoan skirt and wears only a dirty Greek loincloth. His arms and legs are mottled with black and blue bruises and his right hip is gashed down to the bone, the wound crusted with blood. His face is in shadow.

The boy attempts to rise onto his elbows, lets out a yowl, falls back onto the pallet, his left hand clutching at his ribs. Mochlos lifts his lantern to light the boy's face, and feels his own blood rush to his feet. He puts his hand out to steady himself against the wall of the pit.

"Blessed goddess. *His eyes!*" Mochlos falls to his knees beside the pallet. "More light!" he shouts up to the soldiers, and in a moment several men are holding torches above, illuminating the dingy pit. Rah's golden mane is caked with black patches of dried blood. His mail circlet has been ripped from his head, this time by hands other than his own. The white of his left eye is blood red, the right eye so swollen it is closed entirely, the right cheekbone split. His mouth hangs open, his jaw clearly dislocated.

"Do not attempt to speak, angel," soothes Mochlos. "These beasts will tell me what has happened to you, and if they tell lies, you will accuse them by tapping my hand." He gently lifts Rah's left hand and settles his fingers on his own palm. Then he looks up to the audience above, squinting through the torchlight, and addresses Marius.

"You do not have the imagination to understand what price you will pay for this," he says icily. "And I do not have the stomach to describe it, though I once thought I could find my delight in another's pain." He has sunk onto the pallet beside Rah as he is speaking. "You must tell me the names of the men responsible for it."

"Pah!" Ganus huffs. "A man like the Terror knows well the price of disobedience to Greece and would expect no less. He is ours, is that not what matters? We have followed your advice to the letter and captured the little Grain God of Knossos. Our bait is set, our trap waiting to be sprung. I should think congratulations more in order-"

"You half-witted windbag!" cries Mochlos, jumping to his feet. "Did I tell you to disfigure him? Do you expect me to put him back together again as he was? Am I a magician? All because you hadn't the sense to order care be taken in his apprehension? This is on your head, and no one elses. I shall see to it!" He raises a fist at the group above and several soldiers step back, cowed. But Ganus only waves him off.

"He will heal well enough. No broken bones, the surgeon says. Only a dislocated jaw. It should find its way home I would imagine, given time," he thrusts his chin.

"Find its way-" Mochlos slaps his own forehead in disbelief. He turns to Awiti, who has fallen to her knees at Rah's feet. She looks at him and shakes her head, her tears falling freely. Mochlos takes a deep breath, determined to live through this new catastrophe. "I am a priest, not a doctor, Sir, but I have never known a dislocated joint to 'find its way home' without a little help. I beg you, send for that surgeon and have him return to set this jaw. He will need hot compresses, his needle and gut, and clean linen and warm water with which to wash these wounds. And have someone fetch my pack, the one I brought with me from my sanctuary. I have medicine in it to help with the swelling and bruises."

"Very well," answers Ganus. "But he will stay in the pit. I will not have him escape again." He turns and is instantly out of sight, Marius at his flank. The other soldiers turn to follow them.

"Mark me, Ganus!" shouts Mochlos as the last of the soldiers disappears. "There will not be a Greek alive on this island, should this boy's beauty be tarnished by this…this incompetence!"

But the footsteps have receded, and Mochlos can do nothing but settle beside Rah on the pallet waiting for his bag of magical matters and the surgeon. He sits down on the edge, straw poking through the burlap at his buttocks, and pulls his knees up to his chest. And suddenly he feels in his posture the boy he once was, a bare nine summers old, sitting on the bottom step of the temple of Hebe watching while the other boys played sticks, exiled from childhood because his father had presented him to the priesthood as a sacrificial offering. Thusly he began his career as a cleric, first as a Greek apprentice, later a Minoan acolyte.

"He will eviscerate me, and feed my entrails to dogs while I watch," he groans and drops his head in his hands.

"You will save him, Father," Awiti coos at his side. She is petting Rah's foot, tears running down her cheeks unchecked. But her voice is strong. "You will make him new."

Rush has followed the trail south to the Bridge Road. It is mid-morning and the sun is high and hot. He pulls his hood off and tucks it into his belt, turns east and shades his eyes from the glare. There is little to see from his vantage point but across the last mile of open road the sound of stones being pounded and set into place reverberates as the Greek bridge workers toil to rebuild the viaduct.

It is too late to catch the men who took Rah. They are inside the palace by now, and although he can come and go to and from his nest on the roof at night, even Rush cannot slash his way into that stronghold singlehanded. Taking the boy by force would require an army now, and the Greek forces have tripled since his own landed in Malia. It would take time to plan and execute such an attack, and if

Ganus was indeed informed of Rah's worth, he would surely throw him piecemeal off the Bridge before handing him over to his nemesis. This rescue cannot be achieved by force, though force will be put to the test once Rah is recovered. In the meantime, he will need one or two men at the palace to bring him information and perhaps do what they can to keep Rah safe. He has been keeping an eye out for a good informant or two amongst the officers coming and going from the palace, and he has a idea who will do.

Rush remains hidden, moving off the trail to the west to camp on the beach. He fashions a fishing rod out of papyrus reed and fastens a hemp string to the end the same length as the rod. A bit of bronze wire from a spool he filched from Josepha's jewelry making wares, makes a perfect hook. He presses a shrimp on the hook and settles on a rock with his tackle and bait, holding the fishing rod steady while he watches the float. It is not long before he has caught a half dozen bream, which he roasts over an open fire and shares with the kit. At nightfall he beds the kit down in a small cave under the bridge and heads back into the city.

CHAPTER TWENTY SIX

"It's a good name, though," smiles the boy with the hazel eyes. It is a clear night and the bay is still. Lamps along the shoreline remark the silhouettes of soldiers guarding the dock. He has been ordered to take a rowboat out to his ship to collect his things, as well as anything else on board that might be of use to his mission as Steward of the Destroyer. Now, in the light of the oil lamps he dashes about the deck of the warship he sailed in on, gathering his few belongings, and looking about for anything remotely useful to a steward. His old captain, who is called Elm by his crew, is leaning against the bulwark, chewing on dried pumpkin seeds which he picks one by one out of a leather pouch he keeps tied around his neck. He watches the boy rush about as he placidly spits shells out into the water.

"You know what it means?" the captain asks.

"Brave warrior," smiles the boy over his shoulder. He has discovered a length of heavy rope under the yeoman's chair in the cabin and begins winding it into a coil. The captain is aware, by means of the man in the rowboat who accompanied him, that his cabin boy has been given permission to take anything from the ship that he might find handy, and at this rate there will be little left of value on board. The boy's sack is already heavier than he.

"Famed," chuckles the captain, spitting another wad of pumpkin shell out into the bay. It plops into the crystal water several feet from the boat and a school of minnows instantly flies at it from beneath the hull. "Famed warrior," he gives a little chortle. "From a bandage to a famed warrior. Overnight. Quite a leap, Thais."

"You will call me Clovis, now, Captain," quips the boy with the hazel eyes. And with great effort he heaves his sack over his shoulder and trundles toward the gangway.

"I will call you Clovis the day your mother births you a second time, Thais," shouts Captain Elm after him. He hefts himself away from the bulwark and follows the boy midships. "Mark my word, you will meet with a bad end, changing names this way. Never rename a ship!" he gives the boy a light pat on the head as he descends down the rope ladder to the rowboat.

The newly renamed Clovis is marching up the Bridge Road toward the palace when he notices a man he has never seen before standing alone on the side of the thoroughfare as if waiting for him. The man wears a strange, dun colored tunic to his knees and a belt made of deer hide. There are beads of every color sewn into the belt, and tiny beads woven into his headband, which sits above his tawny eyebrows. His hair is wavy and long, caught into two braids at his ears. He wears no beard, or else can make none but the curling fur at his lobes and under his chin. He has a short, matted moustache the color of a foxes brush, and his eyes are sky blue, set with a slight downward drift at the corners, as if the he were perpetually worried, or else infected by too much compassion, a soldier's greatest enemy.

The man stares into Clovis' eyes as the boy hauls his enormous sack behind him with as much dignity as the task will allow. He looks away, a bit embarrassed at his lack of strength, though what he should care what this foreigner thinks is beyond him, when the man is at his side, his burden suddenly lighter. Clovis' fillet knife is out of his belt and on the man's throat in an instant, yet the man makes no move to withdraw or to loosen his grip on the bottom of the sack, which he has taken up and is carrying as if it weighed no more than a small child.

"Peace to you, Sir," says the man in a kind voice. The accent is decidedly northern, all rills and music. No wonder you are nothing but a wanderer, thinks the newly minted Clovis, making a snort of derision. What kind of people could fight with music in their mouths like that?

"I only wish to help. You go to the palace, no? I will help you take your burden a better way."

"Why should I trust you, foreigner?" snaps Clovis, yanking at his pack. A group of soldiers stroll past the two, chuckling. This is none

of their business. Let the boy learn the hard way. Clovis notices the man nod to them, as if they are known to him.
"You must not," says the man, agreeably. "Indeed I am strange to you and to this place. Yet you carry a burden and I am ready and willing to help. You must choose." He stops, drops the bottom of the sack suddenly, causing Clovis to go down with it.
"Clearly, Sir, it is a great burden you carry," smiles the man, "and you will need a friend to help you. I tell you, without help, you will not succeed." He extends a hand.
Clovis looks at the hand warily. If the man had wanted to, he could have easily taken off with the pack by now. He is far stronger than he appears, though he is hardly a hand taller than the boy and more round than broad. Soft, his father, a wiry fisherman who worked from dawn 'til dusk, would have said.
"What other way is there but the palace entry?" asks Clovis, accepting the hand and getting to his feet.
"Just around the west side, where the wave broke the river walls, they have reopened the old shipping entry." The man gives Clovis' hand a shake. "I am Triggvi, Steward of Kapnos the Importer. Well met."
"I am Thais…that is, I was until the General made me his valet. I am Clovis now, and you'd better address me thus else I will make a fool of myself answering to another name." Clovis blushes. This is the steward of the Importer. Gods, how could he have missed it? All the men are talking of him, bravest man in Greece. And how a northerner with strange blue eyes and barbarian dress was with him. Kapnos! The only man courageous enough to dare cross the Aegean to bring supplies to the settlement while the Terror lived!
"I should have realized..," babbles Clovis. "I'm sorry, Sir, I should…"
"Here," Triggvi hoists the sack up on his own shoulders, crosswise. "You have carried it far enough. Come now and let me show you the shipping gate."
Clovis follows Triggvi and his retreating pack around the west side of the palace, avoiding the grand front stairs. They pass through a newly mortared archway and down a passageway along the river's edge. Ahead, peeking around Triggvi's burden, the boy can see that there is indeed a canal running under the palace, fed by the river. The brickwork here is new, and built without excessive embellishment, in Greek military fashion. The passageway becomes

a low colonnade as they reach the walls of the canal. Triggvi steps to his left into what appears to be an alcove and disappears. In the next instant Clovis is suffocating, his nose buried in the cool, dry and ironically pleasant palm of the assassin.

He awakens to the buffeting of his cheek against a black muslin shirt, stretched across a giddily broad, powerful back. His own shoulders are cradled in the blades of that back, his arms trussed and pinned behind him by his own belt. He lifts his head, for there is a torch lit behind him. He is able to make out the smiling face of Triggvi, strolling along after him, in the bumpy light.

"I am not hurt?" is the first thing Clovis can think to say. He is not sure if he is in danger, if he is in luck, if he is in good or bad company. Did he faint? Is this Kapnos carrying him? The Importer's steward appears rather pleased with himself. Perhaps he tripped in the dark over a loose brick, struck his head, the hand over his face, the lack of breath, just a dream. Perhaps these two were taking him up to the surgeon. Not a good idea, though, holding him upside down like this after a blow to the head. Even he knew that.

"Ah, the babe wakes." Clovis can feel the vibration of that deep base humming against his own chest. No one told him that the Importer had a voice like thunder. In fact, wasn't it said that he had a bit of a lisp? Yes! And a limp as well! While this man walked straight as an elm on sturdy legs, though his footfalls along the brick corridor were imperceptible to the ear.

"I am full able to walk, Sir. You may release me," says Clovis. He lifts his head again to get Triggvi's attention, but Triggvi has disappeared. He is alone with his bearer.

"Quiet now," drums the big voice in a whisper. Clovis feels a pat on his rump. "We are there soon."

In a moment the corridor has opened up to the night air. Suddenly Clovis feels himself flying, as if on the back of a monkey, up a heavily vined wall. Leaves and branches, the perfume of blooms, waft past his cheek in a flash of delirious speed. Up and up, and he is certain the man must drop him, that he will tumble now to his death three stories down, when he is hefted with one flex of the man's great shoulder onto his feet. He is on a rooftop! But where? He looks about to find his bearings. There is the bay, shimmering in the half-moon light. There the lamps along the bridge, which is nearing completion, empty now of the masons and slaves toiling to rebuild it. Clovis turns south. There, the mountain, looming like the shoulder of a great beast in the dark, and to his left the oil-lamps of the soldiers patrolling the thoroughfare leading east along the coast.

"We are on the roof of the palace!" he breathes, coming about to face his abductor. A single ferocious ebony eye regards him through a hood of black strips. This is not Kapnos.

Clovis collapses to his knees.

"Good lad." A baritone purr. "You will not faint, then. A sturdy boy." The hood comes off, and the face, though beardless, can only be that of the assassin.

"Kronos, save me!" cries Clovis, falling back onto his haunches and making an attempt to crawl out from under the man's great shadow. But he has seen the face of the assassin!

"Now I will die!" blurts Clovis.

"Pah, a fairytale." Answers Rush, bringing the boy to his feet by one arm. "Am I so hard to look at?"

"No!" Quivers Clovis, "No you are quite handsome, Sir! But all who see your face must-"

"Not all, else who would do my work in secret?" smiles the assassin. "Do you think I mark those I need to infiltrate my enemy? Am I an idiot?"

Clovis sinks to his knees a second time, sobbing.

"Come to your senses, boy, I've much to ask of you." He picks the boy up by one elbow, props him against the wall of a decorative corner turret. There are six of them on the roof of the queen's wing, which is an L shape. They stand atop an ornamental wall the height of the assassin's shoulder. "Snap to, boy!" Rush gives the lad a mild butt in the breadbasket with his knuckles, and the boy gasps and clutches his solar plexus as if he has been stabbed.

Indeed he fears he has. He looks down at his fingers, splays them. Turns his hands over.

"Do you think I would dull a blade on a suckling?" The baritone purrs in his ear. Cinnamon breath tickles his cheek. Still Clovis cannot find his voice in the dry cavern of his own throat. His tongue is stuck, perhaps permanently so, to the roof of his mouth. He feels his chin lifted by a single finger. A sharp nail digs in under his mandible.

"I have been watching you, Thais of Agina," Rush puts a damp kiss on the boy's forehead. "You are a clever boy. Outsmarted old Ganus the Gaseous, did you not? With that story about finding good wine in the palace cellars? Pah! There has not been a drop of wine in that cellar for near two years now. I saw to that myself. It is all in Amega! Got it off the fool's own ship, didn't you? A jug at a time, under your tunic. Then you found an old crate of emptied amphora in the palace kitchens and put The General's own Peloponnesian wine in them. Careful not to disturb the dust and ash and cobwebs that proved the wine was Minoan. Clever little fox, you are." Rush has drawn the boy so close that the lad can feel the hammer of that magnificent heart against his own breast.

"You are forgetting to breathe, Thais," remarks Rush, giving the boy a shake. The boy gasps. "Here now," he takes a small bronze flask from within his tunic and presses it to the boy's lips. "Drink a swallow or two of that." Clovis obeys, his eyes, wide with admiration and wonder, never leaving the assassin's. When he is done Rush recovers the flask and takes a good draught himself. He smacks his lips, returns the flagon to his tunic. "Now you know what real Minoan wine tastes like." He releases the boy and watches him a moment. "Still afoot. Good. I believe you will find it easier to talk now. So tell me, Thais-who-is-now-Clovis, what shall I call you, eh?"

Clovis opens his mouth to speak, closes it. Opens it again. "Your servant, Master," he squeaks. Then, thinking on it a moment, "Your very devoted, most ambitious and energetic servant, who will gladly die in the commission of the most menial task you might assign him."

"Such drama from a suckling, and a fisher's son," Rush claps the boy on his back, sending him down onto his face. "You should have fished yourself to death as your father did, no? That is the way of things. But you chose to save yourself. Your history denies devotion to anyone but yourself, little Thais. Can a perch turn into an octopus? Can you now claim that you will devote yourself to Rush the Assassin?"

Clovis rises with as much dignity as he can muster, brushing dust and ash off his chest. All of his natural instincts tell him to take flight. Perhaps because this man is massive he is not as fast as a scrawny boy such as himself? He feels the thump-thump of fear pounding in his throat, but not the paralytic kind. His feet itch to run, even if it is simply to the parapets where the only method of escape is to fling oneself off the roof into the street. Anything but to meet death by the imagination of this Myth, who has made, they say, the sails for his warships from the hides of his enemies.

Yet another side of him opens his mouth as if against his will. He sputters, "I tell you Sir, I will cut my own throat before I fail you." He lifts his chin, wavering a bit on his legs.

"You will indeed, pup," smiles the Assassin. "For it would be better for you to do so than to fail me, and you are smart enough to say so. Very well, little Thais of Agina. I see there is no need to make you promises regarding our next meeting for you are well informed. Here is what you will do for me." And he takes the lad by the shoulders and draws him close, so that the first half of his instructions are lost on the boy, who is so overwhelmed with hero-worship and wonder that he can only take in what one sense notifies him at a time, the first being the very appearance of the man. But the gist of the matter he grasps, and when the Assassin is finished, he bows three times: first a short, Greek military bow, which he has only recently perfected, then, and to Rush's astonishment, the Amegan, that is, full on his knees, a fist bump to the chest, and finally a servant's bow to a king, which is to say a tragic rendition of something Rah could accomplish with such grace as to cause even the vilest heart to consider if the footfalls of angels do indeed at times settle upon terra firma.

The surgeon's breath reeks of wine. He crouches beside Rah's pallet examining the boy's protruding jaw. He is a man of small stature, his head already greying though he cannot have seen thirty years. He is clean-shaven and his nails are trimmed neatly. His tunic is caked with fresh blood. Mochlos takes the man by his arm and makes an attempt to pull him up onto his feet. But the man shakes him off. He takes hold of Rah's chin, jerks it forward, and the boy releases a heartbreaking yelp.

"Leave off, man!" Mochlos cries, and swats the surgeon on the back of his head. The man looks up at him indignantly.

"Your hands are as good as gone," snarls Mochlos, "If that cry has found the ear of the Assassin."

"Did you wish me to set it or no?" snaps the surgeon, rising to his feet. He turns to recover the tray of sutures and bandages he has brought with him from the surgery.

"Have the girl bathe these wounds now, and I will stitch up what I can. I have only vinegar for antiseptic. Have you a better, Minoan concoction, priest?"

Mochlos turns to his bag. He finds a small packet of powder, hands it to the surgeon. "Use the vinegar first, then stitch, then this. Leave the wounds uncovered."

The surgeon laughs, pouring vinegar over the gash on Rah's hip. "Are all the priests on Crete physicians as well? I could use a good assistant," he ignores Rah's yelp.

"You are good at disregarding the agony of others," says Mochlos, looking upward toward the floor of the Great Hall nervously, as if expecting the great, black-clad shoulders of the Hittite to appear, looming over the ledge.

"One must," the surgeon has begun his stitching. It appears Rah has fainted. He makes no sound, but lies back, apricot lips parted, a single milk-white incisor exposed and glittering in the lamplight. His bitten tongue presses it from behind, plump and pink.

"In my line of work," the surgeon continues, pinching the gash closed with the fingers of one hand while deftly setting a string of stitches along the edge, one loop bisecting the other dead center.

"It was either that or the front." He looks over his shoulder at the priest, who is poised like a carrion bird, fingers set to snatch the errant move of the soused surgeon's hands.

"These Greeks are an ironic lot," the surgeon continues. "It is the gift they gave me for my weakness, my fear of battle. Nor was my terror so much for myself as for the sight of violence upon the person of another. Therefore I was made a surgeon's apprentice, destined to endure my greatest horror for the length of my service, which is to say, until my death: ordered to patch and mop what is broken and bloodied. Thus I keep a flask of strong drink with me at all times," He nods to his tray, and now Mochlos sees that amongst the equipment of his trade sits a flagon.

"I should think it would make your hands unsteady," he turns back to the surgeon's stitching. But the line of gut is precise, the seam flawless.

"He will have a pretty scar." The surgeon slices the thread and begins on the cut under Rah's chin. "Best to take advantage of his faint," he adds.

But Mochlos can hear nothing past that word, 'scar.'

"Is there no chance it will heal without a mark?" He licks his lips, which have become parched suddenly. To hell with it, he thinks, reaching behind the surgeon for the flask. The liquid burns his throat. "Not wine," he coughs.

"Not that, no. During surgery I take a stronger draught," smiles the surgeon. The cut under Rah's chin has required only three stitches.

"That will do." He reaches behind for his tray, finds a wad of linen, puts it under Rah's head. "He must keep his head elevated if possible. Reduce the swelling. And a cold poultice on the eye. Take away this hot food. Fruit only, citrus is best. Cleans the blood." He looks back at the priest. "But I'll bet you knew that."

Mochlos purses his lips, unwilling to give the surgeon the impression that he can leave this burden on his shoulders.

"His ribs are fractured," says the surgeon, setting a hand under Rah's left breast. "Here. You can tell by his inability to take a good breath. You must keep him still. As for his scalp," he brushes aside a mat of curls to show the priest. "He has had some hair pulled out by the roots. Painful, but he will recover."

"He had a crown," Mochlos swallows, noticing for the first time that the Terror's gift is absent. "Dear Goddess, his emerald is gone." He sinks to his knees again, cringing like a beaten child, his arms over his head. "His emerald…" he moans.

"Ah, yes. The soldiers will have taken anything they could without cutting him into pieces for it," says the surgeon cheerily. "But look here," he puts a finger under Rah's collar. "He's still got this," he reaches for Rah's golden belt, "and this," he lifts one of Rah's wrists, "And these. The boy is a walking vault. It is a wonder there is any more left to him than his trunk."

"The emerald," chokes the priest, "A gift from the Assassin. The circlet upon which it is imbedded," he lifts his head, staring full into the surgeon's eyes, "Pure gold. It has been torn from his head. Are you all mad? Do you not understand what you have done?"

"I have done nothing, priest, but reset the poor thing's jaw and stitched his wounds," responds the surgeon jovially, reaching for the flask. He takes a good swig, tucks it back into his tunic. "Now, I do believe my work here is done. I will visit him tomorrow and see how his wounds are healing. I would advise you to stay at his side. He may well waken and thrash about, reinjuring himself." He burps mightily. "He took quite a beating, including a few good blows to the head. I marvel that he was not in the land of Morpheus when we began. Had that been the case, I would not expect him to awaken. But he has only fainted from the pain, now. He will rouse, and rouse hungry." He rises, collects his tray, heads for the ladder.

"Cold foods only for a day or so. I will send a man down with some fruit, and tomorrow he may have bread and cheese, and boiled eggs." He starts up the ladder, takes a misstep, collects himself, and continues to the top where he and his footsteps quickly disappear.

Mochlos brushes back Rah's curls to inspect his bloodied scalp.

"He did nothing for this," he speaks to Awiti, who has remained crouched at Rah's feet. "Be a good girl and wash clean his scalp, would you? Wash it out first with a solution of vinegar while he still sleeps. Then a rinse of cold water." He moves aside, for Awiti has already jumped to her feet to gather what she needs. The surgeon has left a gourd of vinegar and a shallow pan along with clean linens. Awiti fills the pan from the open pipe in the wall and returns to crouch at Rah's head and begin her ministrations.

Mochlos is pacing back and forth beside the pallet, rubbing the stubble on his chin. He remembers his pack, which is still lying beside Rah's head where he dropped it. He opens it, pulls out a wooden box with a bronze clasp lock and a swing hook and unlatches it. Inside are several silk packets. He finds the one he is looking for and hands it to Awiti.

"Here. Make a paste with a bit of water. Use this shell for a mortar and here, this will do for a pestle."

Mochlos hands her a small wooden implement with one thick round end. He taps a quantity of the powder from the packet. "It looks grey now but watch," he takes the linen she has soaked in the running water from the duct and squeezes a few drops into the shell. The powder turns blue.

"Oh!" cries Awiti, a smile brightening her damp cheeks. "Is this magick?"

"In part," answers Mochlos obliquely. "Once you have thoroughly cleansed those head wounds spread the paste wherever the scalp is broken. It will form a scab as it dries and keep the wound clean. We must apply it daily." He sighs, "It is the best we can do."

CHAPTER TWENTY SEVEN

Out on a ridge behind the palace Rush the Assassin is making a fire. He knows it will attract the Greek command guard.

He is roasting a small guinea fowl for himself and the fox, whom he has named Elf. Elf has begun to grow downy fur in place of the mangy crust on her ears. As it turns out, Elf is a female, and her reaction to Rush is like that of any other female. She seems to have no fear of him whatsoever. She burrows into his armpit when he sleeps, licks his face like a dog when he awakens, has even brought him a mouse, which he politely declined, but rewarded her for with a bit of jerky and a pat. She will jump into his arms if he gives her half a nod, run frantic circles around his feet if she senses he is leaving to hunt or fish or return to the city, but dutifully curls up in his soldier's leather when he commands her to stay put.

He has been thinking hard on the legend of the White Elves.

Rush throws another dried branch into the fire. It is taking these Greeks a devil of a long time tonight to send out a response to his bait.

It has been a week since their capture of the Rah. Rush has learned that the boy was injured, though he has no clear picture of the extent of his injuries. The boy, Clovis is a good palace spy, dutifully reporting all that the General is planning, the movement of troops across the north face of the island, and so on. But he has no access to Rah. Apparently the Grain God is being kept in the old Bull pit behind the Great Hall, and the priest, Mochlos, the concubine, Awiti, and the military surgeon are caring for him. He has not been allowed to leave the Bull pit for fear of his escape. And the ladder is only lowered under guard.

The boy, Clovis, hasn't even laid eyes on him, not even from a distance. So Rush has decided to draw out his second choice. The big Ionian.

He has been setting small camp fires on the hillside south of the city for days, and has been successful in luring a handful of soldiers out of the palace every night. Of course, none return, and thus a larger group is sent out the next night. His goal is to eventually come upon the Ionian, whom he knows is assigned a security detail to the south and west of the palace.

Tonight the sky is clear, the vault of stars arcing across the heavens so brightly that a child could find the constellations. A light rain has left the air sweet and moist. Rush has waited until midnight to light the campfire, set slightly further west, closer to the bridge, and further into the hills. He expects a dozen or so soldiers tonight, and so tonight, for the first time, he has set several traps, enough to take at least some of them out of the fight until he has time to finish them off at his convenience.

His position on the hill makes it easy for him to spot the command leave the palace. O hoh! But tonight they leave in not one but three groups! Whoever is in charge of this expedition is more clever than his predecessors.

Rush tosses a handful of dried grasses on the flames. Because of the size of the expeditions thus far he has had the time to torture his captives, hoping to learn the identity of the men who injured Rah, or the extent of his injuries. So far he has come up empty-handed. But he knows that by a simple process of elimination he will eventually obtain the information he is looking for. He knows that the men who took Rah travelled this route up into the mountains. There is no reason that they should be reassigned. Therefore, it is a simple matter of scheduling. And with a bit of luck, he will kill two birds with a single stone, obtaining the man he will use for a spy, and catching the men who took Rah.

Rush notices that one of the three forays is smaller than the rest and taking up the rear. That will be the captain and his men. The other two will walk into his traps first then. He claps his hands lightly and points to his leather, and Elf scrambles to it, yapping and chirping for her treat. He pulls one end up and over her, reaches beneath to give her the treat and a belly rub, then slips silently down the rise toward the closer of the two sorties.

They have been drinking, and as he comes upon the first group, six in number, the stench of metabolized mead strikes his vulpine senses like an oncoming headache. They are frightened, and thus overly hostile to one another and blustering with unfounded machismo. There are two who are nearly as big as Rush himself, but the others are hardly worth a dagger. Still, Rush determines to follow them a way, hoping that their conversation will offer him some information. Presently one of the two hulks gruffs a stage whisper back to his lads. "If it's him up here we'd better have our weapons at the ready. Gallus, Danaus, take up your spears. Lemnus, Stentor, have your double-edges up and at your sides. Mulius and I will rely on you should he manage to get the best of the two of us at once."

"Good luck to him should he try!" snipes Mulius feebly. His bravado is lost on his fellows, who can barely hear him for the racket they are making cutting their way through the bramble toward the assassin's camp fire. They are on an old deer path, but the deer are long vanished from the north side of Juktas. On a hunch, Rush makes a note of these names, in case he should find a talker tonight.

Their progress slows when the one named Mulius, who has taken up the lead, loses his footing in a badger hole. The den is occupied, and the man falls back and cries out, bitten.

"Hold your tongue," hisses the one who spoke first as he yanks him by one arm from the hole. In the light of their torchbearer, the one named Stentor, Rush can see that the man has lost the sole of his sandal and his foot is bloodied. He is already out of the fight, having fatally wounded himself with his own stupidity. "Here, tie off the bleeding with the straps of your sandal and stay here. And keep quiet!"

"Gods be with you, Davius," nods Mulius, "And watch for holes," he adds under his breath.

The others move forward up the brambled deer path. When they are out of his sight, Rush steps out of the wood in full view of Mulius, who opens his mouth to scream, and closes it around the assassin's flying dagger.

"You would have told me much," grumbles Rush, leaning over the man's corpse. "But you are too dim to keep your tongue," he adds, and frowns at this unfortunate irony.

"And there," he wrenches the man's head to the left by the blade of his embedded dagger, the sharp end of which has found its home in the back of the man's skull. "Who put that bite on your cheek, eh?" He takes a moment to examine the wound. It is a human bite, small but male, the incisors quite prominent. Rush plants the flat of Iamhad's boot on the man's chest and yanks his blade out of his mouth. He wipes the brain matter off on Mulius' tunic and sheaths it in his ankle holster.

Farther up the path the two spearmen have fallen back in typical Greek fashion. This is to give their weapons sufficient distance from a frontal attack as to be of better use. However, as their enemy is behind them, it only serves to make his job easier. He takes each down in turn without the knowledge of the other. A choke hold to lift the chin, a single plunge of his short dagger into the clavicle, a shove to send the body off the path and into the underbrush. Now there are only the three: the torchbearer Stentos, Lemnus and the leader, Davius. Rush ducks back into the woods, allowing the three a wide berth. As they crash forward through the brush like wild pigs he soundlessly moves in front of them and plants himself like a tree directly in their path. It takes Davius, slashing at the soft-stemmed greenbrier as if he were hacking a fresh path through a jungle, another five minutes to reach him.

He does not see what stands before him until he stumbles into the assassin's chest and gasps, "Ugh!" Stentos lifts the torch as Rush hauls Davius up by his tunic front, knocking his weapon out of his hands like a man swats a cold fly off his sleeve.

"Now drop those bits of tin you Greeks call weapons, and I will leave this egg uncracked." Rush grins beneath his hood. The man's head is indeed the shape of an egg, and bald but for a collar of fuzz from lobe to lobe.

"Do it!" sings Davius. It is more of a plea than an order, and Stentos and Lemnus hesitate just long enough for Rush to pull his lightest dagger from his hip and throw it into Lemnus' right eye. The man goes down with a soft thud. Stentos drops his blade, lofting it softly toward the assassin's feet.

Rush gives him a nod.

"There's a good man," he says more to himself than to his audience of two. "Now you, torchbearer, continue your climb toward the campfire there. I needn't tell you what will become of you if you do otherwise." He lifts Davius by his tunic and shakes him.

"My instincts tell me I ought to have a word with you, Davius." He cocks his head at Stentos in the direction of his campfire and Stentos, holding his torch high, nods in assent. He squeezes past the assassin and his captive and begins to make his way up the trail toward Rush's fire.

"Take your time," calls Rush softly after him, "And add a few branches to the fire when you get there."

"Bastard!" weeps Davius, who has sunk into such a lump of cowardice at Rush's feet that the assassin must let him go or double over. "You bastard!" cries the blubbering Davius at the retreating Stentos' back.

"Hardly," says Rush, taking the man by his left wrist and wrenching it up and behind him, popping his shoulder out of its socket. Davius lets go a woeful shriek.

"It is you, I think, who are a bastard, Davius. For your mother was an army whore, was she not? Yes, I recognize you, though you had a bit more hair on your head at the time. But underneath? This is the same egg." He gives Davius a sound thump on the temple with the hilt of his blade and the man is out. Rush removes his leather belt, using it to truss the man's wrists and ankles together behind him. He removes an excess strip of black muslin from his leggings, sewn into the garment for just this purpose, and gags him, then shoves him off the path. Satisfied, he starts down the hillside toward the second sortie.

He meets these in a clearing. One has already been captured in a snare and now hangs aloft from a tree. Two others are attempting to free him when a single arrow flies out of the darkness behind them, pinning the two together like lovers, chest to chest. A fourth, grasping what he has stumbled into, halts in his tracks like a frightened deer, looking about for the next arrow.

"There is none," growls Rush, walking calmly across the clearing to the survivor, who has pulled from his belt his short sword. He lifts the blade and holds it dead center, extending it from his solar plexus.

"That is the stance of a coward," advises Rush, and without ceremony he takes his own short sword from his hip and separates the man's weapon from his hands with a flick of the wrist. A fifth man lunges at him from the brush, and with his free hand Rush sends a dagger through his heart.

"But even cowards can be useful." Rush snatches the last man standing by his throat, his sharpened nails digging into his flesh like talons. "Who among you dared to steal the Rah, the Grain God of Knossos, from Rush the Assassin? Speak it quick, while you yet have voice."

The man sputters, "Rush!" is all he can manage.

"My blade will open your mouth for you, worm, if you cannot grow balls to do it yourself," snarls Rush. "I have no time to peel it out of you, as I will that one," he nods at the man who hangs still, squirming, in the snare overhead.

"It was the Commander's order!" cries the soldier then.

"Who took him," whispers Rush, pulling the man closer, so that the heat of his breath stings the man's eyes.

"It was Davius and his men who found him!" whimpers the soldier.

"And beat him? Was that also ordered?"

"They beat him after he tried to escape," answers the man.

"Who?" asks Rush again.

"I do not know, I swear it. Whoever was guarding the soldier's brig that night. There would have been two guards, always is. But I do not know who."

"Ah," says Rush, pulling a crescent blade into the moonlight. "I see it in you now," and his voice is smiling. "There is money involved. Davius, the egg head, he was not about to lose the golden hen once he'd snatched her. That snatch made him something, in his commander's eyes. And he was thinking ahead, thinking of what such a catch could bring him, perhaps from me. And so he paid off the brig guards and set up his own guard, traded places. He and who? His brother? Mulius? Well, Mulius has found his reward. But this Davius, we will let him collect his a bit later."

The assassin's hands are so fast that the man does not know he has been struck, his throat sliced through to his spine. He pulls the body out of the clearing and deposits it in a thicket. Then he returns to the man hanging from the snare.

"No need to waste time skinning you then," he smiles up at the captive, who has time to sigh in relief before his belly is opened and his entrails loosed.

The Ionian and his men have reached the campsite. The Ionian, whose name is Typho, has taken the western fork in the trail leading up the rise, thus bypassing Davius and his moans. He is the first to come upon the assassin's fire and leather, and his big body blocks the trail into the tiny clearing as he stands in awe of the one who lured him here.

"What is it, Sir?" asks the man behind him. His voice is a gnat buzzing in his ear, and he unconsciously swats at it. Across the clearing is a black soldier's leather, which is strange enough in itself, for what did he do? Skin a black cow? Or is it horse? And in it, something is moving.

"Stand back, fool," says Typhos, shoving the man behind him into his brother-at-arms. There are only three in this group: Typhos, and the young twins, Adrastos and Agapias. The boys, who are half Ionian themselves, are just turned twenty and Typhus has taken them under his wing and with him on this expedition more for their protection than his.

"There is something in the leather. A trap. We will fall back and wait." He steps backward into Adrastos, and the three move off the trail into the brush opposite the moonlight. "We will wait," breathes Typhus, but his heart is stampeding with excitement, and he has not felt so alive since the day he was captured, when he was still killing Greeks.

He does not have to wait long. For across the fire a dark bulk appears as if out of thin air. It shimmers in the firelight. How so? Then Typhus sees the thing pull off its own head, and the face of a man appears. Snow white skin, the shadow of a black beard emerging, recently clean shaven. Eyes so pitch as to be almost silver in the campfire light. The black hood is dripping wet. The man wrings it out absently, hangs it on a tree. A red fox emerges from the soldier's leather and fawns at his feet, which are booted. Amorite.

"Amorite?" is all that Typhus can manage, his voice a hoarse whisper.

"No, Typhus of Attica." The man's voice is smiling though he is not. "But I did relieve one of these boots." He looks down, lifting one foot to show off the fine detailing. "They come in handy when one is infiltrating Babylon as the great and fearsome Amorite warrior, Samal-Etatani!"

Typhus falls to his knees, his right fist clenched against his heart. "Master."

"You think them his then?" Rush opens his hands and the kit jumps into his arms to lap at his growing beard. "I could have cut boots off that milkmaid while he still walked in them. These are Iamhad's boots." He sets the kit down and steps toward Typhus, who lowers his head obediently, anticipating the blade that will surely now remove it.

"You are fine," Rush croons, lifting the man's face. "I have watched you." Forced to meet that brittle glass gaze, Typhus takes what he believes will be his last breath. It is long and delicious, scented with island flowers and the salt sea. As we begin, so we end, he recalls his mother's words the day he asked her what would become of his soul after he died. This is not a bad way to die, he thinks. Better the Assassin, than some other paltry enemy of Greece, one that will end a slave no matter what the outcome of the battle in which he dies. *This* man will always be free. This man cannot be tamed and put in harness.

But the blade does not come. The silver crescents he has long feared are not revealed. Rush is looking into his face like a man who loves horses gazes upon the flank of a fine animal.

"I have seen your face," says Typhus finally. "Will you not kill me for it?"

"I am not known for waste," answers Rush. "But tell me first, before I make you mine, who it was who captured the Grain God of Knossos, and who it was who beat him when he attempted to flee the palace."

"The squad leader is named Davius, Master. That night he was with five others, as he is tonight. His brother, Mulius, the swordsmen Stentos, Lemnus, and the spearmen Gallus and Danaus. They are headed this way along the eastern track."

"They are headed nowhere," corrects Rush, who has removed his thinnest blade, the gold and silver dagger, from his weapon's belt. The Ionian barely flinches as he begins carving the Tear of the Bull on his cheek. "All dead but Davius, the egghead. The clever one, who thinks only of his own personal gain," he is speaking more to himself now than to Typhus. A trickle of crimson has begun to flow down the soldier's cheek. "The thing intrigues me. To be so soulless, so sightless to beauty, as to have the disposition to mar such a creature with a fist, a blade." He finishes his work, pulls a bit of fresh raw rabbit meat from a purse hanging within his tunic, and presses it on the wound. "Hold that there. It will stop the bleeding." Typhus obeys.

"I could not do it," he continues, still holding the man's chin in his hand. "And thought it was a flaw in myself that I could not. But I am rethinking this decree against myself. For would I have preferred to be like this Davius? This ugly, envious parasite, death on legs? I am thinking now that I was not flawed. For to look upon such a beauty, and to destroy it....Only envy could accomplish it. And I envy no one, being quite fond of myself and my accomplishments."

Rush helps the soldier to his feet, taking him by one bicep, which even his great hand cannot circle. The man rises, but keep his eyes lowered, his right fist on his breast.

"Tell me, for you have seen him. How badly marred is he? Is he a cripple? Has he lost an eye? Did they scar that cheek? Is one golden hair missing from his head?"

"I have seen him, Lord. But I cannot say if he's been scarred or lost an eye. He is being kept-"

"In the bull pit, I know," Rush turns his back on the man abruptly. "Follow."

Typhus looks down at his own weapons belt. He still has his sword, a short mace, a dagger.

"I will have put them all in your head before you can grasp a hilt," sighs Rush, giving Typhus a bored look over his shoulder. He is already several yards down the path. "We both know you have no loyalty to Greece. Do not struggle with it, man. You are betraying no one who loves you."

"Could you love me?" asks Typhus, gazing with awe at the thick black braid cascading down Rush's back like a horse's tail. "They call you Father of Death now, in Mycenae."

"Ah, Father of Death," Rush has pulled the assassin's hood back on. He turns to Typhus, his one eye slides toward him like a snake. "A misnomer. I did not invent death. Nor did I give birth to it." He turns to continue down the path toward Davius. "It was the other way around, Typhus of Attica. Death invented me."

CHAPTER TWENTY EIGHT

Rah is dreaming.

He is in the House of the Moon, in his own chamber, while the High Priest Mochlos sleeps behind a doorway of strung beads. He is fastened to his pallet with golden chains which are welded to the rings around his wrists, his ankles, his neck and his waist. The chains are so tight that his body is a capsule of pain, and the pain is pulsing like a heartbeat. It pounds in the back of his head, but is also a halo around his crown. It causes each breath he takes to stab him in his heart. His right hip also throbs with fire, and his feet are numb. I will never dance again, he thinks. Why has he done this to me? Does he not love me? Did he not create me?

Rah watches as a shadow forms at the window of his little room. At first it seems no more than a cloud passing over the moon. But as he strains to look over his shoulder toward the apparition it solidifies. It becomes a man, or the silhouette of a man. Featureless, the head a black blur, it rises up over the casement and enters the room. It walks, like a man, toward the beaded curtain. It slips through without rattling the beads.

"Why have you come?" asks Rah. He is speaking a language he has never heard, and yet he knows it well. It is the language in his soul.

Silence.

And then, a flash of light, so bright that he is blinded by it. And he is being lifted up on powerful shoulders. The chains are gone.
He saves, says the language of his soul.

"Goddess, save me, he comes to," breathes Mochlos, who holds a damp cloth to Rah's fevered forehead. "I was beginning to think he never would."
It has been three days since the surgeon stitched Rah's wounds and left him to Mochlos and Awiti. The angry bruises are fading, and the stitches holding. The boy's face is as pale as the clean straw that now covers the floor of the bull pit. His head has been tenderly washed in warm vinegar water every day, and his hair, lightened by the medicinal treatment, is clean and falls in soft silk ringlets on the duck down pillow under his head. His body has been washed daily as well, and his loincloth changed. His lids are lined in crimson and shadowed green as the bruises fade. The inner portion of his right eye still holds blood like a cup.
"Can you speak, Rah?" asks Mochlos quietly. He is not ready to let the guard above know that the boy is conscious.
"Can speak," says Rah softly. The deep tone of his wounded voice is surprisingly sweet in Mochlos' ears.
"There is that bedroom rumble I have been waiting to hear," smiles Mochlos, setting a hand on Rah's wrist. "You are going to thrive, handsome. Do you understand me?"
"Ya, can hear," says Rah. "Priest, he save his Rah, no?"
"I did my best, but magick can only go so far. Now you will be thirsty, but you must drink slowly. Awiti, keep an eye out for the soldier."
Mochlos lifts a small gourd to Rah's lips. "Easy now."
But Rah's hands are up. He snatches the gourd from Mochlos with surprising strength and gulps the entirety.
"You look a mess, Rah," says Mochlos, pushing a tendril of curls out of the boy's eyes. "Do you remember anything about the beating?"

"Head hurt," says Rah, "And here," he puts a hand over his ribs, "And here," and then on his hip. He looks down and sees a poultice there. "Cut," he says.

"You remember?" asks Mochlos again, peering at him in the lamplight. "What do you remember, Rah. Help me now, for the Wolf will come and he will want to know, precisely, and we must have answers."

Rah touches his head. "No crown." He begins scratching at the scabs there and Mochlos quickly snatches his wrist away.

"No, you must leave those to heal. I have put strong medicine on your wounds, but you cannot touch. You understand?"

"Ya, no touch."

"Who hurt you, Rah. What can you tell me? Did it happen during your capture, or here, in the palace. They tell me you tried to escape."

"Rah is no try escape," pouts Rah. "How can escape? Is no window. No light. Put Rah in dark. Shut Rah in. Rah is crazy try get out. Scratch, bite walls. No good. Rah is yell, loud. Call for Wolf. Know Wolf is here. Know he come to Rah if Rah is need him. Rah can no stand this dark box like tomb." The boy has begun to shiver. Mochlos instinctively pulls a sheepskin over his shoulders.

"There now, easy. It is all over. No one will hurt you again. But who put you in the box, Rah? Was it the men who captured you? Or someone here at the palace?"

"One man, he call him Dav-eeoos. Rah remember. Two men look like be brother. One name Mall-eeoos. One Dav-eeoos."

"They told us they put you in the soldier's brig, and that you tried to escape through a high window."

"No brig. What this brig? Put Rah in dark box. No light. Rah is scream so hard no more can talk. Then they come, take Rah up, up. Rah is think, they take to Queen! Is queen chamber. But is no queen. Man with limp he live there now. Dress like general. He ask Rah lot of question. Ask about Wolf. Where is Wolf? What Wolf going to do? Rah can no answer. Never talk Wolf here."

Rah's voice has become quiet. He looks away, so that to Mochlos his right eye is swimming in a blood red tear. Mochlos remains silent, watching the boy's face. A burr has begun in his throat, a kitten's flat-eared defense.

"There is more to this story, isn't there, Rah?" Mochlos offers the boy a second gourd of water, which Awiti has fetched as they speak. This time Rah refuses it. His Adam's apple bobs. His lip lifts in a weak snarl.

"Tell your priest, Rah. If they have defiled you…" Mochlos is sitting beside the boy on his pallet, but his blood has all flushed to his feet. His head swims, and Awiti, seeing her master's distress, steadies him with a hand on his shoulder.

"Ya, de-file. Hit Rah. And Rah is angry. Rah fight. Everybody think Rah can no fight, too pretty. No! Rah can fight. First man, is one Rah bite before. Rah put him on his back, almost have teeth in throat," he puts his left palm on his own throat, "Here, but second man, he hit Rah with something hard. On head. Hit again here," he covers his ribs gently with the same hand. "Pull Rah off this man Rah is want to kill. Too many men. They tie Rah up. Leave with this Ganus Destroying."

"Ganus the Destroyer," Mochlos flicks a look at Awiti, who nods.

"Ya, that one. And other one. He look nice. I think maybe he help Rah. But he do what this Ganus Destroying say." Rah looks down at his hip, "Everything he say."

"And what did-" Mochlos begins.

"The crown," Awiti interrupts suddenly, pressing her fingers into Mochlos' shoulder. "What has become of the crown?" she whispers in Mochlos' ear.

Mochlos pats her hand. "Quite right. Who took your crown, Rah? Were you still wearing it when they took you to Ganus?"

"This Dav-eoos, he try to take but can no do. He get angry, he pull. Rah is bleed. Then he say, 'I tell Ganus we found like this.'"

For a moment Mochlos allows himself to picture Rah, bleeding profusely from a ring around his scalp, the circlet loose but still intact. The image, crimson streams of blood dripping down his pale face, running into the fox-brush brows, into his eyes, into the soft bristles of his immature beard, is horrific.

"There won't be a scalp left attached to a Greek head on this island," Mochlos rubs his own stubble. "Nor likely to me, for allowing this to happen."

But Rah only frowns at him, and reaches to scratch at the scabs in his hair.

"Leave them!" Mochlos snatches his wrist a second time. "It itches because it is healing. In a day or so you'll see, Awiti will wash your head and they will begin to fall off on their own. No more itch. And perhaps no scars."

"Ya, he take Rah to this Ganus Destroying. He say, 'First we bring to Hecuba. She take out. And they take Rah to this Hecuba. Look old but strong. Smell bad too. She take Rah crown, and this Dav-eeoos he say I give you half when we sell. But you tell, I kill you. She say, hah, you no kill Hecuba. Hecuba kill you first, with curse. But Dav-eeoos he no believe in curse. Then they take Rah to Ganus Destroying."

Rah closes his eyes, presses the heels of his hands to his temples. "Can no more talk. No want to talk this. Rah head hurt."

"This is enough for now," Mochlos gentles Rah's head back to the duck down pillow. He pulls the sheepskin up to the boy's chin. He looks up at Awiti. "It is time we moved him to the House of the Moon. He cannot fully recover in this dark hole."

Half way to the spot where Rush left Davius the man he released with orders to stoke his fire is still hacking his way up the deer path. When Stentos sees Rush coming down to meet him from the west he falls on his knees in fear. For how could a child, let alone a man the size of this one, move through this jungle like a leopard, without lifting an axe to clear his way? How did this man beat him to the fire? And then he sees three Greek uniforms following Rush in formation. It is the Ionian and the twins Adrastos and Agapias. And no wonder, for it is no secret that the Ionian hates Greece, and the twins are half-breeds. Now he will take my head, thinks Stentos, imagining the legendary crescent blades coming at his throat from both directions. He drops his chin to his chest, sinks to his haunches.

"Rise," says Rush, and Stentos, stunned, lifts himself to his feet. He is still holding his torch. "Get behind me with that," Rush barks, shoving the man past him into Typhus. "Let us find that egg." And striding off the hacked path that Stentos was making, he leads the four Greek soldiers down an invisible trail through softer vegetation not far from but parallel to the old deer run. Presently the moans of Davius can be heard to their right. Rush nods to Stentos.

"Now cut him loose and take him back to the palace with you. And remember, you are alive because you are mine. You will follow my orders within the palace from here on. I cannot rescue the Rah from a Greek army singlehanded, but I can breach that citadel as easily as a monkey climbs in and out of a tree unseen, and find you in your bed."

Stentos lopes off in the direction of the moans. Typhus, unsure of what is expected of him, remains planted behind Rush, the twins gathered together beside him.

"You will go straight to Ganus tonight. You will give him this message. 'I am marked by the Terror. You have what is his. Everything done to what is his will be meted out to you with greater zest. Send the Grain God of Knossos to Malia, where the Terror's army is gathering, or he will deal with you without his army. There is your choice: die on the battlefield, or in your bed. Tell him to send you back to me with his answer tomorrow."

Typhus swallows. "I am your servant."

"You think he will cut you down for wearing my mark?" Rush scoffs. "Nay, he will hear you out and have much to retort. He is an arrogant fool but he is a general. He will put you to the task of communicating his bloviate to me. And while he is busying himself with talk, I will take what is mine."

Typhus gives Rush a crisp military bow and moves to descend the hill. But Rush lays a hand on his shoulder first, halting him. His fingers have instantly found nerves in the Ionian's neck he did not know he owned, nerves that send bolts of pain down his arm and up into his skull.

"You are my spy now," whispers Rush into his ear, "Do not dare return to me without the condition and location of my property. Do not dare to return to me without finding a means of improving it before you do return."

"I will do all you ask, Master," answers the Ionian, "You have my life in ransom."

CHAPTER TWENTY NINE

Davius calls for the surgeon upon his return to the palace barracks. His head is hammering like a stone mason's mallet from the blow to his temple and he is prepared to speak to Ganus in spite of it. But he can barely put together a thought with his dislocated shoulder. There is no respite, no throb. It is as constant and sickening as a breach birth. He takes a good long draught of the surgeon's strongest mead and cries out in agony nevertheless when the joint pops back into place. Then, with his arm in a sling and Stentos as support, he reports to the General in the Queen's megaron.

"He came at us from out of nowhere," says Davius, panting and intoxicated from his encounter, now that it is a memory. "He took down two of my men from behind, as we were making our way to his camp! He told me who I am, my mother, my father, he is like a spirit! He knows everything, General, he knows that the Cretan god-slave is in your possession, and I suspect he knows that he has been beaten," Davius flinches at the thought.

Ganus nods. "Well, that is the point, isn't it? That he knows we have him? We did not catch him for ourselves, but to barter with," he hooks his thumbs in his weapons belt and puffs his chest. "It is as I planned. Guards, bring me the second captain, Typhus. I understand he, too, met the Assassin, and was given a message to return to me."

"Sir, there is no bartering with that-" begins Davius.
"Nonsense. Everyone has their price," Ganus gives Davius a pat on his good shoulder, which nevertheless sends a fresh shock of pain through his injured one. "Good work, is it Davius? I will remember the name. It is not every captain can say he met the Terror of the Aegean on level ground and lived." He waves Stentos off, and the two leave just as Typhus is escorted in.

After the second interview Ganus turns to his lieutenant.
"Well, what say you now, Marius? We have him! We have him by the nether hairs!" Ganus spouts.
"I don't see how-" begins Marius, offering Ganus a cup of wine from the case the boy, Clovis, brought him.
"No, of course you wouldn't, Marius, it is the thing that makes one a general." He taps his own temple with an index finger. "It's what's up here. The man is done with killing, don't you see? It gets him nowhere. We stood firm. We will not be cowed. And so he sent us back our troops with a message! Negotiations have begun! I have forced him into it."
"But Sir, his … property… is damaged. How can we negotiate with damaged goods?" asks Marius, pouring himself a cup.
All this while the boy, Clovis, stands at attention at the door, waiting on the General. It is difficult for him to hold back a giggle as the two officers pour themselves their own wine in Minoan cups, thinking that they drink what the Terror removed to his own stores almost two years ago. It is even harder for him not to chuckle out loud as the two schemers expose their stratagem in front of his most devoted mole. He bites his cheek to hold back his mirth, and must draw forth into his mind the image of the Assassin in the starlight, atop this very roof. That towering, bull-chested dynamo, more like Hades than Hades himself. More fearful. Not that old man with his curly locks and long beard, leaning on his staff in a senator's robe, as he is portrayed in his statues, but sleek as night itself, wrapped in black muslin death rags, that horsetail braid bisecting his great

wall of a back, his close-trimmed beard silhouetting his strong jaw, and his pitch eyes, glittering, predator eyes.

That image is enough to sober Clovis, who can now stand erect, if shivering, ears open, mind alert. I will recall every word, thinks Clovis.

"He has no means of assessing 'damage' my young friend," says Ganus. "Or do you suppose he can enter this fortress and see for himself the condition of his creature? No, my men are my men and will die for me. And though he may well cut them down on that hill, he will not set one foot inside our perimeter, that is for certain. Nor learn of anything occurring within it which I do not chose to disclose to him. Therefore we will move the creature into the House of the Moon, as the priest suggests, to further his recovery, and continue our little game of cat and mouse with that monster. You see, Marius, if we keep the creature here, in the palace, he will see it as an act of war. But if we can prove to him that the Minoan god-slave is returned to his House, in accordance to his own and his priest's desires, then there is no war. It is only a matter of time before he begins to realize that he will never have him by force. That the creature desires to remain here, where he was made. And then we have him! Compromise! He may have Malia and Gornia, but Knossos? Knossos is ours! And as long as Knossos is ours, his Grain God may remain our guest, secure in his own realm, and under Greek protection!"

The big Ionian has returned to the barracks. The twins assault him instantly with questions. What did the General say to his mark? Are we to return tonight with a message?

But Typhus merely shoos them off. "I am sworn to silence, else I will lose my tongue."

"But the Terror said nothing of silence!" quips Adrastos, which causes Agapias to cuff him on the back, for the few men milling about in the barracks are within earshot.

"Say nothing of the Terror!" hisses Agapias.

"The mark says all that needs be said, boy," sighs the Ionian.

"Now leave me to a few hours' sleep this night. I have much to accomplish tomorrow."

And Typhus removes his leather helmet, loosens his belt and lies back on his pallet to wait for sleep. But he can find no peace. His mind races, not with Ganus' retort to the Assassin, which is enough in itself to get him killed as he stands to deliver it, but with his assignment from the Assassin himself. For what is he to do, to improve the Grain God's circumstances? He congratulates himself for informing the General that the Terror would require his inspection of the creature before returning to him with any messages from Greece. And even Ganus, who is so convoluted and obdurate in his arguments and mechanisms of logic, who is so inflicted with the love of his own anus that his head could be said to be on its third revolution up it, even Ganus could find no reason to deny him that. For who would engage in bartering without being assured that the thing he desires is still intact? Not that Ganus could be made to believe that his own man would admit to the Terror that the creature was impaired, incapacitated, damaged by Ganus' own hand.

"Conceit has its advantages," mutters Typhus, turning onto his side and punching his cloak into a pillow. And shortly he is fast asleep, a soldier who takes his respite when he can get it.

But in only a few hours Typhus awakens and pads past his sleeping comrades toward the great hall. He arrives to see that Mochlos is stalled at the top of the ladder into the bull pit, at the tail end of an exchange with the guard, who, for some reason, has chosen to practice his clearly exceptional skills as a pig-headed prick on the priest.

'Why not bring that pretty bit of black meat up with you, priest, and let me have a go while you're gone? She a virgin? I'll wager she's tight as a crab's-"

Typhus comes up behind the man and slaps him in the back of the head with an open hand, sending his leather helmet into the pit. The man nearly loses his balance and follows his headpiece.

"Jackass," Typhus takes the top of the ladder in his left hand, securing the priest.

"Captain!" the man squares up and salutes.

"I will take this watch." Typhus looks him dead on. The man steps back, nearly falling into the pit a second time.

"Your face!" the man points at the wound on his cheek. "You … you…"

"Get out, ape-shit!" Typhus booms, no longer concerned if he should wake the entire fortress. For what should it matter? He is the Assassin's now. He will do as he has been ordered by the man that could eat Ganus for breakfast, or he will die.

The soldier grabs his weapons belt, which he has for some reason taken off his person and left on the ground, and scuttles away, his sword clattering on the stone floor behind him.

Typhus uses his free hand to help Mochlos up off the top rung of the ladder and clear the side of the pit.

"I am grateful for your arrival, Sir," Mochlos begins, puffing, for the climb up the ladder, carrying the supplies basket, has winded him. "I am not a man used to sleeping on a pallet in what was not so long ago a ditch for beasts, and that young man has given me the same trouble every morning that I rise from this pit to fetch provisions for the Rah. But she is not mine to give, you see, she is-"

"She is his," says Typhus softly, as the priest raises his eyes to see the wound that so silenced the soldier.

"Praise heaven," Mochlos takes a deep breath. "Praise, heaven."

"And you, and I, and the-" he nods toward the pit, "Creature. And all of Crete. I am sent to improve the godslave's circumstances, and to report on his condition. I have found a master worth pleasing, and I intend to do exactly that. I am taking you to the House of the Moon."

"Surely you have not secured the General's permission?" Mochlos whispers hopefully.

"What do I need of the General and his permissions?" spits the Ionian through clenched teeth. "I have been told to improve the creature's circumstances, and I will do so, or die in the effort." He offers a hollow laugh. "Or do you think I should

fear Ganus so long as I wear this mark on my cheek?"
"No, I don't suppose you need fear anyone but the one who made it," Mochlos' fingers have found his own scar. "Very well then, I shall prepare him. We will need some sort of winch."
"I understand he is quite light," Typhus answers as he begins his decent down the ladder. "I will carry him up myself."
But in fact Typhus has the general's permission for the move, in truth, he has been ordered to move the 'creature' to the House of the Moon immediately. And even the General, who commonly views anyone else's suggestions as a personal slight, and at best sees all ideas not blossoming forth from the muck of his own musings inferior, could understand the good of putting this task upon the very man whom the Terror marked. For who could be a better witness than the one he trusted with the Tear? A lie would soon cost him the eye above it.
But Typhus is keenly aware that his first job is to inspect his master's property. This can hardly be done in the near dark of the pit. Typhus descends the ladder, the priest eagerly descending behind him. He will leave no man, not even one marked with the assassin's Tear, alone with Rah, though what he could do to stop this brute from doing whatever he wished is beyond him at the moment. He would think of something.
But Typhus' eyes alight first upon Awiti, not Rah. The concubine is just awakening on her own pallet, which is nearer the base of the ladder. She shades her eyes with the flat of her hand as Mochlos' lamp light the soldier from behind, turning him into a familiar silhouette.
Awiti has scrambled off her pallet in an attempt to dart into the farthest and blackest corner of the pit but the big man's hand closes on her upper arm.
"Not so fast, not so fast now," says Typhus quietly. "I am only here to see that the Rah is safe and to move him back to his home."
Mochlos quickly steps around Typhus, lifting his lamp to illuminate the Ionian's face.
"Oh," Awiti looks up at Typhus, and her fears melt. "I thought

you were he," she murmurs. "You're shape-" she trails off.
Typhus is studying her face. "You have seen him." It is a statement. The girl nods, reflexively hugging her robe about her. "And he, you," Typhus smiles. "But only briefly."
"How do you tell all this?" Mochlos is looking at the Ionian with newfound respect.
"A man may tell much by watching a woman carefully," Typhus grunts. "Most don't," he continues offhandedly, "That was not fright but terror… she had seen such a shadow before. I am a big man, but there is one as big. Bigger. She covers herself, as if she had been exposed to him, yet a woman taken is not so modest before the same man."
"Your powers of deduction are considerable," Mochlos peers at him. "She did have a frightful encounter." He considers his words. Then makes a decision, "In Babylon."
"Babylon?" Typhus turns to him. "Ah, I see. Your story-"
"I think it safe enough to tell a bit more true a tale," Mochlos offers a tigerish grin, "To one who wears the mark. Come, let us create a hammock of these linens. He is indeed as light as air, but that rib is not healed. And I will tell you our story on our way to the House of the Moon."

CHAPTER THIRTY

She has been mad for many years.

And while she understands her world is not the world as others see it, she also realizes that her madness has made her wise, wiser than any who look upon her with pity, with suspicion, with hate. And so she is in love with her madness, and calls it power.

She is here for her magic, and her magic is divination, the conjuring of ghosts and phantoms. And of course, the black art.

Until now she worked for Ganus the Destroyer exclusively. But the crown! The emerald! Woven into the head of the creature who claimed that *her* moon, was *his* mother. Woven into the head of the beloved of the Terror. This was providence, that this treasure should come to her. Should walk right into her hovel, like a thousand golden arrows, sent skyward over the course of a thousand moons, finally returning to her in an enemy's corpse.

Hecate has long heard of the legend of the Grain God of Knossos, the boy-dancer who came to Crete to profit that kingdom and then destroy it. In Greece, among those of her kind, it was believed that he had been killed in the cataclysm, buried under the mud and ash, or washed away in the flood waters. But energy never dies, and already he has reappeared, just as a curse is never really broken, though a good witch can change its direction.

Oh Hecate! she thinks to herself, for to herself she is a goddess and so she prays to herself. Oh, Hecate, your efforts in the arts against the Black Assassin have not been in vain. You will be richly rewarded by the Destroyer. Here is the consummation of your work! Now the thing that can put the Assassin in Ganus' power has fallen into his hands! All because of you! All because of your magic. And in proof, you are already rewarded, before you have even stood before Ganus to demand your reward. Nay, the spirits of the underworld have rewarded us! Look here, look here, his golden hair is still attached. We shall not even wash away his blood, which will be precious against him in magic. And she places the circlet of the Rah on her own grey head and turns and preens like a bird of prey in her mirror. Her long, broken nails comb the strands of yellow hair into her coarse locks, which fall down her back in a twisted mass. Her gnarled fingers stroke the emerald.

His hair is my hair. His blood is my blood. His beauty my beauty. His crown, now my crown. All things are righted at last. For am I not the true offspring of the Moon?

Hecate smiles, a gruesome toothless smile. But the thing that smiles back at her in the mirror is a vision, a beauty. She licks a finger and polishes the blood-caked emerald with her spittle, and then she pulls her mantle up over her head, covering her prize.

The threesome moving along the Thoroughfare toward the House of the Moon are given little notice by the soldiers in the street or the workmen rebuilding the highway and the bridge. A small, covered donkey cart is all that is needed to transport Rah, the concubine and the priest's few belongings. As the little band rounds the last turn in the road a sun shower dampens the dusty street, as if the villa itself has chosen to lay down a carpet before its master. The newly stuccoed southern walls of the house gleam happily in the misty morning light.

"There now, you see?" Mochlos looks over the donkey's back at Typhus. "My home is nearly completed. And I have managed to spare it some of the sobriety of the Greek military staging hall. We have our columns back, our portico, our rooftop balustrade. I've even imported several Minoan statues from Attica for the garden courtyard."

Mochlos prattles on, while Typhus, leading the donkey in hand, ignores his banter and considers his next meeting with the assassin. On the positive side of the equation, he will be able to tell him that he has fulfilled his duty as a messenger. Not a word of the assassin's missive did he fail to deliver. Secondly, he could inform his new master that he had inspected his property and could report of every injury and his exact condition.

Granted this was also a damned dangerous position to be in, since the Grain God of Knossos, while quite breathtaking even in his current condition, was clearly not what he was when last the Assassin laid eyes on him.

Typhus himself had not laid eye upon the creature until he stepped down from the ladder onto the floor of the pit, and the priest, coming behind him, held up the lamp toward the far corner. His first glance cost him a shock, and he jumped back, bumping into the lamp and the priest, for what he saw looked for all intents and purposes to be hanging in midair, a headless ghost, arms extended up and out like the wings of a crane, and standing on the toes of one foot. He was not, as Typhus expected, lying on his pallet. And then the head, which had been tipped forward, rose, rose so slowly that Typhus had to blink and blink again to clear his vision for what kind of creature could stand thus? Balance thus? And why? And now that head came up, ringed with hair so pale as to seem phosphorescent, and in the lamp light, those eyes! Typhus flinched a second time.

"Easy, man," came the priest's voice behind him, "It is only he. He is impossible to keep abed, and has been pushing his body and his brain like this, always to their limits, since he awoke."

It got no easier to look upon the Rah when he (slowly! so slowly) came to rest again upon the pads of both feet and moved soundless across the straw to scrutinize his intruder. His eyes were rimmed in blood from his beating, the lids blue-black, and the inner white of one crimson, giving him a strange, lop-sided look. But it was the not bruising, so clear and defined on such a pale face, that gave the big Ionian a start. It was the eyes themselves. They were silver. Not blue, nor grey, which he had heard of, and even seen himself on the battlefield, but silver, as silver as a leerfish, with spokes of gold emanating from the pupils, like some metalwork statue of the Egyptian lioness, warrior goddess of the sun, come full to life.

"What is this?" whispers Typhus. "This is no Minoan god-slave! The terror has captured Bastet!"

"Rah is no Bastet," says Rah, glowering up into the big man's face. His brows and ears are drawn back, though his lips are twisted in puzzlement. "Who this man, priest? They send more man to beat Rah?" He moves to Typhus left, looking him up and down as if considering the purchase of a slave. He steps behind him, circles back to stand under his gaze, folds his arms over his chest and meets the man's eyes with stubborn hostility. All this while Typhus has remained motionless.

"Big man," says Rah, "Big like Wolf." He spits suddenly at Typhus' feet. "But is no Wolf. Wolf is kill man like you easy." He slaps Typhus' bare belly with the back of his hand. "Need be more than big, to kill Wolf. Better be lot of big man. Army big man." He shrugs, giving the stunned Typhus another back-handed slap, this time on his chest. "Even then, probably you die. Every man touch Rah, Wolf is kill." He lifts his chin at the Ionian, levels his gaze.

He is going to spit on me again, thinks Typhus, and wincing, readies himself to take the insult silently.

But Mochlos has drawn Rah back and stepped between the two. He turns to Rah.

"No, Rah, this man is also owned by the Wolf. Look at the mark, freshly made," and he points to Typhus cheek.

"Ya, people they all want to be Wolf people, maybe," says Rah, "Maybe he do this himself, no? Can cut self too."

"Who would dare, Rah?" asks Mochlos softly, and now he

wonders, has the boy ever even considered it? That no one lives with the mark unless he is the assassin's property? No. Probably not. That brain cannot follow a thought out of a doorway, unless it is bouncing on a woman's rump, or dancing on a colt's. "No one would dare," he assures Rah.

"Ya someone sometime dare, Priest," says Rah. "Hor-oos. He dare. Sometime maybe sometime dare again, so can come make priest think he is friend of Rah, kill Rah. Big brains," Rah chucks his chin at Mochlos, "You think of that?"

Mochlos frowns. "Be that as it may," he turns back to Typhus, "This man is here to take us to the House of the Moon. You want to go to the House of the Moon, do you not? You cannot climb that ladder with your broken ribs, nor can I carry you. Typhus will carry you up."

"Typhoos no touch Rah," says Rah, his lip quivering in a snarl. "Rah can climb. Use one hand. You watch, Priest, maybe learn something." And before Mochlos can intervene Rah has stepped onto the bottom rung of the ladder and, using only his right hand and his extraordinary balance, begins to climb to the top.

When he is half way up he calls down to Mochlos, "Come, Priest, we go home now."

Now, leading the donkey cart over the cleared Thoroughfare toward the House of the Moon, Typhus sighs to himself as the priest continues to prattle on about his newly renovated and redecorated villa. He considers the creature's condition, and what he will tell the Assassin.

His eyes, Lord, were blackened, both. And the priest tells me that his jaw was dislocated. His scalp is shedding blue scabs, the result of someone attempting to yank the band of golden mail woven into his hair out without bothering to unbraid it. Nevertheless he has such an unruly and thick mane of hair that the loss of several handfuls of it has done little to impair his appearance, and the priest tells me (for the creature will not allow me to come close enough to see for myself) that beneath the scabs the hair is growing in dark blonde. Then there is the cut on his right cheek, a single stitch was all that was required to knit it together. It has healed into a small scar, tear-shaped in its appearance, not unlike….no, I will not say that. Let him come to that conclusion himself. And the cleft along his right hipbone, which one should only see if he is naked. Now that was a gash to the bone, but it was stitched up expertly, and has created a…well, a dimple, like those that appear now on his cheek …It is, well you will wonder how I saw it myself, which I did, in fact, and that is because, unless the priest cajoles him into a loincloth or his beloved Minoan skirt, he prefers to be naked. The scar, it is not…unattractive. I know no other way of saying it. It draws the eye…

I tread deep waters here. Shall I tell him that the priest fears that the beating has changed more than his physical appearance? That he says he is no longer the innocent strangeling he once was, but more quickly hostile and chronically suspicious? No. That is not my business. That is up to the priest. For who is to say what a beating did or did not do to a disposition? It may be that he was bent that way from the beginning, and only just now, like the wildcat emerges from the kitten, transforming into a temperament which to be sure his cat-like appearance firmly dictated.

"Bah!" comes the dusky voice of the creature behind him. He has had enough of the donkey cart and is struggling to climb over the front and onto the donkey's back. But his cracked ribs will have none of it. He falls back from the edge, despondent.

"How long Rah can no ride, Priest?"

"I said, 'give him a good going over,'" Ganus the Destroyer puffs, as he swallows the last of the fine Minoan wine from the cask at his feet. "Good heavens, we are out of wine. Send a boy out to my ship, Marius. I've a cask there from Mycenae that will do. Though I doubt it will compare to this," he lifts his empty cup, burps.

"Did you not see his condition after he was 'gone over', Sir? Can we say for a fact that it was not your orders which is to say,

your own hand, that beat him? Cut him? Marred him?"
"We need say nothing of the kind," Ganus sits down a bit too hard on the Queen's bed. Something beneath the mattress snaps, like a cat bone. "We will simply blame it all on that what's his name. Davidae. Davius. The one with a head like an egg. We will return the messenger with his head. That should settle it." He smoothes his moustache.
"Sir it … well it surprises me that a man like yourself has not yet taken a good look at the creature. See for yourself what all the fuss is about. After all, this Minoan god-slave has the Terror's attention. More than that, his protection! Possibly, if one could say he had one, his heart!"
Ganus, mildly inebriated, blurts out a single guffaw. "Heart? That's a good one, Marius. That's rich!" He allows himself a second guffaw.
"But did you evaluate him yourself sir? Did you-"
"Careful, Marius," Ganus snaps, suddenly sober. "You tread on dangerous waters when you question your commander." He sets the cup on the floor, lies back on the bed, his head on his personal pillow, throws one arm over his forehead. "No I did not. I am not such a fool as that. Would I walk into the same trap that my enemy has fallen in? I was born with an exceptional brain, Marius. It's time you noted it. I scarcely looked upon him. Kept my back to him. When he refused to answer my questions, I sent him away with two guards to loosen his tongue."
Marius sighs. Tries again. "Sir, if I may ask, when he came to you, was he wounded? Or was it the work of the guards."
"I've no idea," answers Ganus calmly. "Nor do I wish to. We shall blame it on that Davidae and that is final. Now go and have him beheaded, will you? There's a good boy. Give the head to the messenger for his meeting tonight, and all will be well."

It was his blood, his blood that she needed. An impossible goal, for under what circumstances could she possibly acquire

it? And then, by a monumental quirk of fate, she obtained it!
Hecate paces before her mirror, waiting for the transformation to take place. Blood takes time. It is not instantaneous. She prided herself on her patience, and on her ability to see things at every angle. She was open-minded. She understood that there was a heaven and a hell but also that we made our own heaven and our own hell. She saw with her special gift of open-mindedness that she was a creature, a creation of her mother, the moon, but also that she was a goddess and that she could manifest her own destiny simply by believing in it. She believed in her magic, though she understood that she depended upon fate. She threw her dove bones, she read them daily for guidance. Yet reading them over and over, day by day, sometimes hour by hour, she was awash with confusion. For all of it was true, therefore, truth was a fraud. Just as she suspected. She knew all, by knowing nothing.
Hecate is a furnace of envy, a monumental explosion of hate and greed, but she sees herself as she chooses to believe she is: tolerant and patient, clever and judicious. Only now this mirror, it was mocking her. The spell of her self-delusion was broken. She was no longer beautiful, as she stroked the golden hairs into her own grey and matted locks. She saw her left eye, dulled by the white cloud of age-blindness. Where were the boy's blue-green orbs? Still in his head, and these in hers. The truth was superimposing itself over her grandiose illusions. In a fit of fury she threw her fist of dove bones at the mirror. Truth was her enemy. Confusion her friend. She had been so careful. Had she left something out?
She returned to the moment when all of her wishes seemed at the brink of discovery.
They dragged him in, twisting and snarling like a wildcat. Already Davius had bloodied him, attempting in vain to yank the golden circlet from his radiant head. Rivulets of scarlet trickled from his scalp over his forehead and into his eyes. Those eyes! She would have ruled the world with those eyes alone! Her first impulse was to spit into them. But she was a

creature of premeditation and craft, deliberation and study. Impulse was her enemy. She swallowed her spit and drew closer, unable despite her deliberate restraint to keep her fingers from reaching out to touch. His body is shaking with rage. But his rage only makes him more beautiful, so lean and well-muscled! The golden hairs pointing like an arrow from his solar plexus to his loins are shimmering in the lamplight with his tremors. Her eyes follow the movement involuntarily. She is fascinated by so much gold. Golden down. Golden eyes, shot with blue. Golden skin, golden hairs along the apricot-golden arms. The boy is dipped in gold. In sunlight and honey.

Davius is talking. Spouting his threats and his promises. I cannot remove it! He gives the crown a brutal yank. The boy howls in pain. But Hecate cares nothing for Davius' lies. She hears only that intoxicating howl, that wildcat singing down in that pretty throat. Look at him! Why him, Mother, and not me? His mouth is bowed like a harp, his teeth milk-white pearls. He has the face of a cat.

Her fingers have found his cheek.

And he turns and snaps, faster than sound. Pain! She snatches her hand away. He has drawn blood. The blue-green eyes are riveted to hers. His chest is heaving and despite the pain she can only stare at him, glistening with sweat and rage, panting like a fox.

He spits, and something more than spittle hits her good eye. It is the tip of her ring finger.

Rage swells up in her like a tide. Her hand, the injured hand, becomes a claw, she strikes at that dazzling face, feels her sharpened nail open a gash in his cheek. But she is shoved back. She takes two awkward steps, trips on her skirt, falls back onto her fleshless buttocks. Davius has intercepted her rage, and now she can only rage at herself. She puts the wounded finger in her mouth in vain. The acrid blood gushes. Looking about for something to tie it off she spots the strings of his skirt. Yes, good magic! She grabs at them from the floor. The creature leaps backward, the skirt falls to his feet and the tie is in her hands. Quickly she binds her finger with the white linen cord, and rising to her feet, while Mulius subdues the creature, pinning his arms behind him, and Davius is distracted, she slips her uninjured hand into her skirt and finds her sliver boline and palms it. I will have his blood!

And before the men can stop her she has lunged for him, striking him dead on with the point of the blade into his right hip. The tip sinks through muscle and strikes bone. The creature howls. Davius slaps her hand away, the boline flies. No matter. I will find it and it will be bloodied.

"Enough!" shouts Davius, yanking the witch to her feet. Mulius has bent the creature over her alter, which is the stump of an elm, the top smoothed and waxed to a gleaming sheen. It stands in the center of her tiny room. Mulius pins the creature against the stump with two hands, one holding him by the scruff, the other planted on the dish of his sacrum. Davius has found the skirt and stuffed it into the creature's mouth, gagging him. Rah makes a muffled moan of indignation behind the cloth of his skirt.

"Now!" hisses Davius.

Her fury soothed by the creature's humiliating posture, Hecate positions herself at his crown, where she cannot be bitten, at least not while Mulius holds his scruff fast, and begins the tedious task of unbraiding the mail circlet from his head. When it is finished Davius instructs her to hide it well, and threatens her should she attempt to keep it for herself.

But it is not the crown she is after.

It is the creature's blood.

Of course, it would have been better to have spilt more of it, but magic does not weigh in ounces. The dried ichor on the end of the boline would suffice. She left the palace at midnight and walked up into the woods to a spot she had found one afternoon looking for magical herbs. There was a broken stone archway behind which a little hut sat, as if waiting for her. Beyond it were burial mounds, old ones. The brambles were pouring over the stone walls, but the cemetery itself was clear of trees, giving her a wide view of the heavens. The moon was at the half and waxing. Perfect! She found a spot that might have once been a small garden not far from the hut, and took care to draw a circle of protection with a stick before she started. She had brought with her candles (two red, two black), and she lit these now with her torch before setting them into the soft earth. Then she began drawing down the moon.

She had made no mistakes, she had been careful and precise. But now the moon was nearly at the full and the spell had yet to take its effect.

She was waiting two things.

That the creature should die. And that she should take his place.

CHAPTER THIRTY ONE

"And how fairs my little Thais of Agina?" Rush whispers into the sleeping ear of the boy who is now named Clovis. His beard is growing out, for his business in Mycenae is finished, and he leans close enough to the youth to tickle his jaw with it. Slapping at the bristles, Clovis comes awake with a start, his cranium nearly colliding with the assassin's chin. But Rush is too fast for him. He has pinned the boy by his throat to his bed, as much to avoid a collision as to keep him from crying out in fright.

"Master!" squeaks Clovis, turning his eyes about in his frozen head to look for observers. But the seven other men in his chamber are fast asleep, silent as the dead. Which is odd, thinks Clovis, for at least four of them snore like the devil, and so how could it be that none of these are snoring tonight?

"No need to concern yourself that we might be overheard," purrs Rush into the lad's ear. "So long as we keep our voices down. Now sit up, little Thais, there's a good boy. And tell me what you know."

And so Thais reports to his new master what he has heard of the plans of the Destroyer, how he will bargain with the Terror, drawing a line across the island north to south just east of Knossos, so that the assassin should have the larger quarter, and he, that is, Greece, the lesser.

"Is that so," murmurs Rush, who is standing now, arms crossed over his muslin wrapped chest, feet splayed. His hooded head is turned toward the east, where the window above Clovis' pallet looks out onto an overgrown courtyard.

"He will take Knossos, and I the rest. Malia, Gournia. Cyrus perhaps? Little more than a hole in the earth where a city once lay." He turns away from the window, takes a step, kicks the corpse of the man 'sleeping' nearest to Clovis off his pallet and onto the stone floor. The body rolls, cocooning itself in its cloak. Rush settles himself on the pallet across from Clovis, cross-legged and momentarily boyish.

"So he will give me back the lesser half of what is mine, which he has never taken from me in the first place."

"That is what he said, Sir," answers Clovis, who cannot keep his eyes from wandering over the bodies, still in their beds. Seven dead soldiers, and he sleeping like a babe among them, until the Assassin chose to wake him with a whisper in his ear. He gulps the spit that has collected in his mouth and forces himself to regard the thing that did this. One heavily lashed and downward sloping eye returns his gaze.

"Master, they will know you are here-" begins Clovis.

"Of course," answers the hood. That obsidian eye seems to be reading something printed on the back of Clovis' skull. "Or do you think, little Thais, that there is another as good?" He lifts one hand and sweeps it over his work.

"But I still live," gulps Clovis. "They will know-"

"I do not kill children," answers Rush, as if this would have been obvious. "Nor beardless boys. That is the work of the impotent." He turns and lies back suddenly on the vacated pallet. The corpse in the cloak wrap lies beside him on the floor like a woman lying beside her husband, fast asleep in the knowledge of her safety at his side.

"I do not know that Ganus will see it thus," squeaks Clovis.

"Well," sighs Rush, who seems to be staring up at the ceiling, "He had better see it thus, little Thais of Agina. For he is fast running out of days to live." He draws one arm up to rest his head upon. Even wrapped in the black muslin shroud, the bicep is enormous, and for a moment Clovis' attention is lost on it. How many of mine would it take to compose one of those? he thinks. Dawn is breaking through the window above Clovis' pallet. Soon the barracks will be stirring. Soon men will come to see why C barracks has not stirred. Will they find the assassin here, lying back on a dead man's pallet like he was lying out in a field somewhere observing the stars?

"They will wake soon," whispers Clovis, for the assassin's silence is deafening.

"Awake," murmurs Rush, "They are hardly more effective, these Destroyers." He sighs again. "It baffles me," he adds, studying suddenly the thumb nail of his free hand. "The mind truly boggles with it, how the man has managed to convince himself he is a match for me." He sits up, shaking his head. "For *me*," his exposed eye is studious, sad. And he is on his feet. "No, I cannot bear it any longer." He turns to the window. "I shall have to pay him a visit." And he has leapt through the casement and disappeared, soundless as the dawn glow that follows in his wake.

At the House of the Moon, Rah has been moved to the new Tower. It rises from the flat rooftop, identical to his Tower at the House of Seven Cisterns, overlooking the sapphire sea to the north and the mountain to the south. At the end of a hall past Mochlos' apartments on the second floor, a stairwell rounds to the left, spiraling up to the third level. The stair leads to Rah's tower room, where a mural has been painted around the entirety of the curved wall. And like the tower room in Babylon, the interior walls here curve, though the exterior of the tower is rectangular. But here there is no Enlil standing on a mountain, blowing his golden breath down onto a lush barley field, nor does Ninlil, his consort, bend beneath his enormous phallus.

On this single, circular wall, Mochlos has commissioned a Mycenaean artist to depict the Moon Goddess ruling the tides. Here she is slapping her great tail against the beach, here she holds two writhing eels in each extended hand, and above, in the center of the domed ceiling, she is the moon, smiling down on her son.

The room has been furnished in blue and gold, embroidered drapes hiding an aperture in the north wall where a smaller room, barely large enough to lie down in, hides the tools of the high priest's trade.

Rah stands in his tower overlooking the city. The sun's rays are creeping like yellow fingers across the hills beyond, illuminating Mounts Juktas and Ida through a thin veil of mid-day clouds. The Thoroughfare is moving with slaves and workmen laboring to restore the bridge. Below him, the House of the Moon is empty but for the priest and his concubine. But Rah can imagine dancers practicing in the gymnasium, the laugher of Dimius and Akbar as the newer boys trip over their own feet attempting to imitate him, the giggling of the girls behind their hands as they watch. And he can imagine the yeasty smell Crispo's bread baking in the kitchens, can taste Ting Ya's sweetcakes on his tongue. One day soon he will also feel three new concubines curled against his body as he sleeps on a pallet made of stone with naught but a thin deerskin, two circles of bronze for chaining a slave hanging above.

The priest has done his best to emulate his first chamber as a slave-god at his insistence. There is a basin in the center of the room into which well water can be pumped, and about the walls are several trunks, some opened and overflowing with brightly colored costumes imported from Egypt, Mycenae, even Uruk. There are silks, embroidered and woven linens, feathered head pieces, beaded gloves, fur boots and belts of woven leather. On one wall is a low vanity, and upon it a jumble of face and body paints and brushes. Among them, four tiny decanters of his required perfumes: cherry, myrrh, lotus and hyssop. And across the room a large mirror made of polished bronze rests against the opposite wall.

Rah turns to stand before the mirror.

He has shaved the down from his cheeks and painted his face the color of spring grass. Aegean blue lines his jewel eyes, accentuating their cat-like upward tilt. He has rouged his lips. He is bathed and perfumed, and he wears a white Minoan skirt slung low on his hips so that the solid golden hoop that is his belt lies against his bare belly. The front of the skirt is taut, and skims his thighs, just long enough to cover his loincloth. The back of the garment hangs in folds for ease of movement, the hem brushing his calves. His scalp has healed, the blue scabs turning grey and flaking into his hair before Awiti dared comb them out. The hair coming in behind them is dark gold, creating a shadowy circlet around his head, and the emerald green circle he has painted between his brows appears to be connected to it, as if his crown had never been taken.

Rah studies the god-slave in the mirror for imperfection. He presses the fingers of his right hand into the dimple made by the witch's boline, the wound deliberately exposed by the low slung skirt. He raises his eyes to those of the cat-boy in the mirror. The whites are clear, free of bruising, but the irises are paler, the look less that of an innocent kitten, more that of a wildcat. There is wisdom in them, and secrets.

Rah lifts his chin and shakes back his mane of gold and platinum curls. Then he covers his golden body with a plain linen traveling cloak he has liberated from the priest's own trunk, slips down the stairs, past the priest's chamber, where Mochlos is enjoying a mid-day nap, and heads toward the palace.

At the Palace, soldiers have clearing the last of the bedding and debris of their two months occupation in the Great Hall. Lamps have been lit, although it is early barely noon. There is anticipation in the air, as the Destroyer has announced that there will be a general assembly of able-bodied warriors. He will be addressing them personally, and it is expected that he intends to offer them a fervid call to arms. This rumor was begun at the steward's level, as such things often are. It was the new boy, Clovis, who is said to have heard the Destroyer and his Lieutenant, Marius, discussing plans last night to march to Gournia, where the Terror has amassed his army. Despite the hubbub in the Great Hall, Clovis' bunkmates have not arisen, and the boy has bolted himself in his chamber, complaining of the ague.

"We are all stricken with it, this morning!" shouted the young steward behind the barred door. "We will quarantine ourselves until our infection has passed. You may leave us some cooling foods, citrus and other fruits, and water. But I dare not allow this malady out of our barracks, for you know as well as I that the General will have me skinned alive should I my negligence compromise the vigor of his army!"

The news of impending battle has not been met with the normal bravado and bluster of the Destroyer's men. It is not that the soldiers have not expected to at some point be called up to face the Terror's forces on the island. Battle was always anticipated. Open battle, in daylight, face to face with the enemy. But it is the picking off of sortie after sortie, night after night, up in that blasted hill, like an angler catching fish with a light that has sent a raw chill of reasonable fear through the men. For if a man can accomplish such a thing, is he likely to obey the proper rules of open battle?

Now it is mid-day and the men are growing anxious for their leader, who was expected to arrive in the Great Hall an hour ago. What is Ganus doing? He has been absent all morning, not even joining his men, as he regularly does, for breakfast. In fact, no one has seen him, nor Lieutenant Marius, for that matter, since they retired last night.

Down the hall, in the eastern most quadrant of the palace, the scene in the Queen's chamber is quite different than imagined in the minds of several thousand soldiers now gathered in the Great Hall. For Ganus is not preparing for his speech. Ganus is not preparing for war.

Ganus is not preparing for anything.

Earlier that morning, when the palace was still dreaming, he had had a visitor.

He had been dreaming of his favorite activity, which he rarely enjoyed these days, what with the harsh army foods he was forced to eat, all quite lazy in the gut, hard to put out the other end. But in his dream, he had just consumed a lovely meal of Greek barley cakes, goat cheese and honey to start, then a nice eel stew, topped off with a platter of fresh fruits: melons, peaches, pears, plums, halved and swimming in buttermilk. He had finished his meal and was just feeling the delightful rush of a full-on bowel movement coming, the kind that rushes all of the poisons out of your gut like a flash flood flushes a streambed, when that blasted black cow appeared, once again, to kick him (and now he is a boy of seven attempting to milk that black cow, against his mother's warnings) in the belly. And the food he has ingested is rushing in the opposite direction, towards its entry point.

Before Ganus can comprehend his predicament the black cow, now standing over him, earless and resolute, in the attitude of a man, bashes him in the temple with her fist.

Which is every bit as hard as a hoof.

Dazed and bewildered Ganus the Destroyer completes his dream into the fine imported linens which cover the Queen's mattress. Shitting the bed.

"Foul imbecile," remarks the cow, whose baritone speech rings with a peculiarly Hittite accent. She has moved away from the bed, and now stands on two legs, like a stone giant, near the half wall of the Queen's bath. She is hornless, she is upright. She is a man robed in black gauze like a mummy from the underworld. And she is strapped head to toe in weaponry.

It is the coward, the thief and liar, the fraud and deceiver, who has hit him from the shadows.

But the height of the man, the breadth of those shoulders, the nipped waist, the grace of his smallest movement….

Could it be possible? Has he met this man before?

Now sitting up in his own gaseous releases, Ganus reflects, unhurriedly, on this concept. His effluvia, in any case, keeps the man at bay.

There was the Seven Day Battle of Troy. He lost his left ring and pinky fingers in that one, and the ring he received from the King for his first ten years of service. The beast who took it was a Hittite giant with legs like tree trunks and the shoulders of a brown bear.

But the archer put an arrow in the man's back, which curtailed his onslaught, though it did not stop him from turning and hurling his axe into the archer's chest before he could nock another arrow, and then take the Destroyer's digits and ring as souvenirs.

Ganus groans. He was sure that the arrow had been treated with something evil, a poison.

Yet here stands his enemy. The brute who took his fingers. And once again, it is as if the man is spitting in his face from the moon.

How had his fine brain not seen the similarity? But of course he had never seen the assassin, so how could he? A big man is a big man. One might say the one was a giant, the other a beast. Once a memory, such things changed shape. Was that warrior so trim of hip? So…so graceful?

Ganus' thoughts are broken by the thud of a heavy sack tossed onto his belly. When he realizes, by the shape and weight of it, what it is, he loses the rest of his bowels.

"This is what you would have me believe held the arrogance to mar what is mine?" rumbles the baritone behind the muslin hood. "This egg?"

"Would you kill a man in his bed, coward?" Ganus retorts, shoving the head of Davius in the sodden sack off his lap. He makes to rise, for he is sitting in his own foul flux. But the beast is too quick. He has turned the mattress over on him, and now his liquid shit is dripping on his head.

"See what you have been sleeping on these days, Ganus the Feculent," he roars, and as the great general shoves the fetid mattress from his back, the beast takes him by the hair and pulls his head to rest on the lip of the platform upon which his mattress had been until then resting. There, eye level, is a silken packet, no larger than a sparrow's wing.

"No," says Ganus, feeling the bile rise in his throat.

"Crunch, crunch," whispers the Assassin. "Did you hear it? At night as you turned on my Queen's bed? Open it." He takes the general's right hand and forces it open, then presses the palm over the packet.

"No-o-o…oh, no," groans Ganus, who has begun to weep.

"Have you no stomach for it? Ganus the Gutless? Come now, reunite with thine fingers, lost in the Seven Day Battle of Troy. The ring of service, that remains with me. Greek Kings and their rings of service," he adds with disgust. "A pearl for five, a ruby for ten. As if that were reason enough to indenture oneself to a devil. Nay, this Hittite has thy ten year ring of service, Ganus the Flatulent. And ten years I've kept your fingers hidden under the nose of that king in my own Greek wife's bedchamber in Mycenae. For I am Kapnos, Ganus the Featherbrain. I am he whom your king gave shipload after shipload of army supplies to bring to you here, in my Knossos, and whilst I must admit they are inferior in every way to Hittite materials, nevertheless they have come in handy, and were so easily gained. For I do not plunder my own ships, Ganus the Dimwit. My army is fattened and armed in Gornea, thanks to your king, but alas, though they spoil for war, they will see none. You brought me to your bed with your arrogance, Ganus the Pompous. I could not stomach another foul noise from you. Or did you not know that my spies are everywhere, here in this palace? Or that I slept nightly over your head on the roof of the Queen's bath."

Rush has released the general's hand to turn the contents of the packet out onto the platform before his eyes. There are the broken bones of two fingers, yet linked together with a strand of dried flesh, grey with age.

Ganus is weeping openly. And so removed from the present is he by the sight of his long dead appendages that he feels nothing when the crescent blades meet at the base of his skull.

CHAPTER THIRTY TWO

Below the Great Hall, in her private chamber within the labyrinth beneath the Palace of Knossos, Hecate the witch is knotting the Grain God's skirt tie around her throat. The boy's waist is a wisp, and the cord does not reach around her own thick middle by half, and barely encloses one thigh. Exasperated, she doubles the knot and tucks the ends into the crevice between her pendulous breasts, then pulls her mantle over her head. She has removed the emerald circlet and hidden it deep inside a trunk amongst her magical tools. The nub of her ring finger, spit back into her eye by the little beast, is securely sewn into a scrap of red silk and tied about her neck beneath the skirt tie. She has no current use for it, but she is not one to waste. She prides herself in her thrift, knowing full well that it is precisely when you discard a thing that it becomes most useful. Her chamber, as well as several nearby rooms within the labyrinth, is full floor to ceiling with what another might consider trash. But Hecate will not be caught wishing she had not discarded a thing. That would prove her a fool. And she will not be proven a fool.

This time I will not fail, thinks the witch, smiling a smug half smile into her mirror. I am smarter than he. Smarter than any of them. I will make him pay, oh, nine times nine I shall!

But pay for what, she does not ponder. It is enough that the

Grain God of Knossos stole her rightful place as beloved of the Moon. Had she not served her Queen most all of her life? Or at least as long as she can remember? Hecate does not often think of that Before Time, and mostly it is lost to her. Her mother's doting love, her father's selfless kindness, all disremembered. And in the place of these memories, the sour hate of the spoilt child. For was it not her parents' folly that led to her near death? If she had never been allowed to milk the cow, she would have never been kicked, her skull never cracked, and her soul never expelled from her body and into the dream-life, where she watched from the ceiling her own crumpled form on the pallet by the fire whilst her mother wept.

Hag, she thinks. You wept for yourself, for you had no other living children. But it was your negligence that put me there. My face, no never a beauty but all the same, my face smashed, my nose turned, my teeth forever loose in my head, those left me. It was a week long, that twilight life, wherein she saw her corporeal part from that position on the ceiling above the hearth. She hated life then, forced to watch her parents' maudlin displays of grief while her body lay, a ruined heap of helpless dependence on the straw-stuffed mattress. Did they not know a flying ember could have set me on fire to burn like a live coal in my own bed?

Her hatred for her parents did not abate upon her awakening. And that was how she thought of it. For from the day she returned to her view of the world through her bodily eyes she vowed to spare herself any but the most brutal of emotions: rage, hatred, cruelty, and in turn growing out of these were the precious gems of self-flattery, self- indulgence, greed and love of possessions.

Now she allows herself to imagine how her spell will pull his beauty from him, weakening him, marring him. Did it not already happen? That was the way of magick. Once conceived it is employed, moving circumstances ever forward toward the goal of the spell-caster. The Grain God *was* marred, if prettily so. There was the scar on his hip, the mark on his cheek, like a teardrop, and the strange new crown of amber growing like a living circlet around his head. And he was weakening, surely he was. He had lain in that bed in the bull pit for weeks, until the priest and the concubine, and that

Ionian brute, Typhus, had finally moved him to his Temple at the House of the Moon.

That Temple should have been hers. That beauty, hers, that grace, that face! Hers. But the moon had chosen to shine instead on a creature who had never worshiped her.

Still, this she did not hold against the Moon. Nor the stars, nor the heavens. You are testing me by fire, thinks Hecate. And I will walk through fire. And I will take what should be mine.

And with these stirring thoughts she begins her day by chopping the scraps of last night's meal, to treat her favorite of the many cats that make their home with her under the palace, for the labyrinth is alive with every sort of vermin to occupy them.

Rah reaches the steps of the Palace an hour after sunrise. There is a guard, but in his traveling cloak, his head covered, he appears nothing more than a kitchen slave headed toward his daily chores. He skirts the west flank of the structure, taking the path that Clovis took first beside Triggvi and then hanging from the assassin's shoulder. He is as familiar with the depths of this place as any Minoan palace entertainer would have been, and taking a detour from the Terror's tracks he slips up a stairwell and across a hall, on his way to the Queen's chambers from the servant's entrance. Those coming and going on their way to and from their employments give him little notice, and he is behind the Queen's bath when he stops in his tracks at the sound of the Assassin's heavy whisper.

"Crunch, crunch," whispers the Assassin. "Did you hear it? At night as you turned on my Queen's bed? Open it."

"No-o-o…oh, no," Rah's ears perk. It is the General! The man is weeping.

"Have you no stomach for it? Ganus the Gutless?" continues the Assassin, his booming base subdued but even more horrible by being so. "Come now, reunite with thine fingers."

Rah slips beneath a once-curtained archway, finds himself in shadow, witness to the general doubled over the Queen's bed platform, his head in the assassin's grip, staring at a packet one might carry jewels in. At first he is confused. Does the Wolf bring presents to the devil? But no, Ganus lifts the packet. The contents drop out, like the foot of a bird of prey. No, not a bird. Rah's sharp eyes discern the broken bones of two fingers, yet linked together with a strand of dried flesh, grey with age.

Ganus is weeping openly as the assassin's blades meet at the base of his skull.

It is Rah's imperceptible flinch, the smallest of peripheral movements, which alerts the assassin that someone has joined him. He holsters his blades and rushes at the intruder, a black mass with the speed of a charging bull. He finds not the soldier he was expecting, only a wisp in a dust brown cloak shirking against a mural of dolphins in the bath alcove. A woman? A chamber maid? No matter, another head to loosen.

The assassin plants the knuckles of his left hand against the girl's sternum, draws his right crescent, and is caught mid swing by the chattering hiss of a house cat beneath the hood of the cloak.

"What the?" he flattens his left hand across the intruder's chest, feels a ringed nipple, falls back, his right hand returning the crescent blade to its holster as in a dream.

He pulls the hood back, and he is staring into the blue-green intensity of the Grain God's eyes.

"Rah…" his voice catches. The boy's face is the color of a parrot's wing. Egyptian blue kohl lines his sea-green eyes, pulling them into an exaggerated upward tilt toward his temples. His lips are peach, and in the center of his forehead he has painted an emerald circle, as if he still wears his crown, and the hair in which the mail band was braided is shadowed with dark golden undergrowth, creating a ghost of the circlet that held the assassin's jewel. Rush blinks, his eyes unbelieving. But it is the Rah. And the scent of high worship is on him: hyssop and myrrh, cherry and lotus.

Rush pulls the priestly cloak from the phantom's shoulders and sustains a second jolt. The boy wears only a formal dove-white Minoan skirt, high in front, fuller and calf length in back. It is too loose for him, and sits low on his hips so that the solid golden hoop that is his belt lies against his bare belly. The puckering scar on his hip is like a kiss never planted. Pain pulls upward from the assassin's groin like a lance laying open his heart. Rush pushes Rah from his own grasp, pinning him by the shoulders to the frescoed wall behind him, where a dolphin competes with the aqua of his eyes. Rush drops his head momentarily, fighting for a breath. The boy has seen him behead a man. Has seen him as he is, has seen first-hand what he is. Something akin to shame heats his cheeks.

"What wrong, Wolf?" Rah's voice is a deep rumble, sweet and near, a dark purr. "No want Rah to see Wolf kill?" his hand has slipped from the priestly cloak to settle on the assassin's chest. Beneath the muslin wrap, the big man's heart kicks, as if straining to return the touch. "Kill better thing than this Ganus Destroying, heh? Kill beautiful cat. Kill, kill. Bad wolf. Sometime for no reason. Sometime for good reason." He pretends to look over Rush's shoulder.

He has never voluntarily touched me, thinks Rush. Rah tilts his head as if in question. The painted eyes watch him, the lids at half-mast.

"Why you kill Ganus Destroying, Wolf? Is because is enemy? Big general? Want to take Crete? Or because he take Rah," the voice is sultry, pouting. "Can see he ruin Rah. Rah have cry like Wolf is make on face," he turns his face slightly left, offering the assassin a better view of the tear. Puppy breath puffs against Rush's cheek, mingling with the intoxicating scents of hyssop and myrrh.

"Ganus Destroying he let men beat Rah. Break rib," Rah continues, spreading the fingers of his left hand against his side, "Ya, beat face too, make eye all fill blood." He lifts both hands to grasp his head. "Try to pull crown off head, too, but no can do. Pull lot of hair. Hurt bad." Rah peers up into the assassin's single exposed eye. "Spy, big man, Typhoos, he tell you, Wolf? How bad they hurt Rah?"

Rush flinches.

But Rah only chuckles. "Think Rah stupid. No so stupid, Wolf. Rah is learn. Learn from priest. Learn from Wolf." There is mischief in those glittering blue-green eyes, a mischief Rush has never seen in them before, and he is temporarily stunned. Who is this new Rah? What has happened to the boy. Without warning Rah snatches the assassin's wrists, his grip surprisingly firm, yet dancer soft. Rush flinches a second time, but allows the boy to take his hands off his shoulders and set them lightly on the handles of his crescent blades. His touch sends fire up the assassin's arms.

Playfulness curls Rah's lip, creating a single dimple. He gives Rush a dismissing look, moves to step around him, out of his reach. But Rush blocks him, caging him with extended arms.

"Who cut you, Rah? Who took a blade to you? Answer me or I will kill every last man in this palace."

"Is no man. Is woman. Is witch, Wolf, is witch she stab Rah," and suddenly his face is dark with rage and he is plunging an invisible boline into his own hip. "Yah!"

Rush snatches Rah's wrist, preventing him from landing the self-inflicted blow.

"Stop it now. Who is this witch, tell me, and I will skin the half of her, hang her off the port side and let the fishes feast." The mention of the wound on Rah's hip has brought his blood up. He hears himself babbling his rage, impotently.

Rah brings up both hands and shoves at Rush's chest, attempts to slip under his arms unsuccessfully. He gives a little "ruff" in frustration, seems to think better of it, softens his features.

"Angry wolf, he want to kill?" coos Rah. "Is want to kill now, Wolf? Kill who," he lifts his lip, makes a little snarl and snap, nearly catching the assassin's cheek. Rush recoils. But Rah is still coming at him with his teeth snapping.

"Want to bite Rah now, Wolf?" He lands a vicious punch to the distracted assassin's solar plexus. Startled, and not a little surprised by the power of the unsuspected blow, Rush snatches at the boy's wrists, but Rah is too fast. He lands a second fierce punch, this one to the big man's jaw, inches from his windpipe.

Rush seizes both of Rah's wrists, rage burning with the sting of the blows, palms them in one hand and slaps the boy against the wall.

"Stop it," but the words come out as a hoarse whisper. "Stop it, Rah. What are you doing? What are you trying to do?" Again he steps back, this time at ease, his arms at his sides. Rah gives him an intense gaze, sweeping those lashes up and down his body, a second dismissal. Then he ducks around him, struts to the polished stone bench in front of the three blood red columns leading out to the Queen's courtyard.

He stands there a moment, his back to Rush, as if on a stage awaiting the hush of an audience. Rush plays along, a single silent spectator. And Rah drops the linen cloak to the floor, baring a golden back crisscrossed with healing welts.

It is as if all of the blood in Rush's body has flushed through his feet into the earth. Vertigo, as on a battlefield, as with a blow to the head. He stretches out his hand toward the wall and misses, nearly stumbling into it.

Rah is pacing back and forth. His movements are jerky, rapid and confused. He looks at the floor, the ceiling. He begins to chatter, making small, worried-cat sounds in his throat. What now? Is he meant to interfere? Is he part of this pantomime?

Rush crosses the room and steps in front of him. Rah backs away, head down, but Rush understands now that he is part of the play. He holds his position. And Rah turns in the opposite direction. He knows this dance. Rush moves in front of Rah, blocking him. Now, there is no room left for Rah to move. He turns his head this way, that way, intimidated. He takes a step backward but there is not a full step to take. His wounded back slaps against a stone column. A wavering murmur rises from his throat, the warning of a wildcat. He flicks his startling eyes up to Rush, brow flat. They are full of fear and hate.

And Rush remembers.

That first night, the night Rah was delivered to his compound in Knossos. He'd found Josepha in the boy's room, on her knees and in his embrace. And he had smugly taunted her for falling for his charms.

"You are a bull in a pottery, Antaris," she had said. "He is fragile. It will not serve you to shatter him." She had said.

"I don't mean to shatter him, Josepha," he had answered her, "Just break him."

And then?

The boy is pantomiming it. And here is the slap across that jaw, sparkling with blonde bristles. Rah spins into the wall as if struck by a great blow, holding his cheek in both hands. Something draws his head back and tilts his face upwards. He is breathing short, hard breaths and his body is rigid, as if waiting for the next blow.

"Stop it!"

But Rah's invisible assailant is holding him by the scruff, shaking him. The boy keens and turns full into the wall to settle his cheek against the cool stone, eyes down. His long, thick lashes shading them.

"Stop it, Rah," the assassin hears the defeat in his own voice and feels the rage building again. He reaches for the boy's shoulder, but he cannot bring himself to touch it.

Rah presses himself against the column as if the palm of a great hand were flattened against his injured back.

"Enough," grunts Rush. "Enough of this." He jerks Rah around to face him.

Those sea-blue eyes have turned arctic.

"You remember, Wolf?" says Rah, "Can remember how is Rah?"

Rush swallows.

"Can remember Rah?" Rah asks again.

"Why do you tempt me, boy?"

"Little fire good," mocks Rah, "But too much, Wolf say he take it out of Rah."

Under the hood, the assassin's cheeks burn red.

"Isha nahhan," says Rah. Hittite. His words. *His*. Respect the master.

"Ja," says Rah, "Wolf is remember now. Can see in one eye. Ah but," Rah brings his lips up to the muslin shroud so that his breath puffs against the place that hides the assassin's mouth. "Who is master, Wolf? Eh? Wolf is think is master because can take life away. Even Rah life. But can Wolf he make Rah?" Rah spits onto the muslin mask, cat-quick. Rush can feel the spray dampen his lip. "Wolf he cannot even make chicken. Make egg. Rah is thinking, even chicken better master than Wolf."

The muslin hood is off, and Rah is hanging from Rush's hands against the blood-red column.

"You are impossible," he breathes through his teeth. "You half-witted, feral ingrate." His blood is pounding in his neck, and under the black tunic his chest is slick with sweat. He has killed in passion, he has loved in passion. He has never done both at once. But there is no stopping him this time. This time the thing gets done. This time, by Tartarus, he takes that head.

"Yah," says Rah, nodding. "Wolf is want kill Rah now. Never satisfy. This whole problem. Wolf is like big mouth is always eat, eat never want be hungry. But sometime, Wolf, is better be hungry. You eat what you love, can no have what you love anymore. You take Rah, is no more Rah. Is something else. You understand?"

"You think I don't know this, you little devil? You think you can teach Rush a thing or two about life?" His fingers are boring into Rah's arms and Rah squints at the pain but makes no effort to squeeze out of Rush's grasp.

"Why no?" says Rah. "Why no can Rah teach Wolf some things too? Look what happen Rah because Wolf is always chase, always have to have. Witch, she catch Rah, Wolf is chase right into witch hand. Now she cut Rah, she want to kill Rah with magick, yah, take his place. She think Rah is reason she is no happy. She think because Rah he have this face, maybe because can dance for king, for god, this mean why she no have. But this no why she no have. She no have because ugly here," he lifts one numb hand to press a forefinger into Rush's sternum. "Black heart." He concludes.

"I know of no witch in Knossos," responds Rush, one fury

distracted now by the other. "You will tell me where this witch is, Rah. And we will have our day."
"No threat Rah. Rah tell, but this witch she is make spell, Wolf, even if kill, she curse. Maybe can no fix with kill her."
"You believe in too much magic, Rah. You think you are what you are because of the priest's magic." Rush has set the boy down on the pads of his feet. Without thinking he softens his hands, even makes a little rubbing gesture, as if to bring the blood back into Rah's biceps. A father again, soothing a child. "You are what you are. I have been to the north, Rah. I have discovered who you are. You have always been…were born…magic."
It is the best he can do. He waits for Rah's reaction.
"What you mean? Is nothing left in north. No more family, all gone. Rah is only one left. How you know this thing?" Rah's face has lost that self-protective frown, made comic by the absurd makeup. Rush has hit a nerve behind the powder and paint, has found the younger Rah.
"Rah," Rush puts one hand on his shoulder. And as suddenly as his rage flared, it is gone. He is no longer talking to his nemesis, he is talking to a son. "It is time you meet Triggvi. He is a trader from the north, and he can tell you all there is to tell of your beginnings."
The green mask is still, a portrait, only the eyes staring through it living. But those eyes are glistening.
The boy blinks.
And a single silver tear meets and marries the teardrop scar on his cheek.

CHAPTER THIRTY THREE

In the half-light of daybreak, Mochlos awakens. A red glow illuminates the archway of his balcony, which faces the villa's second story courtyard and, because the acolyte's south wing is a single story, the mountains beyond. Mochlos lifts his head from his pillows. It is good to rise early against a witch. He throws back his embroidered yellow silk sheets, slips his feet into a pair of jeweled Babylonian sandals, reaches for his dressing gown. His movements in a full length bronze mirror against his western wall catch his attention, and he pads across the luxurious Hattushan rug, depicting the now famous Battle of Urgup in shades of gold and blue, to stand before it. His scalp, brows and face are clean shaven. His face is oddly unlined, for a man of his age and experience. His dark eyes have lost none of their depth, none of their cunning. He is not an ugly man, in fact, these years have added something of dignity to his face. His sun-browned skin glows, as if his energy, in his journey toward departure, were not ebbing but expanding.

"Not so bad, you," Mochlos offers himself a smile. But, ah, there is the tiger! Ever lurking behind that forced grin. "Not to be trifled with, eh, priestie?" he says to himself, mimicking Ess's gruff voice. His eyes sparkle. Time for a little mischief. Time for a little magick.

Mochlos turns from the mirror. Through his balcony doorway

he sees that the Cretan sun will soon crest Juktas, and he will be in the Temple of the Grain God when that happens, in the robe in which he created the god-slave, the fine white linen with the five golden heads of grain spreading across his back. Quickly he makes his way to his bath to cleanse, shave and oil his body, and when he is finished he dons the High Priest Of The Moon robe, which he has kept with him, in the bottom of his magical trunk, since he departed from his Villa on the assassin's ship.
By now Rah is down in the newly constructed stables, which flank the Arena. Wearing nothing but a Minoan skirt, he will be talking northern gibberish to the new colt, the one he calls Tut-Ankh-Amen. Image of God, in Egyptian, a name reserved for kings. Tut, for short.
Mochlos climbs the stairs leading up to the Rah's temple, marveling over the new murals covering the curved walls of the stairwell. They have been painted by the finest painters an assassin-general's money can buy, their long-fingered hands shaking with fear at every brush-stroke. But so far the Wolf of Amega is pleased. Here begins the story: Rah, the child, and his sister, Ileah, dancing for the barbarians. Two white-blonde stars twinkling in the center of a sea of fur-clad mongrels. And here is Rah the boy, standing on the back of a dun mare, flanked by four others, all galloping in unison. His curls fly back from his head, depicting speed. He wears the deer-skinned vest and short breeches that Mochlos himself dispossessed him of. These too are tucked away in the magical trunk, though Rah could no longer fit into either. Here am I, the priest, and Ananou, and the Eleven Watchers, climbing the mountain carrying the shrouded boy on a pallet, and here again, proclaiming him the Son of Rah, as the boy stands naked on his alter before the assembly. And here is the Grain God, dancing for Nanaia and her king in the Palace of Knossos, the dove boy. And here, at the top of the stairwell, lying prone on a pallet, being carried down to the ship that would take them all to safety. There, above the doorway leading into the temple, the volcano steams off-shore. It is not until he pulls open the

pearl and sapphire strung curtains, letting himself into the private dwelling place of the god-slave, that the story of the Rah continues on the wall to the right. Here is the golden boy, astride a light-bodied brown mare, approaching the outer wall of the city of Hattusha, and here he is, bound and carried over the shoulder of one of his Amorite kidnappers, deep within those same labyrinthine walls. Now he rides a dun mare, and here, here he has dismounted her though she stands at his side, the royal Babylonian palanquin approaching, and he is bowing in the dust.

The boy's bow bisects the northern curve of the circular wall, just above Rah's mattress. Mochlos strokes his chin, adjusting to the irony. It was the bow that turned master into slave, he thinks, and still the master is pleased to see it there, above the boy's bed of all places. Does it not taunt you? Does it not mock you? Surely you are here, on moonlit nights, standing just here where I stand now, seeing in the dark like the wolf you are, observing your golden god at peace in his dreams. Surely….

Mochlos gives his head a shake. No I will not entertain such thoughts. He has not seen the beast for some time, and hopes not to see him at all, ever again. But if he climbs these vines to view the boy, then he also visits me, perhaps with other thoughts entirely. Perhaps not quite satisfied with the symmetry of things as they turned out, perhaps considering how gratifying my eyeballs on my dresser would be…He turns to the blank eastern wall, imagining the next mural. Following the approach to Babylon, what then? The horseman's whip? The lost pearl? The Dance for the King?

And how will it end? There is the full half circle of the eastern wall to fill, and the Wolf is not such a mindless fool as to complete it while the boy still lives, else he might follow his destiny and end with the last scene.

Never mind the boy's destiny. What of mine? I must make myself useful, else the Wolf….. he has never much liked me, has he?

Mochlos disappears behind the blue and gold beaded curtain

into his alcove of magical items. He retrieves what he needs, and, bowing before the mural of the boy's bow, with a sudden urge for contrition, perhaps even thanksgiving, he leaves the way he came, and heads for the long walk up the mountain.

Several hours later, panting and short of breath, the priest has come to the cave and the altar where the first two Grain Gods were sacrificed.

I did not drug either one of them, thinks Mochlos, and delighted in their cries for mercy. And in my belly I can feel the cat of cruelty scratching at the door of my soul to be let in. I can fairly hear the ghosts of those two innocents mewling still. Repentence. My own medicine. I demanded it of Babylon. Now I must demand it of myself. Else his enemy will have her day. There is no other alternative, for magick, once called forth, will find a mark, one way or the other.

On the alter he prepares his items: a poppet he has made of a straw doll, with a lock of Rah's hair, sapphire eyes and a bit of white linen for a loin cloth. Another made from the hair of a black goat, a mandrake root, two cloves for eyes, a tiny boline made of the bones of a falcon's claw, and of course, his mortar and pestle, his incense, his flint and some dried grass to start the fire, and his magick bowl.

Mochlos arranges the tools of his trade on the altar in the full noonday sun. The air is still here up on the mountain, the sky cloudless. The sun burns with monstrous heat. It is a good omen. He has found favor with the Sun. And how could it not be so? The Grain God, Rah, is the son of the Sun God and the Moon Goddess. He is the god of harvest, of grain, of all that made Crete rich. He has never been better represented than by this golden, sea-eyed boy. It was clear early on that the Moon was pleased by the priest's choice for her son's earthy incarnation. But the Moon was ever only the mother, the vessel of his birth. The Sun was his creator, his father. And had the assassin not learned that the boy was in fact stolen from the Sun People?

And so it is the Sun whom the High Priest of the Moon now appeals. He prostrates himself before the altar. It is forgiveness he seeks, forgiveness for disobedience. He was charged with protecting the Rah, as his priest, and he sought instead to use and to abuse him. But the Lord would not be brought down from his high place to serve the whims of man. It is he who lies on his face in the dust in supplication. Do not take my god, oh God! Do not let this evil prevail, but let your priest prevail, even now, even in the eleventh hour, allow your priest to prevail, that the boy might be saved, that your vessel might remain holy.

Mochlos rises, for a cloud had appeared and blocked the sun. For a moment he believes that he has received his answer, that there is no point in carrying out the ritual. But then the cloud moves off over the mountain, toward the south, so suddenly that the sun burns his eyes. He lifts his arms, opens his palms, faces its glory, which shines in a blinding haze over Knossos. He falls to his knees in thanksgiving, his head bowed, his hands clasped over his breast. And when he rises again he sets his palm down on the altar, ready to do battle.

She has found the hidden doorway.

The sound, the clopping, as of hooves, the snorting, as of bulls, brought her awake at the witching watch, three hours before dawn.

She had never ventured too far into the labyrinth, for fear of becoming disoriented and lost. Her sight was poor, her hearing acute, but hearing did one little good in the dark maze beneath the palace that had been the storehouse of the Minoan city. The wares and goods had long been pilfered, and there was little left but broken amphora, dust and ash. She had tripped over a man's skeleton once, on her way to what she believed was the wine cellar. That had been enough for her. That hollow eyed skull, gleaming up at her from the floor in her rush light, that had been enough. Omen of death. Death here in the storehouse halls among the shards of broken things. No. Not for her. And so she returned the way she had come that time, to her own not-unpleasant chamber beneath the Queen's Wing, full of bat's wings and dried herbs, potions and crow's feathers, and smelling pungently of cat urine.

But tonight she has heard the strange new sound, echoing through the empty halls beneath the palace. Snort, crash, the keening cry of an angry stallion. There is something new in the labyrinth! And she must discover what it is for the labyrinth is hers.

This time she has brought with her an oil lamp, which she has made sure to fill to brimming, for she does not know how long it will take, this mission of hers. She wraps her mantle tight over her shoulders, then thinks better of it and lifts it over her head. Might be she will be glad of anonymity this night. But lo! She spies the boy's golden circlet, his golden hairs still attached here and there, the emerald pulsing in the oil light. She had taken it out of her secret place to gloat over it earlier this evening. Now she lifts it, turns to the mirror, settles it upon her gnarled grey head, combing the blonde curls into her own silver strands with sharp black nails.

Satisfied with her visage, Hecate picks up her lamp and, pushing aside a trunk and a low chest of drawers she pulls open with some difficulty a partition made of two invisible doors meant to resemble a decorative wall. The doors stick, jam, and then, with a grunt and a heft from the witch, release and ease back into the walls on either side. The passage is dark and littered with debris, but Hecate is undaunted now. There is something living in the labyrinth with her. Something large and angry and probably Greek. She has had enough of these Greeks. She had been doing well enough, on her own, living here in the labyrinth of the Palace of Knossos before they came, and when they found her they thought to kill her, like a rat in their pantry. But her magic was too strong for them. They soon found that the labyrinth was deadly, and those that entered it caught fever, vomiting and diarrhea, and then, within a few days, a racking cough overtook them, their hearts beating wildly. Once their breathing became labored they died within a few hours, drowned in their own fluids.

Unable to oust her, and fearing that she carried this illness within her own body without suffering from it herself, the one named Ganus sought instead to contain her. But she would not be contained. She went out into the fields and woods to find the leaves and roots and bark that she needed to cast her spells and cure those who paid her for her medicines. And there were many. People on the outskirts of the city, natives, who had survived the cataclysm learned of her by word of mouth and search her out. She made a good enough living plying her trade, and had no intention of retiring.

But then Ganus the Destroyer sent her a message that changed her mind. It was attached in a little silken packet to the collar of her favorite cat, the big ginger male. His name was Brimstone, and he was a wanderer and a fighter. One ear had been torn half off in a brawl, and his left eye was out, but he had no fear and when the Greeks began broiling and boiling chickens and fish in the palace kitchens he quickly became a favorite of the men, who perhaps missed their own pets at home. They fed him orts and curried his favor, and eventually he earned a braided leather collar for his bravery. One day he leapt up on her lap as she sat mending a tear in her mantel. Attached to the new collar was a silk pouch, and in the pouch was a pearl.

"So," said Hecate to herself, brushing the cat from her lap and standing. "Ready to talk, are we, General Ganus? Very well, I see what you're getting at. Bring the old bat up if she won't be driven out. Strike a deal. She is after all, a witch. And you need a witch, don't you General?"

And indeed he did. For General Ganus needed something destroyed, and though he had never before given soothsayers and magicians much weight, this witches' magic had impressed him. She had, in effect, defeated his army, without losing so much as a hair on her bottle brush head.

"Make for me a spell, one that will give me complete power over my enemies, and I will let you live here under the protection of the Greek army," he said to her when they met. Well of course she laughed. For had she not already proven she needed no one's protection? Least of all his? Still, there might be something more in it for her than protection. A bit of security, perhaps? A nest egg for her later years? These were coming upon her fast, and she had wondered what she would do to put bread and meat on the table for herself and her cats should she become too infirm to wander out into the hills and collect her herbs and roots, her bats bones and crows feathers.

"Is Greece a pauper then?" she sneered up at him from the bull pit, for it was the very pit that Ganus would later put the Rah in that she spoke to him from, shouting up from the dung dust and the moldy straw, a lantern held up over her head so that she might see him, and he her.

"I take your meaning," said the General. "Very well, prove to me that you can put power in my grasp, and I will make you a deal. Your food and shelter for as long as Greece holds Knossos. And whatever else your evil heart desires," he stroked his chin, considering, "within reason."

"So be it," returned the witch. "By the full shall you have more 'power in your grasp' than you can handle."

That caveat, 'more power than you can handle', was not unintended. In the end, had not the Rah been more than he could handle? And the reason he had died at the hand of his worst enemy?

Lamp in hand Hecate makes her way down a dark and littered passage, her bare feet crunching on the carcasses of rat and cat alike. She pays them no mind. There is an intruder in her dark domain and she means to sniff him out.

END

The journey was rough. In the hold of the ship, Minus crouched, terrified, as the rough sea, battered by storm winds, tossed the vessel about. His acute hearing could make out the sounds of the crew frantically fighting the storm above decks. And he discerned more than one "man overboard" among them. No effort was made to save those that the sea had taken. One did not refuse the Sea Goddess her due. The ship bucked and tossed, rose and fell, and Minus crouched in his own vomit, hoping that she would not demand the entire crew and vessel.

But the sea calmed, as seas do, and in the morning, when Minus awoke, there was little more than a gentle lapping alongside the hull against which he lay. Hours passed, and the vessel pulled into a harbor. Minus waited. Food was lowered down into the hold, a basket of the things he was accustomed to: boiled eggs and sliced ham, apricots, dates and figs, a whole roasted chicken, a loaf of good seed bread. He ate complacently, and at dusk, he stood under the hatch though which he had been installed into this gloom by his own brother, and he waited to hear the light tread of his twin.

It was not long after the last footsteps left the ship that the tread he had been waiting for broke the stillness above him. The hatch was thrown open and his brother's voice found his ear.

"It is time, Minus. Your new home awaits you." And Minus,

trusting his instincts, found the ladder up through the hatch, where the assassin waited.

"We do not want to cause a stir," his brother's baritone whisper tickled his ear, and a cloak was tossed over his shoulders, and then a hood over his head, so that his face was completely concealed by it.

"He will be there, brother?" asked Minus, following Rush down the gang plank onto the pier, and then into a wagon.

"He will come and go," answered his twin. "It is his home too, brother." After a moment the assassin added, "It is his shrine, too."

And so Minus was installed in the labyrinth beneath the palace, and the sunken pen, which once housed Knossos' best trained bulls, was now his sacred space, a place where the people of Crete could come to honor him and offer sacrifice: baskets of grapes, figs, apricots, dates, jars of honey, tubs of butter, bushels of fresh breads, cheeses, and his favorite, boiled eggs. There were also flowers to smell: lilies and helitrope, sea daffodil and inula, gladiolas and chamomile. But the assassin's twin was not fed in the bull pit, the walls of which had been stuccoed and frescoed, and were now painted red and blue and gold, as befit a Minoan god, the floor marbled and covered in the finest Hattushan rugs. Minus took his meals at the bottom of the stairwell behind the kitchens, giving Crispo and his army of cooks easy access, and thus allowing the holy one to enjoy his main course direct from the oven and the pan, still sizzling.

Down a corridor not far from the kitchen stairwell where he ate, Minus slept now in comfort in a den furnished with duck down pillows and bear hide rugs, a newly dug cistern providing him a place to bathe.

And not ten feet from where he lay his misshapen head to sleep at night, Hecate too, slipped from the land of the living to the land of dreams. The wall between them was thick, but the years and the shifting earth had pulverized much of the dried mud that sealed the brick and stone, and the monster's rumblings and snoring passed through it like a spell passes through time, losing strength, perhaps, and clarity, but never entirely silenced.

It is on the evening of the of Hecate's excursion through the labyrinth in search of him, that Minus discovers Hecate's hole.

The crone is wandering through the system of tunnels, far from her own bed, when Minus, following his nose, easily sniff out the source of the odiferous climate that is penetrating his own apartment. The hellish mingling of stale incense and cat urine nearly drives him back, but he will not share his new home with this, and so clenching his teeth against her stench he lumbers toward Hecate's unoccupied bed, shoving over her alter and the oil lamp upon it in his haste. The flame swiftly blooms in the pool of oil on the stone floor and catches hold of her bed curtains. In an instant Hecate's mattress is afire, the cats scattering and flying up various stairwells into the kitchens like a family of dislodged bats, while Minus, terrified by the sudden explosion of heat and light against his cheeks, flees down a narrow hall toward the bull pit.

In the kitchens, the smoke billows in from the cellar stairs, and Crispo, aware that his master's brother had been rehomed in the labyrinth just this very day, sounds the great gong that hangs behind the courtyard facing windows. In a moment the kitchen is filled with soldiers and servants, all carrying pails of water hoisted from the canal running along the western wall of the palace to douse the fire.

But for Hecate it is too late.

The hag is found writhing and dancing aflame in her own apartment, where she returned in haste when she smelled the oil smoke, to rescue the emerald circlet hidden deep inside her trunk among her most precious magical contrivances. And her charred and dispossessed hands grasp it still, when it and they are later presented to the assassin.

The dust cloud rising from the training ring is spinning like a waterspout. The herd has been released into the arena, and freed from the day-long journey aboard ship, they canter and kick, buck and twist and fart, round and round the oblong field. There are the twenty white horses from the original group, including Halix, Ileah, and Hali's sister, Ting, as well as Ona, Dias, Pekla and Far, Reh-Kabil's racer, Dashuri, and of course, Hali. But Rah, standing in the middle of the stampeding circle with Rush's fishing pole and line for a lunge whip, can see only one. The black colt Rush has brought back from Babylon, a small, long legged replica of his own Amorite warhorse.

He is not the most aggressive, despite the fact that he is a whole male, just two summers old. Rah watches as he tucks his haunches at the gallop to avoid the teeth of the dominant mare running beside him. It is Hali's dam, and Rah chuckles to himself.

"Is good, Little Warrior, better you be surrender to boss mare. Then you be maybe surrender to me too."

Racing alongside the mare on the opposite side is Halix, his dapples fading to silver-white. He is three years now and has lost his long, baby legs. An easy keeper, his neck has developed a full and muscular crest, his flanks wide, his haunch a veritable trampoline-in-motion for Rah's feet. But despite his girth, his footfalls are as soft as a rabbits. He glides along, a silver-white cloud skimming over the soft, sand-and-soil footing of the arena.

Rah lifts the fishing line and the circle of horses widens, leaving him a wide birth. Behind the stone wall of the arena tiers of seats are being built by stone masons, awaiting the crowds intended for the Rah. But for now, only his concubines, five new girls imported from Hattusha from the King's harem and of course, beautiful Awiti, watch with girlish delight and terror. Rah, enjoying their distress, snaps the whip, and the herd moves in a widening circle out toward the stone walls of the arena.

"You see, Awiti!" cries Rah above the sound of one hundred twelve hooves, "Rah is ride this black! Is ride him no saddle, no bit. Stand on back like can do with Halix someday!" He is smiling, his dimples popping. He stretches out the fishing pole and snaps it as the black thunder's past, and the animal tucks its rump and skids away from the light caress of the chicken feathers Rah has tied to the end of the line.

"Look how is so ….is like dancer!"

"He is a warhorse, Rah!" booms Rush over the roar. "He is bred agile for battle!" He stands on a platform built into the south wall of the arena. On his right Ephtheta, her golden robes fluttering in the dusty breeze, sits on a queen's throne, a pair of swaddled babes in her arms. On his left sits Media, her hair towering high atop her head in an elaborate Minoan construction, a small white cur pup in her lap, whom Rah found one rainy afternoon huddled against the broken wall of the King's pasture half way up the mountain. The pup yelps, delighted at the excitement of the pandemonium below. And Mochlos, seated at her left, rubs its head roughly to take its attention.

But Rah hears only the blow and snort of the new colt, who has left the stampede, skidded to a halt and made a dash toward him. He nips at his skirt pockets insolently, despite the snapping lunge whip.

"This one is be good for chariot! Afraid nothing!" cries Rah, digging a sweet grain cake from his skirt to offer the colt. He lifts the whip, flicks the feathered end at the colt's belly, and the beast leaps back and canters off behind the herd.

Rah rolls his tongue, "F-d-d-d-d-d-d-r-r-r-r-r-h!" to slow the animals to a trot. "H-o-o-o-o-o-h!" he sings the sound down, lowering the fishing rod, lowering his hands and head. The horses slow to a walk.

Rah drops the whip and walks toward the platform. At the base is a small raised area of polished stone. He leaps onto it, finds his balance, and drops into his deepest bow.

And for a moment time slips away, and the noise of the stampede fades. And he is no longer here, in his own arena, but there, where it all began. Back on the Burial Mound Road on a clear spring day. And a great hulk of a man with the chest of a bull and the heart of a lion has tackled him, pinning him in the gravel.

And a shudder of terror melts through his bowels.
He forces himself to rise from the bow, to lift his eyes.
And there stands the man, that beast who took him down so long ago, like a wolf takes down a doe, pursued him across three kingdoms, only to chase him here, back where it all began.
The man stands above him, his gaze fixed on his own, his obsidian eyes fierce in his oddly pale face. Ferocious with fatherly love.

ABOUT THE AUTHOR

Susan Shepherd is a retired law enforcement officer who has spent most of her career interviewing criminals and writing reports for the Court. She lives on the North Fork of Long Island, New York, with her husband, three horses and six cats.

www.ingramcontent.com/pod-product-compliance
Lightning Source LLC
Chambersburg PA
CBHW061950170626
46813CB00006B/2597

* 9 7 8 0 6 9 2 9 7 4 7 6 6 *